RIVERRUN

BEYOND THE FIVE SENSES

Peter Warrilow was raised in Henley-on-Thames, Oxfordshire, and began his working career in engineering, before moving into banking and then sales management in the motor trade. He represented his local amateur boxing club at welterweight and was a keen competitive rower, completing the annual Lincoln to Boston rowing marathon eight times. He is currently working on his third Robert Vere novel.

My thanks to Phil M. Shirley and his dedicated team of professionals at Foreshore Publishing for their help, advice and expertise in publishing The Drysdale Confession.

PETER WARRILOW
THE DRYSDALE CONFESSION

A Robert Vere crime thriller

FORESHORE PUBLISHING
London

Published by RiverRun, an imprint of
Foreshore Publishing 2022.
The home of quality fiction.

Foreshore Publishing
The Forge 397-411 Westferry Road,
Isle of Dogs, London, E14 3AE

Foreshore Publishing Limited Reg. No. 13358650

ISBN 978-1-7395930-8-7

WWW.FORESHOREPUBLISHING.COM

CHAPTER 1

LONDON: November 1962.

GERALD LAMBERT HAD every reason to be nervous. In a little over seventeen hours Stephen Drysdale, his client, would be dead. Hanged for his part in a murder and armed robbery. Gripped with ever-mounting tension he uttered a silent prayer, hoping that the swirling afternoon fog would not delay his taxi journey to the Home Office. Was there hope? Surely, he reasoned, this last-minute summons must be more than a formality. Peering forward, over the driver's shoulder and into the thick fog he could just make out the back of a bus, one place in front of them in the crawling queue of traffic. Its red paint appeared almost yellow as the early November dusk completed the transition from foggy day to foggy evening.

'Home Office coming up on the left-hand side,' the driver called out, 'wretched fog, can hardly see your hand in front of your face,' he grumbled, drawing his cab to a halt as Lambert opened the door.

'Keep the change,' he called out, unaware of the driver's muttered thanks as he walked into the Home Office 'Gerald Lambert to see Mr Davenport,' he announced, nodding

1

to the uniformed official. Moments later Lambert found himself following an aloof, middle-aged lady, down a long corridor. Shortly she stopped before a panelled door, knocking on the woodwork before entering in response to a muffled shout from within.

'Mr Lambert to see you, Commander,' she said, allowing Lambert to enter the room. Stepping forward to extend a handshake he noted how Davenport made use of a walking stick to get upright from behind his desk.

'Lambert, good to meet you after so many months of letter writing,' Simon Davenport spoke firmly as the two men shook hands. 'Sit down, dear fellow,' he offered, waving to the empty chair opposite his desk. 'Miss Roberts, look after Mr Lambert's coat, then see if you can rustle up some tea, please.'

'Commander?' Lambert said enquiringly as the door closed gently behind the departing Miss Roberts. 'I had no idea. It wasn't on your letters!'

'No,' he gave a brief smile. 'It's like this leg,' he patted his right thigh thoughtfully, 'a relic from the last war.' Lambert nodded sympathetically as the older man continued speaking. 'Back then I was a young lieutenant on a destroyer, Russian convoy to Murmansk. That's when it happened then, after convalescing. I ended up around the corner,' he pointed a thumb in the direction of Trafalgar Square. 'No longer fit for sea duties they moved me to the Admiralty, pushing papers well into the fifties. Mind you, they were decent enough to give me another half stripe to boost the pension. Then, before boredom set in, I managed to call in a favour or two. Got myself moved here, winding up as a permanent secretary, three years back. Damned funny,' he explained, 'the old rank thing's a bit popular around here. Guess we're a bit short on Dukes and Earls,' he laughed, 'so who am I to stop them?' Lambert smiled, looking at the bulky, white haired, friendly looking permanent secretary.

'An impressive record, but I'm sorry about the leg.'

'Confounded nuisance,' Davenport muttered, 'but a lot of good chaps came off far worse than me. Anyway,' he paused rubbing his hands, 'enough of that. Let's get down to business.'

'Yes, let's,' Lambert replied, his voice betraying uncertainty.

'Well....to start with, I've been impressed by the fight you and your QC, Bernard Ruskin, put up for your client.' Choosing his words carefully he then asked, 'but aren't you a bit young to be overseeing a high-profile capital case like this?' Before Lambert could reply Davenport continued. 'Must say, I'm more used to seeing people more my own age at times like this.......' He paused, as both men recognised that his words had taken on a questioning pose.

'Fair comment, Commander, it's the handicap I carry for being the only son of the senior partner over at Regency Law. Simply put, my father has always taken a fiendish delight in pushing me to the very limit, which this case has done, physically and emotionally.' Lambert stopped talking, his last words hanging in the air. From across the desk, Simon Davenport studied the young solicitor who, in turn, found how the protracted silence was politely forcing him to continue speaking. 'I'm sorry I was a little late for our meeting, the fog - you know,' he waved absently in the direction of the closed curtains.

'Anyway, I'm here now,' he stated in a sombre voice.

'So, where are you? he challenged, waiting with a certain degree of trepidation for the conversation that he knew was about to develop.

'At times like this,' Davenport tapped a finger on his upright leather-bound desk calendar, upon which the following day's date had been ringed in thick black ink. Sighing, he settled back into his chair and continued speaking. 'Look, I know you were told there wasn't to be a reprieve, but there's always hope.' he paused, looking thoughtfully at Lambert. 'You see, I always make a point of seeing the condemned man's instructing solicitor the day before the....' His speech faltered, reluctant to say the word "execution." 'However.' he resumed, 'as their legal representative, it's good to have a chat, make sure all is in order. I'm sure you know the form, double checking and so forth. That's why I called your office this morning, inviting you here.'

Lambert stared directly into Davenport's eyes, instantly aware of how the use of *condemned man* had somehow seemed to lower the room's temperature. Clearly the statement, bold and unflinching, had been to establish conversational limits. A move that left Lambert feeling uneasy, wondering if more was to come. Uncertain, a loud knock on the door heralded the return of Miss Roberts complete with tea on a silver tray.

Minutes later, after both men had endured an uncomfortable silence, Miss Roberts duly departed. As the heavy oak door shut behind her, Davenport spoke. 'Well, the facts of the matter are beyond dispute. So, unless Drysdale can name his accomplices, the Law, as they say, will take its course. Eight o'clock sharp, tomorrow morning over at Pentonville.' Davenport paused, almost anticipating an interruption but, as none came, he continued. 'Alright, while Drysdale killed nobody, we know that he drove his fellow criminals to and from the robbery. Nevertheless, Drysdale was an integral part of an operation in which two people died. A young female bank employee and a security guard. Of course, it was your man's misfortune to crash the getaway car, trapped in the wreckage as the other two cleared off with the money.' Sensing that Lambert was about to interrupt, Davenport raised the palm of his hand. 'As you know, in such cases, the law takes the view that all parties were acting with a common purpose, regarding all involved as being equally guilty.'

'Yes,' the solicitor acknowledged, 'but Drysdale didn't know the identity of his colleagues. Didn't even know they carried guns.'

'Sorry, but what difference does that make? They're just points introduced by Ruskin in his final submission to the jury. Yet, whichever way you look at it, there are two dead bodies. Murder by a firearm in the pursuit of robbery is a hanging offence, as you well know. The judge, in his summing up, stressed this to be a clear case of *joint enterprise*. They were all in it together, acting in common accord. Whether they knew one another is irrelevant. A point fully endorsed by the appeal judges as well – just weeks ago.' He paused, looking directly at the younger man before continuing. 'Nobody here has a problem with known villains taking an early morning walk to oblivion, but this Drysdale character is something different.' Hardly pausing for breath, he went on. 'Ever since they hanged Derek Bentley, ten years or so back, for a murder committed whilst he was technically under arrest, cases like this don't sit easily around here - I can tell you!' Davenport raised his eyes to the ceiling before slumping back into his chair, lapsing into a pensive silence.

Something different, that's one way of putting it. Aged twenty-two, Drysdale had exchanged his privileged lifestyle for a roller coaster ride to the gallows. Two years earlier he and his elder sister Valerie had become orphans overnight, their parents dying in a plane crash while off winter skiing in Switzerland. Drysdale senior, a prominent surgeon, had a practice in Harley Street with a client list that read like pages from Burke's Peerage, while his younger wife had moved gracefully within the best of London society, making full use of their Georgian mansion. A house seldom without prominent visitors or exclusive dinner parties.

Fuelled by the vitality of youth the youngsters had recovered well, only to end up taking paths that became diametrically opposed. Valerie had continued to maximise her career opportunities in finance while Stephen, armed with access to easy money, had turned his back on Oxford. Joining instead the *jet set*, rowdy night clubs, fast women and even faster cars.

Shocked by her brother's behaviour Valerie had intervened, using legal avenues to curtail his access to the family money. Stephen, deprived of ready cash, had soon become a frequenter of low-quality, smoke-filled bars and snooker halls. Places where the company struggled to rise above the threadbare surroundings. Down on his luck, he'd been a *target*, someone desperately in need of cash. *Just a little driving job*. It had all sounded so straightforward back then.

'As I was pointing out,' Davenport spoke, his voice cutting through Lambert's thoughts, 'we're not comfortable with this. For sure, I can virtually guarantee a stay of execution, followed by a retrial, were your client to give us the names of his accomplices. The Home Secretary is ready to act, even at this late hour, but we must give him something to bite on.' He looked directly at Lambert, 'with names arrests will follow, along with a new trial. Your man will end up with a prison sentence, as opposed to taking a short walk in the morning.' Davenport looked pleadingly at the young man sitting opposite.

'Commander,' Lambert said slowly, 'be realistic. Don't you think that Stephen would name those people if he could? In his place, I'd be shouting my head off to anyone who'd listen! Wouldn't you?'

'Okay,' Davenport conceded, as he looked directly at Lambert. 'Point taken - but without names you must see we've no room to manoeuvre. The sheer violence of the crime caused public outrage, an outrage demanding satisfaction.'

'Damn it,' Commander,' Lambert snapped. 'This isn't about satisfaction; it's about appeasing public opinion!'

'Forget that' Davenport snorted, his weather-beaten face taking on a florid colour reflecting his anger. 'This was a brutal robbery, motivated by greed and conducted without a shred of mercy that left two people dead!' Recoiling under Davenport's ferocity Lambert leant back in his chair, raising a limp hand in a gesture of mock surrender.

'I'm sorry, Commander. Of course, I know just how terrible the crime was, but don't ask me to ignore the fact that Drysdale was simply the driver. The scapegoat if you like.'

'Okay,' Davenport growled. 'Apology accepted, but you must understand that we cannot differentiate here. All three are equally guilty. So,' he questioned, 'where do we go from here?'

'Not far by the look of things,' Lambert offered weakly.

'Well, it's really up to Stephen, you know,' Davenport replied, his hand moving quickly to snatch up the telephone after just a single ring.

'Yes, yes, Miss Roberts, put him through now!' Davenport shouted, his brow furrowing with concentration as he listened intently to the caller. Nodding from time to time, his mannerisms gave nothing away. Less than a minute later, having replaced the receiver, he addressed Lambert. 'That was the Governor over at Pentonville,' he said excitedly, 'told me Drysdale's been busy writing all afternoon. Now he wants to see you as soon as you can get there.' A broad smile crossed Lambert's face as he leaned forward in his chair.

'Names at last,' he said hopefully, 'I'll get over there right away.'

'Yes,' he spoke sharply, 'you do that. Then call me to let me know what's going on,' he snapped, pointing to the telephone. 'But, before you dash off,' he said, his hand returning to the phone to issue instructions. 'Miss Roberts, can you organise a car to take Mr Lambert over to Pentonville? Yes, right away please, oh, and bring in his coat. Thank you.' He turned to Lambert, 'The least we can do. Get the driver to wait, then call me immediately.'

'Right, Commander, I'm on my way' Lambert replied, scrambling from his chair. 'Rest assured I'll get back to you as soon as I can.' Buoyed up by hope he left the building, completely unaware of the horrors awaiting him. Horrors that were to remain lodged at the back of his mind for the rest of his days.

CHAPTER 2

THREE HOURS LATER it was a dejected Lambert who walked across Paddington Station's main concourse. His anguish was compounded by the message plastered across the newsstand placards. *Drysdale to Hang.* A clear statement, incapable of any misunderstanding.

The visit to Pentonville had been traumatic. Although familiar with prison interiors, courtesy of his normal duties as a solicitor, Lambert had experienced something entirely new that late afternoon. Outside, a group of banner-waving protesters had shuffled noisily around a blazing oil drum. Inside words had been kept to a minimum while eye contact with any of the prison staff had been awkward, to say the least.

One look at the Governor's face, upon reaching the prison, had told him that his mission was not going to be successful. Governor Hoskins, with a minimum of words, had told him how Drysdale had been writing for several hours, now insisting that his work be handed over personally. Mindful of his responsibility to keep a condemned prisoner as calm as possible, Hoskins had called the home office. 'Most irregular,' he'd said bluntly to Lambert, 'but I'll take you directly to him.'

Accompanied by a tight-lipped prison officer they had negotiated a labyrinth of soulless corridors, linoleum floors with two-tone walls, green up to waist height, above that cream. Each corridor divided with locked steel grilles, noisily opened by key-jangling warders then firmly closed once they had passed through. Breaking the silence Hoskins had commented. 'At times like this, we ah, find it less distressing for the prisoner to be visited in his cell, as opposed to moving him around.' Lambert had nodded, the message confirming that he would see Drysdale in one of the prison's two condemned cells. The confined space in which a human being was to spend his last night on earth. Fear fuelled by the urge to run had, with each advancing step, tightened the knot in his stomach. Moments later he had nearly bumped into the escorting officer who had snapped to attention in front of a metal door, complete with spy flap. In silence, one curt nod from Hoskins had been enough to have the door opened. The same nod, given at precisely eight o'clock the following morning would send the hangman and his assistant into the cell from another door where they would collect Drysdale before leading him the short distance to the gallows. Seconds later it would all be over.

After swinging the door open the officer had stepped aside allowing the governor and a dry-mouthed Lambert to enter the call. Drysdale, along with two warders, had been sitting around a small table covered with cups, newspapers, playing cards and a half-full ashtray. Of necessity, any conversation had been a brief exchange of words, during which Lambert had taken custody of an envelope addressed to him and carrying a simple message. The envelope was to remain sealed, secure in his custody for the next seven days, before being handed personally to Drysdale's sister. Having taken receipt of the envelope he'd turned, desperate to get away from that dreadful place. It was then that Drysdale had cracked!

Suddenly he'd found Drysdale's arms thrust around his shoulders in a tight grip. Taken by surprise, it had been a matter of seconds before the two warders had been able to intervene. Pressing his face close to Lambert he'd sobbed, pleading that he had not killed anybody. With care the officers had prised the pair apart, settling Drysdale down onto a chair as Lambert, on wobbly legs returned to the corridor. Already tense, he'd allowed Hoskins to take his elbow before guiding him back down the corridor. 'So sorry about that my dear chap,' he'd apologised to Lambert who, incapable of making a reply, had simply staggered forward. What could you say? There were no words – there never could be. Minutes later, back in Hoskins's office he'd sought permission to telephone Davenport, reporting back on the failure of his mission. Choking with emotion he'd been unable to say more as, across the office, the governor had been thoughtfully applying sealing wax to the envelope, pressing the HM Prison Service seal into the molten wax.

***

Comfortable in his corner seat Lambert felt the full burden of defeat boring into him like a drill. The words, scripted on the envelope, had stubbed out any lingering hopes of securing anything. *To be handed by my solicitor Mr Gerald Lambert, unopened, to my sister Valerie seven days after my death. Signed...... Stephen Drysdale.* The carefully phrased words confirming that Drysdale was incapable of saving himself.

Moments later a whistle sounded sending Lambert's train, belching steam and smoke, out into the foggy darkness of West London. Absorbed in thought his mind kept returning to the envelope in his briefcase, daring to wonder if Drysdale really had named his accomplices. If he had, and with hours to go, would the Home Secretary grant a stay of execution? Should I open the envelope to find out? He asked himself. Then, if I did that, how might Valerie react? Obviously, she'd notice, so what might the consequences be? Would she question my professional integrity? Or might she benevolently regard my action as something of a final attempt to bring about a reprieve for her brother? Say Valerie were to tear open the envelope the moment I handed it to her and find that Stephen had named his accomplices? How would she react and just where might she place the blame for that? Then again, what would happen if I just threw the blasted thing away? Only four people know that it's ever existed in the first place: Hoskins, Davenport, Drysdale and me. Please let this be the end of it, the last thing I want is for that envelope to come back and haunt me, the thought refusing to leave him as the train clattered westwards into the night.

CHAPTER 3

AS LAMBERT'S TRAIN was leaving Paddington a man in his early twenties, with swept- back blonde hair above piercing blue eyes, walked into a north London public house. Pausing momentarily inside the squeaking doorway he nodded to the white-coated man behind the bar. Stepping forward he looked around the deserted room, then approached the bar to order a gin and tonic.

'Foul night out there,' he remarked, unbuttoning his expensive camel-hair coat to reveal a well-cut suit, complete with a striped shirt and matching tie.

'S'right,' the bartender muttered, turning to place a glass below the optic. 'Be quiet in here tonight. Won't it?' Moments later the till closed noisily as the man picked up his glass and tonic bottle. Pocketing his change, he considered, and not for the first time, the quirky ability of Londoners to make a statement and then finish it with a question.

Moving slowly the man chose an isolated table, unsighted from the bar yet with a clear view of the door. Settling down to wait his well-manicured hands elegantly placed a silver cigarette case carefully beside his drink. From another, pocket he removed, with corresponding care, a gold-plated lighter which he placed neatly next to the cigarette case. Moments later, aroused by the noisy hinges of the pub door, he looked across as a man entered the bar bringing with him a swirl of fog.

Without any sign of recognition, the new arrival noted the man sitting in the far corner before moving from his line of sight to approach the bar. Minutes later, holding a beer glass in his right hand, he made towards the face he had recognised in the darkened corner. Similar in age with a shock of dark tousled hair, he was wearing jeans and a roll-neck sweater beneath a donkey jacket. His hands were hidden by gloves. After a brief nod to the man already seated, he put his drink onto the table before sitting down. In silence, he pulled the black leather glove from his right hand leaving the other glove in place. Across the table, his companion added a measure of tonic to his gin, then raised his glass before speaking softly.

'Here's to Stephen,' his remark causing confusion for a matter of seconds before the other man regained his composure.

'Oh yes, to Stephen,' he muttered, acknowledging the toast by raising his glass. After taking a modest sip he returned his glass to the table, saying quietly. 'Poor sod. I don't envy him.' Ignoring the comment, the man in the camel hair coat carefully moved the lighter to one side before selecting a cigarette. Then, drawing deeply on his cigarette, his gaze hardened as he addressed his companion.

'Look, don't go distressing yourself. As an ex-army man, you'll appreciate that casualties can be an unplanned consequence in any close action.' The words uttered dispassionately by the man as he breathed out a long stream of smoke. Looking directly into the face of his companion he noted, and not for the first time, the broken nose plus scar tissue above one eye, trademarks that represented the futility of entering a boxing ring without the necessary defensive skills.

'However, George,' he continued, 'it's time to go forward. No point in looking backwards - we can't alter history – we can only make it,' he commented, smiling through a cloud of smoke. 'We must move on, in separate directions that is, after sharing the spoils of war between us. Spoils that are now five hundred pounds to the better because we've not had to pay Stephen.'

'Christ! - you're a hard bastard,' the beer drinker muttered. 'Can't we get his cut to his family - wife, mother or whatever?' Unimpressed, the other man reached inside his coat before speaking.

'Yes...hard I may be, but I'm not suicidal enough to go visiting Pentonville with five hundred pounds in my pocket for Drysdale. He's an unmarried orphan,' he paused before adding, 'but look, should you feel a compulsive urge to drop in there this evening, I've no doubt he'd appreciate a bit of company.' His eyebrows arched in silent questioning as he stared directly at his companion. 'Anyway, time to forget the happy family nonsense as I've got your share here. Half the money, as agreed, in cheques all payable to George Noakes.' Still talking, he withdrew a manila envelope from the depths of his inside jacket pocket. 'Here you go, complete with a covering solicitor's letter, expressing regret at the death of your late Aunt in South Africa but passing over your legacy. It's even got a certificate exempting you from tax!' His last remark produced a fleeting smile that failed to reach his eyes. 'Now isn't that a lovely touch? Everything all nice and legal for you, plus a bundle of cheques!'

'Yeah....but why not just one?'

'Now then, George, don't be naive. How would it look if you popped into your bank, paying in one big slab of money? Questions. Bank managers love people who make big deposits, greedy little sods that they are. It looks good on their monthly returns to head office, helps them up the promotion ladder. Your bank manager would be over you like a fly on a pile of dung. First, he'd want to know where the money came from, then he'd take you out for a slap-up lunch before advising you on how best to invest your money in his grubby little bank.' Sensing an objection, he turned away to delicately place his cigarette into the ashtray. 'Don't forget, questions require answers. The last thing we need is a flaming bank manager sticking his nose into your affairs. So, to minimise any risk, with multiple cheques you make smaller deposits. Use different banks and don't forget the post office. That way no one gets too excited. As added protection, you have the solicitor's letter plus the tax exemption certificate,' he smiled. 'Okay, they'll pass a brief muster, but closer inspection would be most unwelcome, if you take my meaning?'

Gingerly, Noakes accepted the envelope, holding it in his still-gloved left hand while sliding out the enclosed documents with his other hand.

'Bloody hell,' he spluttered, 'so that is what thirty-five grand looks like!'

'Yes, exactly as agreed, so no more worrying about Stephen.' He drew heavily upon his cigarette before continuing. 'Stephen has no idea who we are because I took all necessary precautions before we did the job. The secret of success is to have a safety barrier in place, making sure that none of the crap comes flying your way if the bomb goes off. You know me as Alistair Buchanan, while I know you as George Noakes. But, from the very outset, I made doubly sure that Stephen didn't know who we were, so he's unable to trace us. Let alone finger us in a police enquiry. Relax, we've got away with the perfect crime.'

'Perfect! That's excluding a body count of two, rising to three in the morning,' Noakes countered, with enforced resignation.

'Merely collateral damage, George,' Buchanan replied in a bored tone, peering through a haze of smoke. 'Given the choice of spending all that money or changing places with Stephen, what would you rather have?'

'Yeah well, okay, point taken,' Noakes acknowledged solemnly.

'Right then, stop worrying. It worked well, a one-off job where we got exactly what we set out for. As for Stephen, well he never knew either of us. No names - no trail - no more Stephen. Come eight o'clock in the morning he won't be talking to anybody. No more worries there. The money's untraceable, we're away clean and untouchable,' he stated without emotion. 'Now look, it's unfortunate that your early aspirations to enter the world of professional boxing were, how should we say, cut short. But, not to worry, I'm sure you'll find a way of spending your share of the venture. Have you any ideas in that direction?'

'Yes,' Noakes replied, gathering his thoughts, 'as I can no longer box, what with this damaged hand, I thought I'd apply to the board for a trainer's licence.'

'What board would that be then?' Buchanan asked with scarcely feigned indifference.

'The British Board of Boxing Control of course,' Noakes replied.

'Ah, then what?' came the bored reply.

'Well, with this money,' his gloved hand tapped the envelope lying on the table, 'I should be able to buy suitable premises to turn into a proper gym and training centre.'

'Will that make you any money though?'

'Hmm, yes. There are two ways I've got in mind. The gym thing should make money by charging people a monthly membership subscription.'

'The other way being?' Buchanan prompted.

'Oh, that's where I'd offer my services to the managers of professional boxers, to be their trainer like, for a share of the purse of course.'

'Ah, I see,' Buchanan replied, stubbing out his cigarette as both men shared an uneasy silence.

'Okay,' Noakes asked slowly, 'that's me out of the way, what are you going to do with your share?'

'You'll not be surprised that I organised the robbery to get the money I needed to finance my scheme, one that'll make me exceedingly rich.' He smiled, relishing the prospects of his new enterprise.

'Will it be legal or otherwise?' Noakes asked, taking another mouthful of beer as Buchanan mulled over the implications, answering as Noakes replaced his glass on the table.

'Oh, I don't know. Somewhere near the outer limits of legality I guess, but good enough to stop anybody sniffing around. By the end of next year my thirty-five thousand pounds will have increased by at least five times.'

'Bloody hell,' Noakes gasped in amazement, seeking refuge in another mouthful of beer. 'How the Devil will you do that?' he asked, curiosity getting the better of him.

'Simple. I'll lend it out to poor sods who find themselves unable to afford what they desire, then charge sky-high rates of interest.'

'Loan sharking you mean?'

'Oh,' Buchanan smirked, 'how common. No, this'll be a form of professional money lending, providing a service in areas where banks won't go. You see,' he explained patiently, 'banks lend money against security, property deeds, insurance policies and that sort of thing. However, I find that the fear of a broken leg or worse makes for equally good security.'

'God, you're a ruthless sod,' Noakes uttered. Appalled by what he had just heard, recognising that Buchanan represented the worst kind of person turned out by the public school system. An utterly selfish, arrogant and sarcastic bully, harbouring an overwhelming desire to be *top dog,* exploiting people in his ruthless drive for power.

'As always, in my planning,' Buchanan went on as if Noakes had never spoken, 'I've built in my own special fail-safe system in which I am untraceable, one in which even *my lieutenants* have no idea who I am. After two or three years, I'll have amassed the considerable fortune needed for me to blend into wealthy society, as the owner of a legitimate business operation. You see,' Buchanan continued, gaining enthusiastic momentum as he did so. 'While you know me as Alistair Buchanan, that name is meaningless. Merely a front if you like - a springboard to greater things. As you so rightly pointed out I am a ruthless sod, and that's something well worth remembering.' His voice was hard and unwavering. 'Should you do anything silly, or talk to the wrong people, I shall find out and then come looking for you. Well, not me personally of course,' he smiled, 'but two or three determined gentlemen who do my bidding to the letter!'

With the blood draining from his face, Noakes found himself incapable of forming a reply, grimacing as Buchanan continued speaking. 'But' he laughed, 'no need to bother about that,' he added reassuringly. 'Our future is based upon mutual silence. Come to think of it, either of us could go telling tales to the authorities,' he jested. 'But seriously,' he asked, 'how sympathetic do you think the courts would be? You know, what with having stood idly by while an innocent man got hanger?'

'Bugger all I'd guess,' Noakes mumbled, finally appreciating just how completely pitiless the man he knew as Alistair Buchanan was.

CHAPTER 4

'**RIGHT, I'M OFF**,' Buchanan informed Noakes. 'However,' he paused, 'as I'll always know where to find you, it is only right and proper that you can contact me in the event of a dire emergency. Inside there,' he pointed to another envelope that he'd just placed on the table, 'you'll find the address of a major high street bank, where I've deposited another envelope in their strong room. Inside that, you'll find details of a firm of solicitors who, I assure you, will be able to contact me within days. The envelope I've given you contains a letter authorising the bank to hand their envelope to the bearer of that letter.'

'You've not put my name on the envelope, have you?' Noakes blurted out in alarm.

'No fear,' Buchanan replied, giving Noakes a look of patronising warmth. 'Their envelope has four numbers written on it. No names.' He shook his head slowly. 'In fact, they are the same four numbers that are on the authorisation letter I've given to you. So, once you've withdrawn the envelope from the bank, you can get through to me. Well, not directly,' he explained, 'simply leave a message asking them to arrange for Alistair Buchanan to ring you on whatever number you care to give them. Both the bank and the solicitors will hold this facility for a long time. In that way, after you have asked for them to pass on a message, I'll give you a call back to find out what's troubling you.' Falling silent Buchanan leaned forward, placing his face squarely in front of Noakes before continuing. 'Be sure to make that a public phone box number, stating the time you'll be in place to take my call. Should I not respond immediately, be there at the same time every day because, who knows, I may have been away. Clear?' He looked questioningly into the face opposite him.

'Bloody hell - you think of everything, don't you,' Noakes mumbled.

'Correct,' Buchanan snapped. 'That's why we are not in Pentonville with Drysdale, sitting there like lemons waiting to get topped in the morning!' Then his anger vanished as fast as it had appeared. 'For emergency use only,' he tapped the envelope, 'only a genuine emergency.

'Are you quite clear on that one?'

'Yeah,' Noakes confirmed, 'it makes sense, like.'

'Okay, I can't think of any reason for you to ever contact me again, so I'll be on my way,' he informed his companion, standing up before extending his right hand.

'We worked well together, both getting what we wanted, but it ends here. So, take your time over another beer, and don't attempt to come after me.' Noakes took the offered hand, chilled by the unflinching stare that went with it.

'Yeah,' he replied, 'as you say, that's it.' Remaining seated Noakes watched as Buchanan stepped out into the thickening fog, letting the door bang noisily behind him.

***

Inside the pub, Noakes looked down at his gloved left hand as painful memories of that crowded Hamburg nightclub came flooding back. It had come from nowhere. The jungle knife scything across his left hand, inflicting an agonising wound that instantly severed fingers from the top of his middle finger to the base of the little one. Severely injured, two soldiers had taken him to the nearby military hospital to receive expert attention. During his short confinement he'd not been surprised how the Military Police and nursing staff had downplayed the incident. Under no circumstances could such an incident put Anglo-German relationships at risk by allowing revenge-seeking "squaddies" to rampage around Hamburg.

Noakes, aware of the politics involved, had quickly understood the indecent underpinning his return to England and his inevitable discharge. Four weeks later, on a cold and wet Aldershot morning, he'd found himself unceremoniously bundled out of the army. Disabled, depressed and unemployed, he'd been sorry to leave the army since, to him, military life had represented an organised society. A *family* that had offered companionship denied to him as a single child in a warring household.

During his brief period of military service, he'd volunteered to specialise in bomb disposal, exciting work that he knew he'd miss. Okay, he conceded, up to then he'd not actually seen a proper bomb, but the lectures had been interesting. Especially the way his sergeant had delighted in telling them exactly what made things go bang!

What a bloody mess he muttered, looking again at

his gloved left hand. A senseless brawl over some German tart I hardly even knew. Now I'm permanently disabled, no more soldiering, no more bomb disposal work and no more boxing. The later thought reminding him how well he'd done in the BOAR (British Army over the Rhine) championships. A promising middleweight the sergeant PTI had called him. Now nothing.

With guilt compounding his remorse, he wondered how Drysdale might be managing his last night on earth. Would he sleep – could he sleep? For God's sake, the poor sod's going to die in the morning, trussed up like a turkey with a bag over his head and a rope around his neck! Meanwhile, I'm in a warm pub preparing to spend the money gained at the expense of two innocent lives. He gave an involuntary shudder, sick in the knowledge that another life was to join that tally in a matter of hours. It was supposed to be a simple robbery, clobber the security guard, push a dopey bird out of the way, then scarper with the money. But oh no, not Buchanan. He'd calmly murdered two people, leaving me to grab the money before we made it back to the car. He was still laughing like a drain when Stephen hit that sodding lorry. 'Oh God,' he muttered, terrified by the thought of just how far Buchanan's criminal reach might extend.

Noakes was astute enough to appreciate that their lives now depended upon mutual silence because the temptation to turn Queen's Evidence would be irresistible were one of them arrested. Damn the man, I'm trapped between him and the hangman. Just so long as I'm alive I'll always be a threat but, with me dead, there'd be nothing linking Buchanan to Drysdale, the robbery or the shootings. The truth of this hit Noakes hard, making him aware of just how exposed he had become. Buchanan can blow the whistle on me whenever he likes, but I'm helpless, I've no idea who he is or where to find him, other than that phone number.

Having taken the offered advice Noakes was halfway through his second glass of beer when he realised that Buchanan had just made a glaring error. Weighed down with overbearing arrogance he'd slipped up badly, leaving behind a unique *calling card*. Not the total protection I'd like, but at least it's proof Buchanan was the brains behind that murderous robbery. Gingerly he replaced the glove on his right hand, carefully withdrawing the envelope from his inside pocket. An envelope covered with Buchanan's fingerprints!

CHAPTER 5

THE HOUSE WAS an elegant mock-Tudor building overlooking the Thames a mile upstream from Henley. Called *Montserrat* the magnificent house stood proudly on the sloping hillside just upstream from Marsh Lock. Outside, on the gravelled driveway a little way from the house, two cars stood parked in front of a building that had originally been a stable block. The ground floor of which was now a spacious double garage while the upstairs provided comfortable accommodation for the long-serving live-in staff. Mr Logan multi-tasked as handyman, chauffeur and gardener whilst his wife undertook cooking and housekeeping duties.

That Saturday morning four pairs of eyes watched as Gerald Lambert adjusted his glasses, before picking up a medium sized envelope from the coffee table. Thoughtfully the retired solicitor examined the envelope with care, looking at it with barely concealed amazement.

'After all these years,' he commented, 'it's resurfaced, an almost forgotten messenger from the past. Look,' he pointed out, 'even the wax seals are still intact.' In silence the onlookers took in every movement as Lambert appeared lost in thought, his ageing but still agile his mind travelled back six decades. Still peering at the envelope, through his heavy rimmed glasses, he started to speak softly.

'No,' he said, shaking his head, 'I never expected to see this again,' he rotated the envelope, 'still unopened, its secrets intact. November 1962,' he hesitated, turning the envelope again before replacing it on the coffee table.

Settling back into his armchair he looked around the room, pausing to smile at his younger wife Sarah before turning to face his three seated guests. Two of whom he'd invited to witness the opening of the envelope provided by the third guest, a heavily built man beset with mixed emotions. Of course, everyone was curious, with doubters wondering if opening the envelope might have unforeseen consequences or prove to be meaningless. Only later would they have their fears justified as Lambert, having reached a decision, leant forward in his chair.

'The signature on the envelope, as you know, Mr Lawrence;' he turned to face a heavily built white-haired man in his early eighties sitting opposite him. 'Is that of Stephen Drysdale. And now,' he stopped speaking, interlocking the fingers of both hands across his lap before looking around the room. 'As I remain unsure as to who knows what, let me give you a little background information.' Reaching forward, he again lifted the envelope and began talking.

'Back in the early sixties I was an ambitious young solicitor,' he smiled, 'working for my father's practice, Regency Law up in London's West End. In 1962 we managed the defence of Stephen Drysdale who, having fallen in with bad company, embarked upon a murderous bank raid. An event that led to his execution. During the robbery, Drysdale's accomplices ruthlessly gunned down a security guard and a female bank employee.' Lambert paused, looking around the room, gauging reactions before continuing. 'The robbery,' he said, 'took place as two men from a security firm were transferring cash from their bullion van onto a trolley outside a bank. Young Drysdale was the robbers' getaway driver. Minutes later he crashed the car, left trapped in the wreckage while his accomplices made off with the money, vanishing entirely. Then, once released from the wreckage, Drysdale faced a murder charge. This led to his trial at the Old Bailey where he was sentenced to hang. Then, as you now know, weeks after that he was to meet his fate in Pentonville.' Deep in thought he fell silent, allowing all present to absorb what they had just heard before adding.

'The afternoon before the execution, while I was at the Home Office, the prison governor at Pentonville telephoned to say that Stephen was asking for me urgently. Accordingly, I went to the prison where Stephen personally handed me this envelope, fifteen hours or so before his death. Of course, I'd expected to see him in the governor's office, or an interview room. But no, the governor escorted me to the condemned cell. Oh, dear God,' he mumbled, 'the experience was traumatic! It was horrible - leaving me badly shaken.' Falling silent Lambert gave his guests a haunted look, long suppressed memories rising to the surface of his mind as he resumed speaking in more agitated tones. 'For as long as I live, I'll never forget that terrible place,' his rheumy eyes darting from face to face, 'Everyone there committed to a task for which they had not the slightest appetite! Drysdale was terrified. I'll never forget the fear in his eyes as he grabbed hold of my jacket, crying out that he'd never killed anyone.' He halted for a moment as if trying to reassemble his thoughts into a rational order. 'Then, to my eternal relief, the Governor whisked me out of that dreadful place before any more dramas could be played out.'

Appearing to relax a little Lambert went on. 'As Instructed, one week later I delivered this envelope to Valerie Drysdale. By then she was in a rented flat in Pimlico, having already sold the family home. Our meeting was brief yet, as you can see,' he pointed to the envelope, 'the wax seals are still intact. In conversation she said she'd be changing her name by deed poll before emigrating, I believe to Canada. By then, as our legal responsibilities to her were over, that was the last I saw or heard of her, or this envelope. That was until eleven o'clock yesterday morning when the telephone rang.'

To the right of Lambert, Robert Vere a solicitor in his early thirties, watched his former mentor, worried by the obvious strain the recalled memories were having upon his friend. He'd known Lambert since joining Regency Law, as a newly qualified solicitor living in nearby Shiplake. With Lambert making the daily commute from Wargrave and joining Vere on the same train, it was not long before they embarked upon a growing friendship. Beside him, on the settee, Yvonne Clarkson, a talented fashion journalist in her late twenties, crossed her legs while absently brushing some strands of dark hair away from her face. Like everyone else in the room she remained focussed on Lambert as he cleared his throat.

'Mr Lawrence, perhaps it is time for you to let us have your input,' he smiled across at the big man. 'Because, let's be honest, you are the reason for this little gathering.'

'Dan - please,' he said affably, in a distinct accent that most people would have called American, the more discerning recognising it as Canadian. Leaning forward, he looked from face to face before speaking. 'Okay folks, to bring things into perspective, let me start by saying that Valerie Drysdale and I were married in 1965. Very sadly she died about six months ago, suffering from heart problems.'

'Oh, I'm so sorry to hear that,' Vere spoke, confident he was expressing the feelings of all those present.

'Yeah, thanks. Valarie's death was unexpected and now,' he paused in thought, 'being alone at my age is not that easy. Not after such a long and happy marriage.' From bitter experience, gained when discussing the loss of his soul mate, he smiled at the faces around the room, a ploy he used to relax people whenever the subject of his wife's death came into the conversation. 'Anyway, to continue,' Dan Lawrence said. 'Back in 1963, to dad's regret, I ducked out of college, turned my back on his financial brokerage and opened my first used car lot in Toronto. Dad and I still got on well, despite my jumping ship.' He smiled. 'I was a regular visitor to his offices and, on one such visit, he introduced me to his latest new employee, a young lady fresh in from England. And, as you good folks can guess, Valerie Walsh was the former Valerie Drysdale.'

'Ah,' Vere commented, 'the first piece slips into place.'

'Yes,' Lawrence smiled, 'as you say the first piece, but there's more, plenty more. Not only was Valerie a real looker, but she also had an impressive financial track record, so making her an ideal employee. Over the next year or so we dated on a regular basis, eventually becoming engaged, much to mum and dad's delight, with marriage following in sixty-seven.' Thoughtfully Lawrence then explained how Valarie had originally described herself as an orphan, only years later revealing the name change and how she could arrive, unattached in Canada, with a sizeable fortune. In time she had permitted Lawrence senior to invest her money wisely, the proceeds later funding the purchase of a main dealership in Toronto. Pausing for a moment the room remained in silence, everyone assessing what they had just heard. Taking advantage of the pause, Yvonne quietly said to Lawrence.

'Did you and Valerie have any children, Dan?'

'Sadly no, we were not blessed in that way, but elsewhere we did okay,' he laughed softly. 'We enjoyed life. We had a large penthouse suite, in a block looking right out over Lake Ontario. Quite a view I can tell you. We also had an amazing timber lodge, all mod-cons and miles away up in a forest. The ideal holiday getaway home, that's if you didn't mind the odd bear or two for neighbours.'

All in the room laughed at the picture he was painting, lapsing into silence as a sudden change came over the Canadian, painful memories resurfacing. Breaking the silence Sarah Lambert asked, with the typical English formality that simply outlawed the use of first names at an initial meeting.

'Mr Lawrence, I'd like to ask what brought you to England but, before I do that, please allow me to get everyone some coffee.'

'Hold on Sarah. Surely, Mrs Logan can do that, dear?' Lambert enquired, turning to his wife.

'Nonsense, Gerald,' she laughed in gentle rebuke to her husband. 'Mrs Logan's far too busy preparing a buffet lunch for all of us.' She smiled around the room. 'I've instructed her to set it out in the conservatory. It'll be nice and warm out there in this very welcome sunshine.' Rising gracefully from her chair, she looked around the room. 'Now, how do you all like your coffee?' Once certain of their selections she moved effortlessly from the lounge, still displaying the same confident demeanour with which she had graced West End stages. Yet, as Sarah Lambert left the room, nine hundred miles away in Spain a man was about to die, yet another killing attributed to the unopened envelope in front of Gerald Lambert.

CHAPTER 6

HIGH ABOVE STREET level, the noise from the Marbella bars and cafes failed to reach the top floor apartment of Miguel Ramos, a police officer serving with Spain's elite drug squad. Staring at his laptop Ramos was a fifty-year-old, badly overweight unmarried workaholic, a creature of habit who chose to work from home every Saturday to avoid the daily commute to headquarters in Malaga. A talented officer, appreciated by his superiors and respected by his subordinates and renowned for his logical thought process. Looking thoughtfully at the e-mail on his screen he took a half-smoked cigarette from his mouth, tapping the smouldering end above an already overflowing ashtray.

Another false alarm or was this to be the tip of the iceberg? Ramos wondered, blowing smoke over the top of his screen. Strong feelings were not enough, he sighed. Believing Malaga Airport to be at the heart of a drug-running operation was one thing, but I've no evidence, he muttered, looking again at the e-mail. Could this be his longed-for breakthrough? Earlier, in the airport's check-in area, a sniffer dog had barked excitedly around a pair of tired-looking suitcases belonging to a young couple bound for Gatwick. The police, suspecting drugs, had immediately taken the couple to a secure suite of offices, away from public scrutiny. Ramos then read that while the young couple displayed signs of agitation, they'd seemed more confused than openly frightened. Classic symptoms displayed by those unknowingly caught up in drug running. Known as "mules," these people carried drugs on behalf of the traffickers yet, in the main, had no idea they were doing so.

Ramos, sweating profusely, read how the dog had shown interest in a sealed package of five fifty-gram vacuum-sealed tins of pipe tobacco. Confirming that the tobacco tins were his, the male passenger had produced a Barclaycard receipt from Gatwick, along with a well-worn pipe and leather tobacco pouch. All trademarks of a seasoned pipe smoker. Lacking any drug-related evidence, the police had returned the confused couple to the departures area for their onward flight. As Ramos gave further thought to what he had just read Rosita, his daily help, crossed the lounge carrying a tray with his mid-day coffee and brandy. Without speaking she went out onto the balcony, placing the tray on a wrought iron table before opening a parasol to provide shade. Minutes later Ramos emerged, appearing on the balcony exactly as the man waiting patiently nearby knew that he would. Noon on Saturday.

Settling his considerable frame into the shaded chair, he focussed on the reported incident at the airport. Hard drugs, trafficked from Columbia to North Africa before entering Spain along the Costas, had to go somewhere. But where? he wondered, accepting that getting the drugs to the United Kingdom would be one logical move. There, and diluted with flour or icing sugar, they would have a phenomenal cash value on the drug-hungry streets of Britain. But was this happening and, if so, how?

Suspicious by nature, his instinct had always focussed on the airport's potential to be an ideal conduit for distributing drugs across Europe. Malaga Airport, where hundreds of planes carried thousands of passengers to countless destinations every day. But surely the airport was secure – wasn't it? Unless, that is, someone has found a way around the system! Would being able to refill tins of pipe tobacco with drugs, then reseal the plastic packaging be such a method? Was this possible? If so, it was brilliant, undetectable. Purchase the genuine tobacco tins in England, swap the contents in Spain then have the resealed tins taken onto countless aircraft by unsuspecting "mules." Perfection, no smell, no traces! Hell! if I'm right this could be the most cunningly sophisticated drug smuggling method ever contrived. It's foolproof, guaranteeing that sniffer dogs or customs officials could never detect the drugs.

Acting on instinct he had, in recent weeks, insisted upon intensifying random checks on departing travellers. So far without results, unless creating even longer queues in departure areas counted as a result. Yet, if my thinking is correct, such a smuggling operation as this would require a workshop, backed up by the specialised machinery needed to completely reseal the packages. Not something you'd do in the back bedroom he thought. No, for this to be a paying proposition it must be conducted on an industrial scale. Never mind one pack, imagine thousands of "mules" carrying 250 grams of Columbian pure apiece. The thought made him go cold. Could such an operation be going on right now, in the middle of the patch I'm responsible for? And today, he wondered, had the smugglers made their first mistake, leaving just the merest trace of something suspicious to set the dog off?

Time to see if I'm right Ramos decided, knowing that his proof would be in one of two places, the airport or cruising at high altitude. Not to worry, I'll get our people to check if they're still at the airport. Should that be the case the police can open one of those tins, if not we'll get Gatwick Customs to inspect them. Either way, I'll know. Confident he was on the right track he delayed making the call, unaware that death was just two hundred yards away.

***

'I see you've come in the MG,' Lambert said as they awaited the return of Sarah, 'beats me how a six-foot-something ex-oarsman manages to get into that thing?'

'Bit small for over our way,' the Canadian drawled, 'but I wouldn't say no to a couple of them on the used car lot. Summertime only, you'd lose them in an average Toronto snowfall, never mind a bad one!'

'As for you, Yvonne,' Lambert asked with a cheeky grin on his face, 'just how do you manage in such cramped conditions?'

'Hey, less of the *ex-oarsman*. Robert still manages to make it down to Henley Rowing Club most Sunday mornings. Tells me it keeps him fit but, funnily enough, he always comes home smelling of beer.' All three men laughed, as Yvonne dug him playfully in the ribs with her elbow. 'Getting back to the car,' she explained, 'on days like today, it can be fun. The old wind in the hair bit, and the looks it attracts are brilliant. However,' she grinned, 'getting in and out can be a bit tricky if I'm wearing a tight skirt,' she chuckled, 'but Robert assures me that he likes the leg show. So, who am I to be a spoilsport?' She laughed, teasing Vere who had the good grace to blush. Minutes later Sarah Lambert returned with a large tray, complete with delicate porcelain cups, saucers and a matching coffee pot. After attending to her visitors, she then resumed her seat and addressed Lawrence.

'There now, as I was saying, Mr Lawrence, what brought you to England?'

'Well,' he paused, gathering his thoughts, 'a number of things sort of came together.' He smiled, 'you see, it was only after Valerie's death that I came across that envelope, hidden in the bottom of a closet. Okay, as Valerie had left it sealed, did I have the right to open it?' Describing how he used the internet to locate Regency Law, then learning that Gerald Lambert was alive and enjoying retirement, had only strengthened his desire to know more. Still undecided, the decision about a meeting came about by a chance telephone call. Mark, his nephew currently studying at Durham University, had phoned to ask his uncle if he'd like to come over to his graduation ceremony.

'Well, that clinched it. Getting here was no big deal, then I telephoned here yesterday and spoke with Mr Lambert,' he smiled, 'who kindly set up today's meeting.' Lawrence paused, looking at everyone as Yvonne addressed Lambert directly in a serious tone.

'Gerald, what I am unclear about,' she queried, 'is how come a mere getaway driver is executed, especially when he did next to nothing? It doesn't seem fair.' Lambert shifted in his chair, appreciating the pretty oval face with piercing brown eyes above which slim eyebrows arched in anticipation of an answer to her question.

'Sadly, my dear, fairness didn't come into it. Back then the law was clear, murder with a firearm was a capital offence.'

'But why hang the driver?' Yvonne persisted, 'he didn't shoot anyone.'

'Ah yes, I'm coming to that,' he replied. 'Back then the law regarded a group of people acting together as having a common purpose. Since they were all acting together, the law saw no reason to differentiate from one to the other. With the two killers having made good their escape, only Drysdale remained.' He stopped talking in mid-sentence, as all eyes remained focused on his face. 'The tidal wave of public outrage, following the shootings, was massive. The security guard left behind a wife and three young children, while the bank clerk was a sweet looking girl, due to be married a month later. Instead, she was dead at the age of twenty-two.' Yvonne's expression hardened, her mouth dropping open as she digested the gory information. But, before she could say a word, Lambert spoke again.

'You know,' he continued, 'in this age of enlightenment, the almost daily diet of murders hardly bears out the thinking of those decrying capital punishment as a deterrent. You see, when capital punishment existed no one could ever prove the number of people who, knowing they'd face the ultimate penalty, did not commit murder.'

'Now then, Gerald,' Sarah said reproachfully, 'don't go getting on your hobby horse. You know Doctor Hedges told you to avoid getting stressed as he said it's not good for you.'

'No, dear,' Lambert dutifully acknowledged before turning to Yvonne. 'As you know, while Ruskin the Q C, and I failed to get a reprieve, Stephen insisted upon this envelope remaining sealed. So, there you have it,' he concluded, giving Yvonne a watery smile. 'Stephen Drysdale went to his death without telling us anything further. So, whatever's in this envelope is most likely to be irrelevant.' Lambert concluded with an air of resignation.

Chilled by what she had just heard, Yvonne snuggled closer to Vere, whom she'd had known for just over a year, the couple having met at a dance at Phyllis Court in Henley. During those twelve months they had moved forward cautiously, from routine dates through to spending most weekends together in the secluded cottage he owned close to Shiplake station. During this period, she and Vere had become frequent visitors to Montserrat; the fashion journalist bonding easily with Sarah, a former west end theatrical principal. Yvonne knew that Sarah regarded Vere as the son she and Gerald were never able to have. Seconds later Yvonne's pleasant thoughts came to a sudden halt as, across from her, Gerald Lambert reached out to the coffee table and picked up the envelope.

'Are we all agreed to open this now then? He enquired, looking expectantly at the assembled company.

'Oh, come on, let's get on with it,' Dan Lawrence blurted out, running one of his large hands through his mane of white hair. In total silence Lambert inserted the handle of a coffee spoon under the top edge of the envelope, breaking the wax seal in the process. Setting down the spoon he slipped open the envelope flap with his thumb before withdrawing folded sheets of paper from inside the envelope.

Pausing, only to cast an enquiring eye at the hand-written notes, he leaned forward to speak Vere.

'Robert, I wonder if you would be good enough to read these for us please?'

CHAPTER 7

MIGUEL RAMOS, COMPLETELY unaware that he had seconds to live, relaxed in his chair convinced that his theory on drug-filled tobacco tins was right. One telephone call would be enough, giving him the name of the couple detained at the airport. Then, by contacting Gatwick, he could have the "mules" questioned and any tobacco tins examined. Time enough, he thought, sipping his brandy in the shade of the parasol.

Two hundred yards away a powerfully built man in his mid-thirties moved cautiously inside the framework of a partially completed multi-story block of flats. Slowly he stepped around assorted breeze blocks, timber and cement bags scattered by the construction workers while adjusting his eyes to the partial darkness. Quietly, and wearing white police-issue forensic overalls designed to prevent crime-scene contamination Harvey Dukes, ever the professional, wore them as a precaution against leaving *any* evidence at a crime scene.

With a baseball cap covering his shaved head and his hands covered by surgical gloves, he'd used a series of internal ladders to reach his chosen floor, the one level with Ramos's balcony. He'd left nothing to chance, knowing how the building site would be deserted on Saturday, leaving him free to conduct his task as a hired killer. He was only ever as good as his last job, a job in which "clients" demanded results and paid well for the privilege. He could not afford to get it wrong. Dead or in jail he was of no use to anyone, his clients or indeed himself.

Having moved with care, and staying well within the shadows, he'd retrieved a transparent plastic bag containing a standard US Marine Corps sniper's rifle from beneath a pile of tarpaulins. A Remington 24, complete with suppressor, telescopic sight and a small box of soft-nosed bullets, all left by an anonymous visitor during the hours of darkness. Next, he built a low wall out of breezeblocks, leaving a small gap in the middle. By lying flat on the floor behind this wall he'd have the perfect field of fire through his narrow gun port, right across to the balcony where the creature of habit would appear in twenty minutes.

Sitting on a pile of cement bags, Dukes delicately withdrew the rifle he'd been practising with far away from prying eyes. By making careful adjustments to the telescopic sight, he'd been able to secure the accuracy he'd need to kill Ramos on his balcony, two hundred yards away. Deftly he slipped three of the soft-nosed bullets into the rifle's magazine, sliding back the bolt to chamber a round, making certain that the safety catch was in the 'off' position. Placing the rifle on top of the breeze block he picked up a bag of cement, laying it snugly against the inside of his wall to provide the ideal resting place for the rifle's barrel. From an inside pocket he withdrew a folded sheet of polythene which he spread across the tarpaulin already in place behind his little wall. Not the slightest trace of his presence would remain. No hairs, no sweat and no saliva. Nothing from which the authorities might find a sample of his DNA.

Killing people for money had never been a problem for Dukes, just something at which he was good. His astute alertness, along with his diligence had kept him clear of police forces around the world. In his line of work any attention was unwelcome unless it came from powerful people with troublesome enemies. Those were his people, the people who could meet the high fees he charged for his complete - no nonsense - *removal service.*

Over the years Dukes had read books on former English executioners, intrigued as to how they performed their duties with unswerving loyalty towards their government paymasters. He'd been particularly impressed by the clinical precision of Albert Pierrepoint who, he'd read, could dispatch a prisoner in a matter of seconds. Amazing, but the pay was lousy, just pounds for hanging someone. No, this is far more lucrative he consoled himself, training his rifle on Ramos's balcony. Through the telescopic sight he could see the metal table, the lowered parasol and the well-padded chair. But had anything changed? Just as bankers don't like surprises, I can do without them as well. The repositioning of a chair, the unexpected arrival of visitor or an unplanned object obscuring the line of fire, any of which can negate a successful hit. Always expect the unexpected.

Minutes later, and still peering through the scope Dukes saw a bulky woman step onto the balcony carrying a tray. Coffee and brandy, the precursor to Ramos showing himself. After setting the tray onto the table, she put up the parasol before vanishing back inside. Seconds later, just as the nearby town clocks started to chime the hour, Ramos walked onto the balcony, pausing to look around before lowering himself into the chair.

Two hundred yards away Dukes picked up his rifle, pleased that Ramos had settled and was enjoying his drinks. Always nice to have the victim's full cooperation he smiled, knowing it was time to focus on the target while never ignoring the *bigger picture*. Has anything changed? No, the big guy's motionless, apart from occasional arm movements. Through the telescopic sight Dukes could see how the parasol had shaded his target from the sunlight, he still had a clear view of his aiming point – Ramos's head. Satisfied, he nestled back down into his chosen firing position, weight taken on the hips and elbows, left leg straight back, the right one splayed out and bent at the knee. He was ready. Before him, the rifle barrel rested on the cement bag, while the muzzle protruded just a matter of inches beyond the breeze block wall.

With surgical precision he aligned the telescopic sight's cross hairs on a spot half-way between Ramos's temple and left ear, before going through his well-disciplined pre-firing routine. Mentally he rechecked his calculations, accounting for distance, temperature and compensating for the light breeze. Only then did he take a deep breath before exhaling slowly and squeezing the trigger. The silencer was effective, limiting any sound within the building to a dull "plop" which startled a pair of pigeons, causing them to flap around before escaping into the sunshine.

Through the scope he saw Ramos jerk slightly, a small mark appearing on his temple, followed instantly by a spray of blood, bone and tissue splattering the apartment wall at the back of the balcony. The soft-nosed bullet had done its work with devastating efficiency, *exploding* inside Ramos's skull to blast blood and brains out through a large hole on the far side of his head. Certain that no second shot was necessary Dukes relaxed, knowing it would be at least half an hour before the hired help went out to retrieve the discarded cup and glass. Seconds later, after working the bolt mechanism, he ejected the spent cartridge case along with the two unused bullets before returning them, and the rifle, to the plastic bag. Next, he rolled up the polythene sheet he'd been lying on, placing it alongside the rifle into a canvas bag that he would carry away with him. Satisfied, he returned to the ladders and made his way down to street level before stepping out into the sunshine.

To an observer Dukes appeared to be just another worker slipping into a battered van that had drawn up outside the fenced-off site moments before. Anxious not to attract unwanted attention the driver nodded to Dukes before driving away slowly to join the main road that led towards the Airport.

Standing in the back of the moving van Dukes discarded every stitch of clothing, before wiping his face and upper body with a rag splashed with petrol. A necessary precaution to eradicate traces of cordite on his skin after firing the rifle, the presence of which airport security equipment can detect. To overcome the petrol fumes, he wiped himself down with a soapy cloth, towelling himself dry before applying liberal doses of antiperspirant spray. Only then did he dress, donning fresh underwear, a light shirt, jacket, jeans, new socks and casual slip-on shoes. Next, he placed his old clothes, the petrol-soaked rag and body sprays in the canvas bag containing the rifle, polythene sheet, unused ammunition and the one spent cartridge. Within the hour the incriminating canvas bag would be on a fishing boat heading for deep water.

Moving to the front of the van Dukes told the driver to pull over to the side of the road, stopping to permit him to transfer to the car that had pulled up directly behind the van. Within seconds both vehicles were back on the road. Dukes, in the car's front passenger-seat, turned to recover a flight-bag from the back seat containing his passport, an airline ticket to Heathrow and a pay-as-you-go mobile phone, with which he sent a text message of three Xs to his paymaster. The signal, confirmation of his success, would trigger an electronic transfer of £50,000 to his account in the Cayman Islands. Task completed. The mobile phone was handed to the driver for permanent disposal.

Minutes later, having passed the San Miguel brewery, the car came to a halt outside the Departures area at Malaga Airport. Just another tourist, one amongst thousands. Who'll be taking any notice of me? he surmised, expressing his thanks to the driver.

CHAPTER 8

IN TOTAL SILENCE Vere took the collection of A4 sheets from Lambert, pausing to comment. 'Written in pencil. Why not ink or biro?'

'Ah,' said Lambert, 'in those days' pens were seen as suicide weapons. The authorities went to great lengths to make sure that no one could cheat the hangman. Considered to be bad form,' Lambert laughed softly, his shoulders rising and falling slightly. 'But, before you start,' he continued in a sombre voice, 'remember that Stephen was well-educated, indeed an articulate young man who I got to know well. So, I think we can be sure that his message will be coherent, even if it is now a message from beyond the grave. When writing, he'd absolutely nothing to gain by lying.' Vere looked patiently across at Lambert, pleased to let his friend's well-chosen words prefix his reading of the notes.

'Thank you for that, Gerald. Now,' he looked in turn at the four faces, 'if everybody's okay with this, I'll read what Stephen had to say all those years ago.

HMP Pentonville
November 1962.

I Stephen Drysdale confirm that what I have written below is the complete truth, and the reason that I find myself in this dreadful situation. Last April, due to my own stupidity, I was down on my luck and in urgent need of money. One Sunday evening, at the snooker club I'd been frequenting, an envelope was handed to me by the girl at the entry desk. She said it had been handed in by someone she had never seen before. Inside the envelope I found one hundred pounds in five-pound notes, plus an anonymous message saying that there was another five hundred pounds, just for doing a little driving job if I was interested.

Was I interested? Either way the note said that next day I had to be at a certain point on Clapham Common, sitting on a specified bench at twelve noon. If I wanted the job, the note said that I had to wait for fifteen minutes then walk away as I'd be contacted again. If I didn't want the job, I was to put the hundred pounds in the nearby waste bin then and leave. Needing the money, I sat out the quarter of an hour then walked away. I didn't see anyone, but I guess I was being watched.

Two days later, I was handed a second note at the club, unsigned it told me what I had to do for the remaining money. It also contained two keys, one of which was for a car. At a set time, on a given date, I was to walk down a certain residential road in Croydon. On reaching number 23 I was to unlock the garage. Inside, I'd find a green Jaguar 3.4 saloon with further written instructions on the seat. After shutting up the garage I was to drive the car away, having closed the front gates.

Once mobile, I followed the instruction, heading towards

central London. When I reached the Cromwell Road, I was to pick up two guys who would give me further instructions. At the appointed place two men, wearing flat caps and with their collars turned up, jumped into the back, one shouting, 'drive and don't look at us!' Risking a quick glance in the mirror, I could see the two men were in their early twenties, one had fair hair while the other one was darker. Minutes later they ducked down, then bobbed back up wearing balaclavas. That gave me a bad fright. I never got another look at them. Seconds later, I glanced in the mirror, alarmed to see both men holding sawn-off shotguns. By now I was really scared.

I'm positive these guys were not carrying the guns when I picked them up. Therefore, I can only assume that the firearms were already in the back of the car when I collected it. Up until that point I had absolutely no idea that they were armed. Seeing the guns made me realise this was something far more serious than a little driving job. I said I wanted out - planning to stop the car and walk away. Before I could do anything, a shotgun was pressed into the back of my neck, the man shouting. 'Walk and you'll leave without your head!' Terrified, I carried on driving.

The robbery happened in a flash. They screamed at me to stop the car, pulling up behind a bullion van with its rear doors open. Once stationary, the chap who'd threatened to kill me jumped out of the car. Running straight at a security guard, full on with no warning, he just fired! One shot! It was horrible.

As the guard fell a lady emerged from the bank pushing a trolley. Seeing what was happening she screamed and turned to go back into the bank. The same guy fired again, catching her right between the shoulder blades. There were no warning shouts - just the shots. Be in no doubt, he meant to kill. The second guard, on hearing the first shot had dashed to the front of the van, shutting himself in. Meanwhile, the other fellow grabbed hold of several canvas bags from the van, threw them onto the rear seat and clambered in, joined immediately by the one who'd done the shooting.

Seconds later they were screaming like maniacs - telling me to drive. As we sped away it was that big lorry reversing out of the factory gates that did for us, well for me anyway. I had no chance. The brakes locked and the Jag skidded. The front end of the car slithered under the side of the lorry, crushing the windscreen and trapping me inside. Shocked and confused, all I can remember hearing is one of them shouting 'Get out! Run! Grab the f****** money and run like the bloody wind!'

I told the Police, after I was cut from the wreckage, that I'd no idea who these guys were. As I said at my trial, they only spoke to give me directions, but the one who'd done the killings had an upper class, well-refined, voice. As for the other one, he had a more down to earth London accent. But I did notice something. Just before he jumped out of the car to do the robbery, I saw that he had a damaged left hand. Parts of the fingers were missing. He had to hold the barrel end of the shotgun between his thumb and index finger. I had never seen these two men before, and I don't know who they are. That's the God's truth. Stephen Drysdale.

In complete silence Vere reorganised the sheets of paper into their original order, noting the scrawled signature on the last page. He looked up, glancing in turn from one blank and pale face to another, under no illusions as to how petrified Drysdale must have been. After a lengthy pause Lambert was the first to address the stunned gathering.

'You know,' he said faintly, 'that's exactly what he told

me on our first meeting in hospital. He was hospitalised for a couple of weeks, handcuffed to a bed while the injuries to his legs healed. He told the same story to Desmond Ruskin, recounting the same to the jury at the Old Bailey. Okay, they'd been sympathetic, but their hands were tied. The law was specific. Even the three Appeal Court judges heard the same details of the crime.'

'Didn't the jury make a recommendation for mercy?' Vere asked speculatively.

'No, they did not.' Lambert said emphatically. 'But, even if they had, the outcome would have been the same. Had the judges given Drysdale a reprieve,' he paused, 'well, it would have driven a *coach and horses* through the 'joint enterprise' ruling. It would have set an unenviable precedent. Every *two-bit* hoodlum would have ended up pushing their luck, knowing they had a darn good chance of not getting executed if caught. On this occasion the public demanded justice, they needed a scapegoat and Drysdale fitted the bill very nicely.'

'Oh, that poor man;' Yvonne sniffled, reaching into her bag for a tissue, as a thoughtful silence filled the lounge.

CHAPTER 9

'**DO YOU THINK** they're still alive?' Yvonne asked as Vere swung his MG out onto the narrow Wargrave Road,

'Who do you mean?' he asked, turning his head slightly.

'Those two, the men Drysdale mentioned in his notes.'

'Oh those,' he replied thoughtfully, 'if they are they'll be in an old-folks home and tottering around on walking frames?'

'Don't be so beastly,' Yvonne retorted, 'Should they still be around, they'll be a bit younger than Gerald. And he's far from being a doddery old man.'

'Fair comment,' he acknowledged, as his thumb nail flicked the overdrive switch on top of the gear lever. 'No, the years have been kind to Gerald but, by the sound of it, those two villains will not have improved with age. So, it'll remain a mystery,' A brief silence fell over the couple as they enjoyed the freedom of travelling with the hood down in the warm sunshine. 'Mind you, a little mystery spices up the day,' he called across, having cast a quick look down to where Yvonne's silk dress had slid even further up her thighs. 'That'll spice up my day very nicely,' he added.

Yvonne, having already caught his downward glance,

called out, 'Oh, you're incorrigible!' before falling silent. Minutes later, held up in traffic on Henley bridge, Vere managed to take a quick look around. Away to his right was the famous Leander Rowing Club and, beyond that Lion Meadow, the open space soon to be filled with boat tents for the annual Regatta. Then, with the lights having changed, the traffic moved slowly off the bridge, Vere taking the sharp left turn by the Angel public house.

'You know, in that pub there used to be a small brass plate stating that *Grace Kelly had stood here*. Might still be there for all I know.'

'What....Grace Kelly?' Yvonne teased.

'No, the brass plate, you ninny!' he scoffed.

'How come she came to Henley then?' Yvonne questioned.

'Oh, just after the last war, her brother Jack rowed here in the Regatta, winning the Diamond Sculls.'

'What's that?' she asked in a startled voice, 'sounds like something from a Damien Hirst collection.'

'Oh, thee of little knowledge,' he chided, 'that's scull with a C and not a K. The Diamond Sculls, one of the events that make up the Regatta. It's for single scullers, just one man in the boat with two oars known as sculls. There you are. You see, a little more superior knowledge with which to supplement your threadbare education.'

'Why you.......' she spluttered, turning to look directly at him. 'There are times when you really can be a pompous old windbag,' she spoke with mock severity, trying hard to stifle a laugh.

'Don't knock it,' he replied, 'it's taken me years to get this good. But seriously, before the last war Jack's dad was a good rower. Yet, back then rumour abounded that, as an artisan his application to compete in the regatta was unacceptable since, as a bricklayer the Stewards considered him to be unsuitable. Not sure how true this was but it looks as though the Stewards decreed that such artisans were not the right sort of people for Henley.'

'That sounds a bit arrogant,' Yvonne said indignantly.

'Yes, but as the story goes, Kelly senior determinedly trained up his son so that he could come to Henley and win the Diamonds, which he did.'

'Managing to keep it in the family,' she commented, 'sort of getting his own back on officialdom.'

'That's about the size of it, I guess,' he commented, before sweeping the car onto the Reading Road. Then, in companionable silence, they settled down for the short drive to Shiplake, each looking forward to the weekend seclusion provided by the cottage. For Yvonne it represented two heaven sent days away from her frantic duties with a London based fashion magazine. Two days without the early morning drive from home to Goring station. Two days in which to relax with a loving partner. She tingled at the thought. Oh, how I love the weekends, she sighed contentedly as the MG growled its way back to the welcoming cottage.

***

While Robert Vere was negotiating the busy streets of Henley, twelve miles away a black executive taxi swung through the electronic gates of an imposing riverside house near Wallingford. As the Mercedes glided down the driveway the uniformed driver noted the large pond on his right, where expensive Japanese Koi carp glinted in the sunlight. Moments later, having negotiated the gravelled turning circle in front of the house the driver slowed, coming to a halt under an arched roof supported by pillars affording shelter for arriving guests.

Inside the house Miles Overstone, its sole occupant, stood ramrod straight, gazing through sealed French windows at the Thames flowing across the bottom of his garden. This was his office, secure and away from the city and prying eyes. Yet, the safe beneath his feet contained secrets that he alone was privy to while documentation relating to his sizable property empire was at Canary Wharfe, his city office. Turning, he looked across at thee framed pictures on the mantlepiece, all taken of him at various functions. One with a cabinet minister, another with the Governor of the Bank of England and the other with three senior police officers.

While the old life had been interesting, staying one step ahead of the law had taken all his guile, but this new life was better. Being street wise he'd ruthlessly controlled his first venture, the moneylending that had brought him in millions over the years. Still operational, it was under the control of his chosen *lieutenants*. Men making regular payments to his offshore accounts where questions were rarely asked, and never answered.

Armed with a new identity he'd arrived on the Thames Valley social scene, single, wealthy and anonymous. "*Oh, he ran some sort of business overseas,*" was the polite "gloss" the locals had applied to their new arrival. All frightfully vague but it suited all concerned extremely well. Once settled he'd soon become a target for dinner invitations, golf club membership and the local masonic lodge. Yet, for all the social trappings, he yearned for the excitement that came from generating vast sums of money illegally.

His face, now a little creased with age, still retained its firm lines and piercing blue eyes. Over the years he'd lost much of the hair from the top of his head, yet what remained retained traces of the original blonde colouring. Now, well over seventy, he considered himself to be in good health, having successfully kicked his smoking habit fifteen years earlier. Pocketing the pay-as-you-go mobile phone that had earlier displayed the three XXXs message, he walked out into the wide semi-circular hallway, aware that his taxi had arrived. Stooping, he picked up a small suitcase before swinging open a heavy lockable glass door, the first of two similar sets spaced eight feet apart that led to the main entrance. With security in mind, he'd designed the system so that both sets of armoured glass doors would lock, separately and remotely, by means of a small hand-held device. When entering or leaving the house, everyone had to pass through this short entrance corridor, effectively an air lock. Nodding to the driver, he pushed the suitcase towards him before stepping back inside to activate the alarm system.

'Reading,' he said crisply, 'the station,' as the big Mercedes ascended the driveway, clearing the already open gates which Overstone closed electronically. Minutes later he found himself looking closely at the imposing line of houses facing the river as they approached Pangbourne. One of which he knew that Edward the Seventh had used as a "love nest" nearly a hundred years ago. Pretty isolated spot back then, he thought, away from prying eyes. Couldn't do it now, of course, what with social media and CCTV all over the place. Preserving anonymity these days is a much more complicated process but, nevertheless, that's something I manage on a successful basis.

At Reading, after leaving his taxi, he didn't have long to wait for a fast train to Paddington. Although having a first-class ticket, he soon found a comfortable forward-facing seat in a half-empty commuter carriage which he vacated soon after departure. Picking up his suitcase he walked through to the next carriage before stopping outside a toilet door. Pausing to check that nobody was observing him too closely he stepped inside, securing the door behind him.

Ten minutes later the man who emerged bore no resemblance to the one who had so recently entered. Gone was the lightweight suit, replaced now with a dark business suit, stripped shirt and matching tie. Gone also was the semi baldness, replaced with a well-groomed head of darkening hair flecked with grey. Foam rubber pads pushed out his cheeks while a pair of heavy rimmed glasses replaced the discreetly worn contact lenses. Carrying a small leather briefcase, along with the suitcase, he made his way towards a first-class carriage. Miles Overstone, during that ten-minute transformation, had become Alistair Buchanan. At Paddington he walked briskly towards the left luggage counter where a blonde-haired lady took custody of his suitcase before he headed for the nearby taxi rank.

'Harrods please,' he instructed the driver. Ever one for tight security, he routinely used a planned deception to avoid pursuit or recognition. Enter a crowded place by one entrance then leave by another, a sure-fire method of losing a follower. While Leicester Square underground station was one such example, the pulsating hub of Harrods was ideal for throwing followers off the scent. Entering the building from the front he went up one floor, mingled with shoppers then descended to the ground floor, re-emerging onto the busy Brompton Road from another entrance. Satisfied that he was free from followers he turned into Beauchamp Place, soon flagging down a passing cab.

Half an hour later, in a dingy room above a noisy pub on the Kilburn High Road, he looked thoughtfully at the ten faces ranged before him, the very core of his organisation - his *lieutenants*. No hard-faced criminal types here, just a selection of *mature businesspeople* who all knew him as Alistair Buchanan. Immediately to his right was Bernard Nolan, a successful estate agent from Surrey whom he trusted more than any other. His relationship with Nolan, a man with an insatiable appetite for extra income, had blossomed during the time he'd been expanding his property empire. In Nolan he'd found the perfect partner, one willing to assist in all aspects of rigging land purchases, fixing planning committees, enforcing compulsory purchase orders and executing heartless evictions. Working routines that had soon become their financial glue, cementing the present and guaranteeing their future. Yes, I've got big plans for you Bernard, he thought as he gave the man a confident smile.

Overstone knew that these men were well respected in ten of the UK's major cities. More importantly, they were willing slaves to the criminally extracted funds that kept them all so very wealthy. Yet, without question, they knew the wisdom of giving unerring allegiance to the demanding rules he imposed upon them, rules that had served them well and kept them off the police radar. Nodding curtly to the faces lining either side of the table, he cleared his throat before addressing them.

CHAPTER 10

'RIGHT, I'LL KEEP it brief,' he began, raising his voice to compete with a sudden roar of laughter coming from the bar below. 'My bank manager tells me that all ten payments are still coming through to him on a regular basis. That's good, it keeps everyone healthy.' He paused, looking from face to face before continuing.

'Now,' he enthused, 'the moneylending is still doing well, thanks to you good people. And, naturally, to our banking friends who regard lending money to a section of their customer base as being way beyond their remit.' This brought a little polite laughter from further down the table as he knew it would.

'Tell me.' He paused, breaking into a smile, 'just how many unsuspecting travellers do we have out there in the Spanish sunshine right now?' While waiting for the first man to speak, he considered the genius of his operation. Simplicity personified, be everybody's friend and lend money generously. Not to the destitute, the drunks, the helpless or the smackheads, but to young couples needing help when the going got tough. Help with the mortgage, the utility bill or extra money when an unexpected disaster struck. Desperate people, unable to believe their luck when a smiling money lender had knocked at their door. Unsuspecting people, happy to *sup with the devil* long before questioning the massive interest charges involved. Then, once these "customers" had repaid their loan times over, the *enforcers* were ready for round two.

Round two is where good paying customers have their debt cleared and are to receive a week's self-catering holiday in Spain, free of charge. Overcome with emotion they were hardly able to refuse a polite request from a young lady to bring back *a few tins of pipe tobacco*, were they? 'Our boss is such a generous man,' the girl would plead, 'who enjoys his pipe, but hates paying the duty.' Days later the helpful young lady would return, eager to assist with any necessary documentation, while handing out the tickets. 'Now you won't forget, will you?' the girl would tell them sweetly, 'it's particularly important that you buy him the right brand of pipe tobacco at the airport, before you fly out. When you get back, I'll pop round to pick up the tobacco for my boss.' At no time were travellers told that someone would enter their Spanish apartments to exchange those tins for ones filled with drugs. Then, as the men around the table finished giving their replies, Overstone jotted down their answers before totalling up the numbers.

'Excellent! That's one hundred and thirty mules this week alone, all happy couples enjoying the sunshine.' Further scribbling showed that 32.5 kilos of pure Columbian cocaine would shortly be entering his supply chain, courtesy of these travellers. The drug, mixed with icing sugar to dilute its strength, would create a mind-blowing street value. A figure he knew to be far outweigh the cost of cheap holiday packages compared to this sort of income.

'However,' he said, raising his voice to compete with another salvo of shouting sound released by Guinness drinkers in the bar below. 'For a while it looked as though our little operation, ably yet unwittingly supported by the authorities at Malaga Airport, may have been heading for a problem.'

'May have been?' a man further down the table being the first to assess the implication.

'Yes,' Overstone remarked calmly, looking from face to face along the table. 'Over recent weeks security checking, on passengers heading for the UK, has been intensified. Of course, while our repackaging plant outside Malaga is fool proof, an interfering Spanish police officer has been causing trouble, ramping up security as if he knew something, but could find nothing. Anyway, rather than wait to see what this tiresome little man might do next, I decided upon terminal action. This removal, although expensive, has no links back to any of us here. However, to cover the removal, I shall,' he looked down the table, 'require an extra five thousand pounds from each of you on your next monthly contribution. Should anyone here have a problem with that,' he looked around, 'be good enough to raise your hand now?' For the next few seconds twenty arms remained firmly upon the table.

'Ah....that's good. I was hoping that no one would wish to object.' Not for the first time Overstone reminded himself just what wonderful lubricants greed and avarice were. Here we have ten men able to accept murder and extortion and who regard drug trafficking as a legitimate trade when it comes to making them rich. In selecting his *lieutenants* Overstone had chosen wisely, all married men, solid citizens faithful to their wives. No affairs, no mistresses, and no hidden skeletons in the closet had been the rule. Loving parents, and doting grandparents, made the best social camouflage available.

'Moving on,' he said, recovering his train of thought. 'Don't let's get greedy. The tins of tobacco are doing well because, as you know, I insist upon having a security system in place that's impossible to penetrate. A self-discipline I imposed even before conducting my first successful venture. Indeed,' he paused, 'that was the exercise that provided me with the start-up finance for everything I've now achieved, with your help of course.' He added hastily, thinking back to his first robbery. Loss of life in pursuit of his goal hadn't been a problem then and it certainly isn't now. 'So, before we disband,' he asked, 'are there any other matters that you wish to discuss?'

Fifteen minutes later he offered polite farewells to the ten ordinary faces who represented the beating heart of England's most successful and unknown criminal enterprise. An organisation generating income on an unprecedented scale while staying well clear of the authorities or any illicit operators. His team were professional men, an estate agent, a couple of solicitors, a doctor, a surgeon, an airline pilot, two accountants, the managing director of an engineering firm and the owner of a small chain of hotels. All men of good character, pillars of respectability in their own fields and beyond reproach. Yet each of these men ruthlessly controlled a command structure where no one knew the identity of the next person up or down the chain. In the event of arrests, it was simple, secure, effective and watertight! Yet, despite all his precautions, one man in the room had succumbed to the pleasures of the flesh and was to endanger the entire system!

An hour later, having retrieved his suitcase, Overstone boarded a West Country express scheduled to stop at Reading. During the journey he reversed his disguise. No longer Alistair Buchanan, he emerged onto Reading platform as Miles Overstone. A well-practised routine that formed an essential part of his own personal security precautions.

***

Further across London that afternoon Harvey Dukes paid off his taxicab and entered the imposing lobby to a modern block of apartments close to Hammersmith Bridge.

'Enjoy your break, Mr Carstairs?' the uniformed reception clerk enquired in a friendly tone from behind the counter.

'Yes, thank you, Roger, Cyprus is very lovely at this time of year,' his polished public-school accent creating the perfect balance between master and servant. Although his earlier decision to drop out of university had created a family furore, his later career change remained mercifully unknown to his parents. 'Oh,' he said, calling out over his shoulder on his way to the lift, 'be a good chap, help the cabby with my case. Bring it up with the post.'

'Yes, Mr Carstairs, right away' Roger acknowledged. Minutes later Harvey Dukes was walking through his apartment, busily opening windows to let in some much-needed fresh air. Stepping out onto a small balcony he looked down at the river, noting how the tide was beginning to send a solid stream of water under Hammersmith Bridge towards the sea. Turning away from the bridge, he gazed across the river at the old Harrods Depository, now converted into luxury apartments yet still a familiar landmark. The river both pleased and disappointed him. The pleasure from seeing it at high water, the sadness when low tide reduced the river to a narrow strip of sluggish water framed by yards of muddy sediment between untidy banks.

CHAPTER 11

THE URGENT RINGING of the bedside telephone dragged Vere reluctantly back to semi-consciousness. Normally, on a Friday morning, it was the eagerly anticipated evening arrival of Yvonne that dominated his waking thoughts. But not today as another familiar and highly stressed, female voice demanding his attention.

'Robert, thank God I've reached you!' Sarah Lambert shouted, 'it's Gerald, he's dead!' Vere, gasping in shock struggled into a sitting position.

'What? Sarah, how, when?' he spluttered, trying to clear the fog from his brain. 'Tell me what happened?' he implored.

'I don't know;' Sarah sobbed. 'I've only just found him,' her voice trembled with deep shock, 'sitting there in his favourite armchair. He must have been there all night. He was so cold to the touch. It's awful! I don't know what to do,' she sobbed.

'Oh, Sarah, I'm so sorry,' Vere spoke softly, 'have you managed to call the doctor yet?' he asked, trying to make sense of what he'd just heard.

'Yes. I did that, shortly after finding Gerald's..........' she whimpered, strained emotion cutting short the sentence. 'But Robert, please come, I feel dreadful.'

'Yes, of course I'll come but, oh God, I'm so desperately sorry. I'll be with you as soon as, but meanwhile try to stay calm.'

'I'll so my best but get here soon.' Their conversation lasted a little longer, during which Vere learnt how a friend had collected Lambert the previous evening before travelling to Henley for their regular Masonic Lodge meeting.

'They're usually fairly late affairs,' Sarah told him. 'Over the years I've got used to them, invariably I'd be asleep by the time Gerald got back, so I'd not really see him until the next morning anyway.' But this morning had been different, tragically different, she told Vere in faltering sentences. Woken by noisy birds she'd soon realised that she was alone in the bed, her husband's pyjamas untouched on the pillow beside her. Truly alarmed, she'd rushed through the house in search of him, finally recounting how she'd found her husband. 'Oh Robert,' she sobbed, 'he was in the lounge, slumped forward in his favourite armchair, still wearing his dinner jacket and with a half-full bottle of malt whisky on the nearby table.'

'In the lounge, at that time of night! What was he doing there?' he asked the distraught Sarah who, in reply, explained how Gerald had told her that he wanted to see an earlier televised boxing match on "catch-up" television. Sarah presumed he'd decided to watch it before going to bed.

'Do come quickly, please! Oh, that's the doorbell. Where can Mrs Logan and her husband be?' her voice showed signs of approaching panic, completely forgetting that they were unlikely to be about this early.

'Hopefully, that'll be the doctor,' Vere suggested, having heard the door-bell chime over the phone. 'Just let him in, then tell him I'm on my way. You're not to be alone. Don't let him go until I get there. Do you understand that Sarah?'

'Yes, Robert,' she said slowly.

'I'm sure the doctor will tell you more, so go and let him in and I'll be there just as soon as I can.'

**

Good to his word Vere reached Montserrat within the hour, parking his Jaguar next to an unrecognised 4 x 4, guessing it belonged to the doctor. The thought confirmed as the front door swung open, revealing an older man carrying a black medical bag. Dressed, Vere noted, in an old sports jacket and flannels, a check shirt plus a floral bow tie. A bow tie this early in the morning! Vere struggled to take in the flamboyant attire, hardly appropriate for a sudden death. Approaching the house, he looked at the man standing beside the clearly distressed Sarah. Still in her dressing gown and slippers she called out, 'Oh Robert, thank goodness you're here,' giving him a peck on the cheek before introducing the doctor. 'This is Doctor Hedges, our local man.' A message implying to Vere that Hedges was most likely to be in private practice, dispensing medical care to those with healthy bank accounts. Indeed, someone not above making early morning house calls, complete with floral bow tie, in return for a fee.

'Good to meet you doctor, albeit under sad circumstances,' Vere said pleasantly as Sarah completed the introductions. Pushing out his hand he was rewarded with a cold, unemotional, stare and a limp handshake. Gestures clearly designed to let Vere know that his presence was an annoying irritant. Set below a shock of unruly snow-white hair, the doctor's features gave nothing away. Undaunted, Vere pressed on, asking, for information.

'Heart attack. Quite common in people of his age you know. And, before you ask, I'd put the time of death at somewhere between midnight and two this morning. We'll know more when the pathologist reports back. But anyway,' he remarked, as he paused to put his bag on the ground. 'I'm sure this will all be straight forward though,' he hesitated, 'in cases of sudden death the coroner may require a post-mortem. It all depends, but I've notified the police, of course, as I'm obliged to do in such circumstances. But be aware, it's possible the police may regard this as a crime scene.'

'Crime scene,' Vere spluttered in amazement. 'For God's sake that's ridiculous, I mean….' The doctor's upturned hand cut him short.

'Disregarding the Almighty, cases of sudden death can often trigger police suspicions which, I'm sure you'll appreciate can be quite intense where wealthy people are involved. Be in no doubt, Gerald Lambert was a wealthy man so, if they do get suspicious, they'll want a PM. But let's hope it won't come to all that.' Then Hedges paused, seeming to change of mind as he looked to Vere and gave him a weak smile. 'I'll do my best, have a quiet word with the coroner and try to avoid a PM. In my view, he either died from a heart attack, which I'm quite sure he did, or a slow acting poison. Hardly something he'd be likely to pick up at a Masonic Lodge dinner!' he said haughtily, as Vere struggled to appreciate his offhand manner at such a critical time.

'So, unless this proves to be a case of murder, which is most unlikely, that's me done,' he spoke in a confidential whisper before nodding a brief farewell to Sarah. Having picked up his bag he moved towards his car, pausing to address Vere. 'Sarah's got enough on her plate right now, without the thought of Gerald being sliced up,' his remark issued without compassion was thankfully well out of her earshot. 'Anyway, everything's in order,' he said dismissively, turning to cross the gravel and getting into his car. What a dreadful man Vere thought, more graveside than bedside.

Half an hour later, shortly after Vere had given Mr Logan the tragic news, two police constables arrived from Wokingham. Diligently they spent an hour making a detailed search of the area surrounding the body, later extending their efforts to the rest of the house, without finding anything out of the ordinary. In between bouts of comforting Sarah Mrs Logan made tea for everyone, and later for the bright-eyed Detective Inspector Richardson who'd arrived to oversee events. Sarah, still not dressed, retreated to the kitchen where she gratefully accepted more tea from the equally tearful Mrs Logan.

Not long after that the police, having thoroughly photographed the scene, released Gerald's body to the dour-faced coroner's men in their sinister black van. Inspector Richardson then took time advising Sarah that any decision regarding a post-mortem would depend upon a closer examination, supported by the police reports. 'Mind you, it all looks straight forward to me,' he said, 'but I'm so sorry for your loss, Mrs Lambert. I'll say that I don't see the need for any further investigation, hopefully that'll avoid a PM,' he added kindly. Before taking his leave, Richardson told them he was going to interview Lambert's fellow Mason, the one who'd brought Gerald back to Montserrat for the last time yesterday evening.

'Now then,' Vere said kindly, turning to Sarah as the front door closed behind the departing police officers. 'You need company, someone to come and stop with you for a while. I hate the idea of you being on your own at a time like this,' he suggested, 'I'm sure you'd find it a comfort having someone here with you. Is there anybody you can call?'

'Well,' she replied, acknowledging Vere's concern, 'there's my younger sister, Molly, we're quite close. She lives near Beaconsfield.' Guiding Sarah back into the lounge Vere thought the sister sounded well suited at this time of crisis.

'Do you think she'll come? Has she any dependent children?'

'Good Lord no!' Sarah managed a weak smile. 'Her two have long since flown the nest. Desmond, Molly's husband, is a retired Civil Servant,' she managed a watery smile. 'You know the type, bags of money, self-opinionated and full of wind. Lives on the golf course. Probably not even notice she's missing, well not until he finds his dinners not ready. I'll give Molly a call now.'

Later, as silence again descended upon Montserrat, Vere went out onto the terrace where he shuddered, painfully aware that it was less than two weeks since they'd all gathered here to read Drysdale's notes. Now this, he paused to look at his watch before ringing Regency Law to pass on the sad news. Still on the line he asked to speak with his secretary, advising her that he'd not be going into the office that day. 'Oh, Mary,' he said, 'can you call Blanchard's, you know, the firm of accountants we use? Have a word with their head man, his name's Turnbull. They manage all Gerald's affairs. Ask him to get someone down to see Sarah, today if humanly possible. Get them to make sure that she's okay for money, them check on the Lamberts' banks, see who can sign cheques, withdraw money, that sort of thing. Tell them to make sure she'll be okay for money, while we get things sorted on the legal front. In the meantime, I don't want Sarah to have any more worries than necessary. You okay with that?' he asked before disconnecting.

He then dialled Yvonne's number, disappointed to hear a 'call me back' message. Rather than return to the lounge he paused, looking down at the river. Away to his right Marsh Lock lay bathed in sunshine while upstream, to his left, the river ran straight for a while before curling its way round to Shiplake. All this beauty, yet a man has died, reminding Vere of a lovely film he had once seen about an otter that had been killed, leaving behind the empty rock pools where it had played. Only the rocks remained, not unlike Montserrat, still here but without Gerald. The buzzing of his mobile interrupted his thoughts, pleased to see Yvonne was returning his call.

'Robert, what's up?' she said sharply, 'I'm already late for a meeting. Don't tell me you want to change our weekend arrangements, not at this late hour?' she asked, her voiced laced with annoyance.

'No, darling, it's nothing like that,' he replied, trying to remain calm, 'but thanks for calling back so quickly. Sadly, it's more serious than our comings and goings. Right now,

I'm with Sarah at Montserrat. She called me earlier to tell me that Gerald had died during the night.'

CHAPTER 12

THE ATMOSPHERE IN Vere's cottage that evening was sombre when Yvonne arrived a little after seven, having first called at her Westridge Green home to collect essentials for the weekend.

Despite her obvious sadness Vere thought she looked stunning, hair swept back into a ponytail, a plain white blouse, skin-tight black ski pants and low heels. Lightly applied make-up, while adding to her beauty, did little to disguise her feelings of profound sadness. Vere, having spent all week in suits, was more informal in an old sweatshirt, jeans and trainers. Deciding against their more traditional Friday evening stroll to the local pub for a meal, they both felt the need for private time in which to share their grief for the sudden loss of Gerald. Decision made. A visit to the freezer unearthed a pizza while the fridge yielded up enough ingredients from which Yvonne made a salad. Half an hour later they settled down to eat beneath the well-worn ceiling beams in the kitchen, late evening sunlight giving the room a welcoming glow. Clinking wine glasses, Vere made a softly worded toast to the man who had guided him through his early years in Cavendish Square, later to become a firm friend.

'Now he's no more,' he spoke softly, 'gone, not giving us the chance to say thank you or even goodbye.' In reflective mood Vere remembered a saying that he'd heard a while ago. *Life is like a bank account, every day you draw out but you've no idea what remains in the account.* Wise words to reflect upon at a time like this.

'Poor, Sarah,' Yvonne said, cutting through his thoughts. 'I'm glad her sister's staying for a while. Hopefully, that'll ease things for her but, oh I don't know,' she sighed, 'Gerald looked so well when we saw him the other Saturday, didn't he?'

'True,' he agreed, 'he was in good form, I don't think anybody could have seen this one coming. He didn't smoke, drank a bit, but not to excess and he certainly wasn't overweight either.' He offered these words thoughtfully, somehow seeking to explain away the unexplainable. 'And he told me how Sarah watched his diet, plenty of greens and fish.' He paused for a moment, still trying to find an answer. 'We'll never know. Just too many miles on the clock,' he said, reaching out for his wine glass. 'Mind you, I didn't rate his doctor, miserable old sod. More like a ruddy undertaker,' Vere added thoughtfully as he swilled a little wine around his glass. 'Perhaps if he'd been more on the ball, this might have been preventable. Who knows?' he muttered, morosely.

'Well, at least they've accepted it as a heart attack. That's something I suppose,' Yvonne commented, wrinkling her brow, 'although it doesn't tell us why. Did he have a shock or something?'

'Sadly, these things can happen at any time, that's what the old fart of a doctor reckoned.'

'Robert!' Yvonne said reproachfully, before breaking into a grin.

'Sorry, but you didn't see him. Mind you, I'll bet Gerald dined well at the Lodge, all washed down with a glass or two of decent claret. Then he totters back home, flops into his favourite chair, complete with a night cap. No doubt nursing what he thought was chronic indigestion. Huh, like as not relying upon a belch to shift it. Who knows?' he said, carving his way into a large slice of pizza.

'What was the fight he wanted to see? Was it that important?

'Not really,' Vere looked across in surprise, 'I don't think so, although it'd been well publicised in the press beforehand. It involved Danny Bates, a promising English middleweight, and an American "has-been" looking for an easy meal ticket, so the papers said. All a bit boring, ten rounds with a narrow decision going to Bates who was looking to claim a valuable scalp on his way up the ladder.'

'Oh, I see,' Yvonne said, finding little interest is the matter.

'Don't get me wrong, the O2 Arena had been fully booked for weeks. Saw a report on-line at lunchtime, said both men were back peddling which had the crowd doing a fair bit of jeering.'

'Boxing,' Yvonne sighed, 'hardly likely to give Gerald cardiac arrest,' she offered philosophically in the hope of more stimulating conversation.

'Anyway,' Vere replied, 'just in case we missed anything, we can watch it on the laptop later.'

'Must we?' Yvonne groaned with an evident lack of

enthusiasm, rating boxing on a par with the gratuitous violence associated with the Coliseum in Rome.

***

Less than an hour later Yvonne, comfortable on the settee in the lounge, grudgingly watched as Vere booted up his laptop on the coffee table.

'I can see Mrs Jackson's been busy today,' Yvonne commented, sniffing furniture polish, having already noticed how tidy everything looked in the cottage.

'Yeah,' Vere commented, 'worth her weight in gold, that one. Every Friday she drives over from Reading, does two or three other places while she's here in Shiplake,' he added before returning to his laptop. Above them darkened oak beams dissected the ceiling, while slightly uneven floors bore testimony to the age of the building. At the far end of the lounge an imposing floor to ceiling stone fireplace was the room's prominent feature. In winter, a roaring log fire threw out the welcome heat, but tonight nothing more than a two-bar electric fire was being relied upon to manage the task.

Vere, leaning over the laptop, connected to the I Player before selecting the boxing from the offerings available. After minutes of expert comment, plus a brief interview with a former British champion, proceedings got under way. Both fighters starring unflinchingly into each other's eyes as they steadfastly ignored the referee's final instructions. Touching gloves, they returned to their corners to await the bell.

It took less than two and a half minutes for Vere to agree that the lunch-time report had given a realistic account of the event. While both men were agile, neither looked to have any inclination to deliver a proper fight, so denying the spectators value for their money. As the countdown for the end of round one approached, he stood up. 'I'll nip into the kitchen and open another bottle, while those two have a rest after all that exertion.'

Knowing that a South African Merlot suited them both he selected a bottle from the wine rack on the kitchen wall. Double checking the label, he removed the screw cap before pouring the dark red liquid into the first of two glasses. About to fill the second glass he jumped, startled as a penetrating scream made him splash wine across the worktop.

'Bloody hell fire! What's that about?' he shouted, rushing back into the lounge to find Yvonne on her feet, ashen faced and shouting at the screen.

'For God's sake, Robert, that man's hand, it's him!' she cried, pointing at the screen.

'Who?' Vere question, uncertain as to Yvonne's obvious concern.

'It's him,' she shouted, 'the one described in Drysdale's notes. I'm sure of it,' she gasped, still pointing at the screen. Vere, struggling to take in what she'd said, stepped around the settee and thrust an arm across her trembling shoulders.

'What do you mean - it's him?'

'Oh, Robert,' she spluttered, 'it's him,' her index finger pointing at the screen. 'He's gone now, the old person in Bates's corner. He's got a damaged left hand, just as described by Drysdale. Next time the cameras on that corner, look at his left hand.' She paused, breathing heavily. 'At first, I wasn't really paying attention, but when I saw him place his hand on the boxer's shoulder, while giving him a drink, I screamed. Did I frighten you?'

'Not half, like the shower scene in Hitchcock's Psycho. Frightened me to death, made me spill wine all over the place.' Turning he guided Yvonne back onto the settee, before settling down beside her. 'Are you sure about the hand?'

'Of course, I am,' she snapped, frustrated that the cameras refused to return to show the man's hand. 'From the top of the second finger to the base of the little finger on the left hand, all missing' she confirmed, leaning back into the sofa. 'By the look of him, he's the right age as well. About where the man mentioned by Drysdale would be now.'

'Okay, don't let's get too excited, probably just a coincidence,' his suggestion lacking conviction. During round three Vere went back to the kitchen, returning with two full glasses of wine to wait patiently for the next interval to see what had so disturbed Yvonne. Sure enough, moments after Bates returned to his corner, an older looking man with a thick mop of grey hair climbed stiffly onto the ring apron. As he leaned into the ring the camera clearly showed his left hand on a rope for support while using his right-hand to smear grease around his fighter's eyebrows.

'Hmm, I see what you mean. No wonder you let out such a scream. I damn near dropped the ruddy bottle.'

'It's the same,' Yvonne retorted angrily, annoyed that her companion failed to show any real enthusiasm for her discovery. 'Who's that guy anyway?' Yvonne asked, not really expecting an answer. Then, as if by divine intervention, the television commentator supplied the answer. 'As you can see, "Knocker" Noakes is busy slapping Vaseline around the fighter's eyes to prevent any cuts developing.'

'Noakes,' Vere muttered, 'you reckon seeing that damaged hand's what gave Gerald his heart attack?'

'Yes, I do,' she said firmly, before folding her arms across her chest. 'It jolly well could have done,' she continued. 'We all saw how tense he got when talking about Drysdale the other day, how those notes brought back so many terrible memories, forcing him to revisit things he'd rather have forgotten.'

'That's true enough,' he agreed.

'Okay,' she replied, 'I'm no doctor, but I reckon seeing that would have given him a huge shock. Just imagine, I'll bet he was trying to get up, desperate to share the news, when he had the attack. I'm sure the shock of seeing that hand would have been enough to bring one on.' She paused, looking Vere in the eye when she raised her next point. 'Let's say that it did bring on the heart attack. What shall we do about it?'

'What do you mean, do about it?' he asked cautiously, aware that Yvonne was not in a mood to ignore such a chance sighting.

'We can't just let this pass us by,' she queried before leaning across to settle her head on his chest. 'We owe it to Gerald to do something. Can't we go to the police, now we've got additional information?'

'The police,' Vere said with a sigh, 'they'd want facts, hard evidence before even thinking about doing anything. Really, love,' he tried to placate her, 'you must see that an old document, and an equally old trainer with a damaged hand would hardly count as evidence.'

'Robert,' she snapped, 'stop being so sanctimonious. I know the police need facts,' she added, 'but they also need a place start from. From what I've just seen this'd be as good a place as any.

'Oh, but do be practical, love,' Vere pleaded, 'imagine the police turning up and asking Noakes what he was doing back in April 1962?' He offered the scenario, hoping to head off any argument. Yvonne, recognising an impasse, decided to keep quiet rather than spoil their weekend. Accepting her silence as vindication for his argument, he lowered his head and kissed the soft fresh hair on the top of her head. As his mind turned to happier thoughts, he eased his right hand to undo the top button of her blouse, gaining the space he needed to softly fondle her well-rounded breasts. Lovingly, he lightly kissed the nape of her neck, trusting that well-applied TLC might divert her mind away from damaged hands, a long-hidden document and a recently departed friend.

CHAPTER 13

THE SOLITUDE OF her usual Sunday evening drive back to Westridge Green had given Yvonne time to think, recalling how Robert had chosen to see Gerald's devastating death as an untimely but natural ending. *Whereas for me is it about unanswered questions? Are my journalistic instincts making me look for a story that's just not there? No. This is not about coincidences* she reasoned, *it's way beyond that. Blow you Robert, fly off to Madrid on Friday for your cosy little legal conference because, if you are not going to follow up on this, I most certainly am.*

After watching the fight on the Friday evening, she'd felt annoyed by Vere's distinct lack of enthusiasm since, to her, the circumstances had been obvious. Yet, with her partner steadfastly refusing to accept her viewpoint, she'd wisely refrained from revisiting such potentially dangerous ground. From the outset Vere had stressed that any links between Drysdale's notes, the trainer's damaged hand and Gerald's death were, at best, sheer speculation. Further emphasising that her argument was based upon the assumption that Gerald had seen the damaged hand in the first place. 'What if he'd had the heart attack before then?' he'd questioned, arguing against dashing off with a half-baked theory. His "leave it alone." had been firmly emphatic, ensuring that their parting that evening had verged on the frosty.

Next morning, and refreshed after a good night's sleep, she set the ball rolling by taking one of the two office juniors into her confidence. At seventeen Wayne was a typical sports mad youngster, yet he worshipped the very ground she walked on. Unsure of his feelings, he guessed they were a heady cocktail of adoration, lust and raging testosterone. Her tight skirts, thin blouses, occasional visible panty lines and a tell-tale glimpse of her slip would set his pulse rate rocketing as, from afar, his big eyes took in her every curve.

Despite what he took to be manly feelings, his unshaven cheeks soon turned an uncontrollable pink whenever addressed by Yvonne who, that morning, had done her best to help him overcome his habitual shyness as he carefully listened to her request.

'Yes...yes... Miss Clarkson,' he'd stammered after listening to what she wanted, his eyes alternating between her face and her mildly provocative tight sweater. 'You want to know where you can find Noakes.' In confirming her request, he was relieved to find that his randy thoughts, fired by that oh so tempting sweater, had prevented him from helplessly blurting out, *you mean Knocker Noakes.*

Half an hour later he returned to her office, bursting with pride at having found her the relevant information. Pushing a hand through his straggly hair he resisted the temptation to take another look at that inviting sweater. 'It's all here, Miss Clarkson,' he said proudly, pushing two pieces of paper across her desk. 'I went onto Google, then looked at a couple of websites, a national newspaper and Boxing

News. With Noakes's gym being in Acton, I've printed off this street map, stapling it to my notes.' Beaming with pride he risked one last lingering glance at the sweater before leaving her office.

***

Later that day it was an excited Yvonne who sipped her coffee while digesting the results of her foray into Acton where, thanks to Wayne, finding the gym had been easy. Once inside, and having seen Noakes on the television, spotting the trainer hadn't presented problems. Arriving without an appointment she'd relied upon feminine charm with which to confront the old trainer. And it had worked. Even if it had involved walking into an all-male preserve to become the centre of instant attention, recalling the prevailing aroma of sweat, damp leather and massage oil that had assailed her nostrils. And the noise. Shouted instructions, skipping ropes slapping the floor, the rhythmic drumming of the speedball and the heavy thuds coming from well-pounded punch bags. Noakes, at the far end of the gym, was supervising a sparring session as she had walked up behind him.

'Keep that jab going, Tony,' he'd shouted, leaning on the ring apron and absorbed in his work, unaware of the advancing female. She'd known that entering a men-only environment would have its drawbacks, yet playing to the gallery had certainly helped because, in a matter of seconds, everyone her had stopped what they were doing. Skipping ropes had fallen silent and punchbags were suddenly motionless as more than a dozen pairs of eyes had bored hungrily into her back as she approached ringside.

Alerted by the unexpected silence in the gym Noakes had turned to see what had caused the activity in his gym to cease. Moments later he been even more confused, stunned to find the smiling Yvonne approaching him with her right hand outstretched. Noakes, regaining in his composure, had recognised her discomfort at being in such an alien environment and had reacted promptly by escorting her towards the privacy of his narrow wood and glass office at the back of the gym. As they'd made their way there, Yvonne had commented on Noakes's limp.

'Touch of arthritis in the right hip,' he'd muttered. 'Not too serious, but it's a bit difficult nipping up onto the ring apron in between rounds, you know when you've only got a minute.' After mentioning that, he'd stood aside to allow Yvonne to go through the glass panelled doorway before him. 'Don't get many ladies round here,' he'd joked, pointing her towards a chair. 'So, what can I do for you, miss? Thinking of taking up the noble art, are we?' he'd asked her as she had settled into the offered chair.

'No, nothing so drastic, Mr Noakes, I'm just after a little help, please.' Yvonne had smiled, preparing to destabilise Noakes and gauge reactions. Carefully she'd explained how she was hoping to compile an article on professional boxing, as seen from the female point of view. 'It's something I've wanted to do for ages,' she'd explained, 'and finally my editor has agreed. Next I took advice from my "macho" colleagues,' she'd smiled, 'told unanimously that speaking with a well-respected trainer would be my best way forward. They suggested that you, with all your experience, would be ideal.'

'Well thank you, miss,' the old trainer had welcomed the praise. Flattery gets you anywhere she'd thought, as

Noakes had shown enthusiasm for her project, agreeing that she could return in a week's time to conduct an interview. Good, she'd said to herself, ready to see how he'd react to her casually injecting a selection of well-chosen words or phrases into her conversation, before playing her trump card. *'Thanks for seeing me so quickly, it's saved me hanging about,'* had been amongst her opening lines while, in other sentences, she had managed to insert such expressions as *'sticking my neck out,' followed by 'a short drop' and 'putting my head in a noose.'* Throughout Noakes's demeanour had remained bland, leaving Yvonne to wonder whether her ranging shots were falling hopelessly wide of the target.

Ever since she'd first seen Noakes's damaged hand on the screen she had known that there had to be a link somewhere. Initially disappointed at not having been able to unsettle Noakes, she'd them allowed herself to innocently come out with the name of Drysdale. Her "acid test" as she'd liked to call it, aware it would either fall flat or hit a nerve. *In fact, I hit a whole load of them* she smiled, remembering how the blood had drained from his face, coupled with a temporary inability to speak coherently. *Point made,* she'd thought, before glancing at the trainers damaged left hand. Tormented by doubt, she'd wondered if this man really had been one of the robbers mentioned in Drysdale's narrative. For Yvonne, proving such a link had been the very purpose of her visit.

'Mr Noakes,' she had asked hesitantly, 'forgive me for asking, but what happened to your hand?'

'Oh that,' he'd replied nonchalantly, 'happened a long time ago, way back in the early sixties. An accident, in the army you know,' he'd then shrugged, having become used to such a question. 'Put paid to my boxing career, and my time as a soldier. This,' he had held the damaged hand inches above the desk, 'was the result of an explosion, I copped it while working in bomb disposal. Normally you don't get away when things go wrong, but that time I was lucky.' Once said, he'd known that this highly embellished distortion generated more sympathy than telling the truth would ever do.

Within seconds of Yvonne leaving the gym, Noakes had yelled out to an older man casually sweeping the floor. 'Lefty,' he'd said, pulling a twenty pound not from his wallet, 'follow that bird. She's a journalist, from a woman's magazine. Like as not going back to her office. Says her names Clarkson, just got married and now says she's a Drysdale. Check her out and ring me back as soon as you've got something to tell me.'

***

Shortly after lunch Noakes put down his mobile phone, pleased that his twenty pounds had been money well spent. Lefty, having just phoned in, reported that he'd followed Clarkson to the offices of a national women's magazine close by Vauxhall Bridge. He'd then told Noakes that he'd made enquiries at the front desk, yes they did have a Miss Clarkson in the building but no Mrs Clarkson. Further delicate probing confirmed that nobody by the name of Drysdale, married or single, had been employed there in recent years.

As he digested this l information, the badly worried Noakes knew that he'd nowhere near enough facts to assess the danger. To do that he needed accurate information. Silently he asked himself exactly what Clarkson might know. There had to be method in her madness. A smart looking dame doesn't just walk unannounced into a gym full of sweating bodies. Not unless she is on the game, and that she certainly wasn't! No, she is up to something, all those clever remarks: hanging about, head in a noose and so forth. No, she knows something – but what? And as for mentioning Drysdale – well bugger me – that could make her dangerous. Can I really afford to wait until we meet again next week? No way, she's too big a risk - action now rather than later. As in boxing,' he smiled at the comparison. Attack is always the best form of defence, but I need more information before mounting my attack.

Fifteen minutes later he'd made up his mind. Reaching for his mobile he called Lefty, passing on more instructions. 'Look, he began, 'there's another twenty pounds in this for you, but I want you to hang about there until that Clarkson woman comes out after work. See if she's with anyone or try and get hold of one of her friends. See if you can pump them for a bit of info. I can't tell you anymore, but I need the "inside track" on this bird. She's up to no good, could cause trouble. Call me back later.'

After disconnecting Lefty was totally at a loss to understand how a smart looking bird could cause 'Knocker,' or his stable of fighters, problems. Still confused he pocketed his mobile, pleased that another twenty would be coming his way.

CHAPTER 14

MILES OVERSTONE WAS in a jubilant mood on Tuesday morning, smiling as he watched a tugboat and barge power its way through the fast-flowing river along Canary Wharf. Eight feet behind him, on his leather topped executive desk, lay the reason for his feeling of well-being. An e-mail confirming that thirty-two million pounds would be in his bank a week on Monday.

Happy to enjoy the moment Overstone had known that all good things must come to an end. For years he'd happily pushed the boundaries of luck in pursuit of wealth, but now it was time to leave it to others, to his *lieutenants*. Entrepreneurs, especially criminal ones, must know when to call it a day. No, he concluded, leaving all this behind for a life in the sun will be painful but financially rewarding. Time to cash-in that leaving present. But there's still work in need of doing he reminded himself, revisiting his masterplan for making the perfect exit-strategy. He'd always known that *proper preparation prevents poor performance* and in planning this, his swansong, he had made no exceptions.

The derelict corner site, within a mile of the Olympic Park, had proved to be the perfect bait for the trap. Not only did it have position, but it also had the potential to make a huge sum of money from something that he'd never owned. Establishing the bogus company in the Isle of Man had been key to the entire enterprise. Providing, as it did, the perfect trail of documentary evidence needed to convince bankers to support his plan. For months, the flow of official looking documents had intensified, setting out how the fictitious company wished to open a share-dealing office in London. Somewhere close to the financial centre, in and around the Docklands area, would be their preferred location.

Photographs taken of the vacant corner site, midway between Docklands and the Olympic Park, had reached the Isle of Man. And, weeks later, Overstone was far from surprised to hear how this location met with the full approval of the non-existent directors of the mythical client in the Irish Sea. Further bogus letters from the Isle of Man confirmed how the board had agreed to pay an annual rent of more than four million pounds for the fictitious building. Four floors of open-plan offices would, they had said, be ideal. Later adding that were such a building to have six or seven floors, with suitable meeting rooms, secretarial suites and executive accommodation, paying higher rentals would not be a problem.

Indeed, as Overstone had planned, this proved to be a mouth-watering proposition for a number al of the big banks. Supported by drawings, the proposal had contained a false letter stating how local planners had approved planning permission for a seven-floor structure. Next the signed "letter of intent," agreeing to pay enhanced rent on the completed building was the finishing touch. The icing on the cake! It had proved irresistible to three major banks.

What a proposition, lend thirty-two million plus interest, secured against prime land and a building where the owners would be guaranteed to receive millions a year in rent!

With a smug smile of self-satisfaction Overstone knew that his reputation had helped to smooth the way. Previous experience having shown him that bankers were pussy cats when it came to high-quality bluff and bluster. The bigger the bluff, backed by plenty of bluster had proved to be a winning formula. Forget the petty cash. Go for the big hit every time. At recent meetings he'd received warm assurances of solid support from all three financial institutions. Their eagerness reinforced by executive lunches, concessionary theatre tickets and director's box invitations to Premier League football matches.

Now, after weeks of infighting, he had identified the bank willing to meet his criteria, the unsuspecting partner needed to play the pivotal role in his swindle. Already informed that the deal was going to go through, the bank's e-mail confirmed the transfer of the whole thirty-two million.

Then I'll be away with their money, having it safely tucked up in Panama by nightfall, followed by me twenty-four hours later. What could be better? Those greedy banks could go whistle for their money. He smiled, why worry about the very institutions that had recklessly caused so much financial damage to the UK within recent memory. No, stuff it, he grinned, gleefully considering how he'd use their money to build the perfect home where he could live like a lord. Even if the money runs a bit low, it's only a short trip across to the Cayman Islands for a top up.

The sudden ringing of the telephone startled him, a sharp reminder that he still had a fortnight to go before being able to capitalise upon his master- plan. He took five steps back across the soft pile carpet before sitting down to pick up the handset.

'Oh, Mr Overstone it's Susan in reception. Look, I'm sorry to trouble you, sir, but I have a caller on the line that I don't understand. He says his name is Williams, calling from a firm of solicitors. He tells me he's been given this number as a point of contact for someone called Buchanan.' The man behind the executive desk gasped, unable to speak as Susan continued. 'Of course, I told him we'd nobody here of that name here,' she gushed. 'Quite honestly, sir, I just don't understand any of this,' she stalled, 'what shall I do?' Overstone slumped back into his chair, pole-axed, his chest thumping and his breathing difficult. God almighty, he mouthed silently between gasps.

'Mr Overstone, what shall I do?'

'Oh, put him through,' he snapped, 'it's obviously a mistake of some kind. I'll sort it,' he blustered, desperately trying to control his racing pulse. Fear gave volume to his voice, startling Susan as he almost shouted down the line.

'You say his name's Williams?'

'Yes sir, that's correct.'

'All right then, let me speak to the wretched man,' he barked, wrestling with the fact that only one person had ever known how to contact him as Buchanan.

'Mr Buchanan?' the caller questioned in a firm voice.

'No. Not at all, I'm Miles Overstone. Now what can I do for you? My girl says your name's Williams.'

'That's right, Mr Overstone.'

'Sorry, but I can't recall your name at all. Should I know you?

Undaunted by the barrage of questions Williams mentioned the name of his firm. 'Never heard of them either!' Overstone said bullishly, lying whilst recalling the name from the back of his memory.

'Sir, that's not a problem,' Williams replied politely. 'It is just that I have been asked to relay a call we had today from a Mr George Noakes.'

'Never heard of him either,' Overstone gave a false laugh, hoping that his blatant denial would deter his caller, yet painfully aware in which direction this conversation was heading. Desperately he tried to rally his mental defences, hoping to put up enough firepower to divert Williams from his purpose.

'Over the 'phone,' Williams persisted doggedly, 'Mr Noakes told me that someone on this number might be able to contact this Buchanan chap? Is that correct?' Without waiting for an answer Williams continued. 'I'll say you've taken a bit of tracking down, what with new buildings going up all over the place and the telephone exchanges getting ever bigger. Must say the phone people have been extremely helpful, backtracking on which numbers superseded the originals. Took a bit of doing, but they managed it in the end.'

Williams paused as Overstone gasped in disbelief, horrified that his earlier fears were now turning into hard facts. George bloody Noakes, crawling out of the woodwork after all these years, he muttered to himself.

'Are you still there, sir?' Williams asked. 'This is the result of a convoluted messaging service, set up years ago whereby Mr Noakes could contact this Buchanan chap, via our firm and you. Is that correct?'

'Bloody hell' Overstone spat out. 'That was at least fifty years ago. I'd forgotten all about it.' Struggling to collect his thoughts, his mind went searching for more bluster. 'Yes. Now you mention it, hmm, I do seem to remember something about it. Nothing to do with me,' he rounded on Williams, 'yes, I do seem to recall saying I'd function as a sort of link between those two chaps.' Deciding that this sounded plausible, he gave it a little more embellishment. 'That's it, can't remember who, but one of them was off to travel the world. Wanted to use my help, should they ever need to contact each other.' At least it sounded believable he reckoned, before continuing. 'Anyway, you said his name was Noakes, do you know what this chap wanted?'

'Oh, nothing much, he's just wondering if someone on this number might be able to reach this Buchanan person. If possible, could they ring him back today at noon. If you've got a pen, I'll read the number out to you.' Badly flustered Overstone reached for a pen, scribbling the number down on his desk pad.

'Yes, got that, leave it with me,' he said, putting down the phone, not at all convinced that his vagueness had satisfied the badly confused Williams.

CHAPTER 15

AN HOUR LATER it was an angry Overstone who dialled the number supplied by Williams. Recognising that the dialling code was for somewhere in the west London area he waited for, and then heard, the ringing tone.

'Is that you Alistair?' a muffled voice asked.

'Yes. This had better be good. I told you, all those years ago, only to use this contact system in an emergency. So, what do you want after all these years?' Noakes paused, then started to tell the man he knew as Alistair Buchanan what had taken place in the last twenty-four hours. Starting slowly, he prefaced his comments with a brief overview of how he had established himself as a boxing trainer, building a successful gymnasium for fighters, later setting up a popular health club on the ground floor.

'Yes.' Overstone butted in, blustering impatiently, 'do get on with it.'

'Well,' Noakes continued, 'yesterday morning a most attractive young lady waltzes into my gym. Said she's a journalist or something, from a women's magazine, interested in doing an article on boxing, wanting to get a perspective from the wives or girlfriend's angle.'

'For God's sake, Noakes, you bloody fool. What's this got to do with me?' Overstone bristled in frustration.

'Cut the insults, Alistair,' Noakes shouted back. 'I'm coming to that,' as he went on to explain how he had been keen to cooperate with such a nice-looking lady.

'Good, so you can still pull the birds at your age. What did you want to do, get into her knickers?'

'Don't be so ruddy crude, you overblown public school twit.' Noakes snapped back before confirming how he had arranged to give her a more formal interview in a week's time. Agreeing to let her take some pictures on her next visit, he'd noted the meeting in his diary, along with a reminder to get the place tidied up.

'All very pretty, I'm sure,' Overstone said sarcastically, 'but I still don't see what the hell this has got to do with me.'

'Well, this'll take the wind out of your sails because, as she was leaving, she spotted the local Boys Club collecting tin on my desk, asking if she could contribute. Happy to accept, she proceeded to make out a cheque for twenty quid but, as she went to sign it, she laughingly told me that she'd got married a couple of weeks ago. Told me she still had problems remembering to sign in her married name. She's now a Clarkson but, before that, *her maiden name had been Drysdale!*'

Overstone went icy cold as his brain digested the information before he found his voice. 'Where did that come from? How did you react?'

'How do you think I reacted? I went as white as a sheet and was nearly bricking it,' Noakes replied in total honesty. 'I was bloody dumbstruck, I could hardly breathe, let alone speak.'

'Was her name printed on the cheque?' Overstone asked, attempting to get a grip on things.

'Oh, as expected, Clarkson with the initials Y L. Oh, and before you ask, it was the first cheque out of her new book, with her new name on it.'

'What do you think the bitch knows?' Overstone snarled in uncontrolled nervous anger.

'I don't know. What could she know?' Noakes offered weakly. 'But I'm sure she'd have clocked my reaction, like when she dropped out Drysdale. You'd need to be a ruddy good poker player not to flinch at that one! Anyway, she's coming back next Tuesday to do an interview.'

'Fuck me,' Overstone bellowed down the line, 'are you completely mad?'

'Well....what else could I say to her?' Making the effort to control his thoughts Overstone replied slowly.

'Okay, we'll worry about that later. But what did you do, after she'd gone, I mean? apart from getting into a blind panic and buggering up my day.'

'I slipped one of the brighter hangers-on around here twenty quid, told him to follow the woman. See where she went like, and what he could find out.'

'Okay,' Overstone muttered. 'It doesn't sound like terminal damage, well not just yet anyway. Be on the same number tomorrow morning, at ten then give me an update. We can then decide just how serious this might be and what we need to do,' he demanded, before banging the 'phone down.

***

By nine that Tuesday evening Noakes was deep in thought, silently weighing up every word that Lefty had relayed to him over the phone earlier. Clarkson, he'd said, had come out of the office at around 5.40 pm, accompanied by a young lad. Respectful and attentive the youth had spent two minutes in conversation with her before parting in different directions. Lefty had then explained how he'd approached the youth, guessing he'd be more likely to respond if questioned discreetly over a drink.

'Excuse me but wasn't that Miss Clarkson you were talking to?' he'd asked a startled Wayne. 'You see, we met a year or so back at a fashion show over in Chelsea. I'm a photographer, take fashion pictures for an agency.' Wayne nodded, agreeing to go to a nearby pub as anything to do with Clarkson stirred his interest. Once settled Lefty Archer had soon found how the young lad's supressed lust for Clarkson had given free rein to his tongue. Wayne, Archer told Noakes, had known the basics, confirming that Clarkson lived in a small Berkshire village, commuting daily to work from Goring Station, where she left her car. And no, he couldn't recall the number.

'What about her love life?' Noakes had then asked, 'anything there?'

'Not much, the lad's a bit vague, thinks she might be quite involved with some fellow, a lawyer of some sort, or so the kid reckons.' Noakes had flinched at that. An interfering journalist was bad enough, but a bloody lawyer as well! Concerned, Noakes had then pushed Lefty to find out more because a plan was already forming in his mind, for which he needed to know the number of Clarkson's car and when it might be at Goring station.

CHAPTER 16

9.00 AM WEDNESDAY and Wayne was in a quandary. Anxious to retain Yvonne's favour, he felt honour bound to let her know about the mystery photographer, plying him with beer and asking questions. Aware that he had done something foolish, he nervously tried to balance any indiscretions against the more worrying thought of incurring her serious displeasure. For the first half an hour, after reaching the office, he had suffered in silence before an incoming call had helped to set his mind at rest.

'Look,' his caller said, 'after our chat last evening, I realise that I'll be going by Goring station tomorrow as I'll be attending a fashion shoot at a posh country house nearby. Thought I'd like to put a note on her windscreen, you know, leave my number and ask her out for a drink. Don't say a word. Give her a surprise like. What sort of car's she got? You know, make, model, petrol or diesel, registration number? Will it be there tomorrow? Don't want to get the wrong car. That would make me look like a right dope.'

'Hang about,' Wayne said, 'that's a shed load of questions, where do I start?'

'Take your time mate,' the caller said. 'I don't want to screw this up.' An unfortunate turn of phrase, one that jarred with the lovelorn Wayne. Uncertain as to whether any action of his might be helping a possible 'love rival,' he hesitated, silently forced into accepting the futility of his emotional position. *I'm a seventeen-year-old on the minimum wage and fancying my chances with a divine goddess like Clarkson.* Get real. Dream on, he conceded. Brightening up a little he thought, well at least I can still look.

'Tomorrow you said?' Wayne questioned, attempting to overcome his lustful imagination. 'Let me check her diary, see what plans she's got. It's all here on the computer. Hold on.' Minutes later Wayne was back on the line. 'You're okay. She's in the office tomorrow. That means her car will be at the station in Goring, be there all day.'

'That's handy,' Lefty acknowledged, waiting to see if there was more.

'Okay, now for the other info you wanted,' Wayne said into the 'phone. 'It's all down here, car details and home address. Oh, and hers is a petrol model. Each staff member, with their own car has a breakdown and recovery policy paid for by the firm. The boss says she can't risk having her staff standing by the roadside, or stuck at home, when they should be working. She's a right old sergeant major, I can tell you.' Then, as if feeling compelled to justify his importance in the scheme of things he continued, 'hang on, here it comes. I update this every so often, part of my job like, so I know the info's right. Okay here's all the details you asked for but,' he said forcefully, 'don't you dare tell her how you got any of it, particularly her address. Okay?'

'Of course not, that's our little secret.'

'Well, make sure it stays that way. She'll chew my balls if she ever finds out.'

'Wow! From what you said I reckon you'd secretly enjoy that,' his caller jested, laughing down the phone.

'If only,' Wayne commented, suddenly starting to blush. 'Now shut up and write this down.' Unaware of any potential consequences, he then proceeded to innocently give away information that would shortly place the girl of his dreams in mortal danger.

***

Later that morning it was a nervous George Noakes who waited for his twelve o'clock call from Overstone which, at one minute past the hour came through. Hesitantly Noakes updated his caller, this time without any interruptions or curses. An improvement.

'Don't like the sound of the boyfriend,' Overstone stated, 'could end up being a right pain in the backside!'

'Yeah,' Noakes concurred, 'but look, they know nothing.'

'Wrong!' Overstone barked. 'The girl must know something, coming out

with that damned name! Think about it. Your man said that no one called Drysdale has ever worked at that office, so her performance the other day was just that, a performance designed to get you rattled, which it's done all right. There's no smoke without fire!'

'Well, okay then, what should we do?' Noakes whined.

'Do?' Overstone snapped irritably. 'We don't do anything, well not until we've got the facts needed to work with. Nothing's altered, the truth still holds good. Drysdale never knew us. If he had of done,' he paused, 'we'd have been hanged flaming years ago,' he stated firmly. 'So far, all we've got is a fashion journalist playing silly buggers. Okay, she may be sharing a bed with a flaming lawyer, but so what? Relax, they know nothing. All we've got to do is sit tight and see if anything else crops up. My guess is we're over-reacting, but at least we're forewarned of possible trouble. I'll ring you on Friday, same time. Be there!' The line went dead, leaving Noakes stunned and alarmed, but pleased that he'd managed to avoid mentioning the unintentional help given indirectly to him by the besotted Wayne.

***

That evening George Noakes struggled to assemble his thoughts. Without doubt the woman knows something, but what could she know? After all these years was her sudden appearance a menacing threat or just a pure coincidence? Surely, given the fact that no one called Drysdale has ever worked in her office must rule out coincidence. No, the more I think about this woman the bigger the threat of prison becomes. Having dodged the death penalty, while an innocent man was less fortunate, we'd go down for ever if caught. I'm well over seventy, far too old to go to jail, besides, I'd never come out, well only in a wooden box. Nobody would miss me if I went down, not even Terry, that useless son of mine. Drugs, alcohol and benefit cheques are his currency in life. Yet, he did come to the gym the other week, he recalled thoughtfully. Nice to spend a bit of time together, especially as he was sober and looked to be drug-free. Maybe I do him an injustice, but he's got me down as a useless father. As for his mother, the ex-wife, completely useless, shacked up God knows where with anyone she sees as a half-useful meal ticket. '

Suddenly he laughed as a vision of a TV show flashed before his eyes with the host saying: 'George Noakes, *This Is Your Life.*' Shock horror! Well, at least the gym and health club are doing okay, and I'm still managing with one and a half hands, and a dodgy hip! Okay, Danny Bates did me no favours, even if he did win the other night. But that young welterweight from Battersea is a real prospect for a title, if I can get the best out of him.

Later, as he recovered from his mental ramblings one thing became clear. No matter how big a mess his life had become, it was still worth fighting for. He hoped that a planned meeting with Terry, over the coming weekend, might just promise a new beginning. I've got far too much at stake to risk having it mucked up by an interfering busybody in a skirt. No, she's a dangerous liability, a threat to my freedom that I reckon needs taking care of before she goes any further. Deep in thought he reached across the kitchen table and poured himself a small whisky.

As the fiery spirit gripped his insides Noakes knew that Clarkson needed elimination, his more acceptable euphemism for *murder*. A task he had to complete sooner rather than later. Any delay would only increase her potential to become ever more dangerous. No, I've got to get to her before she has the slightest opportunity to bring her lawyer boyfriend into play or, worse still, drop into her local police station for a chat.

The fact that he was contemplating killing someone didn't seem to trouble Noakes as he balanced out the equation. The possibility of getting away with murder, set against the certainty of life imprisonment were the truth to come out. Crunch time. With his options severely limited, Noakes appreciated that a defining moment was fast approaching. Could he commit a murder and not be detected? Or could he risk Clarkson uncovering the evidence she'd need to bring about long-overdue justice? He trembled as another terrifying prospect crossed his mind, might Buchanan now see me as a threat to his freedom. A frightening scenario that he knew could only have one inevitable outcome.

Finally, as if by a mystical process, he realised that he'd made his decision. Murdering Clarkson represented his safest option which, if committed without Buchanan's knowledge, would be all to the good. Present him with a done deed. Taking another sip from his glass he knew that the success of such an enterprise depended upon getting three things right first time.

To Noakes, Clarkson had suddenly become an iceberg. Plainly visible on the surface, yet far more dangerous by not knowing what lay beneath it. Her arrival in my gymnasium didn't just happen. It was deliberate and driven by information she must possess. But what does she really know? Dealing with facts was not a problem, but the unknown terrified him since the dread of the penal reckoning was ever present. Add to that the unknown quantity of Clarkson's boyfriend, a toxic mix if ever there was one. The duo from Hell. No, she's got to go, before she becomes even more dangerous!'

For Noakes, genuinely frightened by the re-emergence of his criminal past, disregarding Overstone's demand to do nothing was the lesser of two evils. It was time to act because, as with boxing, getting you blow in first was essential. Power dominated and Noakes knew that knowledge was power. Reassuringly, he told himself that he possessed the power and knowledge needed to eliminate Clarkson. With what I have in mind she will be dead within twenty-four hours he though, believing it possible that not a single thread of evidence would lead back to him. Refreshed by these beliefs he then analysed the moves needed to secure a successful hit. The blessed trinity; where, when and how. Well, he thought, the "where" would be simple, the "when" could be tomorrow. As for the "how" - well that'll be easy enough, thinking back to his army days when he'd been fascinated by learning how things could be made to go bang!

CHAPTER 17

HAVING DECIDED UPON his plan Noakes spent the
final hours of Wednesday busy in his kitchen, carefully
setting out a small collection of items on the table. Each
item on its own was harmless enough but, when put
together correctly, represented the components he'd need
to bring about the timely destruction of Clarkson and her
car. Using the knowledge gained in the army he set to work.
Painstakingly he began assembling the delicate mechanism
that would ensure Clarkson and her car were no more. No
need for any explosives. Thanks to Clarkson they'd already
be there! All he had to do was to assemble a device capable of
igniting the vapour in the car's petrol tank. Done correctly
this would unleash an instantaneous and devastating
explosion, the likes of which have been known to bring
down aircraft. So, he smiled, a Ford Fiesta shouldn't be that
much of a problem.

Looking down he surveyed the components needed
to bring about such an explosion: A short piece of plastic
tube, a glass mercury tilt switch assembly with electrical
connections, a stun-gun the size of a cigarette packet and a
roll of "gaffer" tape. For tools he had a small lithium battery

powered drill, fitted with a circular ring saw blade exactly matching the diameter of the plastic tube. Fearful of street violence he had armed himself with the illegal stun-gun over a year ago, managing to buy it anonymously online. Whereas the mercury tilt switch had been a gift, left over from a major plumbing job at the health club. At the time he had shown great interest in the gadget and its workings. "Keep it, mate," the plumber had said when packing away his tools, "we've got dozens back at the workshop."

Fifteen minutes later, after slipping on a pair of tight rubber gloves, he fitted the stun-gun snugly into one end of the plastic tube, its twin prongs pushed down inside the tube itself. Pausing, Noakes knew that he had to complete any further work needed to bring about the desired explosion once he was underneath the car. For this to happen, he'd have to use the ring-saw to cut a small hole into the side of the car's plastic fuel tank. Through this opening he could push the end of the tube into the tank, so exposing the

stun-gun contacts to fuel vapour. Then, and only then, could the tilt switch be securely attached to the tank and the contacts wired up. After that, when the car encountered a slope, gravity would cause the heavy mercury to flow from one hinged chamber to the other, covering the contacts and making the circuit. Instantly thousands of volts would flash through the vapour at the top of the fuel tank. Good night Miss Clarkson and no more bleating about Drysdale! Finished, he packed everything into an old, paint-stained, haversack with a grubby canvas shoulder strap. Perfect, he'd just be another old worker, complete with flask and sandwiches.

Before retiring he powered up his lap top computer, and using Google Earth, familiarised himself with the layout of Goring village which lay nine miles upstream from Reading. Directly opposite Goring, on the other side of the Thames, was the smaller village of Streatley. He could see how the river divided the two communities but noticed how a long road bridge joined them together. Next, he looked for, and found, Goring railway station. The map showing that it lay a little further back from the river, easily accessible on foot with the car park on the far side of the railway line.

Needing to cross the railway line to reach his objective he started to form a plan, knowing success would depend upon him remaining unobtrusive and unrecognised. Travelling there by train would be the easiest way, but that was out of the question. Station staff can remember passengers, especially those with unfamiliar faces. No, I need to reach the car park on foot, he told himself, and a leisurely approach through Streatley must be my ideal route. All right, while this looks straight forward enough, it's a fair way with this arthritic hip, but it does mean I can reach the objective without having to stop and ask for directions. An encounter with a well-meaning citizen, gifted with a retentive memory, would not be at all helpful.

Re-examining the map, he noticed how a shorter route through Goring village would take him to the station. From there the footbridge, over the tracks, gave access to the car park. Although taking this route meant less walking, he assumed that the platforms would have CCTV cameras. While these were a known deterrent to late night troublemakers and drunks, they would be a ready source of information to the police making enquiries into a murder.

Driven by the compulsive need to kill Clarkson he realised that the route through Streatley, and up Goring High Street, had to offer the best chances of anonymity. A further look at the map showed that taking a right turn, coming off the road bridge, would take him the short distance to the station building and car park. Yes further to walk but that's nothing compared to being seen and remembered, even if my blasted hip does give me more grief.

Before switching off his laptop, he scrolled further up the map looking for the village where Clarkson lived. Westridge Green was, he noted, was three or four miles out of Streatley on the back road towards Newbury. Using Google's Street View' facility he observed how the road, having left Streatley, climbed steeply out of the Thames Valley. Perfect. Driving up a good steep hill will tip over the mercury tilt switch, meaning that the explosion would take place in an isolated spot devoid of witnesses. Then, as he anticipated his killing ground, he had a thought. What if I positioned the tilt switch the other way around? Set it to activate when the car is going downhill as opposed to uphill. Braking sharply, while descending the steep hill into Streatley, would be even better. Timing the explosion for Friday morning, rather than Thursday evening would, he knew, give him an extra twelve hours or so in which to cover his tracks. He could be well clear of the area before anything happened. Okay, Clarkson you're still going to die, on Friday and not tomorrow. Happy that he'd just improved his chances of avoiding detection he shut down his laptop.

CHAPTER 18

THE DECISION TO commit murder had left Noakes in a determined frame of mind. Utterly convinced that he was about to do the right thing he boarded a mid-morning train from Paddington armed with a return ticket to Reading. Wearing paint-stained overalls, a cloth cap and a lightweight raincoat he was just another worker travelling to or from a job. Beside him the tatty haversack completed the image, hidden behind the Daily Mirror even his gloved hand didn't look out of place. Silent and "faceless," he was just one of those people that nobody ever seemed to notice, yet alone remember.

Leaving the train at Reading was, he knew, a sensible precaution since travelling directly to Goring would have been a big gamble, a risk he was not prepared to take. Confident his device would wreck Clarkson's car away from the area, he could not entertain the possibility of anyone being able to recall him being anywhere near Goring or Streatley. For certain, he knew it wouldn't take the police long to determine that the explosion was no accident. After which they'd leave no stone unturned in their search for the culprit, with Goring Station being the first "stone" they'd be turning over!

Following the planned Friday morning explosion, Noakes knew how the police would immediately back-track for evidence, checking first where the car was on Thursday night. Had this been outside Clarkson's place at Westridge Green? Then, before that, they'd find that her Fiesta had spent twelve hours parked or more parked at Goring station on Thursday. After that amount of time in a very public place, logic dictated that the car park would be the starting point for their investigators. As ever, Noakes set about taking every precaution needed to ensure that his journey in and out of the car park was as unobserved as possible.

Walking away from Reading station he headed in the direction of parked buses. Happy to be unnoticed in the crowd he took several minutes to study routes and timetables, eager to relate the printed information to his studies of the previous evening. Unobtrusively leaving a bus some way from the target had to be his best and safest choice. Okay, it'll involve a bit more walking he reasoned, soon identifying a bus that was due to leave in twenty minutes, passing through Streatley on its way to Wallingford. That route dovetailed perfectly with his planning, allowing him to get off in Streatley and walk through the village on his way to Goring Station.

***

An hour later he left the bus, stepping down just a few yards in front of the Bull public house. With the haversack over one shoulder he took advantage of the traffic lights to cross the narrow but busy main road. Seconds later he was on Streatley High Street, the road he knew that sloped all the way down to the river. On either side of the road, neat cottages and well-presented houses fronted the busy thoroughfare.

Courtesy of a gap in the traffic he crossed to the left-hand side of the road, making his way down towards the old bridge in the distance. Grey clouds overhead threatened rain, encouraging what few pedestrians there were to seek out shelter. The sight of a seventy something old man, wearing a lightweight raincoat over well-worn overalls failed to attract any attention. With his right hand resting lightly on his paint spotted haversack he was just another worker, moving slowly through a village where most of the population invariably made use of such faceless workers. Feeling close to invisible, he shuffled slowly onto the slope of the bridge, occasional stabs of pain from his arthritic hip causing his stride pattern to falter at times.

Absently he looked to his left, down onto the water where he could see two palatial motor cruisers moored alongside the terrace of the Swan Hotel. Leaving the Swan behind he crossed the first stretch of water before the bridge dipped slightly onto the support provided by the small, wooded island in the middle of the stream. In a few more yards he'd reached the next part of the bridge where, looking to his left, he could see water rushing noisily over the curving weir before tumbling down a series of concrete steps. Beside the frothing weir Goring Lock provided safe passage for craft navigating the river.

Once off the bridge he entered the Goring village, passing the Miller of Mansfield hotel on his left while to his right the church was set back a short distance from the road. From his earlier map-reading he knew that he now had some three hundred yards further to travel, all slightly uphill as he progressed towards his next objective. The steel sided bridge that crossed the railway. Not too far now, he reassured himself, as the suspect hip joint once again registered an uncomfortable protest.

Turning right, after crossing the bridge, the road then ran slightly downhill which allowed his walking to become a little easier. In a further hundred yards the pavement became the station entrance, in front of which yellow lines marked out space for taxis to pick up and drop off fares. From there the main road curved away to the left, leaving the car park entrance directly in front of him.

Seconds earlier, when passing outside the main building, he'd cautiously looked around for possible CCTV cameras. Although none were easily visible he remained convinced that they were there, watching over travellers and as a deterrent to troublemakers. Further along he felt sure there'd be more cameras to monitor the parked vehicles. Before him, two long rows of vehicles stretched into the distance. 'Now to find her car,' he muttered, reminding himself of Clarkson's registration number. To his right, parked vehicles were close up to the mesh fencing that faced the 'Up' platform. Glancing across he noticed a large sign saying that CCTV cameras monitored the platforms. And the car park as well he reasoned. Not a problem since the presence of cameras tended to deter crime or provide information after an event.

Approaching the end of the line of cars parked on the platform side he smiled, sure that any CCTV footage would be at least twenty-four hours old by the time the car exploded. So, who is going to remember an old boy in raincoat and cloth cap.?

After surveying the first line of vehicles he then doubled back, crossing the car park to concentrate on the vehicles lined up on the opposite side. These, he could see, had been parked up against a grass covered slope, some having been driven into position, whereas others had been reversed into their slots. The positioning, he guessed, represented the driver's arrival time. Late arrivals driving straight in, while the more organised had the time to reverse neatly into place. Please let Clarkson's be one of the organised types. Was she a Virgo? The neat and tidy type, reversing up to that nice and oh so convenient grassy slope?

Nervously he paced slowly along the line of cars, very much aware how important Clarkson's parking habits could prove to be. Had she driven her car in nose first, on either side of the car park, working on the fuel tank would have left him exposed to anyone in the car park. At least she's not reversed up to the fencing by the platform. Had she done so, I'd have been plainly visible to any passengers waiting for a train, or even to those blasted cameras. Not good he muttered. Had that been the case I'd have had to abort the job, rather than run the risk of detection. Quietly he cursed himself for not having given more thought to the risks of exposure posed by the driver's parking preferences. Working on a car that had been reversed up to the bank would be okay, but everything else would be highly risky!

Minutes later his mood of despondency vanished, hardly believing his luck as he found what he was after. Clarkson's Fiesta, all neatly backed up to the grassy slope and close to a sprouting bush. Bless you, he uttered in silent thanksgiving, even if you're not a Virgo. The subtlety of invoking a blessing for the person he intended to kill escaped Noakes entirely.

Although rain threatened, the ground, at the edge of the tarmac was firm and puddle free. Before getting down onto his knees, prior to sliding under the car, he walked into the gap between Clarkson's car and the one next to it. Casually leaning against the journalist's car, he took one final look around to be certain he was away from for prying eyes. Returning to the rear of the car he stopped to put on a pair of thin rubber gloves. Then he slipped off his raincoat, dropping it onto the ground before using his foot to push it under the back end. Dropping to his knees he rolled onto his back and began to wriggle underneath the Fiesta. With the tilt switch in one hand, he wormed his way further under the car, pulling the haversack beside him with the other hand.

Once in the right place he got to work, first taking his hand-made device from the haversack and laying it beside him. Next, from the haversack, came the small battery powered drill, fitted with the ring saw blade needed to cut into the plastic tank, making a small hole as high up its side as possible. This was the tricky part because, unable to know just how full the petrol tank was, he ran the risk of boring his hole below the level of the fuel and being soaked with petrol. On public transport, which he'd need for his return journey to Acton, everyone within breathing distance would have smelt the petrol and, worse still, would have remembered him.

Exercising great care, under the most uncomfortable conditions, he probed gently with the small circular saw, holding it at an angle to make only the smallest exploratory cut into the plastic. Stopping just as soon as he felt the saw-teeth make the merest penetration into the tank. Holding his breath, he waited to see how successful he'd been, fearful of dripping petrol. Then, as no petrol seeped through the small cut he relaxed, believing that he was cutting above the fuel level. Yet, troubled by the noise generated by the small cutter, he worked as slowly as he could, giving the drill just a few turns as a time. Soon, to his eternal relief, he watched as the ring saw left a neat circular hole in exactly the right place.

Totally absorbed in his task the thunderous noise created by a high-speed train barrelling through the adjacent station made him jump. In the limited space he smacked his head sharply on the car's underside, causing him to swear spontaneously in the process. The train's harsh roar, followed by the blast of its ten accompanying coaches, produced a shattering wave of unexpected sound. 'Hell!' he cursed loudly, dropping the device that only seconds before he'd had so gingerly picked up. Desperately hoping that no passers-by were near enough to have heard his outburst, he remained stock still for several seconds, filled with dread and fearing that he might hear the voice of a small child. 'Daddy, what's that man doing under that car?' But there were no excited cries, and no curious eyes. He was safe, unseen and unheard.

Still cursing under his breath, he rolled onto his side in the confined space and rubbed his stinging head. Satisfied that he was not bleeding, he stretched out to try and retrieve the device. It was tantalisingly close, but just out of reach. By further twisting, and ignoring complaints from his hip, he succeeded in placing a shaking right hand on the assembly. Once in his grasp, he carried out a careful examination, anxious to check that the glass tilt switch remained unbroken. Feeling relieved, he resumed his work. Spurred on by the knowledge that his device had not suffered any lasting damage, he forced the open end of the plastic tube into the hole he'd cut in the tank. Once he'd got that firmly in place he applied the heavy "gaffer tape" needed to hold the tilt-switch tightly against the petrol tank. Finally, and after double checking that everything was in the right position, he coupled the last remaining wire from the tilt-switch to the stun-gun. With his device securely in place, and only in need of a steep downhill braking motion to complete its deadly purpose, he remained unaware that he'd made a profoundly serious miscalculation!

Minutes later, standing upright behind the car, he again checked for any unwelcome watchers before bending to recover his raincoat and haversack. After slipping into the raincoat, and knowing he was unobserved, he cautiously stepped from between the parked cars before walking towards the car park exit and the main road.

CHAPTER 19

WALKING SLOWLY TOWARDS the station Noakes watched as a small van pulled up on the yellow lines reserved for taxies. Head down he absently recorded the name of a local garage, sign written along the side of the van. Seconds later, and hearing voices from behind, he turned to see a white-haired elderly man in dark overalls leave the van, stooping to shout back to the driver through the still open door. Then, as the door closed, a man in railway uniform emerged from the building to engage in friendly conversation with person in overalls. Moments later the van driver, seeing smiles all round, stepped out to join the light-hearted banter.

Unconcerned, Noakes walked away from the station, intent upon reversing his route back to Acton. Ten minutes later he was in Goring, just short of the bridge and allowing himself a quick smile in satisfaction of a job well done. One interfering journalist less to worry about, no more trouble in that direction. And, more importantly, I'll have Buchanan off my back. So, even if there are CCTV cameras in the car park, what can they show? Nothing more than a blurred image of an old chap; it could be anybody. I've worn surgical rubber gloves throughout, so no fingerprints. Despite my injured hand the installation process had gone to plan, apart from that bloody train frightening me witless!

Freed from anxiety Noakes advanced onto the bridge intent upon making his way up to the Bull where, with luck, he shouldn't have long to wait for a bus back to Reading. As for Clarkson, well she's not due to be picking up her car until later, much later. Safe as houses.

After leaving Goring the bridge crossed a strip of water before reaching the large island in the middle of the river. From there he could see the Swan Hotel standing proudly on the Streatley side of the far bank. With the threatened rain having failed to materialise, dappled sunlight filtered through broken clouds making a perfect backdrop to a lovely view. Noakes, pausing for a second, soaked up the view and had no idea that this tranquil picture postcard village was about to become the stuff of nightmares.

Initially, unseen by Noakes, the sign written van he'd so recently seen outside the station crawled onto the bridge in a line of traffic heading towards Streatley. Once, within his field of vision, he failed to attach any significance to the van's reappearance as he moved further onto the bridge.

Seconds later he was struggling for breath. Directly behind the van was Clarkson's Fiesta. The very car he'd just fitted with a firebomb! His legs buckled, forcing him to grab the upper timbered handrail of the bridge with his right hand. For fuck's sake, what's it doing here? he mouthed. And who the hell's driving it? He screamed inwardly. If it isn't that bloody woman, who is it? Not in a million years is that Clarkson, it's an old boy! What's going on? Numb, and hanging onto the bridge rail for support, he stared in disbelief as the Fiesta almost vanished from sight, descending in pursuit of the van down the gentle slope off the bridge. This is wrong, his brain screamed. A mistake! The words tried to leave his parched mouth as he battled to make sense of what he'd seen. Knowing exactly what might occur, given the right conditions, he dare not cry out. Doing so would attract unwelcome attention, followed by questions that, if answered incorrectly, would condemn him to die in prison.

Deep within him a calming voice was pleading for reason, the voice of logic fighting against the inner turmoil caused by having so unexpectedly seen the two vehicles. Hang on the voice told him. All right, so the Fiesta is on the move, but the device cannot go off just yet. Don't get so alarmed. It needs to be going down a steep hill to move the mercury. Telling himself that the incline off the bridge was nowhere near steep enough to tilt the mercury, he watched as the two vehicles moved away from him.

'I say, are you all right?' One of two white haired elderly ladies walking towards the staggering Noakes thoughtfully enquired, having seen him lurch and grab hold of the wooden handrail, mumbling nonsensically.

'Leave him Emily,' her companion said in a prim voice, giving the man a withering look of utter contempt. 'It's dreadful. He's either drunk or on drugs. It really is quite appalling, and at this time of day!' she chided, extending an arm around her companion's shoulder. 'Now come along dear. We don't want to become involved with anything unsavoury do we?' So, they moved on, completely unaware how they were the only two people to have even given Noakes more than a second glance that fateful day.

***

William Turner, Bill to his friends, having long since retired from the railway was a spritely eighty-two-year-old who had never married. Not known for being idle he enjoyed bowling, outdoors in the summer and indoors in the winter. Regular trips to his local British Legion club were also part of his social scene. And, on most weekdays, he would be at the local garage, sweeping up, making tea, taking the van out to collect parts, driving customers back home or picking cars up for servicing. While Bill looked upon these labours as his job, it was very much part-time and conveniently cash in hand. Was it only half an hour ago that the owner had called out through his open office door?

'Bill, quick, get hold of young Sid. Get him to take you to the station. Damned near forgot, we've got to pick up Miss Clarkson's Fiesta for a service. She'll expect it back at the station by six. Got her spare key here,' he shouted, tossing it quickly to Bill who, despite his age, caught it deftly with his left hand.

'Should've had me behind the stumps for England,' he quipped back over his shoulder as he'd headed off in search of Sid. And now, he thought, ten minutes back to the garage, time to brew up ready for the lad's lunch break. Nice to see old George at the station, he said to himself. A quick natter and we've managed to fix up the transport for next week's bowls match at Marlow. He smiled, completely unaware that his executioner was waiting, primed and ready to take fatal action at a moment's notice.

Had he looked to his right Bill Turner may have noticed an elderly pedestrian totter on the footpath before frantically grabbing the bridge's handrail for support. Yet, even if he had witnessed this bizarre happening, it would have meant nothing to the old railwayman as he drove slowly down the slope off the bridge. Yet Noakes, still clutching the handrail, tried to reassure himself. No, he muttered, the angle's nowhere near steep enough to cause the switch to tilt.

From the outset he'd been confident that the winding descent from Westridge Green, coupled with hard braking, would cause the heavy silvery liquid to move forward at the right time, covering the wires needed to fire the stun gun. Milliseconds later, an arc of high energy electricity would flash into the vapour laden petrol tank to create an all-consuming fireball. Fine in theory but Noakes had failed to factor in the unexpected.

CHAPTER 20

IN SINGLE FILE the Fiesta and the van began their slow descent off the bridge into Streatley. Unseen by Noakes, but clearly visible to Sid, a stray dog careered across the road directly in front of him. Instinctively he braked, locking up the front wheels and coming to a sudden halt. Behind him Bill, reacting just as quickly, managed to stop inches behind the van. Tragically this sudden stop was violent enough to tip over the tilt switch, sending the mercury surging forward. Bill, pleased not to have run into Sid's van, never saw or heard the glass tube fill with mercury and topple on its axis. A fraction of a second later the mercury bridged the electrical contacts with devastating efficiency.

From the middle of the bridge Noakes had seen the Fiesta dip down the slope. Moments later the sound of sudden braking confirmed how Sid was reacting rapidly to avoid the unexpected canine interloper. Noakes then heard the unmistakable sound of an explosion. Horrified, he watched as a large fireball bellied out from beneath the car, flames coming from where the windows had been blown away by sheer pressure from the explosion. Even from his position on the bridge Noakes could feel the wave of heat given off by the inferno. Gaping, open mouthed, he watched as the flames produced by burning rubber, plastic, and upholstery leapt upwards.

Stunned pedestrians gasped in horror, while reflex action alone made the driver of the nearest car approaching from Streatley swerve left into the Swan Hotel's car park. Other vehicles approaching the bridge came to a stop, stunned by the frightening appearance of the fireball before them. Inside the van Sid, certain that he'd neither hit the dog or the car in front, wondered why his vehicle had suddenly shaken badly. Has old Bill been caught napping and run into me? he thought, glancing into his rear-view mirror. The thought dying instantly as he saw the Fiesta blazing furiously behind him. Seized by panic he jumped from the van, staring open-mouthed at the burning car. Ignoring danger he ran towards the fireball, screaming out before the invisible wall of intense heat stopped him in his tracks.

On the bridge the car following the Fiesta had swerved to the right, yards in front of Noakes before mounting the kerb and embedding itself into the stout woodwork of the bridge parapet. The sound of escaping steam from its smashed radiator only adding to the chaos.

Following drivers, sensing immediate danger, abandoned their vehicles while uttering startled shouts and cries of disbelief. Some of whom preferred photography to flight, avidly taking pictures rather than call the emergency services. Yet, in their haste to make sense of what they were avoiding, no one gave any attention to the elderly man clinging to the bridge's handrail and muttering incoherently. Minutes later the sound of a police car's siren reverberated in the High Street as the driver skilfully threaded the car through the stationary traffic, occasionally mounting the kerb in its efforts to get closer to the inferno.

Numb with shock Noakes edged his way further forward, stumbling amongst pedestrians and drivers who had abandoned their vehicles in confusion. As the curious moved forward the more prudent retreated, fearful of another explosion. People screamed in terror as, away to his right, Noakes dimly registered those drinkers on the Swan's riverside terrace had begun jumping up from their tables and pointing upwards while others ran inside.

The horrifying shock of what he was witnessing rendered Noakes incapable of movement. Still gripping the bridge's heavy timbered handrail, he gazed in horror at the sight of the ferociously burning car whose panels were already glowing red hot. Dully, his mind registered the various sounds around him, screaming people, police sirens and shouted instructions. Above that the roar of the flames dominated, broken by small and intermittent explosions as components reacted angrily to the blisteringly hot temperatures.

Not close enough to hear the words, wildly pointing arms and horrified expressions left Noakes in no doubt that the car's driver remained trapped inside the blazing inferno. Despite his inner turmoil, Noakes noticed that the burning car was far enough away from the nearest houses to avoid further damage, although flames had managed to set the branches of a nearby tree alight. Tottering on unsteady legs, and still gripping the bridge's handrail, he had the appearance of a badly dazed boxer desperately clinging to the ropes. Barely upright his mind was unable to comprehend the enormity of what he had unleashed.

'Must have been a terrorist bomb' a man standing nearby called out, oblivious of Noakes.

'Bloody hell!' someone else called back, 'reckon there might be more?'

'No point in hanging about,' the first man responded, 'those buggers don't do things by halves. I'm off.' Noakes turned sideways and, while still clutching the rail he leaned out over the river, his body shaking as he retched. Beside his arched body an upper-class voice cut through his thoughts.

'I say old boy, any idea what's going on?' Noakes turned, giving the speaker a quizzical look while taking in the smart blazer, well-pressed flannels and open-necked white shirt.

'No.....no....,' he managed to splutter, saliva running from the corner of his mouth.

'Ah well,' the speaker replied, accepting Noakes as some sort of half-wit village idiot out of whom he was unlikely to get any sense. 'Not to worry old boy, I'll just nip down there and see what this is all about.' With that he was gone, epitomising the British stiff upper lip, unflappable and only mildly curious.

Peering beyond the departing speaker Noakes could see a fire engine making its way towards the burning car. Soon brown coated firefighters were spraying foam onto the wrecked Fiesta, damping down the flames as a lone police officer struggled to holding back ghoulish sightseers. Noakes, along with the other shocked people, watched as uniformed authority went about restoring order from disorder.

From the bridge he could see how lines of police 'Do Not Cross' tapes were already in place around the wreckage. Making to leave, he felt the bile rising in his throat again, sick with the knowledge of what he had just done. In the twisted depths of his mind, he'd seen killing Clarkson as necessary and justified. But not this, the brutally horrific murder of an innocent human being that was never meant to happen. How, he asked himself, did this all go so dreadfully wrong?

Although tormented by this thought Noakes found that his survival instincts were beginning to override his traumatised state. With absolute certainty he knew that getting clear of the bridge had to be his number one priority. Under no circumstances could he be there when the police started taking names and addresses, a prospect that filled him with dread. How could he explain his presence on the bridge? What was a well-known boxing trainer from Acton, dressed in workman's overalls doing in Streatley? What could he say? What name would he give if questioned? Already two police officers, nearer the scene were beginning to take statements from stunned drivers and pedestrians. Close to the scene cameras were in use and, while facing police questioning would be bad enough, having his picture flashed across the media would be disastrous. So, with the police now blocking access into Streatley, a return over the bridge to Goring was his only option. One he had to take before escape became impossible.

CHAPTER 21

FOR YVONNE THURSDAY morning had been hectic. With Vere due to fly out to Madrid early on Friday she'd spent a leisurely Wednesday evening at the cottage, later driving home to prepare for an early start. Following a mad dash by taxi to Great Portland Street, to interview a noted fashion designer, she was back in her office by one, ready to receive a planned call from a New York fashion house. Breakfast time for them, early afternoon over here. Wayne, ever attentive, waited until she came off the phone before appearing with a welcome coffee, along with a scribbled note asking her to ring her garage.

'Not something wrong with the car? That's all I need,' she sighed as the teenager left her office. In anticipation of a large and unexpected bill she reached for the phone, recoiling in shock.

'What do you mean it's blown up'!' she'd shouted in alarm. 'Cars don't just blow up. Where did this happen? What about the driver then?' At that point, realisation sunk in as she'd absorbed the bare facts. Her car was a burnt-out wreck on Streatley High Street, with a dead man trapped inside it.

'Sorry, Miss Clarkson,' the garage owner said, 'but I think you should get down here as soon as possible. I've just come back from the bridge, it's chaos down there, what with the police crawling over everything. But look,' he continued, 'don't worry about transport. I can fix you up with something to for a bit, you know while the insurance people sort things out. We offered to remove the car, but the police say it stays put. Might have something to do with it being a crime scene, so they said.'

'Crime scene?' she muttered to herself, slowly returning the handset to the docking station. Seconds later she snatched it back and dialled Vere at Regency Law.

***

Three hours later, Yvonne, clutching Vere's hand, was standing open-mouthed and looking at the burnt-out wreck of her car inside a taped off ring of isolation. Totally confused, neither could produce answers to the questions that were uppermost in their minds. Blankly they gaped at the charred metal skeleton, noting how the four bare wheel rims were already starting to sink into the fire softened tarmac. Outside the cordon a dazed group of onlookers pointed and muttered, yet eager to speak with the first television news crew who'd reached the scene. More were to follow.

In shocked silence both gratefully appreciated that the police had already authorised removal of the driver's body. Or what was left of it, for onward transport to the mortuary and the pathologist! Standing alone, and hand in hand, a dark haired scholarly looking man in his early forties approached and introduced himself.

'DCI Ted Crowland,' he said perfunctorily, 'from Reading CID. I understand this is your car Miss....?'

'Clarkson,' Yvonne added unsteadily. 'But that poor driver;' she sobbed slightly. 'How could this happen? I mean....'

'That's what I intend to find out,' he replied formerly in his most professional DCI manner. 'And you are, sir?' he asked inquisitively, abruptly turning to Vere and fiercely determined to ward off any unwelcome interlopers.

'Robert Vere, solicitor and Miss Clarkson's partner,' he replied, extracting his wallet and handing over a business card. Sensing that the DCI was about to launch more questions Vere interrupted.

'Look, Mr Crowland, Yvonne here,' he nodded in the direction of his badly shaken partner, 'is not in a fit state to answer questions. I'm running her back home to Westridge Green. I'll write her address and phone number on the back of the card for you. Right now, I'm guessing that you know as much as we do. Yvonne, Miss Clarkson, left her car at Goring station early this morning, as she does most mornings. The local garage, they hold a spare key, were down to collect the car for a service. They were due to return the vehicle later in the day, leaving it in the car park for when Yvonne arrived back from London. That's as far as we can go with it now.'

'Thank you, sir,' Crowland said politely, trying not to bristle at Vere's attitude. Something not helped by the solicitor's next remark.

'Remember, Mr Crowland, Yvonne is also a victim here. She's just found her car blown to smithereens, along with someone she's never even known burnt to death inside it. The girls in shock, distressed and confused.'

'Quite so, sir,' Crowland responded with due formality, recognising that Vere would never permit him to tackle the girl in such a fragile state. A situation where both men knew just how easily the shocked or unwary can say the wrong thing in an unguarded or pressurised moment.

'Of course, Miss Clarkson, I'll need to have a more formal session with you later,' he said, giving her a weak smile, 'once I've got a bit more to go on. So,' he said examining the back of Vere's card, then smiling at Yvonne. 'I'll give you ring to fix a time. Is that okay?' As Yvonne nodded her silent consent to the officer, Vere stepped forward and put a hand companionably hand on the Detective Inspector's shoulder, steering him away a little distance before speaking.

'Look, I know you've got your job to do, but go easy. She's had a hell of a shock. This is rotten timing I'm afraid, but I've got to fly to Madrid in the morning, a conference on International Law. Can't get out of it, even with this mess,' he sighed, waving his hand towards the wreckage. 'But I'll be back by lunchtime on Tuesday. Can wait until then?' Detecting a thaw in Vere's approach Crowland responded in similar form.

'That's okay sir. But, until I know more, this may well turn out to be a crime scene. You understand, sir, a murder investigation?' Vere paled at the implications as Crowland continued, 'in that case I'll certainly need to speak to Miss Clarkson before you return. In fact, if I find out we've got a car bomber on my patch we'll be pulling out all the stops. I'm sure you can appreciate that?'

'Yes, okay, but please go easy on her.'

'Of course, we will sir. But Miss Clarkson, well she's a key player here, one way or another, you understand?'

Sensing a little confusion, Crowland spoke again. 'Let me spell it out, sir. This was her car and if this was an accident,' he pointed at the wreck, 'an electrical fault of some kind, while deeply regrettable, it's understandable. But, on the other hand, if this was deliberate it's a fair bet that Miss Clarkson may well have been the intended victim. And, if she was, I want to know why and very soon. Even if she wasn't the target, and it wasn't an accident, it still leaves me with a murder on my hands.' Shocked by the DCI's words, Vere mumbled something before turning away to re-join Yvonne. As he did so he was painfully aware that this was the second time, in the last few days that a police officer had mentioned crime scene to him. Even more worryingly, Crowland's remark highlighting Yvonne's status as the intended victim had truly terrified him.

Earlier on, after meeting up at Paddington, they'd travelled by train to Shiplake to collect Vere's car before making their way to Streatley. Hearing of the bridge's closure, on the car radio, forced them into take a longer route. Finally, upon reaching Streatley, finding the High Street closed to traffic only added to their frustration. After stopping by the traffic lights, they managed to persuade an agitated police officer that Yvonne was the owner of burnt-out car and that they had to reach the fire scene. Only then were they permitted to park a little further down the High Street. This meant that after parting company with DCI Crowland, they only had a short walk before reaching the seclusion of his car and its comfortable leather seats. Minutes later they were at the garage were Yvonne, wiping tears from her eyes, listened in shock as she learned more about the unfortunate Bill Turner.

'But why?' she kept saying. 'How does a car just blow up? It must have been a fault with the car. Is that possible?' She asked the equally confused garage owner, fearful of hearing the truth. Shuddering with realisation she voiced her inner fear. 'Oh God! I might have been in the car, and not that poor man.' Her words making her cry out in alarm and throw her arms round Vere's neck. Over her shoulder a confused Vere looked at the garage owner with pleading eyes.

'Well, is it possible? Could a car just blow up?' he asked, afraid to hear the answer. The garage owner, balding and a little overweight, looked thoughtfully back at Vere before answering.

'Possible, maybe, but in my view not very bloody likely.' Then with forced cheerfulness he turned to Yvonne, anxious to get away from speculation. 'Come on Miss, let's get you fixed up with a set of wheels, you know, just while we get things sorted out here for you.'

CHAPTER 22

LATER THAT EVENING, as Yvonne sat quietly in the lounge of her small, detached house, she tried to make sense of what had happened. Good to his word Vere had followed her back to Westridge Green and had then taken care to make sure she was settled in her own familiar surroundings. Yet, as he had fussed about, they'd both felt uneasy, only able to make stunted conversation. For his part he'd felt wretched about his forthcoming trip to Spain, desperately pleading with Yvonne to accept that he had to go, even under these harrowing circumstances.

'Look, I've called the firm again,' he'd told her. 'The senior partners, even knowing what's happened, insist upon me going.' He'd mentioned higher authority hoping to add weight to his defence. 'In fact, they're adamant!'

'Oh, bugger the senior partners!' she'd hurled back, tears running down her cheeks, 'what if I'd been killed in that fire? Would you still be running off to Spain?'

'But thank God, you weren't killed,' he had offered in appeasement. 'It was an accident of sorts, a technical fault of some description. DCI Crowland will sort it out. We'll know the truth in a day or so.' Vere had tried desperately to believe his own words yet, deep down, the DCI's assessment of the basics had shaken him badly. Yvonne, the intended victim! How do I get around that one? I can't say anything like that to her or she'll go berserk!

On that note they had parted with Yvonne remaining resolute. 'How can you go away at a time like this?' she had pleaded. 'Surely, if you really loved me, you'd stop here,' she had sobbed uncontrollably? But now, curled up in her armchair, she tried to be more circumspect. If I really loved him, I should have come clean, telling him about my visit to Noakes's gym and our meeting next Tuesday. While these pangs of conscience made her feel depressed, she knew that Robert had been equally despondent, upset that she could not see the necessity of his trip to Madrid. On such shaky ground their parting had been devoid of the usual loving embraces and emotional conversation.

***

Rallying herself after Vere had left she'd walked next door to see her neighbour. Edith Frobisher, an elderly widow, habitually welcomed the company of the bright and bubbly lady from next door. Despite the age gap, they got on well together. Yvonne delighted in listening to her neighbour's experiences and, as always, Mrs Frobisher found the younger woman's company enlightening and refreshing. Never one to dwell in the past, Edith loved hearing about Yvonne's fast pace of life and exacting work schedule. For the last twelve months, as neighbours, they had made a point of being there for each other, when in need of help. Just next door, in the event of trouble had been their little rallying cry. Each had a key for the other's front door, for deliveries, meter readers, plant watering and in cases of emergency.

But that evening Edith Frobisher had been visibly shocked when hearing about Yvonne's car bursting into flames and killing the innocent man from the garage. With automotive technicalities being well beyond the elderly widow's understanding, she was not short of common sense. She'd seen just how worried Yvonne had been but, by what she could not tell Yet she did know fear when she saw it. After a while, and despite Yvonne's obvious tensions, they'd managed to share a cup of tea and memories of more pleasant times.

An hour later, back in her own armchair and clutching a much-needed gin and tonic, questions without answers filled her mind. Being able to talk through events with Mrs Frobisher had given temporary relief but now and alone the demons were back. Was this just an accident? But what if it had been deliberate? Who then might have been responsible? Do I really have enemies who hate me that much? Might it have involved Noakes? Did I really rattle him that badly by mentioning Drysdale the other day? But then again, if Noakes was not involved, who was? Why would anyone want to target me?

Okay, she reasoned, with a million or so women reading my articles each month I expect I've upset one or two of them. Had my odd rant about anorexic models appearing to be aggressive really been so upsetting? Mildly offensive to some, but grounds for a firebomb? Never. A snotty e-mail or even a 'yours disgusted, Tunbridge Wells' letter to my editor would have sufficed. No, she concluded, this had to be deliberate. By a process of elimination, she deduced that someone firebombing a vehicle had to fall into one of two categories. They were either a raving lunatic or so badly frightened that they needed to commit murder to silence the truth. If not the former, could the latter involve anyone else apart from Noakes?'

But, as one gin and tonic became two, and the evening light began to fade, she could come to no sensible conclusion. Absently she reached out for the telephone, dialling a number in far-away Cornwall, anxious in case television news of the Streatley fire-bombing had alarmed her semi-retired mother. Okay, she thought, that nice but very formal Mr Crowland had given assurances that my personal details wouldn't be released to the media. Well, not until they had a much better picture of events. Yet, she had no illusions that hungry news hounds would go to any lengths in their quest for a story. How long before reporters set up camp in the lane outside, yelling at me every time I open the front door? How traumatic would that be?

Oh, how I want to be in Cornwall, she sighed inwardly, her mind already there in that lovely bungalow in Falmouth, just behind Pendennis Castle. My parent's place. My home for so many happy years with that fantastic view from the bay window, looking right across the Fal estuary and over to St Mawes Castle. As the shadows lengthened, she became more emotional, remembering her late father and how they had joined seasonal visitors peering down into the huge dry dock, watching ant-like men walking underneath giant ships. Oh, she sighed, remembering those far off days. One day soon, she thought sipping the last of her drink and wiping away yet more tears from her cheeks.

CHAPTER 23

IN WEST LONDON Noakes, badly shaken by events had no doubts. For him it was certainty. The certainty of knowing that he had murdered an innocent man with a cruel device that had claimed the wrong life. More whisky went into his glass as he struggled to make sense of how his well-made plan had gone so disastrously wrong. It had been the right car, but tragically not in the right place, at the right time or with the right driver. Scoring only one out of four was nowhere near good enough! And, because of that a harmless person is dead, Clarkson's alerted, and the police will have a field day. Then there's the media, they'll be all over this lot like a rash. God what a bloody awful mess!

Piece by piece his stunned mind reassembled the facts. Had I missed something? The garage vans arrival at the car park, the old guy getting out? he questioned himself. Then, what about the person who'd come out of the station building? Clearly a railway worker, judging by his uniform then, lastly, he recalled the young driver who'd joined the pair beside the van. Had any of this been significant? No, he concluded. Perhaps if I'd lingered in the car park, I might have been able to do something? But what he asked himself?

Even if I'd seen that fellow drive off with Clarkson's car, what could I have done about it?

In his mind he could see the two vehicles, nose to tail on the bridge. *Without doubt, my timing had been wrong. I can only assume that the garage van and the appearance of Clarkson's car meant something. Were they taking it in for service or repairs? If so, why did it have to be today? For God's sake, how was I supposed to know that? This day of all days, the one day in the year when Clarkson has her car serviced.* Downhearted, he slumped back in his chair, his injured hand on the table and a whisky glass in the other. *Who cares?* 'Well, I do,' he shouted at the empty room. *That poor bloody driver, yet another innocent victim, just like Drysdale.* He shuddered, unaware that his meticulous planning had been set at zero by a stray dog. On the verge of being suicidal he gave thought to Buchanan's telephone call scheduled for next morning. *Will it be praise for showing initiative, or abuse for his stupidity?* On balance he knew the answer. His face creased with apprehension, realising the implications caused by his abject failure to take out Clarkson which would invite police and unwelcome media attention. Shuddering with fear he wondered exactly what the police forensic people might uncover, aware that his limited knowledge of Buchanan only made matters worse. *For God's sake this is the man who cold-bloodedly gunned down two innocent people right in front of me. But who is he really? Where is he from?* The questions fizzed in his head, made worse by not knowing just how far Buchanan's criminal reach extended.

Plagued by unmitigated fear, he cherished a forlorn thought that Buchanan may be forgiving. If not, he realised that sudden death could come from any angle or at any time. Reaching out an unsteady hand he poured more whisky from the bottle, thinking back to his original defence strategy.

Might the envelope with the incriminating fingerprints be good enough to keep me alive? Could the threat of revealing it be strong enough to keep me safe? But now, if the police can tie me into the firebombing, Buchanan could never take the risk of me turning Queen's Evidence. He'd have me dead and diced long before that. As his befuddled mind bounced these ideas around like a pinball machine, he had a welcome thought. The contact system set up by Buchanan all those years ago is still there. It worked for me the other day. What if I were to give the number to Terry when he's here next weekend? If I tell him everything, he'll at least know the score and go barmy! Be just like him he thought, banging his empty glass onto the table. Then, as his thoughts cleared, he realised the sense in setting out the facts to Terry. Putting him in the picture, no matter how unpleasant, and telling him where to find those fingerprints had to be the answer. From there Terry would be in a great position to bring Buchanan to justice, were the bastard to strike first and have me killed.

Threatening to hand over the envelope covered with Buchanan's fingerprints might, he reasoned, be just enough to keep me safe, more so if backed up with details of the telephone contact. Not much of an insurance policy is it? he thought, pushing his now empty glass across the table. Not for the first time that day he found himself wondering just how good the forensic people in Reading were likely to be. Is there any way the police could link me to that burnt out wreck? Hopefully, they won't be able to do that, even though Clarkson had managed to track me down. Just a lucky shot or was her information good enough to give to the police? Pouring more whisky into his glass he knew it'd not be long before the police were talking to her. They'll want answers because cars don't just blow up. How far will they go with that one? Will she mention coming to see me and, more alarmingly, tell them how I'd reacted when she'd come out with the name of Drysdale?

***

Waking after a disturbed night Yvonne felt downcast, a mood not improved by pulling back the curtains to reveal grey clouds and squally rain. Still drowsy she made her way downstairs, confident that a 'caffeine fix' would aid recovery. Black coffee followed by a shower and a leisurely breakfast of toast and fruit juice added to her belief that the day could only get better. First things first though she sighed, walking through to the lounge to telephone her office.

'Good morning, Wayne,' she greeted him. 'Look, I know this is a bit sudden, but can you tell everyone that I'm taking time off. Just a couple of days. You remember how I got called away, yesterday?'

'Yes, something to do with the car wasn't it?'

'That's right, but it was more serious, I'm afraid. Oh, it was awful. It caught fire just after the garage people collected it from the station car park. It's now a burnt-out wreck. The police tell me it somehow managed to blow up. Oh, I don't understand any of it,' she gulped. 'It killed the man driving it back to the garage, not to mention causing a fire right in the middle of Streatley High Street.' Yvonne fell silent as she heard Wayne catch his breath, stunned by what he'd heard.

'That was your car!' he said incredulously. 'It was on telly last night, on the ten o'clock News. I watched it with my mum.' Greatly alarmed by the news, his latent admiration for Yvonne surfaced in a rush. Anxiously he blurted out 'But you're okay, aren't you, Yvonne?' Despite herself, she smiled at Wayne's unaccustomed familiarity. 'Oh, I'm sorry, I mean Miss Clarkson,' he stammered, trying to cover up his unintentional error.

'Don't worry Wayne,' she replied, suppressing a tiny smile at the lad's embarrassment. 'Shaken, not stirred, as they say in the Bond movies,' she laughed before continuing in a more sombre tone. 'The police want to speak to me,' she paused, 'this morning I think, that's why I'm stopping here and waiting for their call. After that, I'm going to disappear for a couple of days. Call it compassionate leave or whatever, no contact numbers, no nothing. All things being equal I'll be in first thing Tuesday. And Wayne,' she added before disconnecting, 'please ask Fiona to look after things for me until then.'

After disconnecting Wayne, shocked by what he'd heard, began walking around the office, quietly passing on Yvonne's message. Collectively work seemed to stop, with groups of people going into huddles across desktops or around workstations as they absorbed the information. Like Wayne, those having seen the report on television were devastated to realise how it had involved a colleague. And those, previously unaware of events, stood open mouthed in shock, universally expressing relief that Yvonne was unharmed. Wayne, once his messenger duties were complete, began a lengthy discussion around the coffee machine with his equally young opposite number, David Adams. Quietly, in the corridor, they took turns in trying to promote their own theory as to how a car could catch fire so dramatically.

'No way,' Adams said dogmatically, 'it had to be a bomb. Stands to reason, don't it?' he said in a forthright and knowledgeable manner. 'Be honest, yeah, a leaky fuel line could cause a small fire under the bonnet but not a bloody great explosion like what they said on the news last night. Straight up, the bloke on the telly said one minute the car was fine, next it's a ball of fire that killed the driver instantly!' He decreed, warming to his theory. 'Fuck me! That could have been the lovely Clarkson, toasted in her own car'

The words caused Wayne's legs to buckle beneath him, forcing him to place a steadying hand on the coffee machine. Memories of his recent conversations came flooding back, compelling him to face the question that had suddenly exploded into his brain. Did I say too much to that chap in the pub the other day? Or did I give too much away on the phone when he called? Leaning against the drinks machine the thought burrowed down into his brain, demanding that he confront what may have been the error of his ways. Did I supply information that had put Yvonne's life at risk? Have I been responsible for that old chap being murdered? Oh no, this was never meant to happen, I believed that chap, genuinely thought that he was an old contact of hers. Fear gripped his insides, filling his bowels with ice water. Horrified, he turned on his heel, moving rapidly in the direction of the gent's toilet.

'Blimey mate, you look terrible! You've gone all white. What's up - seen a ghost?' Adams shouted in surprise at Wayne's departing back.

'Oh, no!' he called out in mid-stride, 'I'm about to be caught short.'

CHAPTER 24

WHILE WAYNE SOUGHT relief, isolated in the men's room, Yvonne was reaching for her telephone. In far-away Falmouth Mrs Jean Clarkson pushed her aging Labrador to one side as she answered the call.

'Mum, it's me again,' Yvonne called out to her mother. 'Look, I've wangled time away from the office, two or three days, and wonder if I could come down?' she asked forthrightly. 'To tell you the truth I'm tired out, what with that dreadful business yesterday.'

'Of course, dear,' her unflappable mother replied. 'You know your old room is always ready for you. Will Robert be coming with you?' She enquired diplomatically.

'No just me,' she hesitated, 'just a solo effort this time. Can you believe this? He's cleared off to Spain, says he's got to attend an E U conference to discuss the health and safety implications of watching paint dry,' Yvonne said sarcastically. Mrs Clarkson, who knew her daughter only too well, refrained from further comment. Intuitively, and suspecting underlying bother, she tactfully kept such thoughts to herself.

'When will you be down? Are you driving or taking the train?'

'Well, after yesterday, it'll be the train. The local garage owner's been a dear, loaning me a vehicle for a while. But honestly, I don't want to drive all that way in a vehicle I'm not used to. So, it'll be the train.'

'Of course, how silly of me,' her mother said apologetically.

'That's okay. Don't worry. As I say, I've got local transport, at least a temporary run about for the time being. I've got things to tidy up here first, then check the timetable. I'll give you a ring when I'm on the train. Is that okay?'

'Of course, dear, that'll be fine. As you've guessed, I'm not working today, so just ring me with the details.'

'Right, thanks. I'll try to get something to Truro, then a local one to Falmouth' she paused for a moment, 'but, if a through train to Penzance is my best bet, can you pick me up from there please, mum?' Children, Mrs Clarkson thought, no matter how big they are you still end up running around after them.

'No trouble, dear, just let me know when and where. I'll be there.' She didn't pause for a moment, content that a fifty odd mile round trip to pick up her daughter would still be well worthwhile. However, a train to Falmouth station would bring her so much closer to the front door, far more convenient. But then, she asked herself, when did children consider a mere thing like parental convenience?

***

Minutes later, thanks to the wonders of the internet, Yvonne was busy finalising her planning, when the telephone noisily demanded attention. Busy morning, she thought, a little annoyed at the unwanted intrusion.

'Miss Clarkson?' the caller asked formally.

'Yes,' Yvonne said guardedly.

'Hi, good morning. DCI Ted Crowland, Reading CID, we met yesterday. You remember?'

'Of course,' Yvonne acknowledged, detecting a little more warmth in the policeman's tone. 'Not likely to forget that one, am I? What a day that was!' Yvonne replied, anxious to know what was coming next.

'Very true, and that's the reason for my call as I need to speak to you soonest, something's come-up.' The policeman's words hung in the air as Yvonne tried to figure out what was coming next.

'Well yes, okay, I suppose,' she said hesitantly, 'but I'm just arranging to go away for a day or two.'

'Not leaving the country, are we?' Crowland smiled.

'No such luck. I'm travelling down to Cornwall, going to spend two or three days with my mum, but I'd like to be on a train by late morning if possible. I'm trying to book it now.' At the other end of the line Crowland looked at his watch.

'Not a problem,' he replied, 'it's only just gone nine and we'll be with you well before ten. Go ahead and book your ticket, say for any time after twelve thirty.'

'Okay, I'll do that, but did you say we?' she questioned.

'Yes, that's right. I'll be bringing my sergeant along and a WPC, nothing to worry about - promise we won't keep you too long.'

'Okay,' she said, 'ten it is then.' She laughed a little, 'and if you promise to be nice, I'll even make you all a coffee.'

'That'll be fine. Of course, we'll be on our best behaviour. Oh, just before I go, will Mr Vere be with you?'

'No,' Yvonne grimaced slightly, thinking back to the solicitor's defensive tactics of yesterday, and to the DCI's brittleness. 'No, in the confusion I expect you've forgotten that he's on his way to Madrid, as we speak.'

'Oh, yes. You're right. He did mention it but it'd slipped my mind.'

'Don't worry, Mr Crowland, I'm just a little girl all on my own some,' she smiled, 'no legal bulldog to chase you off.' In return Crowland chuckled, seeing the funny side.

'I'm relieved to hear that. See you later then.'

***

By ten-fifteen all four had settled in Yvonne's small, but comfortable lounge and enjoying the promised coffees she'd made for the DCI, his sergeant and the WPC he'd introduced as Natalie Phelps. Sergeant Baxter, she thought was a little bit on the chubby side, with deep penetrating eyes, dark hair and smelling strongly of aftershave. As his DCI had settled into one of the armchairs, Baxter wasted no time in commandeering the other one. Facing the two men Yvonne perched nervously on the edge of the settee next to Phelps, an attractive slim blond-haired police officer with a ready smile. In a matter of seconds Natalie Phelps had a pleasant surprise, finding out that this Yvonne Clarkson was the very Yvonne Clarkson she routinely followed in her monthly magazine. The discovery allowed youthful enthusiasm to take over as the two girls engaged in fashion gossip, oblivious to the men in the room. Crowland, nodding subtly to Baxter, permitted the banter to continue knowing that it was helping Yvonne relax while letting her establish a good rapport with his WPC. Pleased, he knew the decision to bring Phelps along had been the right one.

'All right, ladies,' Crowland interrupted with a smile, 'having now confirmed that Milan is set to have hemlines at least an inch below the knee this autumn, let's get down to business.' He looked directly at Yvonne; his gaze rewarded with a smile.

'Baxter, can you take notes, and' he turned to address Yvonne, 'is it okay with you if Phelps clears away the cups? We'll need the coffee table for my laptop;' he offered by way of explanation.

'Fine with me,' Yvonne confirmed, watching as the smartly uniformed Phelps placed the empty cups onto a tray and headed for the kitchen. A minute later, when she returned, a business-like atmosphere prevailed in the room. Crowland, ready to lead the charge, was busy booting up a small laptop on the coffee table, while Baxter sat poised to record events. Phelps, as a trained family liaison officer, was ready to support Yvonne in case of any distress. With conversation on hold, Crowland made a series of keystrokes on the computer which, after seconds, displayed a full colour picture of Yvonne's burnt-out car, taken within a secure police workshop.

'Right, Miss Clarkson,' Crowland addressed her stiffly. 'I'm sorry to have to tell you this but, even after a preliminary inspection, our forensic people have confirmed that it was a bomb of some description that destroyed your car.' Yvonne gasped at the revelation, the news confirming her worst fears. 'Tragically, as you know it killed William Turner who was driving it at the time. Pardon me. I should've said murdered Bill Turner.' He paused and looked intently at Yvonne. 'So, we're now investigating two crimes, both related of course, a murder and a firebombing.' Crowland paused, before going for the jugular. 'Who do you think would want to do this to you, Miss Clarkson?' Yvonne gulped, the colour draining from her face. Suddenly she was staring at the truth. A bomb had deliberately destroyed her car.

'I've no idea,' she started to sob, her shoulders shaking gently. 'Oh, this is terrible!' she whimpered, her face contorted with grief. Yet, in that dreadful moment of facing stark reality she felt a soft hand give hers a gentle squeeze.

'That's okay, Yvonne,' Natalie Phelps said gently, 'just take your time and tell us what you know. Anything at all, no matter how trivial you think it might be.'

CHAPTER 25

AS YVONNE GRAPPLED with trying to absorb the devastating information from Crowland, George Noakes stood trembling in an Acton 'phone box, not at all ready for Buchanan's call. Fired by the sudden urge to run, common sense told him that going into hiding was not worth considering. Buchanan will surely find me, the thought rapidly becoming a certainty. Frantically he raced through the various permutations, the ones he'd mentally rehearsed for letting Buchanan know what had happened. Still undecided as to which approach might serve him best, he jumped as the ringing bell shattered his nerves. Wishing to sound confident he grabbed the phone yet riddled with doubt and fear he failed miserably.

'Tell me that burnt out car, I saw on the television last night, had nothing to do with you?' Buchanan demanded, firing off his opening gambit. 'You know the one, right in the middle of Streatley High Street.' He sneered sarcastically, almost as if television News bulletins were inundated with burnt out cars.

'Alistair, don't blame me,' he spluttered in reply, 'I was trying to do my best for both of us.'

'So, it was you!' he exploded. 'Bloody hell Noakes, don't drag me into your hair brained schemes!' Buchanan thundered down the line. 'I told you to do nothing! All you've done is stir up a hornet's nest. The coppers will be all over this and they won't let go,' his warning emphatic. 'Burnt out cars maybe common place on some sink estates, but not bang in the middle of a Tory stronghold like Streatley. I'm telling you they'll want answers. For crying out loud, half the people down there take sherry with the Chief Constable. This is Streatley on Thames not fucking Baghdad!'

'Look,' Noakes wilted under the barrage, 'it all went wrong. How could I have known the bitch was having her car moved? But look,' he offered seeking, appeasement. 'Nobody saw me, and I've not left any fingerprints, managed to avoid any CCTV cameras as well. Even if they did pick me up - what would they show? Blurred pictures of an old chap in a raincoat and cloth cap. Anyway,' he continued talking, 'as I told you, she's coming to see me on Tuesday, to do an interview. All set for 1pm at the gym. I can soon find out what she knows, then send her off with a flea in her ear.'

'For God's sake, you silly demented old bugger,' Buchanan blasted down the phone, 'you're missing the whole point. While I appreciate that you may not rate Miss Clarkson as Mastermind material, she's only got to tell the police that she came to see you the other day. Christ, they're probably interviewing her right now,' he shouted, 'they'll be checking her recent movements, where the car was parked, that sort of thing. They're bound to.'

'But.......Alistair,' Noakes tried to interrupt.

'No buts, you dimwit, listen to me. Even the "plod" will think it odd that a bloody fashion journalist just happened to drop into a boxing gymnasium! Think about it! What if she tells them that she dropped out the name of Drysdale? Well, they'd sink their teeth into that lot, wouldn't they? They'll check their records, find out that Drysdale got himself hanged while his two accomplices vanished with the money. Never to be seen again! If she then tells the police how you reacted, when hearing that name, they'll be across to your place like a rat up a drainpipe. Then you'd sing your bloody head off, turning Queen's Evidence to save your own skin. Wouldn't you?'

'No, Alistair, I'd never do that' Noakes whined, desperate to think of something to placate Buchanan's raging temper.

'In your dreams,' Buchanan snapped, 'you'd see me sent down for life to save your own arse. I know you, you're a slimy little toad. Do you think I'm going to risk my future on you keeping quiet when being turned over by a bunch of coppers? No way, you'd talk!'

'No, I wouldn't do that, honest!' Noakes shouted into the mouthpiece, feeling claustrophobic inside the confined booth. Desperately he sought relief from Buchanan's pressurised assault as he battled to find the right words. Finally, after deciding that now was the right time to play his ace he carried on talking. 'Okay, Alistair,' he said with deliberation. 'I didn't want to use this, but I've had an *insurance policy* on hand now for years. It's something you should know about. Because, you see, I've never really trusted you.' There he'd said it.

'Not trusted me!' Buchanan fumed, 'an insurance policy. What the hell do you mean?' he shouted, confusion adding to his anger.

'Ah, that's got you,' Noakes rallied, turning his head to see a couple of middle-aged ladies waiting patiently outside the phone box. Wanting to make a call they glared at him intently through glass panels. 'Do you remember the envelope you gave to me, all those years ago?' Noakes continued, 'you know, the night before young Stephen got the chop. Well, I've still got it and your fingerprints are all over it. So, think on! That's my bit of protection.' A long pause followed before Buchanan's icy cold and flat calm voice came down the line.

'George,' he said patronisingly, 'as for you not trusting me, well that's ridiculous. I could have had you killed years ago. That's how much I trusted you.' In a smooth voice that Noakes found chilling, Buchanan continued talking. 'Seeing that car fire on the television yesterday evening, I knew it had to be down to you. So, I spent last night working on ways to resolve the mess you've made, and to keep you away from the police. Now, with that ill-advised last remark you've just signed your own death warrant. You've now become a complete liability. Goodbye!' The line went dead, leaving Noakes in shock as he stumbled out of the 'phone box, mindlessly pushing aside the two grumbling women.

CHAPTER 26

BADLY SHOCKED, YVONNE pulled a face as she digested the DCI's leading question as to who would want to kill her. Who indeed, she thought and, more to the point, why for heaven's sake? Trying to stay calm under the scrutiny of three pairs of eyes she struggled for answers as the DCI posed another question.

'Is it okay if I call you Yvonne?' Crowland asked, hoping to ease the tension as he smiled at the visibly stunned young lady sitting across from him.

'Yes, I suppose so,' she said, managing a wry smile as she agreed to his request.

'Thank you,' he returned the smile. 'Now,' he paused, 'as I see things, we have three possible scenarios, based upon knowing the attack on your car was deliberate. They are,' he indicated by sticking out the first three fingers on his left hand. 'One, as I pointed out, is that the attack would appear to have been deliberately aimed at you.' Adding emphasis to his point, he tapped the first finger of his left hand with the index finger of his right hand, making Yvonne gasp at the brutality of the remark. 'Next, might this have been a case of mistaken identity?'

'What do you mean?'

'Well, Miss,' Baxter cut in before his DCI could speak, 'say someone wanted to set fire to a Fiesta but got the wrong one? You know, thinking your car was the one they wanted.'

'Thank you, sergeant,' the senior officer added tersely, not best pleased at being interrupted at such a critical point.

'So, that's point two,' Crowland added, repeating the finger touching exercise.

'And point three? Yvonne questioned.

'Highly unlikely, but was Bill Turner the intended target all along?' For a few seconds Yvonne grappled with that one. But, as she looked up at the DCI in astonishment, he gave her a weak smile, before nodding to Baxter and Phelps. 'Don't worry, we've already kicked that one into touch. So that leaves us with just two possible, either you were the target all along, or this was a case of mistaken identity. Sorry to be so blunt, but we've narrowed it down to those two and, fact is, I'm inclined to throw out the mistaken identity one as well.' Taking his time, he explained that whilst the forensic checks were not yet fully complete, the nature of the device was known.

'Despite the intensity of the fire,' he paused, 'enough evidence has been found to show that a detonating mechanism, of some description, had been fitted to the cars fuel tank. We know it had to be some sort of tilt switch device, as opposed to an electrical timer being wired up to an explosive charge.' Crowland paused for a moment, before giving Yvonne a brief description of a tilt switch and how it operated. 'Forensics found traces of glass and mercury at the scene, but no trace of any explosive material. The device, they believe, ignited the petrol vapour in your fuel tank. Highly explosive stuff. Anyway, it's their opinion that it was fitted to your car not long before the explosion, most likely designed to detonate when the car was going up or down a steep gradient. Given that your route to and from the station is all up and down hill, it had to be fitted shortly before it blew up.'

'You mean?' Yvonne grappled with the permutations, 'here, outside my house, or at the station. They're the only two places where the car was left, during that time frame.'

'Are you sure of that?' Gary Baxter enquired, making Yvonne hesitate before making her reply.

'Oh, hold on, yes, that's right. I was over at Robert's place in Shiplake, for a couple of hours on Wednesday evening, now I come to think of it. But' she looked startled, 'that doesn't make sense. After I left Robert's place, I drove up several steep hills on the way back here. Then, as you know, I had no problems with it yesterday when I travelled back down through Streatley to the station.'

'Well,' Crowland thoughtfully tapped his teeth with his pen, 'that really confirms Forensics thinking,' he said, turning to address Baxter. 'Start making enquiries around here first, before looking around Vere's place over at Shiplake. Ask the usual stuff, any strangers hanging about, unfamiliar vehicles and the suchlike. But' Crowland he added, 'don't waste too much time on that because my money is on the station. You've already told us your car was there, by about seven-thirty yesterday morning. That would've given anyone plenty of time to attach the device, long before the garage people collected it anyway.' Yvonne noted that Crowland had used the word device a couple of times rather than bomb.

'Yes, I see,' Yvonne said softly, reassured by another squeeze from Phelps.

'Right then, sergeant, let's cancel those last instructions, the device had to have been fitted at the station. What with all the driving you did on Wednesday, as well as yesterday morning, it would've gone off by then,' he concluded, being careful to avoid stating the obvious that she'd have been the victim in such a case.

'You mean....,' she struggled with the words, 'I'd have been in the car?'

'Exactly,' Crowland said gravely. 'Be in no doubt that device was primed to kill, leaving me convinced that you were the intended victim.' The DCI's bluntness shook Yvonne badly, forcing her to accept the very conclusion that she didn't want to accept.

'Right, as a first step, I've already got a couple of officers trawling through the station car park, in search of any similar cars to yours. Just to be on the safe side, and to rule out the mistaken identity bit. Should any similar cars be found we'll contact the owners, just to ask if they'd any reason to believe that they might have been the intended victim. And next,' he said, tapping the computer back into life, 'we've got CCTV footage from Goring station.' He fast forwarded for several seconds, pausing the pictures after a while. 'Here you are, arriving at 7.32am, backing into a vacant space.' Looking carefully, Yvonne watched the grainy images of herself leaving the Fiesta, pressing the remote locking button on her key ring then crossing the car park to move out of the picture. 'So, we'll get the bay where you parked cordoned off, let Forensics get on their hands and knees, hopefully picking up any traces.'

'Why?' Yvonne asked naively.

'Well,' Phelps replied, gently stroking the back of Yvonne's hand, 'after what you've told us, the DCI's certain that's where the device was fitted to your car.'

'Yes,' Crowland acknowledged, 'if we're right on this it narrows the period down to between when you arrived and when your car caught fire. I'll bet good money that'll be when the device was planted. We've already scoured the station's CCTV tapes, but to no avail. All we've got are vague images of people coming and going, even shows one or two folks near your car but nothing definite. Certainly not enough to take to Court, but whoever got in there knew exactly what they were doing.'

More fast forwarding took place, after which Crowland set the computer back to its normal pattern. 'And now,' he said, 'here we have Sid and Bill arriving in the van. Then we've got Bill who, having got out of the van, is joined by Albert Wallace his friend who still works at the station. He and Turner were big pals, played bowls together. Then, here we have Sid, the driver, getting out and joining them for a friendly little chinwag that lasted for the next ten minutes or so.'

Yvonne stared at the screen, painfully aware that she was watching a man just minutes away from death. Horrified, she stared at the blurred images, three innocent people chattering away, harmlessly and unconcerned. For Yvonne, who knew exactly what was to happen, the pictures were unreal. Unwilling to prolong her agony, Yvonne turned away feeling Phelps give her hand a squeeze of reassurance. At least you understand what I'm going through she thought, appreciating the WPC's support. As Crowland began to

finish with his laptop, morbid fascination made Yvonne
return her eyes to the screen, snatching one last glance at the
scene of normality. For a fleeting moment it was the back
view of a man that filled the screen. An older looking man
walking awkwardly away from the car park. She shuddered,
her jaw dropping as the screen faded into blankness. The
person she had just caught sight of was wearing a raincoat, a
cloth cap and walking with a slight limp! Her heart missed
a beat as an image of Noakes, limping towards his office
flashed into her mind. Might that just possibly have been
Noakes? But then, why should it be?

Momentarily flustered, she wondered if any of the others
had detected her sudden agitation. No reactions. She sighed,
debating whether to raise her thoughts concerning Noakes.
But then I'd have to tell them about Gerald, mentioning
Drysdale before telling them about the fight and spotting
the damaged hand. Oh, and my trip to Noakes's gym. No
way she decided, getting through that lot would take forever
and, like as not, considered to be nonsense. Damn it all,
even Robert doesn't know any of this yet. On top of that
Crowland will think I'm being paranoid, and I'll never get
away to Cornwall.'

'Right,' Crowland spoke, his voice lancing through
Yvonne's quandary, 'that's all for now. I'm afraid we know
what happened after that, no point in turning the screw
any further. In ten or twelve minutes we'd have seen Sid
drive off in the van, with Bill Turner following in your car.'
Crowland snapped down the computer's hinged screen,
looking directly at Yvonne. 'Did you say you were planning
to go away?'

'Yes,' she replied brightly, 'that's right, I'm going down to Falmouth on the train. It's where I grew up,' she offered by way of an explanation. 'I'm going to spend a long weekend with my mum, but I' must be back at the office first thing Tuesday. Three days away, out of the limelight.'

'Good idea,' Baxter offered, 'the break will do you good. But, just in case, can you leave me a contact number please, Miss?'

'Not a problem. Let me have a piece of paper and I'll jot the numbers down, my mobile plus mum's number in Falmouth.' Tearing a page from his notebook Baxter handed it to Yvonne for her to write down the numbers. Returning the slip of paper to Baxter she continued to outline her plan. 'I've checked, there's one or two fast trains from Reading, around lunch time, all heading for Cornwall. Hopefully, I can make one of those but,' she raised a concern, 'can you still manage to keep my name out of the papers?'

'We'll do our best. We've asked the media not to go chasing the car's number with the DVLA. And your local garage, who seem like a good bunch, has promised to say nothing. So, with any luck we can keep the lid on this for a little while.' Preparing to stand up Crowland looked at his watch and smiled at Yvonne. 'Hey, if you get a wiggle on, we'll take you to the station. We're on our way back to the office and the stations on our way. See, we're not all bad,' Crowland joked.

'Never thought it for a moment,' Yvonne laughed, jumping up. 'Give me ten minutes and I'm ready, five to get packed and another five to nip next door to see my neighbour, Mrs Frobisher. She's such a dear. I always let her know what I'm doing.' Whilst exuding false bravado,

Yvonne struggled with her conflicting emotions. Had she been right not to mention Noakes? Airing such a vague suspicion would have taken up valuable time, make me miss umpteen trains as well. No, they are the detectives, not me, she told herself heading for the stairs and a suitcase.

CHAPTER 27

MILES OVERSTONE SLUMPED back in his comfortable executive chair, letting out a long sigh. It's been years since that ruddy bank job and I'm just days away from getting out, making a clean break with money to burn. Now this, he cursed. George Noakes, damn the man, he said to himself. After all these years he comes out of nowhere, like a long-lost shipwreck managing to resurface. Picking up the telephone he made an internal call.

'Susan. No phone calls for the next half an hour, understood?'

'Very good, Mr Overstone, no interruptions for the next half an hour,' she said, repeating the instruction. In silence Overstone, having already sent a text to Dukes containing just a single letter X, prepared to make the next move. To the assassin the single faxed letter would place him on standby for another job, the details of which Overstone would now send to an accommodation address in nearby Putney, a newsagent's shop not all that far from the killer's Hammersmith apartment.

After slipping on a pair of thin rubber gloves he walked across to a delicately carved antique wall unit, from which he withdrew a sealed pack of A4 copy paper. This he placed on his desk before using a steel letter opener to slit open one end of the packet. Using his thumb, he fanned down the plain sheets before stopping to withdraw a single sheet, which he then placed in the feeder tray of his printer.

Taking similar care, he selected the envelope needed to carry the message. Both paper and envelope had to be sterile, free from fingerprints, DNA samples and any other incriminating elements. In other words, totally and utterly untraceable. Using his computer, he set out all known details of George Noakes, emphasising Tuesday's planned meeting. One o'clock with the Clarkson woman at his Acton gymnasium.

Convinced that he had covered the relevant points he watched as the completed document slid clear from the printer. Next came the envelope, nearly addressed to a Mr Colindale, care of the Putney newsagents.

Although he had no reason not to trust the newsagent in Putney, he and Dukes were not ones to risks because they knew the shop keeper needed extra cash to support his drug habit. For the newsagent, funding this habit had been easy once he'd discovered exactly how well blackmail paid.

Whereas one or two "customers" might complain, he'd always known they'd never dare to take things any further. He was safe in his shop, surrounded by papers and magazines, safer still in his back room. That special place where illicit stock catered for the more deviant or depraved tastes of some clients.

For years he had been constantly amazed at the sums of money people would pay to retain custody of compromising pictures, pornographic magazines and odd shaped packages. All I'm doing is sharing their secrets and being paid a nice little retainer for keeping them safe. Those people, what with their murky backgrounds, perversions and fetishes pay because they dare not complain. It's called business he muttered, leaning contentedly on his counter and thoughtfully handling a small bulky brown package. Even so, the newsagent was wise enough not to classify all customers as being in the same boat. Take that shaven-headed Mr Colindale, him with the piercing eyes. Now there's someone I'm not going to mess with.

***

Aware that daily temptation faced the newsagent, Overstone and Dukes had installed a final safety net, one designed to show if their communication conduit remained safe and uncompromised. In keeping with this well-tried procedure, Overstone took a ten-pound note from his wallet and then, with the aid of scissors, he cut a tiny sliver from the edge of the note. Not more than a millimetre wide and two centimetres long. This he carefully placed on the envelope, leaving about four millimetres between the two self-sealing surfaces. Anyone opening and destroying the envelope en route, and typing out a replacement, would never see this tiny trap. Likewise, anybody in receipt of the envelope and finding the small piece of bank note missing, would know immediately that their messaging system had been penetrated.

Then, by using a self-sealing postage, the possibility of leaving DNA samples could not exist. Most unlikely he thought, secure in the knowledge that once read both letter and envelope would be incinerated. Finally, he placed the sealed envelope inside a plastic document wallet, then into his briefcase for posting later that day. Doesn't look much like a death sentence, he thought, clicking shut the briefcase.

CHAPTER 28

TWO HUNDRED MILES west of London Yvonne, having changed trains at Plymouth, settled into her seat on the rail car unit bound for Truro. Once there she'd take the branch line for Falmouth Noisily her train rattled slowly over Brunel's famous Saltash Bridge, crossing the Tamar into Cornwall. On one side of her traffic sped in both directions across the modern road bridge while, on the other side the river headed for the Dockyard and then out to sea.

The waterway below had, she knew, provided countless fleets with the perfect anchorage. Ideal for storage and development in times of peace, perfect for repairs and refurbishment in times of war. Sadly, the once powerful Devonport Dockyard was now a shadow of its former self. Gone were the days of the big fleets, battleships and cruisers now replaced by submarines. These she knew were regularly docked here for servicing and recalled her father saying how they were always referred to as boats and never as ships.

For the fourth time since leaving Reading, she flipped open the clasp of her shoulder bag. Once again, she took out her mobile phone, debating whether to ring Robert. For the fourth time she angrily pushed the phone back into her bag. Damn him to blazes, she stormed inwardly. Why should I be the one to ring first? He's the one that's cleared off to Spain. I'm the person that someone's tried to kill. I'm the one frightened out of my mind, terrified of what might happen next! No. If he wants me, he can jolly well ring first. Cross, irritated and frustrated she turned her head quickly back to the window, lest a fellow passenger should notice the unwanted tears running down her cheeks.

***

Further away still, Robert Vere stepped out of the shower and slipped into the towelling dressing gown provided by the hotel. He felt wretched, knowing that he had been a lousy travelling companion for his office colleague on the flight out to Spain. A greasy lunch followed by an afternoon lecture had not improved his mood. Now, with the light fading and dinner beckoning, he felt dejected and alone. Why for God's sake didn't I have the guts to stand up to the firm? I should have insisted. Told them that I couldn't leave Yvonne like that, frightened and on her own? As he tried to justify his action he imagined, and not for the first time, a scenario involving the senior partners. *Look I'm sorry, sir, but I can't go to Spain because my girlfriend's car has caught fire.* It sounded pathetic, they'd have laughed out of the office and told me to grow up. Yet, for God's sake, what if Crowland's right, and the explosion had been deliberate? Was someone really trying to kill Yvonne? These thoughts spiralled through his mind, each one more sinister than the one before. But who'd want to knock off a fashion journalist? Get real! Okay, none of this makes any sense.

169

There must be a logical explanation. Deep down, another thought penetrated his brain. She must think I'm a prize rat for deserting her at a time like this.

Moving into the bedroom he sat on the side of the bed, looking again at his mobile. In hope, he checked for messages. Shall I call her now and apologise? Was it wrong of me, expecting her to understand that I really had to come to this conference? Surely, if she loved me, she'd have understood. But, then again, if I really loved her, I should have stood my ground, stayed with her and damn the consequences. But would I really have had the guts to do that?'

Standing up, he walked over to the minibar, muttering absently. Bugger it, I'll be seeing her on Tuesday when I'm sure she'll have calmed down. By then that DCI will have found out the whole thing was a proper cock-up, dodgy wiring or something. He found these thoughts comforting, a sub-conscious policy that made him feel better. Safe as houses, a nice bottle of her favourite perfume and all will be forgiven! Come on, it's only four days away, Tuesday will be a breeze. Okay, tears I guess, then a good dinner out somewhere and back to the cottage. What could be better? Unused, he replaced the mobile telephone on the bedside table. Neither him nor the impersonal instrument having the slightest idea what sort of day Tuesday would be.

***

As Yvonne fretted her way to Falmouth, and Robert Vere moodily prepared for dinner in Madrid, a mobile phone buzzed in a large apartment block, close by Hammersmith

Bridge. In anticipation of an eagerly awaited evening date Harvey Dukes had spent more time than usual with his personal grooming. His cleaning-lady, well accustomed to the ways of rich and single men had, as always done a first-class job in making the flat look perfect. Everything was clean and well-polished. Fresh flowers were everywhere, even in the bedroom. Clean towels, luxury perfumed shower gel in the bathroom and bubbly on ice. What more could a girl want? Yes, he grinned, everything was ready for the much-anticipated late-night action.

Stepping back into the lounge he picked up his buzzing mobile. Short and to the point, the single letter X on the screen made Dukes tingle with excitement. Another job! Who and where this time? Ah, hold on, he said to himself, tonight will be about pleasure, tomorrow can be about business. In an instant his best efforts to focus on seduction techniques had nearly vanished, the spell almost broken. Dukes knew this meant a trip to that slimy newsagent in Putney, a guy he wouldn't trust further that he could spit. High time he learnt that Harvey Dukes is not one to mess with, that's unless he has a sudden urge to become part of history. But that's for tomorrow.

Smiling, he replaced the mobile on the table as his mind returned deliciously to thoughts of his attractive companion. We'll have a fantastic meal, followed by champagne in the bedroom. That sure beat thinking about work and hiking over to see a low-life newsagent in Putney. Tomorrow's another day.

CHAPTER 29

'YOU DID WHAT?' Terry Noakes's jaw dropped in horror, his eyes wide with disbelief. Stunned, he struggled to take in what had his father had just said. Across the kitchen table the older man pushed aside the Sunday paper, set down his coffee cup and watched in silence as his son grappled with the information. After so many years apart he was pleased that Terry had agreed to the weekend meeting. What should have been a pleasant occasion was now turning ugly, marred by having to impart so much bad news. Dressed in combat trousers, boots and an open-necked shirt Noakes thought his son appeared alert and confident. Was it the 'wire brush' haircut? Well, it did give him something of an Action Man look. Whatever, he was pleased how Terry was looking more like his old self.

He liked what he saw, expressing pleasure when Terry had told him about his new flat in Reading, just off the Oxford Road. So, he sighed, were things starting to get back to something like normal for him? Terry had said earlier how the last spell 'inside' had finally shown benefits. He had responded well to the helpful and trained staff, people that had worked tirelessly to wean him off drugs. Also, with the help of civilian workers, he had started to acquire the basic skills he'd need to get meaningful employment. Okay, at forty-one a late start is better than no start. Even better than the one I tried to give him all those years back, Noakes thought as Terry's harsh voice cut through his memories like a whiplash.

'Hold it, you're telling me you took part in a robbery where two people died? Gunned down in cold blood. God, that's terrible,' he shook his head in disbelief. 'That's bad enough but you say one of the other blokes, Drysdale or whatever his name was, ended up on the gallows. How could you? Three deaths,' Terry snarled in disgust.

'Yes, I know it sounds crazy, but that's just what happened. But honest, I didn't kill anybody!' he halted, uncertain how to continue. 'Well not then anyhow.' Terry jumped up from the table, sending his chair flying behind him.

'Why are you telling me all this now? For God's sake, it was ages ago. Do you think I'm a priest - here to give you absolution?'

'No, of course not,' Noakes replied weakly, 'but things went oh so wrong the other day. I'm a dead man walking and need someone to talk to. I'm now a target.'

'What do you mean, a frigging target?' Terry shouted, bending to pick up the upended chair before calmly questioning his father's reference to now being a target.

'Okay,' Noakes sighed, pleased to have a chance to explain himself, 'I'll tell you everything, but no more interruptions, okay?' Opposite, his son nodded his reluctant consent.

'I want the lot,' he growled, prodding his finger at

his father in anticipation, 'the whole nine yards. Don't go missing anything out. All right!'

'Yeah, okay then. It's like this,' the older man began slowly, hoping that confession might bring him much needed relief, yet aware that it was far more likely to spark further reactions. 'Back in '62 I was struggling, what with this,' he raised his damaged left hand off the table, 'the army chucked me out and was down on my luck. All I could manage was the odd bit of thieving, fiddling to make ends meet. No proper job, like. Then one day, in a pub down Streatham way, I met this bloke. Told me his name was Alistair Buchanan. Ex public school, spoke all posh like, didn't give a toss for anybody, or anything for that matter. He was just after money, didn't give a stuff where it came from.' Noakes stopped talking, trying to read something in Terry's blank expression.

'Anyway, this Buchanan chap said he'd had a tip-off about making easy money from a bank job. Just turn up and help yourself like! So, he puts the job together, managed to recruit this Drysdale bloke to drive us. Buchanan and I,' he hesitated as memories came flooding back. 'Well, we both carried shooters but, up until that moment, Drysdale had no idea we were armed. More importantly, he didn't even know who we were. Buchanan had made damned sure of that. Said if he didn't know us he couldn't finger us to the law, you know,' he shrugged, 'like if the police picked him up afterwards. Good thinking that turned out to be, given what happened.' He stopped for a moment, wiping his forehead with the back of his hand.

'Buchanan, the crafty so and so,' he continued, 'managed to hide the guns in the car before Drysdale even picked it up. Like I said, the poor sod never even knew we had the shooters. Well, not until the job kicked-off. Then Buchanan was out of the car, blazing away at everything before him.' Silence descended as Noakes recouped his thoughts. 'A security guard and a young girl went down, straight away. I grabbed the money bags from the back of the bullion van. Within thirty seconds it was over. We were back in the car, and out of it. Then, down Chelsea way, this big lorry backs out of a works yard like. Drysdale, the flaming idiot, crashes right into the side of it. Got his legs trapped, as the bonnet and dashboard caved in on him. Buchanan and I were in the back, so we buggered off sharpish like, then separated. For weeks after that we laid low, leaving Drysdale to cop the heat while the papers were full of it, but he knew sod all. One day he even arrived at court with his face cut and badly bruised. The lying coppers made out that he'd fallen down the steps at the police station. Total hogwash. They'd hammered him senseless, but that was of no concern to the Judge. Didn't stop him putting on his black cap and sending Drysdale off to get topped.'

Another long pause followed. 'The night before Drysdale was due to hang Buchanan and I met in a pub, up Hampstead way. I was sick with worry. I couldn't stop thinking about Drysdale, what with him sweating away his last hours on this earth like.' As he stopped talking, Terry noticed a slight shaking of his father's hands. 'Anyway,' Noakes continued, 'he gave me my share all legitimate, well as legitimate as it could be. I got thirty-five thousand, in cheques, plus a solicitor's letter explaining that the money was an inheritance. And, up until this week, we'd never spoken to each other since that evening up in Hampstead.'

Again, he paused, this time looking pitifully at his son, seeking just the slightest glimmer of compassion.

'However,' he continued, 'as you can guess, the money set me up with the gym, and later the fitness club.' True to his word Terry had maintained his silence throughout but, by the worried look on his father's face, he knew there was more to come. He wasn't wrong either, as over the next few minutes, his father recounted how Yvonne Clarkson had arrived at the gym, shattering his nerves completely by mentioning the name of Drysdale. 'For crying out loud Terry, it was like a bloody nightmare, everything just came flooding back.' Pausing to collect his thoughts, he then detailed how Buchanan had given him an emergency contact procedure. Without another word Noakes stood up and left the room, returning minutes later clutching a slip of paper.

'There you are,' he said, tapping a finger on paper, 'ring that number. Get them to leave a message for Alistair Buchanan to ring you back on a public box number at a set time. It worked for me, the other day, should work again if you ever need it.'

'Why should I want to speak to that piece of low life?' Terry scowled.

'Well,' Noakes repeated himself, 'I'm now a marked man.'

'Yeah, so you said. What do you mean?'

'It's like this. Only last Friday Buchanan told me that I'd signed my own death warrant,' he said calmly and without emotion.

'Oh God, this just gets worse!' Terry blurted out. 'He can't do that. Not just kill you like. Surely you can find him?' Terry's earlier promise not to ask questions collapsed. 'What else haven't you told me?'

'Yes, there's more, which I'm sure you guessed;' the older man spoke dejectedly, 'lots more.' Minutes later Terry knew everything, his father having explained Buchanan's reluctance to take things seriously, in the belief that Clarkson knew nothing. 'Flying a kite, he'd said, flying a kite I ask you? Okay Buchanan said we were untouchable.' He then fell silent and peered intently at his son.

'Me. I wasn't that ruddy confident I can tell you. I was in a blind panic. I could see this Clarkson bird as a real threat,' he implored, 'believe you me, I was scared witless. Say she'd gone to the police, told them what she knew? I'd have ended up in jail with a full life tariff.'

'But what does she know?' Terry stormed, 'you still haven't told me.'

'That's because I don't know, well not exactly,' he spoke calmly, as if seeking justification. 'Whatever it was, it was enough to bring her to the gym and that worried me. Not only that, but she's also more than friendly with a flaming solicitor. So, I acted. I had to!' Terry's bushy eyebrows arched in expectation, listening as his father began to detail the events of last Thursday. All of which culminated with the horrific explosion in Streatley and the death of the innocent Bill Turner. Both men then fell silent as Terry, stunned by the disclosures, watched his father's facial muscles relax. Was this what the relief of confessions looked like he wondered, marshalling his thoughts before trusting himself to speak.

'What a bloody awful mess,' he concluded softly, 'four people dead, if you include Drysdale.'

'Well, you've got to include him. He's dead for sure,' his father snapped back.

'Yeah, right, and now you've got yourself lined up to be number five. That's bright, sitting here like a rabbit in the headlights, not knowing when or even where the threat's coming from.'

'Yes, but don't forget,' his good hand pointed to the slip of paper in front of his son. 'If anything happens to me, you can at least contact the bastard.' To this Terry gave a brief smile before responding.

'Hey, come on now, that's not the brightest of moves. Look where it got you?'

'Alright, I'll give you that, but there's still one piece of evidence left that I've held onto. Frightened the crap out of him when I told him about it last Friday. I know.' Noakes shook his head slightly, 'not twenty-four carets, but it could be enough to keep me alive. You see,' he said thoughtfully, 'I told him I've got a full set of his fingerprints and wouldn't the "Old Bill" like that?' He smiled, going on to tell his son about the sealed plastic wallet fixed to the back of an old boxing print on his office wall at the gym.

'So, if anything happens to me, ring that number. Tell him you've got his fingerprints and you're going to the police. Blow him out of the water, make sure he rots in jail. At his age he'll never come out, that's if you do things properly. Anyway, that Clarkson woman's coming to see me on Tuesday. I'll see what gives, then I'll let you know. Anyway, enough of that,' he remarked, standing up slowly and keen to stop talking about recent events. 'How about a spot of lunch at the pub across the road?' he smiled down at his son.

'Sounds good,' Terry said absently, his devious mind already working on how NOT to do things properly. Bugger the police. He could already smell an opportunity to rake in some real money for a change, should his father be murdered.

CHAPTER 30

SUNDAY LUNCH FOR Yvonne and her mother was a leisurely affair taken at the Lemon Arms, a cosy public house set in a pretty village some five miles out of Falmouth. 'A favourite watering hole of mine,' her mother had explained earlier, saying that she'd managed to book a table for one o'clock. The drive out to Mylor Bridge, in warm sunshine, had taken them through Penryn and then another two miles down a narrow road to the delightful village itself.

Although Yvonne had told her mother how an electrical fault had wrecked her car, and that the devastating fireball had killed the driver, it had now become the *elephant in the room*. A subject upon which Yvonne had not wished to elaborate while her mother knew better than to pry. The garage and the Insurance Company would be sorting it out she'd said. Subject closed.

Jean Clarkson, having left well provided by her late husband still enjoyed working, albeit part-time as a receptionist for a big hotel on Falmouth's Sea front. Although kept busy on Saturday by her shift rota, she'd been free to enjoy the next two days in the welcome, but totally unexpected company, of her daughter. Despite recent pressures, Yvonne had soon begun to relax, feeling less stressed as she'd settled into familiar surroundings. A feeling made more satisfying by having spent a relaxing Saturday on self-indulgences. Firstly, she had taken Patch up to the Headland, walking the Labrador in dappled sunlight under the trees that lined her route. Away to her left, through the foliage, she had caught glimpses of the River Fal as it went out to join the sea at Carrick Roads. Reaching the Headland, she'd walked into the car park below the Coastguard Station, letting Patch off the lead. Free, the old dog had enjoyed romping around the grassy slopes, scurrying off to root around in the odd rabbit burrow.

Away to her left, across the water, St Mawes Castle and St Anthony's Lighthouse had glistened in the sunlight. To her right the whole vista of Falmouth Bay was spread out before her. In the distance the land curled away towards the Helford River, then further round towards the unseen Lizard Peninsula Easily visible in the sunshine had been the tips of the treacherous Manacles, the partly submerged rocks that had claimed countless lives in the days of sail.

After settling the exhausted Patch down onto his bed, she took a brisk walk into town, passing Events Square - an open forum encircled by shops, bars and eating establishments. A little later she'd been pleasantly surprised to find a salon, one that could 'do something' with her hair as she had hopefully explained to the young assistant. Later, and feeling much better, she had set off for a little retail therapy before taking a light snack in a small harbour side restaurant Fortunate enough to secure a window seat she'd idled away an hour overlooking the busy harbour. In the distance she'd been able to see the docks, while below her hundreds of yachts and motorboats had bobbed jauntily at anchor in the sunshine.

Casting an approving eye over the Lemon Arms menu she was content, yesterday had been a good day. As her mother reminded her not to forget the "specials" board on the wall she relaxed, ready to enjoy the rest of Sunday, and indeed most of tomorrow. The train journey back will be a pain then, after that, things will be what they are, she accepted tipping a little more tonic into her glass. I'm damned if I'm going to worry about Tuesday, until it arrives. As for Robert Vere, even her mother had displayed the good sense not to raise that one!

***

For Harvey Dukes, Sunday lunch was far more business-like. Relaxed and well satisfied from the previous evening's activities, he was now comfortably seated in his lounge. Three items competed for space on the coffee table: a cheese sandwich, a copy of the London A to Z and an opened envelope. The latter having contained Overstone's letter, complete with the sliver of bank note, that he had earlier collected from the newsagents.

Collecting the letter had involved an enjoyable walk, taking him across Hammersmith Bridge to reach the embankment where, shortly after joining the towpath, he'd passed the University Boat Race mile post. Approaching Putney, and still on the embankment, he'd walked in front of the many boathouses that lined the river front knowing they belonged to several of the major banks, universities and college rowing clubs. With Sunday morning being a popular time for getting out on the river, several of the fragile looking but deceptively robust craft had already been placed outside in canvas cradles. Away to his left the river had lapped contentedly against the long sloping concrete ramp from which boats were launched and recovered. Of the crews that had already taken to the water, some were making for Putney Bridge as others headed towards Hammersmith, staying close by the Fulham wall.

Memories of the walk vanished as the printed sheet before him commanded full attention. Carefully he read, then re-read, the instructions. His target was one George Noakes, boxing trainer and gymnasium owner. A person his *employer* wanted removing at the earliest opportunity, even going so far as to suggest that a planned Tuesday lunchtime meeting might offer a good opportunity. Might be worth looking into he thought, folding up the piece of paper. As always, his instructions were precise, giving a good description of Noakes and highlighting the damaged left hand. No point in hitting the wrong guy, he said to himself, it really mucks up their day and ruins mine as I don't get paid. Smiling, he picked up the A to Z and committed to memory the location of the gym in Acton. Never mark a map was another of his rules. If the police come checking and find an A to Z marked with a place where a hit's taken place, well even they can work that one out! No, he thought, I'll use the motorcycle courier routine. In, bang, and out! Carried out in seconds, black leathers, black helmet complete with black visor. Reaching for his mobile he sent a double X text message to a number held in his memory, letting his paymaster know that the instructions had been received and understood.

***

Shortly before one o'clock Dukes was releasing the up-and-over door of a lock up garage about half a mile from his apartment. Once inside he flicked on the light, lowering the door behind him. Stepping forward he carefully removed a protective white sheet covering a gleaming black and silver Honda VFR 750 motorcycle. To Dukes, this beautifully cared for piece of equipment was nothing more than a tool of his trade. A machine used to ride to and from jobs. To maximise anonymity Dukes had, in his possession, three different sets of number plates for three legitimately registered and identical motor bikes. These bikes were owned by three unsuspecting riders, each living in the Home Counties. With so many number plate recognition cameras around, the false plates gave him the time and protection needed when carrying out 'jobs.' Within seconds of being 'clocked' by any one of these cameras, electronic checks would show the bike to be legally owned, taxed, insured and with a valid MOT. Any further checking by the police would, he knew, leave some unsuspecting 'Joe' having to answer some awkward questions. So, this deception gives me the necessary time to get clear and away following a hit.

Precautions, always precautions, Dukes reminded himself as he removed his outer clothing, before slipping into a full set of motorcycle leathers, plus boots, gloves and a black helmet with an equally black visor. After taking a last look at the A to Z he slipped the book inside his jacket, pulled the zip up to his neck then flipped down the visor. Opening the garage door, he took a quick look around before lifting the bike off its stand and pushing it outside.

Leaving the bike supported on its footrest, he returned to close and lock the garage door. Like a true thoroughbred, one press of the self-starter fired up the engine. Seconds later he slipped out of the side street before turning onto the main road. Ahead of him lay an easy journey to Acton where, in a slow cruise along a narrow street, he'd familiarise himself with the surroundings. All essential for next Tuesday, ready to identify potential hazards and to take note of possible parking positions. Not that he'd be there that long!

Later, when satisfied with the results of his Acton survey, he let out the clutch and applied a small amount of throttle and re-joined the traffic stream. On balance, he reckoned the whole thing looked feasible, with space to park the bike outside the gymnasium, with a tee junction fifty yards up the road. So, within seconds of the kill I can be out of sight, slicing through the traffic, comfortably protected by the false number plates. No problem. Tuesday it is then, he said to himself, paying no attention to a guy in camouflage combat trousers stepping out from a nearby pub doorway, helpfully supporting an old guy on one arm.

***

The receipt of the double XX text message came as a welcome relief to Overstone since Noakes had become a total liability and had to go. Blowing up that damned woman's car had been the mark of a dysfunctional fool. Just a few miles down the road from my house in Wallingford, the stupid sod. Now's the time for steady nerves, not for giving way to impulses. No need for me to get into a spin. If Dukes does the business in a day or so that'll be that. With

Noakes gone it's the end of the line. Even if the police do end up with my fingerprints, so what? They're not on file. With Noakes out of the way, that'll be just another dead end for the police with no possible feedback to me.

God only knows what made that Clarkson woman go to the gym, and then come out with the name of Drysdale? She knows nothing because there is nothing for her to know. As for her boyfriend, he's probably just another flaming ambulance chasing solicitor on the lookout for a fast buck. Of course, she could have read about Drysdale, or maybe she'd seen the name on some website or in a book somewhere. But why go bouncing it off Noakes? That just doesn't make sense, but I'm not taking any risks at this late stage. Certain that his meticulous planning would see Noakes consigned to history in a matter of days he relaxed, unaware that that Vere and Clarkson had been witnesses to a document that some people would later call the *Drysdale Confession.*

CHAPTER 31

ALTHOUGH ARRIVING HOME tired on Monday evening next morning Yvonne had a spring in her step. While she'd enjoyed her time in Cornwall, it was the planned meeting with Noakes that now fuelled her motivation. Making her way through the open plan section of the office smiles and good wishes s greeted her while Wayne, she noted, looked drawn, even a little sheepish. Minutes later, in the privacy of her office, the size of her e-mail Inbox damped down her good spirits. Not to worry, she thought, I'll deal with those later. Right now, George Noakes at one o'clock is my priority.

Calmly she assembled the things she would need for the interview: a fully charged pocket-sized digital recorder, secretarial note pad and a good supply of sharp pencils. After slipping these into her shoulder bag, alongside her mobile phone, she then spent half an hour running an eye over three fashion articles she had been preparing. Finally satisfied she pressed the button, sending them into cyber space to reach the printers in time for their next monthly editions. Next up a summons from the *Iron Lady* – one floor up, in her executive office. Usually, such meetings with the editor were on a one to one, face to face across her desk. Pleasantly surprised, Yvonne had found herself steered towards the informally relaxed area in the corner of the editor's office. A space normally reserved for influential clients, and where comfortable low chairs and a stylish table awaited.

Over a welcome coffee Yvonne's editor expressed her shock at the events of last Thursday, again asking the same questions. How did it happen? Was she injured? What did the police think? Did she need any time off work to recover from the shock? Yvonne parried these well-intended probes with the skill of an Olympic fencer, politely answering No, No, not sure, and yet another No. And, after a while, the conversation returned to business, fashion business that is with Yvonne assuring her boss that her workload was well in hand, with no more unforeseen interruptions.

'In fact,' she concluded, 'as the police are investigating a *murder,* they seem a bit devoid of ideas. Well, they've not told me anything, apart from saying they know the attack on my car was deliberate.' Anxious to be getting on Yvonne stood, smoothing down her skirt before making for the door and calling over her shoulder. 'Anyway, the garage owner's a sweetie, lending me a Volkswagen Golf while the police and insurers sort out the mess.' With that she departed from the office, leaving her editor none the wiser, but more reassured as to her employee's well-being.

Later, just as she was double checking her handbag for the things she needed, Wayne tapped tentatively on the glass of her office door. Standing beside the desk, she pushed down the leather flap, flicking over the small gold coloured retaining clip. Her long hair falling softly onto her shoulders as she turned to face the young man.

'Yes, Wayne, what is it?' exasperation giving an edge to her normally calm voice. 'I'm late for an interview. Can't this wait?' Although mildly annoyed at the interruption, she noticed that Wayne seemed even more flummoxed than usual in her presence. Intrigued, she moderated her tone, and stepped around the desk. 'I'm sorry, but I've got to dash. You've obviously got something on your mind, so I'll see you when I get back. You okay with that?' she asked as in the doorway Wayne blushed.

'Yes, Miss Clarkson, you …you're right,' he stammered. 'For days now something been worrying but I'll tell you when you get back then.' Before Yvonne could reply to Wayne he had departed, leaving her none the wiser. Slipping on her jacket and sliding the bag's long strap over her shoulder, she idly wondered what could be troubling the office junior. Is this serious or is he going to blurt out *overtures of undying love?* she thought a touch unkindly. Even so, the sudden thoughts of love made her think of Vere. A thought she dismissed just as quickly.

***

That same morning Harvey Dukes began his preparations with a visit to a central London safety deposit storage company. There, below ground in an isolated vault, he donned surgical rubber gloves before placing one of his numbered boxes on the central table. Out of habit, he then spent the next few minutes walking around the confined space looking for signs of any hidden cameras. The ABC of management, he muttered to himself, *accept nothing, believe nobody and check everything*. Having failed to detect any intrusive equipment he unlocked the box, taking out a Glock 9mm pistol, suppressor and a packet of ammunition from which he proceeded to load the magazine. Satisfied, he slipped the loaded pistol into a shoulder holster before returning the unused ammunition to his safety deposit box. Finally, after slotting the locked box back into its allocated space in the secure units, he pressed a buzzer to signal that he was ready to leave the vault.

Outside, he flagged down a taxi, directing the driver to within about three hundred yards from his lock-up garage and motorbike. While making the short walk to the garage he paused by an overflowing waste bin, carefully easing out an empty porridge oats packet after again donning the rubber gloves.

Back inside his garage he set to work. Using a Stanley knife, he cut around the already open end of the packet, leaving a hole large enough to get his hand in. He then picked up a roll of heavy black tape, which he proceeded to wrap around the box. Finally, and using clear tape, he attached a blank white label to the black box. Using a biro, he then made a series of illegible marks on the label, marks that would pass as an address in the eyes of the unwary.

Next, he removed the Glock from his holster, placing it inside the taped over porridge oats box which then went into the top box fitted to the back of his motor bike. Then, for the last time, he rehearsed his routine. Open the top box, take out the packet and slide the right hand inside and grip the pistol. People, surprised by the unexpected arrival of a package, would never notice that one of the courier's hands was inside the package being delivered. Simple. Enter the gym, identify Noakes, stand directly in front of him while calling out, "package for Mr Noakes." Then, with just inches between us, one, two or three shots would do the job. Dead. Quite dead! Back down the stairs, on the bike and away, he said to himself as he started to get into his leathers.

CHAPTER 32

YVONNE CLIMBED THE familiar stairs shortly before one o'clock and pushed open the door into the gym. This time, she noted, that only two or three people were using the facility. Even the ring, normally bustling with activity, remained silent. Casting her eyes around she detected no immediate sign of Noakes, making her wonder if he might have *bottled out* and wouldn't show up for the interview.

'Mrs Clarkson,' a voice called over her left shoulder. Startled, she turned to see a pale faced Noakes standing in the doorway of his office as, for a second, she struggled with the married prefix. Quickly regaining her composure, she smiled at the trainer before holding out her hand and stepping forward.

'Good to see you again,' she acknowledged, 'and thanks for making the time available.'

'Come into the office, and it's nice to see you too,' Noakes replied with little conviction, before stepping aside and ushering her through the door. The office, a narrow structure built along the back wall of the gym had wood panelling up to waist height. Above that, glass gave a full view across the gym, while below the window a long worktop provided space for files, papers, telephone and a laptop computer. As she eased further down the narrow office a framed picture on the end wall caught her attention. Well painted, it showed two old-style bare-knuckle boxers squaring up to one another in a roped off area of grass. In the brief silence Noakes tried to assess just what sort of potential threat his visitor might be. Could she really be dangerous? Hell, she looks harmless enough. Yet she did seem a bit surprised when I called her 'Misses, and with no band of gold on that left hand either. Was she really married? If so, had her birth name really been Drysdale? These thoughts ran through his mind, as he watched Yvonne moving further along the confined space.

'Do take a seat, Mrs Clarkson.' Noakes indicated towards a tired looking swivel chair. This time his use of the married prefix came more naturally.

'Thank you, Mr Noakes,' Yvonne said graciously, as she managed to turn and settle herself into the chair, now squeezed awkwardly between the wall and the desktop. Once seated she looked back towards the now closed door, watching Noakes as he positioned himself on an equally worn chair facing her.

'Thank you once again, Mr Noakes, for this privilege,' Yvonne smiled, placing her bag onto the desktop in front of her. 'During the interview I'll take shorthand notes,' she pointed to her notepad. 'However, to ensure I don't get anything wrong, do you mind if I record our conversation on this?' she tapped a finger on the small digital recorder she'd taken from her bag. For a moment doubt clouded the trainer's eyes but, after a thoughtful silence, he gave his answer.

'No, that's okay,' although uncertain of any implications.

'Where do you want to start then?' he asked, as Yvonne pressed the button to begin recording the conversation.

'Well, as you know, I'm with a leading woman's magazine,' the name of which she then gave. 'And' she smiled, 'while boxing has been a male preserve for years, the female angle is certainly widening these days. Why it's even an Olympic event now; isn't it?'

'That's right, although I'm not too sure about it myself. Bit of an old dinosaur I suppose' he laughed, 'but who am I to stand in the way of progress?' Noakes smiled at the beautiful woman before him, mixed emotions churning away behind his forced and placid exterior. Could this woman really be the one to nail me for murder, or is she still flying that blasted kite? Time for something different, he thought. Attack is the best form of defence.

'Mrs Clarkson,' Noakes spoke softly, peering directly into her eyes, 'a married lady, but not wearing engagement or wedding rings, I see?' Curious, he waited for a response, noting the sudden appearance of a small nervous twitch in one corner of her mouth. Yvonne, blushing, looked across at Noakes, having just taken a furtive glance at the outstretched fingers on her left hand.

'Oh, no, will you look at that? I've done it again, coming out in such a rush I......' her words cut short by an urgent knocking on the office door.

'Oh, excuse me,' Noakes said, turning in his swivel chair before getting up to open the glass panelled door. Glad of the interruption, Yvonne looked up as the door swung outwards giving her a partial sighting of the new arrival. Tall, broad shouldered and wearing a black leather motorcycle jacket and black helmet and visor it could have been anybody. Absently she looked down at her note pad, dismissing the interruption as a minor inconvenience, confirmed as a muffled voice came from within the helmet.

'Special delivery for George Noakes.'

'That's me, pal,' she heard him say. Although unable to see exactly what was happening, she assumed that Noakes was in the process of reaching out to take delivery of a package. Still looking down she heard two soft plopping noises, followed by a muffled gasp. Instantly she was alert, staring open-mouthed at the back of Noakes as his legs buckled beneath him. Falling awkwardly, he collapsed onto the floor, wedged squarely in the open doorway. Semi-paralysed with shock Yvonne screamed, gaping in horror as the man in black stepped forward, straddling the fallen Noakes. Now she could see clearly. He had a gun in one hand and stood poised with his legs astride the fallen body. In horror she watched, mesmerised as the gun barrel swung menacingly down towards Noakes's temple. Rigid with fright she babbled incoherently, knowing exactly what was going to happen next. But it didn't.

Before he could fire another shot the courier staggered forward, shoulder charged from behind by a large and heavily sweating boxer. Unable to move his feet, because of the body lying between his legs, he toppled forward. Struggling to control his balance his arms reached out in search of support. Forced to release the pistol he watched as it clattered to the floor and went spinning towards Yvonne's feet. Thrusting a hand onto the desktop for support the killer managed to free one foot while half turning to see what had caused him to stagger. One look at the perspiring giant facing him was enough. Escape became his priority.

Of the two, the boxer was the more surprised, hesitating and barely able to take in what he had just witnessed. Open mouthed he stood still, giving the killer precious seconds in which to regain the initiative. Managing to free off his other foot he turned, adroitly sidestepping a swinging right hand punch. Upright, and in now control, he was away, rushing through the door and onto the stairs. Relieved at seeing the leather clad man disappear, Yvonne got unsteadily to her feet. Stepping over the fallen Noakes she stumbled out of the office, scared and badly frightened, yet knowing it was necessary to be taking control.

'Ring for an ambulance!' she screamed at the shocked man in the doorway. 'He's been shot.' For one moment the big man stood nonplussed, rooted to the spot as she frantically repeated the instruction. This time her high-pitched yelling cut through his confusion. Turning, he spun round and headed for the dressing room and his mobile, completely ignoring the telephone on the desk.

Stunned by what she had seen, but aware of the need to react quickly, Yvonne dropped to her knees beside the gravely injured man. Cradling his head in her lap, the sight of frothing blood dribbling over his lower lip alarmed her. A sure sign that a bullet had punctured a lung. In desperation she looked around, seeing two more anxious and sweaty faces looking down at her. Aghast and confused they stared at the oddly positioned couple on the floor. One, a beautiful woman on her knees, the other their old trainer with blood seeping from a corner of his mouth.

Although fatally wounded, Noakes had his eyes open and started to speak, his voice just above a whisper. Hearing these sounds, Yvonne shouted to the nearest of the two men in the doorway. 'Quick, that voice recorder on the desktop. Pass it to me, now!' she yelled in desperation. Responding to her shouted command the man clumsily pushed past her, stepping over the stricken man in the process. To the other boxer she yelled, 'fetch a towel.' As he vanished from sight, the first man thrust the recorder into her hand. Stunned and unsure, he pushed her awkwardly to one side in his haste to get clear of the office.

Shuffling closer Yvonne pushed the instrument up against Noakes's mouth as he gasped for breath. With her head held low, she just managed to hear his garbled words. 'Yes, it was me with Drysdale. Don't know how you got that name,' he spluttered as more frothing blood trickled onto the hem of her skirt. 'We did that bank job,' he gasped, 'me and Buchanan.' The voice was getting fainter. 'He's the one what's done this.....I just know,' he spluttered. Although listening intently, Yvonne managed to use her free hand to push the now proffered towel between her knees, supporting the back of Noakes's head.

Holding the recorder as close to him as possible, she then managed to hear him say, 'It was me.....last week..... your car......the fire.' He gurgled, blood rattling in his throat. 'See........the picture......on the wall...his prints, they're on the back.....' He gurgled again, his one last effort to speak failing as his eyes closed. Horrified Yvonne then felt his body stiffen, racked by a seizure of some kind before it went completely limp.

CHAPTER 33

MINUTES LATER, NUMB with shock and oblivious to the tears running down her cheeks, Yvonne was still holding Noakes's head when she heard an ambulance's siren. Shortly after it had stopped, two green clad Paramedics entered the gym. Instantly spotting the injured Noakes on the floor they got to work. Rigid with shock Yvonne watched as they unzipped their heavy canvas bags before speedily removing vital equipment. Moments later she found herself pushed unceremoniously out of the office and into the gym by one paramedic as the other began a frantic search to find a pulse.

Giving way to the professionals she staggered around the gymnasium, shocked and disorientated. In one hand she held the voice recorder, in the other the blood-stained towel. Turning, she looked down to where both paramedics were working fast, one injecting a colourless liquid into an upper arm as the other administered oxygen. After a further two minutes of watching this drama, Yvonne was shocked when the female Paramedic stopped working. Looking up at her from the floor she shook her head in a definitive and unspoken statement.

'It's no good, Miss, he's gone. Sorry, but there was

nothing we could do.'

'Oh no,' Yvonne muttered, grabbing hold of the office door frame for support, 'surely, he can't be ....'

'Yes, I'm so sorry. Our Dispatcher told us it was a shooting.' Pointing towards the trainer's blood-stained T shirt she added, 'not much for us to do, after shots like that. You know, up close and personal into the chest cavity. Look,' she pointed; 'you can see the powder burns.' Yvonne stared down, looking in the direction indicated by the paramedic's gloved finger, both holes singed with black, around which a little blood stained the white surface of the T shirt. 'One bullet must have gone close to the heart, stopping it right away. Instant loss of blood pressure, hence little bleeding.' The dispassionate appraisal doing nothing to calm the shaking Yvonne.

'Anyway,' the paramedic continued, 'the police will be here in a minute or so. Automatic like when a shooting's mentioned.' Yvonne, on uncertain legs leaned back heavily against the wall.

'Here, Miss,' the other paramedic said, seeing her totter, 'let's have a look at you. Are you injured?' he asked, pointing to the towel she still clutched. Gratefully making use of the offered arm she looked blankly back, before managing to speak.

'No, I'm okay, scared but thankfully unharmed,' she told him, dropping the towel on the floor. 'The blood's his,' she nodded towards the office doorway.

'That's the ticket, miss,' he acknowledged, guiding her to a nearby chair. 'The 'old bill' will want to know what happened. Take statements, I expect.' Shocked and confused, Yvonne found his words and manner strangely comforting, pleased to find one human being who could spare time to care for another.

Grateful for the chair, she tried to clear her head. Confused, she struggled to understand what Noakes had meant about Drysdale. Had he really confessed to being party to that robbery? She flopped back into the chair gasping for breath, realising that Noakes had also confessed to blowing up her car. But in God's name why? She muttered to herself, desperately trying to make sense of what she had just seen and heard. I don't understand. Suddenly she felt very alone, mere feet away from a dead body and sitting in a boxing gymnasium. Scared and vulnerable, she needed Vere. Thoughts of their rift paling into insignificance when set against the present scenario. He would know what to do, she thought, even if he did go and leave me when I needed him so badly.

Minutes later Yvonne physically jumped as the gym door bursting open to admit a determined looking police sergeant followed by a pair of constables. Noting the two paramedics, and the body on the floor, he instructed his colleagues to secure the area. 'Check for other exits, the changing rooms, showers and the like. Round up anyone you find there. DI Robson will be along shortly. We need to get a grip on things before then. So, let's get on with it.' Turning he then addressed the paramedic, asking what had happened.

'Not sure, we arrived minutes ago and this guy,' he pointed to the body blocking the office doorway, 'had taken two bullets, directly into the chest. He was dead when we got here, seconds after, for the technically minded. The gun, it's still on the floor, in there,' he pointed towards the office. Next, he looked down at his colleague, who nodded her confirmation. The sergeant then looked at the seated Yvonne, surprised to see a young lady in a boxing gymnasium.

'And you are?' he enquired bluntly.

'Clarkson, Yvonne Clarkson,' she spoke softly, alarmed at how badly her hand shook when holding out the business card she had taken from her jacket pocket.

'Bloody hell,' he muttered, studying her card, 'a fashion journalist in a blasted fight emporium, along with a dead body. You saw what happened then?'

'Oh yes, I saw it all right,' she sobbed, as her shoulders shook slightly. 'It was a motorcycle courier, helmeted, all in black. It was horrible,' she stammered, pulling a tissue from her jacket pocket and dabbing her eyes.

'Okay, Miss,' the sergeant spoke in a more moderate tone, recognising the trauma the young woman in front of him was experiencing. 'Just tell me what you saw?' At that point, the two constables reappeared.

'All clear,' one of them announced, 'only a fire escape with an alarmed door. No one's been that way. Nobody else out there either.'

'Right then, Appleby!' he shouted, 'get outside. It looks as though our killer came on a motor bike. See if you can grab any witnesses, anybody who might have seen *anything*. Well, get on with it!' he bellowed as the constable headed for the door.

'And you,' he turned to the other police officer. 'See these guys,' he waved at the four semi-clad boxers. 'Take them to the changing room, let them get them into warm gear. Round up all their mobile phones, keep them apart until the DI gets here. I don't want them talking to each other, discussing what they saw or didn't see,' he barked out to his man before giving Yvonne a quick smile.

'Now, Miss, where were we? That's right you were going to tell me what you saw.' The sergeant's brief distraction had given Yvonne a chance to think about what to do next.

'In a moment,' she replied, standing up, 'but first I need my handbag. It's in the office, down the far end.'

'Sorry, you can't do that I'm afraid, it's a crime scene.'

'Don't be so ridiculous,' she snapped. 'I was in there when the shooting took place, and I've come out. So, if you won't let me go in, will you get my bag for me? My mobiles in it. I need to ring my boyfriend. He's a solicitor and he'll know what to do and advise me.' The sergeant, taken aback by such a forthright manner, looked closely into the pale, tear and mascara-streaked face. Frail looking, he thought, but certainly showing plenty of determination. As for a bloody solicitor coming around here and calling the odds, that's all I need. If I upset his bird, we'll never hear the end of it. Police brutality, harassment, human rights violations, oh bring back the good old days.

'Okay, Miss, I'll fetch it,' he said relenting, turning to walking towards the office. Moments later he reappeared, clutching her bag in one hand.

'Is this your bag?' he asked politely as Yvonne, despite the tension, gave a small laugh.

'Yes, thanks, that's the one. Not sure how many handbags you'd expect to find in a boxing gym?'

'Fair comment,' the sergeant smiled at the humour, watching as Yvonne undid the clasp. Seconds later she had the mobile in her hand, urgently dialling Vere's number, aware that she was trembling from shock. After three rings she was thrilled to hear the familiar voice.

'Robert,' she shouted with emotion, 'I need you, now! For God's sake don't ask questions, but something terrible' just happened. Someone has just killed a man right in front of me. Just get to this address now and hurry. Please?' she pleaded.

'Yes, of course' he answered, momentarily stunned by the bluntness of

Yvonne's terse message. 'You're timings perfect. I'm just walking out of Heathrow. Look, are you okay? And where exactly are you?' Quickly she told him, almost choking on a sudden and uncontrolled sob.

'Right then, I'll grab a taxi and be with you ASAP.'

CHAPTER 34

HARVEY DUKES GUNNED the big motorbike into action, swerving out into the traffic and cursing at his ineptness. A skilled contract killer caught out so easily, he fumed. That should have been a simple job, a piece of cake. It would have been, had it not been for that stupid woman screaming her head off and that oversized goon hitting me like a train and making me drop the flaming gun. Unforgivable.

Slicing neatly between a car and a van he dropped a gear then, squeezing more revs, he managed to clear a set of lights as they went from amber to red. Could they trace the gun? No, with the serial number ground off it should be safe. Yet, in the back of his mind, a thought emerged to taunt him. He recalled reading somewhere how scientists had managed to electronically trace a gun where the number, although ground off had still left impressions below the surface.

Something to do with shockwaves, he seemed to remember, how they could leave a deeply imprinted pattern in the metal. But, even if they did find the number, they couldn't get back to me. Feeling a little better he acknowledged the positives. Whatever else had gone wrong that day, George Noakes was well and truly dead. Job done! Soon be time to tap in triple X on the mobile. Happy days! Now to get the bike tucked up in the garage, safe after another good pay day.'

As the powerful engine purred beneath him, he thought about the bullets he had just fired. Okay, they'd be able to match them with those taken from the merchant banker I shot in the city twelve months ago. So what? They've got the bullets and now the gun. Where can the police go with that? These thoughts failed to worry him as he moved slowly through the traffic. 'No! I'm home free,' he sang contentedly to himself, riding happily by yet another CCTV camera. Thanks to the false plates, another old boy will be crapping himself in an hour or so when an armed SWOT team starts kicking in his front door. Just not his day!

***

Within minutes of constable Appleby departing, in search of witnesses, the gym door crashed open admitting Detective Inspector Sharon Robson, followed by a limp looking young man in a suit. Yvonne watched the pair with interest, noticing how the uniformed Sergeant visibly stiffened as the DI glared around the gym. Robson was about five foot six, a couple of stone overweight, hatchet faced, and with minimal make up beneath her close-cropped hair. She wore a crumpled looking trouser suit whose buttons around her midriff were under considerable strain. Not one of my readers Yvonne surmised, watching as the limp looking young man accompanying her hovered to one side. Her luckless sergeant Yvonne thought, taking in his terrified expression.

Robson scowled around the gym, noting the hanging punch bags, weight benches and a selection of speed balls. Next, she spared a glance at the body, wedged across the office entrance. Her stance reminding Yvonne of a ferocious Rottweiler, sniffing around and sizing up where best to cause the maximum amount of trouble. It was the uniformed Sergeant who became her first victim, as she snapped out orders and asked questions.

'What about the paramedics?' she barked.

'They've gone. Had to get back on duty, but I've got their details.'

'Oh, well done,' she said sarcastically, 'wouldn't have surprised me if you'd just let them swan off.' Yvonne noticed the sergeant bristle from the unwarranted remark, his neck above the collar reddening. *What a first-class so and so* she concluded. *I just hope Robert gets here soon; he'll know exactly how to put the silly cow in her place.* Just then the door swung open again, this time admitting three men in white forensic suits. Seconds later a fourth man followed, similarly suited but carrying an assortment of cameras and flash guns. More clipped orders came from the 'Ayatollah,' as she responded to the arrival of the crime scene specialists. Yvonne watched and listened to Robson as she snapped and snarled in bursts of clipped conversation. *Man-management skills zero and entitled to a refund on her course at the Charm School.* Moments later another suited individual entered the gym, tall, grey-haired, well-groomed and carrying a medical bag.

'Ah, doctor,' Robson saw fit to address this new arrival, but only with a hint of deference. In return the doctor's curt acknowledgement plainly indicated that he preferred to keep his distance from the surly DI. No doubt based upon previous encounters Yvonne surmised, watching as the doctor slipped into a white fabric suit before kneeling beside the body. Still seated, Yvonne looked up as Robson walked across and glared down at her with obvious disdain.

'Your name?' she snapped, awaiting a reply as Yvonne stood up and looked her in the eye.

'I'm Yvonne Clarkson, and you are?' Robson paused for a second, taking in the tear stains and the streaks of eye shadow coursing down her cheeks. Initially stunned by someone who looked vulnerable, she snapped back.

'I'm Detective Inspector Robson, Acton C I D. What are you doing here?' Yvonne pulled yet another business card from her jacket pocket, passing it to Robson.

'Business, I came to interview George Noakes. That's the dead man on the floor, in case you're interested.' For a split-second Yvonne's response stunned Robson, coming as it did from someone she had already judged to be a lightweight. Yvonne managed a faint smile, an effort wasted on the DI. Seeing her gesture fall on stony ground, she quickly followed up. 'And you, your identity please,' Yvonne asked formally, drawing upon years of the journalistic interview techniques needed to wrong foot awkward or defensive people. On this occasion she was desperate to compose herself before this fat inquisitor bored in again. Momentarily flustered by the request, Robson reached into an inside pocket, produced her Warrant Card and flashed it in Yvonne's face.

'Satisfied, smartarse,' she snapped curtly, before replacing the warrant card in her pocket.

'Thank you,' Yvonne replied, looking back, but this time minus any smile. 'And now what can I do for you?'

Robson fumed with indignation, further annoyed by having seen a brief smirk on the Doctor's face.

'Well, you can stop pissing me about, to start with. Of course, I realise a man's been murdered here. We are the police you know,' she added sarcastically. 'I intend to find out what happened here and to get his killer. Now, start talking before I really lose my rag with you!' Yvonne, under this onslaught, felt her resolve begin to crumble'

'You can't speak to me like that,' she cried, giving way to a small sob. Robson, now, fully confident that she'd got the upper hand, bored in relentlessly.

'Oh, can't I? Well, listen up sweetheart, I've got news for you, I can talk to you any way I like!' Yvonne felt as though she had received a slap in the face from hard-featured DI who gave a glare of satisfaction, poised and ready to pounce.

CHAPTER 35

'**NO, YOU BLOODY** well can't.' The firm and familiar voice slashed through the charged atmosphere as Robson, shocked by the unseen speaker, spun round to see who had dared to challenge her authority.

'Thank goodness you've arrived,' Yvonne cried, launching herself into Vere's arm to receive a welcome hug while glaring scornfully at the badly bemused DI.

'I'm Robert Vere,' he said, gently setting Yvonne to one side as he stared at Robson, 'Miss Clarkson's partner and her solicitor. Now, if you'll be so good, we'll do this properly and politely. Shall we? Or do I ring your superiors?' Both the open challenge, and veiled threat hung in the air, causing Robson to falter in her approach. For Yvonne, relief flowed through her like an electric current. Now we can fight on even terms. Across the room she caught a glimpse of both sergeants exchanging grins of delight. For them, seeing the obnoxious DI metaphorically shot up her well upholstered backside was a rare treat for them to savour.

'Now,' Vere said calmly, 'having got that out of the way, I remain unsure as to what has gone on here. Clearly someone has died,' he pointed to the body, 'and, equally well, we both know that Miss Clarkson's not your killer, although she could certainly be a material witness, isn't that so?'

'Well, yes,' Robson admitted grudgingly.

'Good. I'm pleased we agree on that. So, having established that Miss Clarkson is not under arrest, she now has the right to fair treatment as a material witness. Isn't that so?

'Well yes,' Robson conceded again.

'And believe me, I intend to see that you fully adhere to that. Is that clear?' he said in a raised voice, ramming home his point. By now Robson knew that she had climbed into the ring with someone who had her measure, and with someone who could land heavy punches.

'Yes,' she responded, with marked reluctance.

'And now, before you start I need to speak with Yvonne in private as I need to establish what she knew, and why she was here in the first place. So, the quicker I can do that the faster you can move,' Vere stated flatly. 'Therefore, I'll thank you in advance but, should you deny us time together, I shall be advising my client to take the *No Comment* route. A position I'm sure you'd find most unhelpful, when all you want to do is get to the facts as soon as possible.' Without more ado he placed an arm around Yvonne's shaking shoulders, guiding her away from the simmering DI.

They walked a little way further down the gym, settling into chairs either side of a table close to the ring apron. Yvonne, realising that Vere's final verbal shot had completely floored Robson, expressed thanks for his speedy arrival.

'Thank goodness you came, I did wonder, following last Thursday's unpleasantness…..' she whispered, reaching out to touch Vere's hand across the table.

'Of course, it'd take more than last week's nonsense to stop me from ever seeing you again. Now,' he smiled confidently, 'as I'm completely confused, tell me what the hell you've been up to?' Still holding his hand Yvonne began to unburden herself, starting with them watching the fight together on television.

'Oh, Robert, I'm sorry, but I could see a story and all the time you wouldn't even talk about it. Never mind thinking of following it up.' She sighed, before going on to recount how, with the help of the love-struck Wayne, she had tracked down the unfortunate Noakes. 'Right here in this very gym,' she looked across and waved her free arm in an expressive arc across the room. Turning back to face Vere she recounted how she'd contrived to mention the name of Drysdale, and the reaction it had caused. Then, using the excuse of an interview, she had arranged today's follow up meeting.

'I'm assuming the body on the floor is Noakes?' he asked, watching as Yvonne nodded her silent confirmation, before going on to recount how Noakes, in his death throes, had admitted to the firebombing of her car. 'But why, why do that?' Vere asked, struggling to make the connection.

'We never got that far,' Yvonne looked up, 'but I'm sure he saw me as a threat to his liberty, what with bouncing Drysdale across him. He must have wondered just how much I knew. Of course, I never got to tell him about the notes that Gerald had recovered after all these years. But' tapping her left-hand jacket pocket, 'I did get it on tape, the firebombing plus his confession to the robbery, along with a chap called Buchanan.'

'Oh, you're a crazy, lovely, beautiful fool,' he said

laughing, 'you nearly get yourself blown up then come back here for more. Why?'

'Oh, I don't know, maybe I thought I was onto a story. Yes, I did wonder if Noakes was behind the fire. But honestly, I couldn't see how he knew which was my car. I only saw him on Tuesday, for the first time, then forty-eight hours later my car's destroyed.' She looked directly into Vere's eyes. 'How could he have known it was mine, and where to find it? And then, with you going to Madrid, I almost gave up. Was I wrong and were you right in thinking the fire was an accident?' She paused and looked into his eyes. 'But you're here now, and that's what matters to me.'

'And to me,' Vere said tenderly before suddenly becoming all business-like. 'Now, does the old dragon down there know any of this?' He nodded to where the DI was busy alienating people, firing off questions, reprimands and insults in equal proportions.

'No! All I told her was that I'd an appointment to interview Noakes for my magazine. Mind you, she must believe that I saw something of the shooting. Oh, Robert,' she sobbed, 'it was horrible.'

'I'll bet,' he replied with feeling. 'Does she know about the recorder?' Vere asked, desperately trying to remain unemotional.

'No, not yet anyway.'

'Okay, before we go and tackle her, tell me what happened?' Vere probed, anxious to know the whole story. In reply Yvonne related exactly what she had seen, and what she did immediately after Noakes had fallen to the floor, stressing that identifying the killer would be impossible, given his attire.

'What with black leathers, black helmet and dark visor, it could have been anybody,' she explained, feeling helpless as Vere patiently digested her information.

'Look,' he said as he stood up. 'I know this has been one heck of an experience but, if you feel up to it, I think we should make a full statement to old sour puss over there. Under *no circumstances* can we risk a charge of withholding evidence. She'd just love to have a pop at me for that one. Agreed?' Yvonne nodded her compliance before standing up slowly, her legs wobbly from delayed shock.

'Yes, okay,' she said managing to smile, her tear-stained cheeks still smeared with streaks of mascara 'but I really need the girl's room to do a repair job. I must look a real mess.'

CHAPTER 36

ONCE INFORMED THAT a full statement would be forthcoming, DI Robson decided upon a retreat to the familiar surroundings of her own police station. As such it was a while before Yvonne had found herself ushered to the 'ladies' by a somewhat concerned WPC to affect "repairs." While warm water, creams, lipstick and mascara took care of her streaky and tear-stained face, it needed the efforts of a damp cloth to rinse the blood from the hem of her skirt and the knees of her tights.

Fresher and more presentable she geared herself up for round two with Robson, buoyed up by knowing that she now had Robert in her corner. From the 'ladies' she was escorted into to what she recognised, from watching television programmes, as an interview room. Standard issue, high windows, steel table bolted to the floor, four plastic chairs and a large mirror. Vere was already in the room when she arrived, seated and sipping coffee from a foam cup, his brief case open on the table. He got up and gave Yvonne a hug, whispering in her ear.

'Say nothing, the room may be bugged.' He then guided her into the chair next to his, where they remained in silence while Vere resisted the temptation to pull faces at the mirror, confident they were under surveillance. But, ever the gentleman, he remained calm. Antagonising D I Robson any further, while tempting, would be unwise. After a further delay, the door opened and Robson strode in, followed by the limp sergeant. Vere deliberately stood up, knowing that Robson would react.

'Stay seated, Mr Vere,' she snapped before taking the chair directly opposite him.

'Oh, I'm sorry, I was always taught to stand when a lady entered the room.' First round to us, Yvonne thought, as the sergeant began fiddling with the twin tape machine on his right-hand side.

'Now, what do you want to tell us, Miss Clarkson?' Robson ploughed in without preamble. Yet, before Yvonne could open her mouth to speak, Vere cut in.

'My client is going to make a statement of her own free will, describing in full what she witnessed this afternoon. She is doing this in the firm knowledge that it will assist you in your enquiries. Naturally, you will be taping proceedings and we will be handed one of the two tapes,' he nodded to the machine. 'My client will be willing to return here to sign the statement when it's ready. And, once Miss Clarkson has finished, I shall be sending a copy of our tape to DCI Ted Crowland of the Thames Valley Police in Reading. And, at the risk of telling you how to do your job, I'd advise you to liaise with Mr Crowland directly after we have gone. The reasons for this will become obvious.' Vere paused to let his words sink in, surprised that the sour-faced DI hadn't tried to score a point or two during his introduction. Getting no response, he began talking again.

'However, before Miss Clarkson begins, allow me to provide much-needed background information about myself and Regency Law, the company I work for. And, more importantly, about a young man executed for murder back in nineteen sixty-two. His name was Stephen Drysdale. I, or rather, we,' he smiled at Yvonne, 'would like to bring to your attention certain information regarding the written material that Drysdale put together on the afternoon before his execution. Believe you me, this is the reason we are all here now.' Instant attention, Vere noted, pleased to see the effect of his words.

By four o'clock Robson, recognising that Yvonne was exhausted, send out for coffees all round and offered a ten-minute comfort break as well. Back in session they once again listened to Yvonne's recording of Noakes's dying words that referred to the set of fingerprints taped behind the picture in his office. After a couple more questions Robson picked up her mobile and dialled out, addressing Vere as she did so.

'Just calling the SOCO guys, they'll still be working at the gym.' Seconds later, Vere and Yvonne heard her ask about any framed pictures in the gym.

'No,' Yvonne interrupted her,' not in the gym, it's in the office. Look behind the picture, an old painting of two bare knuckle fighters.' Robson relayed this information to the officers in the gym and, after a short delay, barked out another order.

'Bring that over here immediately. I'm in interview room three.' The 'phone went down sharply onto the table. Robson back on form Vere noted. Taking advantage of the silence, he looked at his watch.

'Now, if you'll permit me to make a 'phone call to my

office, I can get a copy of Drysdale's notes faxed over to you? Would you like me to do that?' Robson thought for all of two seconds.

'Yes, Mr Vere, please make that call.' Vere, slightly surprised by her using the word "please," reached for his mobile, soon speaking with his secretary. Looking down he noticed that the sergeant, anticipating his need for the police station fax number, had already scribbled it down and was in the process of pushing it towards him.

Ten minutes later a police constable handed the faxed copy of Drysdale's notes to Robson, who began reading avidly. Just as she reached the last paragraph another interruption occurred. This time it was a burley sergeant holding a clear plastic wallet containing a white envelope.

'Just arrived at the front desk, Ma'am.' Robson took the awaited delivery and placed it flat on the table. Her attention immediately drawn to the small note attached to it with clear tape. In stunned disbelief she read out the terse message. 'This envelope has on it the fingerprints of the man I knew as Alistair Buchanan. Together we robbed a bank in April 1962, where he shot and killed two people. Signed George Noakes' The silence that followed held everyone spellbound, broken eventually by Robson addressing the sergeant.

'Take this to fingerprints now. Tell them I need to know if any of the prints on this envelope are on file.' As the Sergeant left, Robson almost smiled. 'If they're on file, we've just got ourselves a murderer.'

'Let's hope so,' Vere replied lightly, 'good progress all round. Now, and if you don't mind, Miss Clarkson and I would like to go?' As Robson failed to respond to his request, Vere stood up and helped Yvonne to her feet. 'You okay if we go now?' he repeated. The DI looked a bit vague and began collecting her thoughts.

'Oh, yes. But look, there is something else we need to consider, or should I say contain.' Robson stopped talking as Vere and Yvonne looked down at the thoughtful DI. 'In a word – the media,' she explained to the couple. 'We can't keep the lid on this for much longer. The papers and television will want the story, you know the sort of thing, top fight trainer shot dead in his own gym. It'll certainly be on the television news this evening, and in the papers tomorrow.' Robson looked up and suggested that they sat back down again, which they both did as she continued to speak. 'Right now, I'm proposing that we keep your names out of this, yours in particular,' she nodded to Yvonne.

'Oh,' Yvonne uttered, aware of just how intrusive the press could be.

'I'm scheduling a Press Conference for seven this evening, which I'll keep short. Just give them the basics, describe the killer as best we can. Those chaps in the gym, well they're still there and will not mention your presence at all.' She gave a rare smile. 'They all know just how difficult life will be if they let anything slip. But the press, that can be another problem altogether, just a sniff that a fashion journalist was in the gym and witnessed the whole thing. Well, you won't want that now, will you? Her piercing narrow eyes bored into Yvonne as she considered the prospects.

'No way,' Vere said sharply, answering for her.

'That's good because, without any further leaks or disclosures, the story will die in a day or so. To-day's news is tomorrow's history, that sort of thing. But should they get hold of you,' she warned, 'it'll be like putting petrol on a fire, it'll run and run forever.' Vere nodded and took hold of Yvonne's hand as she remained silent.

'Okay, we've got that. But look, once the media find out that the burnt-out car in Streatley belonged to Yvonne, the press will have a field day. So far Ted Crowland's managed to keep that out of the media but yes, we can see the three-ring circus that'll develop if the press found out Yvonne was in the gym today. Fear not, there'll be no comments from us. So, if that's all? he looked directly at the DI, 'we'll be on our way.' Rising from his chair and helping Yvonne up, he smiled down at Robson who was quick to offer her thanks.

'No, that's fine. But thanks for your help, it's not very often we get so much information. Well, not all in one go, it's usually more akin to pulling teeth.' Vere looked down at the still seated DI, before carefully enquiring.

'Do you reckon this Buchanan chap was behind today's incident gym?'

'Yeah,' the D I said thoughtfully, 'a fair assumption, but knowing our luck we'll just have to wait and see. Oh, and before you ask, my next move is to give DCI Crowland a call in Reading. I'd say there's got to be a fair amount of common ground here. Anyway, bye for now. I'll give you a shout when the statement's ready. I'm guessing you'll want to check it before letting Miss Clarkson anywhere near it,' she smiled, pushing out her hand.

'Count on it,' Vere replied, laughing and taking the offered hand. Minutes later, walking side by side down the corridor Yvonne snuggled up to him.

'I reckon you've just made a conquest there.' She gave a little giggle, nudging an elbow lightly into his ribs.

CHAPTER 37

A SURPRISED TED Crowland took the call from D I Robson shortly after five-thirty, unsure as to why he was being contacted by an officer from another force. 'Look, I'm sorry, but what's this got to with me? he asked Robson.

'Hold on, sir, just bear with me for a few moments then I think you'll understand why it was suggested that I make this call.'

'Go on,' he sighed, 'I'll listen, but this had better be good.' And so, he'd listened, becoming absorbed by hearing about the shooting of a prominent fight trainer in a West London gymnasium. All thoughts of an early evening get-away vanishing as Robson passed on her information. Good job I'd not promised to take Susan out this evening. After fifteen years of marriage, he'd long ago learned that it was always better to surprise her by coming home early, as opposed to making promises and then having to break them. Far better to avoid that difficult telephone call, 'sorry, love - I've got to work late, something's come up. It's just the job, the damned job!'

'Once we'd secured the area,' Robson's voice cutting sharply through his thoughts of domesticity, 'both in the gym and out on the street, we started the interview process. In fact, I believe you know our star attraction? The one person who witnessed everything, a young fashion journalist called Yvonne......'

'Clarkson,' Crowland snapped, 'how did she get in on the act? She lives down this way.'

'As we now know, sir,' Robson acknowledged.

'And works in London,' Crowland added. 'I only met her for the first-time last Thursday, then spent an hour or so with her on Friday. Did she tell you that her car was firebombed just a few miles down the road from here? A total tragedy, an old guy got killed.'

'Yes, we got all that as well, sir,' Robson confirmed. 'But look, I'd only just started to question her when her boyfriend turned up, a solicitor called.....'

'Vere,' Crowland growled, 'what going on over there? I've not heard anything about this at all.'

'No. We've managed to keep it under wraps – well, for a while anyway, sir, as I don't want the Press stealing a march on us, at least not until we've a bit more to go on.'

'Well, that's something, I suppose, but where do we come in? That is apart from the Vere and Clarkson angle?'

'At the moment, the best link we've got for you is from a couple of the lads the gym. They told me Noakes has a son. Said his name was Terry. Mind you, they didn't reckon the two were that close. From Noakes's diary, we've got an address for him in Reading'

'Ah, my turf,' the DCI said.

'Yes, we really need to get to him first, you know, before the media circus gets involved. That's one of the reasons behind this call. I'm wondering if you'd do the honours, sir, break the bad news. Perhaps you could send someone round?'

'Not a problem. Got the address?' Crowland enquired.

'Yes, as I said, Terry's his name and we checked him out. He's got a bit of form. GBH and drug possession, been inside a time or two. I expect he'll be on your list of regulars.' Robson added, hoping the background information might be useful before speaking again. 'So, if you've got a pen handy, I'll read out the address.' Dazed by the information, Crowland wrote down the address, mentally conjuring up a picture of the area. Just off the Oxford Road, busy, thriving and multicultural, home to a few of our *regulars* as well. Smiling, he put down his pen and asked Robson for some help.

'Look, run that lot by me again? I'm bloody well confused. As I said, I only came across Clarkson four days ago. Her car was firebombed right in the middle of a local village, a true-blue Tory enclave, I can tell you.'

'Yes, sir,' Robson acknowledged, wondering by his tone if Crowland regarded the firebombing of cars as being acceptable, but not in safe Conservative strongholds. 'As I said earlier, sir, she told us about that. But hang onto your hat, sir, as Noakes lay dying he confessed to causing it.'

'He did what?' the DCI exclaimed, stunned by the revelation.

'Yes, sir. Clarkson managed to record Noakes's dying words. He even confessed to taking part in an armed bank raid with some chap called Buchanan back in '62, during which two people were murdered.'

'He did what? Oh no,' he moaned, 'I'm more confused than ever.'

'Don't worry, sir, it gets better,' Robson paused, giving Crowland a few seconds to focus on what she was saying. 'We *now* know the person who drove Noakes and Buchanan to that robbery was a young person by the name of Stephen Drysdale. Not much of a get-away driver, crashed the car shortly afterwards, got himself trapped in the wreck and was promptly arrested. Noakes and Buchanan escaped on foot, with around eighty thousand in cash. Drysdale ended up being hanged, the old joint enterprise routine, all in it together. But now, according to Vere, he left a set of notes which have only just come to light.'

'Who left the notes, Noakes?

'No, sir,' Robson said patiently, 'it was Drysdale who left the notes, writing them the day before he was executed. Since then, they've been in Canada for the last fifty years. Then,' she pressed on, 'the notes were finally opened – a few weeks back - by Gerald Lambert in the company of Vere and Clarkson. Back in nineteen sixty-two Lambert was Drysdale's instructing solicitor, eventually going on to become Vere's boss at some outfit called Regency Law. Lambert died the other day, suffered a heart attack after seeing Noakes's damaged hand on television, so Vere reckons.'

'Robson!' Crowland said loudly. 'I'm going dizzy – on information overload. Take me through it again because, right now, you're throwing names at me that are meaningless. So, please, nice and slowly?'

'Yes, sir, I'll do that, right from the moment we got the call from the ambulance people and arrived at the gym.'

As Robson began methodically repeating the day's events Crowland groaned, this is the stuff of nightmares,

Clarkson everywhere, with Vere running a close second. Noakes's taped confession made him ask why an ageing, and much respected fight trainer would want to blow up a fashion journalist's car. Crazy, but at least some parts are starting to become a little clearer. Up until a minute ago all I had was a burnt-out car, a victim, the car's owner Clarkson, and Vere of course. Mustn't forget him, or a Chief Constable terrified that a fire bombing in Streatley signified the end of civilisation as we know it. Then, he wondered, had Clarkson really been smart enough to put two and two together and got anywhere near making four.

CHAPTER 38

AS ROBSON CONTINUED speaking, Crowland found himself thinking about the other man involved, this Buchanan character. Was he still alive and in touch with Noakes? If so, had he encouraged Noakes into taking his ill-advised action with the car? As for Clarkson. Even if she'd had the slightest suspicion of Noakes's involvement, going back to Acton would not have made sense. Surely one dose of that lot was enough. Bravado, stupidity or was she hoping to find out more? Crowland sighed, shuffling the information around in his head. Trying to make feasible connections he addressed the DI.

'So, you finally managed to sit them down. Did you get what you wanted? Is this the full story?' Crowland asked hopefully.

'Yes, sir, I believe so and that's after nearly three hours hammering away here in Acton nick.'

'Let's hope you've got it all because, if what the dying Noakes said is correct, that gives you a link to Buchanan.'

'True enough, sir, and I don't reckon Noakes was going to be telling lies, not with his last few breaths.'

'I guess you're right there,' he acknowledged as another thought crossed his mind. 'Those notes, the ones left by Drysdale, have you seen them?'

'Indeed, yes sir, Mr Vere organised a copy for me. I've got them here and I'll Fax a set across to you.' Robson then explained how Yvonne, after having read Drysdale's notes, reacted when seeing Noakes's damaged hand during a televised boxing match. 'It was the damaged hand that made the connection for her, especially as their friend Lambert had died watching the fight the day before. 'Now,' she continued, 'in answer to your earlier question, we can see no trail back to this Buchanan person. But, as I said a minute ago, having now got those fingerprints we may just get a match from the database.'

'You should be so lucky with that,' Crowland replied, 'fairy stories are for grandchildren, and I haven't got any of those either. Okay, I think we'll wrap this up for now. Meanwhile I'll get someone round to break the news to Terry Noakes,' he told her, pleased to help a colleague. 'No, dash it,' he said forcefully, 'after what you've just told me, I'll go myself. It's the least I can do. Anyway, thanks for your call and let's stay close on this one, as I've absolutely no idea where it's going.'

'Oh, before I go, sir,' Robson said cautiously, 'do you reckon I'm way off track here by thinking that Clarkson and, by implication her solicitor friend, may be in any form of danger? We've checked Noakes's diary. He had an appointment with Clarkson, for one o'clock this lunchtime.' She paused, giving Crowland time to consider this new angle.

'Hard to say,' the DCI commented, 'but, thinking about it, the killer had the perfect opportunity to shoot Clarkson while he was taking care of Noakes. But he didn't. Was that because he didn't need to, or that he wasn't being paid to do it?'

'Valid options I guess, sir, but just for a moment, say the killer was acting on Buchanan's orders? Of course, we have no way of knowing that right now, so just bear with me. The fact that Clarkson's still alive, might that just indicate that Buchanan didn't know about her? Or if he did he didn't rate her as being of any importance?'

'Could be. Anyway, I can see where you're coming from, given that Noakes was the only one shot. Let's assume that Buchanan doesn't see Clarkson and Vere as problems. Or anyone else for that matter. Well, not yet, so we'll keep an open mind on that one. No point in causing unnecessary panic.' Deep in thought he continued by asking Robson if she could give him any assistance with his enquiries into the Streatley murder and firebombing.

'Yes, sir, if I can I most certainly will.'

'Thanks for that,' he paused, 'you see I'm stuck with the problem of finding out exactly how Noakes knew which was Clarkson's car? With around one hundred plus cars parked at Goring station every day, how did he know which one to go for? To the best of my knowledge Clarkson first met Noakes on Tuesday then, on Thursday, her car gets blitzed. I'm puzzled. If you get a minute, might you make enquiries at your end? You know, call in at her office, have a chat with the people she worked with. Anyone been asking questions? Hope I'm not teaching you to suck eggs, but you know the form?'

'No worries there, sir,' Robson agreed, 'I'll have a quick word with my "super" and see if I can get around to those offices first thing in the morning.'

***

Miles Overstone took one look at the screen and broke into a broad smile. The triple X message was unmistakable, his instructions had been carried out. Uncertain as to when Dukes might act, he'd thought that Noakes's one o'clock meeting seemed to offer promise. Yet, that afternoon he had logged onto the BBC News channel on three separate occasions, anxious to see if contained any reported shooting incidents. But nothing! For years he had regularly accessed the BBC's on-line News facility, finding it to be an up-to-the-minute conduit for data: national, international or financial. Yet the absence of any media information coming from Acton had made him wonder if Dukes was working to a different timetable. Almost resigned to waiting, the late arrival of the triple X message had set Overstone's mind at rest. Noakes was now dead, he smiled at the news, now unperturbed by not seeing it as an item on the BBC's website.

***

An hour later, after clearing Heathrow's Long Stay car park, Vere nosed the Jaguar onto the West-bound carriageway of the M4. Upon leaving Acton Police Station their priority had been transport, or, as Vere had so succinctly put it, the lack of it. His Jaguar was at Heathrow, Yvonne's borrowed VW was at Goring Station and his cherished MG remained at Shiplake. Now, with his eyes looking firmly ahead, he slid his left hand across and lightly squeezed the top of Yvonne's nylon covered right thigh.

'No arguing, you're moving into the cottage this evening. Given the sort of day you've had I'm not leaving you on your own tonight?' Despite being exhausted, Yvonne was thrilled to find their recent differences now seemed to be behind them. Time together in the cottage was just what she needed, the squeeze on her thigh sent a pleasant tingle through her body that made her smile.

'Well, at least you didn't say you were going to leave me alone tonight,' she responded impishly.

'Shameless hussy,' Vere laughed, his left hand giving the warm nylon another gentle squeeze.

An hour after clearing Heathrow they were in Goring, having left the motorway at Theale, before driving up through Pangbourne. Moments after turning right in Streatley, Yvonne gave a shudder as they drove over the spot where fire had destroyed her Fiesta just days ago. Vere, detecting the mood change, expressed concern.

'Sorry about that, darling, unthinking of me to come this way. I should have realised.'

'No, don't worry,' Yvonne said tenderly. 'I've got to pick up the car, and besides, I come this way to the station every day, don't I?'

'True,' he conceded the point, as they made their way towards the car park. More ghosts here he thought. With the car park close to being empty spotting the VW was easy. It stood in splendid isolation allowing Vere pull up directly in front of it. For a moment Yvonne baulked at getting out of the car, flooded by an irrational fear that somehow this vehicle might also have received unwelcome attention from the unknown firebomber.

'You okay with this?' he asked, slightly concerned as his companion remained firmly in her seat.

'No, not really. It's silly, given that Noakes is dead but, just for a second, I got that feeling that someone has walked across my grave. Have you ever had that sensation?'

'I think so,' he acknowledged. 'I know what you mean,' he grinned across at Yvonne. 'Look, don't worry. I'll drive the VW and you take the Jaguar. I'll follow you to the garage. We'll leave the car, lock it up, and drop the keys through the letter box.'

'Would you?' Yvonne asked quietly.

'Of course, then we'll head for your place so you can pick up anything you'll need for the next few days. Take five minutes to have a word with Mrs Frobisher, let her know what you're doing. And' he said grinning broadly, 'make sure you bring plenty of lacy underwear.' Vere added the last bit firmly confident that the grin on his face would dispel any lingering tensions. And it worked.

'Oh, you're impossible,' she giggled, 'you've got a one-track mind. Cold shower for you when we get to Shiplake.'

'Ugh' he grimaced, 'come on, let's get cracking. The light will be going soon.'

CHAPTER 39

THE STREET LIGHTS were already on as Baxter parked
the unmarked police car on a side street off the busy Oxford
Road. Earlier, Crowland had spent time bringing him up
to speed following his conversation with DI Robson. Once
over the disappointment of not getting home early to his new
wife, Baxter had settled to the task. Over coffee and canteen
sandwiches the two men had analysed the information,
fitting it together with what they already knew, factoring
the unknown Buchanan into their thinking. While digesting
the information both men had been all too aware of the
unpleasant duty they were about to undertake.

'What do we know about Terry Noakes,' Crowland
asked as Baxter searched for a convenient parking space.

'Not much really, sir. Bit over forty, got a bit of form,
as the Acton DI told you. He's done three terms inside - a
couple of six-month spells, and a two year one for robbery
with violence. Records show that he got out a year or so
back, been clean since then.' Crowland thought about
that for a moment, as Baxter reversed into one of the few
remaining parking spaces.

'Ah, not always as simple as that,' Crowland said, his mind clouded with doubt. 'Does that mean he's really been clean for a year, or that we've just not managed to catch him for a year?' Turning off the ignition, Baxter looked across at Crowland, considering the alternatives.

'There you have me, sir, I don't know. Mind you, Terry's father was a good bloke.'

'Good bloke,' Crowland sniffed, 'that's an understatement if ever I heard one. Look, say Robson's right and I see no reason to doubt her, your "so called good bloke" is a killer and that's without adding Bill Turner to the tally. Choose you words more carefully in future.'

'Yes, sir, I will,' Baxter accepted the rebuke, squirming uncomfortably in his seat as he struggled to find the words to justify his assessment of Noakes. 'What I meant to say was that he's a good trainer, like he's got three British title holders in his stable?'

At first Crowland wasn't surprised by the open hostility Noakes displayed when confronted by the unexpected arrival of two police officers. For Terry, and based upon previous experiences, such events had invariably been the precursor of nasty things to follow. However, once realising that Crowland was not there to feel his collar, he visibly relaxed before reluctantly admitting the two officers into his untidy flat. Dressed in a sloppy roll-neck pullover and torn jeans he flopped down on a weary settee, not bothering to invite his callers to take a seat. Comfortable and controlled in his own environment was how Crowland assessed Terry's demeanour. Staring upwards at the two police officers he waited for them to begin. Crowland, judging any polite and social conversation to be unnecessary, broke the news to Noakes of his father's sudden death. For several seconds Terry remained motionless, before sitting up and acknowledging the news.

'Yeah, dad said something like this might happen,' his words uttered so casually left both officers tongue-tied and rooted to the spot. Never had Crowland, or Baxter for that matter, received such an unemotional response when delivering news of a death. Reporting fatal accidents, or unexpected deaths, to friends and family was bad enough. But having to tell someone that a loved one had been murdered was at the top end of the scale for reactions. But not here.

'Say that again,' the DCI asked, taking an uninvited seat and shocked that Noakes was so unconcerned by the news. Might just as well have told him it's going to rain later, the DCI reflected as he awaited a reply.

'Look,' Noakes said expressively, 'dad and I were never close. Fact is I hadn't seen him for ages. Never came to see me when I was doing time, did he? Mind you, we were just starting to patch things up a bit, I suppose.'

'Well, that was good, wasn't it?' the DCI said, looking carefully at Noakes as barrage of thoughts exploded in his brain. Confused by Terry's bland acceptance of his father's death, Crowland struggled with the obvious. He hasn't asked the one most natural question. How did my father die? Does this mean he already knows? Impossible, there's been a news blackout so was he there? Am I looking at the actual killer? Holding this maelstrom of doubt in check he looked directly into the eyes of the man on the settee before speaking.

'Terry, you'll have guessed that we checked you out before coming here.'

'Well, there's a surprise,' he said sarcastically.

'Okay,' Crowland replied, speaking slowly. 'I appreciate that you and the police have been on opposite sides from time to time. Anyway, I'm not here about that but, believe me, I'm sorry about your father. Anyway, as of now, we need all the help we can get to find out who killed him. Are you up for that?'

'I guess so,' came the lethargic response from the settee.

'Okay, I'll take that as a yes, so when did you last see your father?'

'Last Sunday, coach up to London then a bus across to the old man's flat in Acton, near to his gym. He'd done all right there, training them boxers like. And that health club thing's turned out to be a real winner. What with all those rich geezers, you know paying a fortune to be like Peter Pan, not ever wanting to get old.' Crowland absorbed the information, a little thrown by Terry's variations in diction. One minute he seemed to border on the educated, next managing to sound like a barrow boy.

'Yes, but what did you talk about? What made you say that he thought he might be killed? Why would anybody want to kill your father?' Crowland watched and waited, determined not to let Noakes know what he knew about Drysdale and Buchanan, courtesy of DI Robson. But, for a fact, he knew that Noakes was holding back to protect his position.

'Terry, for God's sake, somebody shot your father!' Crowland blurted out, frustration adding a sharp edge to his words.

'Oh, did they,' Terry nodded nonchalantly. 'Dad said he'd done serious stuff, years ago like with another guy called Buchanan, something about a robbery.' Terry went on as if he had not even heard Crowland's outburst. 'Yeah,' Noakes sighed, 'reckoned something had crawled out the woodwork. Started to spook him after all these years. Didn't say what it was, or that he really knew this Buchanan person, you know the chap what he did the robbery with.' Noakes scratched his ear, looking from Crowland to Baxter and back again. 'Mind you,' he said conspiratorially, 'he did tell me that he wondered if this bloke might be coming after him now. You know like, after all these years. Didn't make sense to me, but that's all I know. Honest, like.' He paused, before starting to speak again, this time a little excitedly. 'Hey, do you reckon it was this Buchanan bloke that did for the old man?'

'Early days, Terry, that's if we can find him because we've next to nothing to go on, no leads at all. But anyway, look we'll get back to you if anything develops. Oh, but look,' Crowland asked, rising from his chair, 'can you tell us where you were around lunchtime today?'

'Cor, that's an easy one,' Terry laughed. 'I was down the Job Centre, had an interview at twelve-thirty with some stroppy bird.' He paused, laughing, 'even had the bleeding nerve to tell me to get a job. Me, with my record! Okay, I manage the odd cash in hand job, here and there, working for builders, labouring like, but nothing permanent.' He laughed again. 'Not something I was going to tell that nosey-bloody-parker about was it?' Crowland caught Baxter's eye, making sure the Sergeant understood that he required confirmation of that meeting first thing in the morning.

***

'Well, we both managed to keep our powder dry,' Crowland said to Baxter as their car pulled away from the kerb. 'Damned if I was going to tell him what we know about Drysdale, Buchanan and the fingerprints. And I certainly wasn't going to tell him about Clarkson and the Streatley firebomb, but I'll bet his old man coughed the lot. Can't see them having had a cosy chat about summer holidays, can you?'

'As if, sir,' Baxter gave a low chuckle as Crowland stretched out comfortably, stifling a yawn before continuing.

'I reckon his dad would have told him everything, saying something like he'd become a marked man. No, that lad's holding back on me. I intend to give his cage a damn good rattle in the next few days. In the meantime, have a scout round, see if Noakes left a will and if that bit of low life back there is in line for anything. What, with the gym and his health club, our George must have been worth a bob or two. Money. Hmm, might just be a motive I suppose, especially if the Job Centre can't confirm his alibi.'

***

Having escorted the officers out of his flat, Terry thought a reward for seeing off the coppers was in order. Walking into his debris-strewn kitchen he opened the 'fridge door, carefully removing a can of beer from the large stockpile. No room in there for food, so thank goodness for take-away meals. Nevertheless, a shame about the old man. He didn't deserve that, memories of their time together last Sunday flooding back.

Unable to find anything resembling a clean glass, he flicked open the ring pull and drew deeply on the chilled liquid. Belching loudly, he ambled back to the front room and flopped onto the settee. Silly old sod, he thought of his father. Fancy him getting into all that mess – an armed bank robbery. He smiled woefully. If they'd caught Dad and then topped him there'd have been no me. So, it's not all bad. "Cheers, Dad," he said loudly, taking another swig of the beer and satisfied with his handling of the police.

'Coppers,' he scoffed, happy not to have told them thing. Let them do their own work. And, as for asking me where I was, do they think I need an alibi? Surely, they don't reckon I did the old man in. That's funny, they'll end up getting that old bag at the Job Centre to confirm where I was at lunchtime today. That'll be the first time she's ever been any bloody use to me. He laughed at his humour, belching loudly while taking comfort from not having revealed his telephone contact method for reaching Buchanan. Okay, the cops know his name, but that's all. Sounds a nasty piece of work but there could be a few quid there if I play my cards right. No. The coppers can go whistle, I'm telling them nothing. He smiled at his own thought process, knowing that police officers no longer had whistles.

Humour quickly faded, as he wondered if the police would find his father's killer. Despite all his faults, the old man didn't deserve that, not just when we were starting to get something going. Anger started to mount inside him as realisation set in. Last Sunday should have been the beginning of a new togetherness – something for which he had hoped. Instead, it was the end. Those few hours in the pub had been smashing. Why couldn't we have had more of them? No. Somebody's going to pay for that he promised himself. If the coppers can't find Buchanan then I will.

CHAPTER 40

'WHO CAN THAT be?' Vere asked, dropping a half-eaten slice of toast as he walked from the kitchen to answer the ringing telephone in the hall. Half past eight in the morning, but at least he's dressed. Yvonne smiled, accepting that his old tracksuit was far more suitable for public display than her nightdress and negligee.

Yesterday, while she'd kept her part of the bargain, Vere had managed to escape the cold shower treatment. Just as well she reflected, looking back on their evening together. An occasion where wine and a leisurely meal had preceded intimate embraces on the settee, later followed by a satisfying retreat upstairs to bed. There, between the sheets, shared intimacy had helped conquer the anxieties of the last few days. Casting those tender memories aside she failed in her attempt to listen to one half of the conversation drifting back from the hallway. Moments later he reappeared in the kitchen, laughing down at her.

'Come on girl, jump to it. That was Ted Crowland on the phone, he and his sergeant are on their way here now. We can't have them seeing you in a state of near undress, make them forget what they came for. End up arresting you for indecent exposure instead.' Still smiling he resumed his seat, picking up the toast he'd discarded in his haste to answer the phone.

'All right, sexist pig,' she giggled, putting down her coffee cup and standing up. 'What about you? Hardly an example of what the well-dressed man about town's wearing. A shave wouldn't come amiss,' she laughed, 'we don't want them mistaking you for the back-end of a badger.' Floating gracefully around the end of the table she laughed, nimbly sidestepping to avoid the flat of Vere's hand as it swung playfully towards her curvaceous and silky rear end. Turning to face him, she stopped laughing and became practical.

'Okay, but seriously we've got to start thinking about this afternoon, you know, Gerald's funeral.'

***

Following the arrival of the police officers Yvonne headed for the kitchen as Vere directed Crowland and Baxter through into the lounge. Vere settled on the settee as the visitors took the armchairs. Idle conversation followed for a short while before Yvonne reappeared with coffees all round.

'Right,' Crowland began once everyone had settled. 'I had a conversation with DI Robson from Acton Police, late on Tuesday afternoon. She put me in the picture regarding her take on the incident at Noakes's gymnasium. Hopefully, with every detail included.' Staring hard at Vere, his next words left the couple on the settee in no doubt as to the purpose of his visit. 'Mr Vere, I'm sure I don't need to remind you, of all people, how seriously we take the withholding of evidence?'

'Of course not,' he replied sharply, looking the DCI straight in the eye. 'As far as Yvonne and I are concerned, the statement we made to your colleague in Acton was the full and frank containment of all our knowledge. Isn't that so, darling?'

'Of course,' she agreed. 'It's absolutely true in every detail, nothing's been left out, I can assure you.' Leaning forward to pick up her coffee cup she looked directly into Crowland's eyes, as if challenging him.

'Thank goodness for that,' he smiled, visibly relaxing. 'Sorry to sound a bit heavy handed, but I had to be certain because I think we're playing for bigger stakes.'

'What do you mean?' Yvonne snapped angrily, 'bigger than an old chap burnt to death in my car, plus a cold-blooded shooting?'

'Hold on,' Crowland replied, taken aback by Yvonne's outburst. 'Yes, tragically, we know all about those, but here's something you don't know. Noakes had a son, Terry and he lives in Reading and, so I'm told, they've been estranged for years, and they'd only just started talking to one another again.'

A silence fell over the room, but the pair on the settee knew there was more to come. 'Baxter and I,' he nodded to his sergeant, 'went to visit him late on Tuesday evening, to break the news about his father. His reaction, or lack of it, was startling. He simply told us that his father had mentioned that something like that might happen.' Vere remained tight lipped, as Crowland looked from one to the other.

'Oh, that's dreadful.' Yvonne spoke quietly, remembering her late father with great affection as Vere, after a pause, enquired thoughtfully.

'As Yvonne says, that's dreadful, but where do we fit in?' Crowland considered the question for a moment before admitting to a degree of uncertainty.

'I'm not sure, that's the problem. Our best guess, Robson's and mine that is, centres around the assumption that it was the unknown Buchanan who killed Noakes. Or, alternatively, did he hire someone to do the job for him? But, then again,' he paused, looking directly at Yvonne, 'despite having had the opportunity to shoot you, over at the gym, the killer chose to ignore you.'

'Small mercies,' Yvonne responded, 'all right he didn't kill me, thank goodness. But who knows what he might have done, had it not been for that big heavyweight charging into him?'

'As you say, thank goodness, and that's absolutely correct. No doubt about it, that big bloke saw off the killer and saved the day. Now, with Noakes confessing to trying to kill you with the firebombing, the man sent to kill Noakes ignores you. Why?'

'Surely that confirms the obvious,' Vere pointed out before Yvonne could get a word in. 'Noakes and Buchanan were not acting in harmony. While one saw Yvonne as a threat,' he turned slightly and patted her knee, 'the other clearly did not.'

'I can only agree with you since I believe that Noakes regarded Yvonne as far more of a threat than Buchanan ever did.' Crowland looked thoughtful before continuing. 'To that extent, I hope this Buchanan now regards any trail back to him as being well and truly closed off.'

'So there,' Vere added, 'you don't think we're on his hit list then?'

'Probably not,' Crowland responded carefully, 'but don't go taking any stupid risks. Particularly you, young lady,' he said, wagging a parental finger in Yvonne's direction.

'Have no fear there,' she said, affectionately catching Vere's eye. 'Tuesday took care of that,' she grinned, 'from now on it's the quiet life for me. from now on.'

'Good for you,' Crowland smiled back, 'and make sure you stay that way.' Yvonne nodded in response as the sound of a mobile phone took priority. 'Now, if you'll excuse me,' the DCI said, standing up and pulling the phone from his inside jacket pocket, 'I'll take this out in the hallway.'

Two minutes later he returned and resumed his place. 'That,' he looked at Yvonne, 'was DI Robson, tells me she's been busy talking to people in your office.' Yvonne cringed inwardly at the prospect. Dear Lord, she sighed, Detective Inspector Robson stomping around in the delicate world of a fashion magazine office! Instantly visions of the proverbial bull in a china shop flashed through her mind.

'I suggested that she made the visit,' Crowland looked across at the clearly puzzled Yvonne, 'for one reason only. Simply put, we have no idea how Noakes identified the Fiesta as being yours. That's been troubling me all along. How could he have known which car to attach his device to? Where did he get that information?' he asked looking directly at Yvonne.

'Hey,' she challenged, 'don't go looking at me,' she replied defensively. 'I've not got the faintest idea how he knew which car was mine. Unless he'd been following me,' she added as an afterthought.

'No, I can't see that being likely,' Vere suggested, 'knowing how you only met Noakes two days prior to the car fire.'

'Alright then,' Yvonne reacted, turning to face Crowland, 'did DI Robson find anything out? Did she get anything out of my people?' Yvonne probed, almost fearful of getting a reply. In response the DCI fiddled with his tie before casually firing off a question to Yvonne.

'Who's Wayne?'

'Wayne?' Yvonne asked, momentarily confused. 'Oh, he's one of the office juniors, we've got two of them.' Yvonne gave the information easily, before having a sudden thought. 'Oh, my goodness, what's the little prawn been up to? He's a seventeen- year-old youth. He drools over me. Oh, I don't know he's harmless enough, could even be he fantasises that he's in love with me.'

'Hey, that's my job,' Vere chipped in lightly, causing Crowland to laugh.

'Oh, so it's just a fantasy is it? Yvonne laughed along with Crowland.

'Okay, you two' the DCI responded jocularly, 'knock it off, I'm not here to sort out a domestic. But seriously, getting back to Wayne, by all accounts he's harmless in one sense, and dangerous in another.' He made this observation before explaining that Wayne, under questioning from D I Robson had broken down, admitting to talking to a stranger about Yvonne, and to passing over the information about her car.

'We know Wayne and this guy had a chat the other evening in a nearby pub, a place where they get a fair bit of trouble, so loads of CCTV. Wayne's watching the pictures now. Also, according to Robson, Wayne's being most helpful.' Yvonne shuddered at the thought of Wayne and Robson together. More images sprang into her mind.

A virgin on a troopship would stand a better chance, she reflected crudely.

'However, on the bright side,' Crowland continued, 'if your friend Wayne can possibly identify the chap who contacted him, it might give us a bit more to go on.' In the ensuing silence, Yvonne arrested her wandering mind and squeezed Vere's hand.

'Mr Crowland,' she spoke slowly, looking directly at the detective. 'A minute ago, you intimated that Noakes's killer might have been Buchanan himself. Sorry, but I think you're off-course with that one.'

'And why would that be?' he asked, clasping his hands.

'Don't forget I was there! You see, there's no way the killer could have been Buchanan,' she stated firmly, 'so, allow me to explain my thinking. If I'm right, this Buchanan must at least be in his mid-seventies by now. You agree?'

'Well yes,' he responded, 'based upon what Noakes confessed to you in the gym, along with Drysdale's notes saying the two guys with him were of a similar age. Yes, mid-seventies would seem to be about right. Why?'

'Okay,' Yvonne continued, 'well, if that's the case there's no way that a person of that age could have moved so fast, recovering as quickly as he did after that big guy charged into him from behind. Not to mention being able to duck to waist-height to avoid a wicked looking punch. No! Sorry, but that could not have been Buchanan.'

'Yet,' Crowland smiled, 'I read that a number of medical people are now of the opinion that being seventy is today's equivalent being fifty,' he remarked, trying to look serious.

'No. To my mind whoever shot Noakes had to be a very much younger person. But should it turn out to be

Buchanan, let me know what he drinks as I could do with a glass or two of that stuff myself.' Her jovial comment, made under such serious circumstances, produced a chuckle from Baxter

'Okay, Yvonne. If it wasn't Buchanan, who was it then?' Crowland teased.

'No way, that's as far as I go.' she laughed, 'that's your job, not mine.'

CHAPTER 41

TWENTY MINUTES LATER, as Crowland and Baxter were saying their farewells the senior man called out over his shoulder. 'Take care and the pair of you stay out of trouble. Oh, and I hope everything goes all right this afternoon at your friend's funeral.'

'Yes, thank you, they're never easy,' Vere acknowledged as he and Yvonne stood next to one another in the cottage doorway. Turning on his heel Vere was about to usher Yvonne back inside when the sound of a ringing mobile phone cut through the still air. In a silent tableau three people stood motionless, all watching as Baxter fumbled inside his jacket to respond to the familiar ringtone. The ensuing conversation, such as it was, lasted for all of ten seconds, after which the police officers held a short conversation across the roof of their car. Yvonne and Vere watched in silent fascination, unable to hear what was being said. Returning the phone to his pocket Baxter opened the driver's door and prepared to get in as the DCI made his way back to the watching couple in the doorway.

'That call,' he said, nodding towards the car, 'was from the Acton fingerprint people. You remember the envelope they recovered from Noakes's gym?'

'Yes,' the couple answered in unison.

'Sadly, the fingerprints don't match anything on the national database.'

'No further forward then?' Vere commented, disappointment in his voice, 'I know, but D I Robson was hopeful.'

'What,' Crowland said quickly. 'With our luck if we had a bloody goldfish it'd drown,' he spoke sharply, 'whoever Buchanan is we're none the wiser. As I said, I'll keep in touch,' his voice lacking enthusiasm. Seconds later he joined his sergeant in the car, muttering quietly. 'More dead ends than Hampton Court fucking maze.'

'Sorry, sir, 'did you say something?'

'No, just thinking aloud,' he answered.

***

For Terry Noakes Wednesday had been a day of remorse and anger, making him continually plunder the contents of his fridge. By late afternoon, his alcohol intake had finally transported him into a drink-sodden sleep. Next morning, and badly hung over, it was the thought of picking up easy money that sloshed around in his befuddled brain. Like any seasoned drinker he subscribed to the "hair of the dog" theory, making him return to his fridge in the hope of finding relief. Peering into the near-empty space the angrier he became, mentally adding revenge to the money he felt entitled to collect from his father's killer.

Despite emotional attachments to his father having been on the thin side of slim he felt cheated and denied any chance of reconciliation. I don't give a toss what he did all those years ago, he didn't deserve to die now. So, just who is this Buchanan anyway? What right did he have to kill my old man? Just as sand, agitated inside an oyster, can become a pearl, the anger inside Noakes hardened off and, by late morning, was demanding retribution. No, Mr Buchanan you've gone too far. I'll have you for this.

The sudden urge for action became overwhelming. Fully motivated, he kicked on a well-worn pair of trainers and struggled into a grubby jacket, complete with hood. Before reaching the door he picked up an old envelope and a biro, ready to find a 'phone box and make a note of the number. This, he remembered, was the first part of the routine outlined to him last Sunday by his father. Get a phone box number – leave a message with the solicitors – wait for Buchanan to ring back on that number. Simple, what could be easier? Then I'll have him, stuff going to the coppers, this one's mine. And he's going to bloody well pay, he repeatedly told himself. Buoyed up by alcohol, and in the belief that he had right on his side, he tottered into the street.

On unsteady legs he headed towards the Oxford Road, certain of finding a phone box somewhere along the busy thoroughfare. Hope it's not been vandalised he muttered, continuing his short journey and shunned by other pedestrians. To them he was another piece of unshaven flotsam. Consumed by hatred he remained unaware he was about to invoke the law of unintended consequences. As for warning people to be careful of what they wished for, well that wasn't on his list either.

***

By the time they arrived back at Castle Street Police station, Crowland's mood had not improved. Irritably, he listened as the duty sergeant relayed a message.

'A DI Robson, said she'd like a word, sir. when you have a minute. Said it wasn't urgent, or she'd have called you on the mobile.'

'Thanks sergeant, I'll get onto it now.' He acknowledged the message, wondering why Robson wanted to speak with him again so soon. At that moment Baxter appeared and, when advised of Robson's call, he looked hopefully at his DCI.

'Hope she's got something useful this time,' Crowland growled. 'Grab two coffees and join me in the office.' Minutes later, settled behind his desk he used Robson's direct line and quickly reached the D I.

'Thanks for calling back, sir. I've got more info, but it doesn't get us far, I'm afraid.'

'Come on, Robson,' he said gloomily, 'tell me your worst,' painfully aware that this was not going to be a good news call?

'Well, as I said earlier, sir, that Wayne is a spineless little dick. He's head-over-heels in love with Clarkson, from a distance of course.' Crowland listened, thinking there was a sentiment to which he could relate. Patiently he waited for more. 'We've had Wayne watching the CCTV recordings. After a bit of shuffling about they got the right pictures, showing Wayne chatting with one of our known regulars, Lefty Archer. He's about thirty-five, an old boxer hence the handle. He's got form. The usual stuff, burglary, car theft, deception and caught with stolen goods. All minor league, been up in court and sent down three times. Sadly, he's one of life's losers.'

'Okay, but where is this going, Robson?'

'Sorry, sir, but a bit of probing showed us that Archer regularly spends time helping out in Noakes's gym.'

'Ah, I see,' Crowland replied. Looking up, he smiled as Baxter entered the office, complete with coffees. 'So, it's a fair bet to say that this Archer chap functioned as Noakes's leg man? Doing the follow-ups on Clarkson and checking things out. Would that be your take on things?'

'Yes sir, as sure as we can be that is. Wayne says it was the same man who phoned him on Wednesday morning. The one to whom he gave Clarkson's car details. Also, as a final check, I showed Archer's picture to the girl on reception at Clarkson's office. She's a smart one, recognised Archer straight away. Said she remembered him coming in and asking about a Mrs Clarkson, or a Miss Drysdale. Did either of them work there? She thought it was a bit odd.'

'Thanks, Robson, you've done well. I'll leave you to have a chat with this Archer chap, and make sure he's not been hawking Clarkson's details all over the parish.'

'Will do, and I'll get back to you, sir,' she said before disconnecting. Crowland replaced the telephone and looked despondently across at his sergeant.

'Yet another dead end,' he sighed. 'Alright, so we now know how Noakes identified Clarkson's car, but we're still no closer to finding Buchanan.'

CHAPTER 42

ALISTAIR BUCHANAN, ALIAS Miles Overstone, the focus of Terry Noakes's burning hatred, looked out across the splendour of the revitalised Docklands and marvelled at what he saw. Long gone were the ships of a thousand nations, the nautical legions that had brought commerce to England from the far corners of the world. Gone too were the sweating stevedores, the fussy hooting tugboats and the cranes that had lined Hayes Wharf on the approach to Tower Bridge. The very cranes he recalled dipping so solemnly over the motor launch *'Havengore,'* as it had carried the body of the late Sir Winston Churchill on his last journey across the river. Recalling a cold and blustery Saturday in 1965 that had marked the passing of a great political leader. Had it also marked the ending of an era, the day when post war blues gave way to the swinging sixties?

What had once been a thriving centre for international shipping had transitioned into the centre of new money. Here, and fathered by the advent of global computerisation, banking and share dealing had changed overnight. Gone were cheque books and banker's draughts, replaced by plastic cards and flashing screens as money now circulated the world in milli-seconds. And it all stemmed from here he thought, the financial centre where the knowledgeably brave could make fortunes just as quickly as their reckless counterparts could lose them. Not for me, those risks, Overstone mumbled. While it's good to be greedy, only when you know how to control greed can it become an asset.

Not long now, a week on Monday and I'll be away free. But, even after my departure, life will go on. Why should what I've built up go to waste? Of course, once that bank discovers they've been well and truly stuffed all hell will break lose. Overnight, I'll become public enemy number one. Well, for a while anyway. Then again, as banks hate bad publicity might they simply keep any fuss to a minimum?

Memories are short but I'm sure the banks will sell off my tangible assets slake the public thirst for revenge. My Wallingford home will fetch a fair bit, as will this office block. Yet, in the grand scheme of things, they are just loose change. Okay, my staff may have a rough ride once I've gone, a number may even face charges of guilt-by-association or, worse still, be prosecuted under the old joint enterprise banner. That all-encompassing swipe of justice that did for Drysdale, but now nowhere near so terminal. Ah well, let them worry because I'm about to activate a little more of my exit-strategy. Reaching for his mobile phone he knew it was time to let his faithful second-in-command know that his long overdue promotion had arrived. And, with that elevation, will come the responsibility of heading up my entire operation while I adjust to a perfect life of wealth and luxury in Panama.

'Hello, Bernard,' he began, 'we need to be seeing each other very soon as I'm in need of your help. Oh, and I've also got good news for you,' he said encouragingly. Yet, even as he spoke to Nolan, a scruffy forty-year-old man in a Reading phone box, and reeking of stale beer, was about to spoil his best laid plans.

***

Sergeant Baxter clattered excitedly into DCI Crowland's Castle Street office without bothering to knock. 'Hey Gov,' he called out, 'I've been through the custody suite, just to see who the boys pulled in last night. Guess whose name I came across?'

'Go on, surprise me?' Crowland growled and looked up, distracted from a report he was considering. 'And one day you might even remember to knock, now that'd be something.'

'Sorry, Gov, but I thought you'd like to know. The boys on duty last night pulled in Terry Noakes,' Baxter informed his superior. 'It's right there in the charge book, blind drunk and causing a disturbance down near St Mary's Butts.'

'Now, why doesn't that surprise me, sergeant?'

'Well, okay, he's running true to form, hauled in around midnight and bad-mouthing the police,' Baxter concluded.

'As you say, true to form. Be honest, he's hardly what you'd call a loyal supporter of the constabulary, is he?' Crowland offered sarcastically.

'Yes, but he wasn't just vilifying the police in general, you know the usual bilge, speeding fines, parking and harassment. No, he was far more specific, banging on about the shooting of his dad. Saying that we'd never catch Buchanan, the chap who organised the killing. He'd built up quite a fan club in the tap room before the landlord had him chucked out, bemoaning his lot and blaming us for everything.'

'Ah yes, quite the little conversationalist is our, Terry.'

'Not this morning, Gov. He'll have a head like a bucket. Had a right skin full, serves him right,' the sergeant said, his words devoid of any sympathy.

'Okay then,' Crowland frowned as he considered the information, 'time for that action I mentioned. Now, sergeant!'

'Hang on, Gov,' he replied, shocked at the change in his boss's manner, 'what's got into you suddenly, sir?'

'Chop-chop, sergeant, this could be our big moment.'

'How do you mean, sir?' Baxter looked sceptical, deep creases lining his face.

'Get back down and see the Custody Sergeant, right now! Hopefully, he's a friend of yours. Tell him I want Noakes held for a few more hours. No court appearances and not soft-hearted duty solicitor is to get near him. Understood?"

'Yes, sir, but what about his rights………?'

'Sergeant,' Crowland snapped angrily, 'right now I don't give a bugger

about his rights. Make up any excuse you like. Get him full of black coffee because I want him sobered up. Any problems refer them to me. I told you the other night that I'd give his cage a jolly good rattle and,' he paused, 'I reckon this could be as good a time as any.'

'Sir,' Baxter concurred, still unsure what his chief had in mind.

'This couldn't be better, I know very well that he's holding back on us, and this time we're fighting in our own backyard. And I'm in the mood for shock tactics.' Crowland slapped the desk to emphasis his point.

'On my way, Gov,' Baxter called as he left the office, with his DCI deep in thought. Minutes later, Crowland arrived at a decision and reached to pick up his mobile phone.

***

'You know,' Vere said thoughtfully over a late breakfast, 'aren't funerals meant to be about closure, you know, celebrating the deceased's life, giving comfort to those left behind and moving on? Yet, I don't know,' he commented, rubbing the back of a hand across the stubble on his chin, 'somehow that lot yesterday missed me completely. It was far too stage managed, not the respectful formality that Gerald deserved. Oh,' he let out a gentle sigh, 'I don't know, he was worth more than that.'

'You and me alike,' Yvonne confirmed thoughtfully across the cluttered table, her face pale and without makeup, 'but, on the plus side yesterday's service was, as they say, well attended.'

'True,' he remarked, thinking back to the previous afternoon's events, 'what's euphemistically referred to as a good turnout. The great and the good were on parade, which I guess is what Gerald would have wanted, but I thought the speakers were poor. Okay, they might have given the relevant facts, but there was no passion there, not one of them got down to the real man. You understand what I'm trying to say?'

CHAPTER 43

SARAH LAMBERT HAD arranged for Gerald's funeral service to take place at Saint Mary's Church close by Henley bridge at two in the afternoon. Knowing how parking space near the church would be at a premium, Vere had arranged for an old rowing contact to reserve space for his Jaguar on the far side of the river. 'What are friends for?' he had informed Yvonne, as they'd driven along the tarmac roadway by the entrance to Leander Club. In another fifty yards he'd spotted a "Reserved for Mr Vere" notice nailed to a post on the nearby grassy area. From there it had been a short walk over the bridge, then up the steps by the Red Lion Hotel before taking the stone-flagged pathway beside the church around to the main entrance.

Sarah had explained that the Henley service was to allow all of Gerald's local friends, associates and Masonic brethren to say their farewells before a private cremation in Reading. Further to that, in a month's time, a memorial service was to be held at All Souls Church in Langham Place, close by the BBC buildings and near the Cavendish Square offices of Regency Law.

All-in-all, perfect arrangements Vere had to agree, perfect to mark the passing of someone who had been such an influence on his life. Sarah had organised a post funeral reception at Phyllis Court, the country club on the Marlow Road just outside Henley. A gathering that all those eager to share treasured memories of Gerald had found comforting.

After an hour or so the young couple had discreetly slipped away, passing through large French windows onto a well-manicured lawn that had led down to the riverbank.

'Good job it's been dry,' Yvonne had commented, 'otherwise these heels would have been lost from sight by now.'

'True,' he had agreed casually, as they had reached the awnings covering the terraced riverbank. In front of them, and stretching away to their left, twin floating wooden booms spaced sixty feet apart marked out the Regatta course. At the far end they had seen Temple Island and the small white building with its domed cupola glinting in the sunshine. Like the carved figurehead on an old ship, the building stared straight up the course towards Henley, just under a mile and a half away. Vere, pausing, had then hugged Yvonne, kissing her gently on the cheek.

'This is where we met. Do you remember?'

'As if I'd forget,' she had replied, hugging his waist. 'Let's walk down that way a little, towards that small bridge,' she'd suggested.

'Ah, you mean the hole in the wall.'

'What's that?' she had enquired.

'You see,' he had explained, 'a stream runs out of there, through a small opening in the brick lined riverbank. Racing crews, out there,' he had pointed to the middle of the river, 'use it as a marker. When they see that opening, what they call the hole in the wall, they know they're near the end of the race. Time to wind it up for the big finish.' He had then smiled at her, happy to explain the 'technicalities' of racing to Yvonne who had listened patiently, still not able to understand the logic of being in a race that involved facing the wrong way!

***

'Come on,' Yvonne said, finishing off her toast. Memories of yesterday fading fast. 'We've both been through a rough patch lately, but at least we've got a few days to recover. Let's be positive. How about a drive out, stop off for a pub lunch somewhere?' she suggested.

'Yeah, could do, I suppose,' he answered, showing little enthusiasm for her idea and, about to say more, the telephone ringing out in the hallway demanded attention before he heard a familiar voice on the line.

'Mr Vere, Ted Crowland here. Hope I'm not interrupting anything?' Assuring the police officer that his call was neither unwelcome nor untimely, Vere listened intently to what the DCI was suggesting.

'No, I don't think what you are proposing is wrong, a little close to the outer limits, but who's arguing? In fact,' he continued, 'as you're not charging Noakes with anything he is, as you say, helping with your enquiries. What he knows, and how far he'll go, well that's another matter entirely.'

Grateful for Vere's confirmation the DCI expressed his thanks before suggesting they meet in a couple of hours to discuss tactics. Minutes later they had settled upon a riverside hotel at nearby Sonning, for lunch around noon. Replacing the receiver, he returned to the kitchen.

'Come on then,' he spoke to the still seated Yvonne, 'posh frock job, Ted Crowland's buying us lunch.'

'Oh, that'll be nice,' she smiled before another thought occurred to her. 'Hold on, you of all people should know there's no such thing as a free lunch?.'

'Funny you should mention that' he replied, smiling for the first time that day.

CHAPTER 44

SHORTLY AFTER TWO o'clock Terry Noakes, still the worse for wear, swore loudly as two police officers led him from the Castle Street cells and into an interview room. Already seated, when he entered, were DCI Crowland and Sergeant Baxter. Sitting beside them was a solidly built, smartly dressed dark haired man in his early thirties.

'Sit down, Terry,' the DCI began conversationally; 'relax, you're not facing any charges, indeed, you're free to go. But, before you walk out of here, we could do with your help.'

'Hah...that's rich, me helping the coppers,' he scowled. 'Who's he then?' Noakes gave a surly nod in Vere's direction. 'Another copper I suppose?'

'No, Terry. Mr Vere is not a police officer. In fact, he's a solicitor,' Crowland informed him.

'Huh, don't be silly. You say I've done nothing wrong so why do I need a bleeding solicitor?'

'Indeed, you don't,' Vere responded, leaning across the table and extending his hand, a gesture ignored by Noakes. 'Look,' he continued, undaunted by the rebuttal. 'I'm sorry to hear about your dad, as I know the DCI is as well,' he nodded towards the police officer. 'He's just as anxious as you are to see the killer brought to book. Yes,' he waved his hand to cut short what looked like being a snarled insult from Noakes. 'The police have told me how your dad was involved with a fair bit of criminal activity years ago. And, for a fact, they know he was working with someone called Buchanan.'

'That's right,' Noakes admitted, feeling the need to say something. 'Dad told me that, said he was the bastard that did the shooting, all those years ago. All my old man ever did was to pick up the bags of money, like.'

'Quite so,' Crowland cut in, not prepared to argue the finer points of stealing bags of money from beside dead bodies. Falling silent he waited as Vere sought another approach that might appease the disgruntled Noakes.

'Of course,' he began, 'we all want to get hold of Buchanan but look, before we go any further, why don't you just sit back while the DCI here tells you what he knows so far?'

Fifteen minutes Crowland stopped talking, having presented Noakes with a detailed overview of the evidence they had gathered so far, including the notes left by Drysdale. Crowland also informed Noakes that they now had a set of Buchanan's fingerprints, while explaining exactly how Yvonne Clarkson had managed to locate his father and introduce the name of Drysdale into their conversation.

'As you now know,' Crowland continued quietly. 'Stephen Drysdale was the young man who drove Buchanan and your dad to that robbery. He crashed the car during the getaway and then, trapped in the wreckage, the police arrested him and later charged him for his part in the enterprise. For Drysdale this led to a trial, a death sentence and summary execution. Did you know any of that?'

'No!' Terry lied forcefully. 'Dad told me about the robbery, but honest, I knew nothing about some guy getting hanged.'

'Well, whatever,' the DCI acknowledged, certain that Noakes was lying continued. 'Anyway, the long and short of it is this. Your father had Yvonne followed by one of the hangers-on in the gym, a person called Archer. We also know that Archer managed to coerce a young employee called Wayne, the junior in Yvonne's office, into passing on information that resulted in the firebomb. Yes!' He said emphatically, 'we know that your father fixed an explosive device to Yvonne's car! Did you know that?'

'Course not!' Noakes stared defiantly back at the DCI, refusing to let himself become flummoxed. 'What do you mean, firebombed? For God's sake, he was bloody fight trainer.' Crowland, undaunted by Noakes's refusal to accept the truth, remained silent as his information penetrated Noakes's addled brain. Seizing the moment, he pressed home his advantage. 'In fact, Terry, it's our firm belief that your dad managed to contact Buchanan, after all these years before the attack on Clarkson's car. How did he do that, Terry?' the DCI asked. 'Did he tell you that he'd done that?'

'No. Course not! It was days later that I saw my dad, last Sunday to be exact.' Terry became flustered by Crowland's persistence, along with his change of attitude.

'And you know,' Crowland barked across at the badly troubled Noakes, 'an innocent old-aged pensioner died in that fire!' He slammed his fist on the table. 'Now, come on, tell me what you know!'

'No, that weren't meant to happen – not that old boy,' he stammered.

'So, you did know about the car catching fire?' Crowland pounced, knowing that his persistence had forced Noakes into a partial admission.

'No, that weren't meant to happen,' he said again.

'Damned right it wasn't!' Crowland snapped back, before continuing in a softer tone. 'So, Terry, now let me show you something that *was* meant to happen,' he said quietly, pushing a button under the table. Seconds later a uniformed WPC entered the room. After the briefest of nods to the DCI she picked up a chair which she then carried across and set down beside Vere before leaving the room. Seconds later Yvonne appeared in the doorway, all eyes watching as she came in and sat in the vacant chair. Poised and perfectly composed, she looked slowly from face to face before her unblinking eyes finally settled on the decidedly agitated Noakes.

'Well now, a bit of skirt,' he blustered, 'the day just gets better. Who is she then?' Noakes asked with forced bravado, ever fearful that this was another attempt to wrong foot him.

'This bit of skirt,' Crowland's voice was icy, 'as you so crudely put it, is the young lady your father deliberately set out to murder! This is Yvonne Clarkson.' Ashen faced, Terry Noakes looked across at Yvonne. His mouth opening and closing but no words came out as Yvonne maintained her demeanour, silent, aloof and distant. Finally, Noakes managed to speak but not the words those present had hoped to hear.

'So, you're the meddlesome bitch that panicked my old man, getting him shot. Thanks' a bunch lady! I really owe you.'

'Sergeant,' Crowland roared in anger, jumping up from his chair. 'Get this piece of pond life out of here before I spoil my manners.'

'Sir,' Baxter snapped back, standing up and walking around behind Noakes. 'Come on you, shift yourself,' he shouted, pulling the surprised Noakes none too gently from his chair. Then, as the duo reached the doorway, Noakes turned to look dispassionately at Yvonne.

'Sorry, miss, but if you'd been dead, I'd still have a father.'

'Out,' Crowland shouted in rage as his plan to get Noakes to say more disintegrated in front of him. Baxter, obeying Crowland's order, bundled Noakes unceremoniously down a long corridor. Feeling awful, and on unsteady legs, he tried to cheer himself up with the knowledge that the police had got nothing from him. Help the coppers? Over my dead body! Huh, that's not so funny. I feel half dead now. Stumbling slightly, a thought came to him. I have an advantage over the police. Okay, so the coppers want this Buchanan chap, but they don't know how to reach him. But I do. Should the police find him first a daft old judge will sentence him to three square meals a day and colour television. But he'll still be alive, not dead like my poor old dad.

Shoved along by an uncaring Baxter, Noakes's befuddled brain continued to gnaw away at the possibility of turning this mess into a financial advantage. Okay, the police want Buchanan found, charged and jailed. That's understandable yet, for Buchanan, the opposite must hold good. His need to stay clear of the law must be all consuming. Indeed, paramount and something that must have financial value.

Okay, he grinned at Baxter, the first thing I do now is to get Buchanan on the phone and name my price.

***

Determined to put his masterplan into action Terry Noakes returned to his flat bursting with aggression. Hungry for revenge he could hardly wait to begin his quest, having already decided on the amount of money he was going to screw out of Buchanan. Compensation, he chewed on the word, mentally seeing it in terms of a double reward. Money for the loss of my dad, and even more money for my on-going silence.

Within minutes of entering his flat he was on the move again, making a return visit to the telephone box on the nearby Oxford Road. Eager to contact

the solicitors, on the number his father had given him, he was ready to contact Buchanan. Excited by his own boldness it was only a matter of minutes before his plan began to unravel. Upon reaching his chosen phone box he saw how the confined space was occupied by two teenage girls giggling nonsensically. For Noakes annoyance turned to frustration since the girls were showing no inclination to finish their call. Scowling through the glass he mouthed comments to show his impatience before tapping angrily on the scratched panes. Shortly, the door was pushed slightly open by a girl with bright red hair, too much make up and a low-cut blouse who shouted out at him. 'Piss off.' Job done, she let the door close to resume her gyrations and shouting.

Noakes, inwardly fuming, knew that were he to stay there any longer he would cause trouble. So, determined not to end up back at the police station, he walked away. No point in doing anything silly over a pair of slappers, planning their next drug crazed orgy he muttered, moving further away along the pavement.

Ten minutes later he returned, thankfully finding the phone box empty but reeking of cheap perfume. No matter, at least that's overcome the more lavatorial stink so often associated with such public facilities. After fumbling with his piece of paper and loose coins he steeled himself to dial the number, primed to set the contact procedure into action. Seconds later the line clicked a couple of times before a taped message began playing.

'While we welcome your call our offices are now closed for the weekend. We will reopen at nine-thirty on Monday morning, when we shall look forward to taking your call. Thank you for calling our offices. Have a nice weekend.'

Noakes stumbled out of the phone box, shimmering with rage. Have a nice weekend, he spluttered. Here am I, moments away from a huge payday, and those idle sods have closed for the weekend. Stepping away he looked at his watch, five past five.

CHAPTER 45

OVER THE WEEKEND Vere, and particularly Yvonne, had managed to unwind after the tensions of the Noakes interview. During this quietly fulfilling break they had managed to review recent events, each giving thought to their future. A future they had felt even more confident to face given that Crowland now considered that Buchanan had no further interest in them.

'Well,' he had said thoughtfully, relaxing beside Yvonne on the sofa. 'Whoever Buchanan is, it now looks as if he's away free. Crowland's no idea where to find him. And' as he had slid his arm around Yvonne's shoulders, 'he can't be interested in us.'

'I guess you're right,' she had whispered, snuggling closer, welcoming the strength of his encircling arm. They had both been thrilled to find that their emotional attachments, having survived the upheaval of the last few days, were stronger than ever. Now they simply felt an unspoken desire just to get back to their normal routines, agreeing that these provided the right balance between work and leisure. For Yvonne, her working week might well include attending fashion shows, both at home and abroad.

Add to that magazine functions, lunch with an editor now and again and being present at countless photo shoots. Overall, she had a demanding routine, and that's without going into the office to draft out those endless articles. Mustn't forget the articles she told herself.

Vere's working life was far more predictable. The daily commute, office work, client meetings in and around central London, court appearances and infrequent prison visits. When working the occasional late night, a nearby hotel offered convenient accommodation. Whilst this freedom of movement suited both parties, Yvonne was aware that it could not last indefinitely. Ever practical she knew it was only a matter of time before a permanent move to the cottage loomed large on her horizon. Now, there's a thought, she smiled at the prospect as she drove back to her house late on Sunday evening. Well, at least I've still got his Jaguar, she told herself lightly.

Yet she knew how any permanent move to the cottage would involve a lifestyle change. Clipped wings and reduced independence. Would Robert, she wondered, be quite so willing to make similar concessions, were we to set up home together? Tired, yet content, she felt sure that this was one sleeping dog she could safely let lie for a little bit longer anyway.

***

On Monday morning, these thoughts were far from her mind, as she settled behind her desk, looking dolefully at the number of documents already filling her In-tray. Switching on her computer, the size of her Inbox was equally daunting. Top of the pile was an internal e-mail, direct from the 'Iron

Lady' upstairs, entitled *Wayne*. Oh no' she sighed, pressing the open button and beginning to read.

Yvonne. Following last week's visit from the police, and the discovery of Wayne's duplicity, I've had no option but to fire him forthwith. Of course, the excuses he made in his defence were many and varied. But my decision is final. I cannot, and will not, have staff members divulging personal information to anyone outside of these offices. With any luck that dreadful policewoman will honour her side of the bargain, keeping our name out of any proceedings. Please do not waste your time, or mine, in trying to get me to reverse this decision. See me when you have a minute, on other matters only. J. M. Brief and to the point, Yvonne thought as she deleted the e-mail before consulting her diary.

***

By nine-thirty that Monday morning, Terry Noakes had worked up a fine head of steam, the weekend having given him two days in which to stoke up his anger. Frustrated by the lack of immediate action his habitual shortage of cash had seen the stock of beer in the fridge run dangerously low. On Sunday afternoon, having managed to cadge twenty pounds off a friend, he had gone to a local off licence for supplies. Aided and abetted by an old coat with deep 'poacher's pockets,' he had quietly 'lifted' a litre bottle of scotch, whilst dutifully paying for a pack of beer tins. Walking home afterwards, now stocked with beer and whisky, Sunday evening looked to be far more promising, giving him time to work out the amount of money he could take Buchanan for.

As expected, while the alcohol had produced the desired effect on Sunday, it had predictably left the undesired result on Monday. Despite feeling that Reading Football Club had played their last game with his head, he managed to make the short journey to the phone box, arriving just before ten. By five past the hour, he was walking back to his flat, his mood improved after a word with the switchboard lady and a short talk with someone called Williams. Following his father's advice, he'd introduced himself as Mr Noakes, asking if a Mr Alistair Buchanan could contact him on this number at 12 noon today. 'Should Mr Buchanan not be available today,' Terry had informed Williams, 'I shall be on this number, every day this week at 12.00 noon, expecting his call. Thank you.'

***

The working day started early in the city. By eleven o'clock on Monday morning London's world of finance was well into its energetic stride. Although Miles Overstone, while trying to maintain an appearance of normality in front of his staff, tension was stretching his every nerve and sinew. Around the office everyone knew, and accepted, that their ageing yet dynamic employer would blow up long before he wore out. They had always known that retirement would never be an option as he had always set a blistering pace, uncompromisingly demanding that his staff maintained it with him.

Pausing to look up from a document he was reviewing, he slumped back in his chair and sighed. Roll on, just one week to go. Only seven more days, then it will all be over. No, he thought abruptly, that's wrong. Next Monday will be a new beginning. *The old order changes and gives way to the new.* Recalling those well-chosen classical words from his public-school days gave Overstone pleasure, evoking memories of his youth. Had he thought more, another well-known poetical phrase might have come to mind and caused him concern. *A doubtful throne is ice on summer seas.*

Briskly he flicked the desktop mouse, reawakening his computer to stare again at the e-mail that he had just received from his bank. One reconfirming that the money they had agreed to advance, for the land purchase and subsequent building programme, would be in his bank account first thing next Monday morning. Perfect, by Tuesday the pair of us will be in Panama. Still relaxed, he thought back to his weekend meeting with Bernard Nolan, his designated second-in-command. A meeting held in a secluded car park on the Lewes to Newhaven Road offering views across the rolling South Downs. As ever security had taken priority, away from prying eyes and beyond the range of any electronic eavesdropping equipment. Thinking back to their time together, he remembered how Bernard had been openly shocked by his news.

'Bernard,' he had said, 'I want you to take over where I've left off. The money lending business is in fine shape, as you know. The drug smuggling is as near perfect as it could be. Just keep the screws on everything and everybody. And' he'd laughed, 'the money pouring into the Cayman Islands. While a forthcoming bank coup will take care of my pension, do keep my share of the other monies rolling in. I don't want to run short now, do I?' Overstone fondly remembered how Nolan had laughed at his little joke. Suddenly the ringing telephone cut short these memories.

'Call for you, Mr Overstone,' Susan stated from the outer office. 'It's that funny Mr Williams again, the chap who can't get your name right.' In a second, Overstone's manner changed dramatically. An inability to manage words held him in a vice-like grip. 'Mr Overstone, are you there?' Susan persisted, surprised by the lengthy silence. 'What shall I do?'

'P – P - Put him through,' he rasped.

'Very good, Mr Overstone,' she acknowledged.

'Is that you, Mr Overstone? The now familiar voice of Williams came down the line. 'You remember we spoke a while back?'

'Yeah,' Overstone struggled, his mind in disarray, 'what do you want this time?'

'Oh, nothing too serious, it's just that I've had that Noakes fellow back on the phone.' Overstone gasped in disbelief as Williams continued. 'He wants you to arrange for this Buchanan chap to give him another call. You obviously managed it the other day after we spoke, finding the contact details needed to get hold of him.'

'Yes, yes I did. That's correct,' Overstone blustered. 'But look here, I don't want this to become a regular occurrence.'

'Fine by me,' Williams cut back quickly; 'no need to tell me, just make darn sure you let Buchanan know that.'

'Okay, sorry about that, Mr Williams. But look, I'll sort this out it with Buchanan, so we'll not be needing you again. My word on it.'

'Very well then, but he's got a different number this time. If you've a pen, I'll read it out to you.' After writing down the new number he carefully replaced the phone, struggling to make sense of the situation. Noakes was dead.

Even the television news had finally covered the shooting, and it was in my morning paper as well, he told himself repeatedly. I've even bloody-well paid Dukes, he muttered, so for fuck's sake, how can a dead man want me to ring him up?

CHAPTER 46

BADLY SHAKEN, OVERSTONE reached into the top drawer of a filing cabinet and took out a bottle of whisky and a glass. Pouring himself a generous tot he wondered if it was too early in the day for such an activity. But no, sod the time, I need this he told himself as he absorbed the implications of the call and tried to rationalise its meaning. After a while he honed this down to one of two alternatives.

Firstly, he wondered if the police had somehow got hold of the number, the one he had left for Noakes to make contact, via the bank and the solicitors in case of emergency. Certainly, he had used it the other day, but has the silly sod left the number hanging around for the police to find? If so, are they using it to flush me out? Secondly, he considered the possibility that another party altogether had got hold of the number. In this case, as the saying goes, are they pulling my chain? After a while he concluded this had to be the only viable possibility because, had the police penetrated the contact procedure, they'd be clambering all over the place by now.

Having further examined the options he felt a little better, the feeling improved by a second measure of whisky.

But, despite his optimism, he knew for certain that someone else must have found their way in. Even Noakes isn't clever enough to be making calls from beyond the grave, he thought by way of consolation. Settling back into his chair, his original concerns about Clarkson and her solicitor boyfriend began to intensify. They've got to be in there somewhere. So, what should I do? Ignore the call, or ring that number?

Faced with a simple choice Overstone made his decision, dialling the phone-box and having his call answered on the second ring.

'That you, Buchanan?' a surly voiced demanded.

'No. I'm Miles Overstone,' he stated forcefully, 'it rather looks as though I've been asked to ring an incorrect number.'

'No, you bloody well haven't,' Noakes shouted. 'Overstone, Buchanan or whatever you're calling yourself, you'd better listen up!' he shouted down the line.

'Look,' Overstone said defiantly, 'I'm putting the phone down, whoever you are.'

'Okay then, but before you do that there's one thing you should know. I'm Terry Noakes, George's son. Bet you hadn't bargained on that one, had you?

'A son,' Overstone spluttered, reeling at the implications.

'Yes, a son, and not a happy one because you've just murdered my dad. Okay,' he pressed home his advantage, 'I'm guessing you didn't do the job yourself, but I know you were behind it. Now, as I've got you bang to bloody rights stop all this Overstone cobblers or I'll go to the police and tell them what I know.'

'Oh, will you now.' Overstone replied, trying to stay calm by asking a question. 'And, since we've never met, what exactly what do you intend to tell the police about me? I get the feeling you're just not plausible.'

'Plausible,' Noakes exploded, 'we'll see who's plausible when you're up before a judge at the Old Bailey.'

'Judge, Old Bailey, what are you on about?' Overstone asked firmly, making one last attempt to sound defiant.

'Yes, I'll tell the police that my dear old dad told me how you and he robbed a bank together, back in the sixties. Not only that, but you also shot two people, a security guard and a young girl, gunned them down in cold blood, didn't you? Oh yes, Mr Buchanan, I know all about you. Okay, my dad tried to blow up that bird's car the other day, after she'd been round the gym trotting out the name of Drysdale. Oh yes, I know about him as well, your getaway driver, the bloke what got hanged after you ran away and left him. That Clarkson bird scared my dad so badly that he went for the girl's car. He was desperate, trying to save the pair of you but he failed, so you had him shot.' Noakes finally stopped talking as Overstone, shaking like the proverbial leaf, finally managed to ask the question that was uppermost in his mind.

'Are you going to put the police onto me, then?'

'What? Don't be silly. No way, you're far too valuable to me.'

'Valuable! What in God's name do you mean?' Overstone snarled, fear carving up his insides.

'You've robbed me of my dad, so it's going to cost you. That's what I mean by *valuable*. So, let's stop mucking about because I want twenty-five grand, and I want it now. Mess me about and I'll tell the police about this contact procedure.' Noakes paused and smiled, fully enjoying his moment in the sun.

'Oh yes, I had a long chat with the cops the other day, over in Reading nick,' he continued. 'Get a load of this, they asked for my help in trying to find you. That's a laugh, I'll tell you.'

'Well, what did you tell them?' Overstone asked tentatively.

'Sod all of course. If I had of done, you know given them the contact routine, you'd already be starting to like the taste of porridge. No worry. But now, try and guess who else was there at our little gathering?'

'How should I know?' Overstone snapped.

'Now you're bothered. I can tell that, by the tone of your voice,' Noakes laughed.

'Okay, smart arse' Overstone shot back, 'why should I be worried?'

'Well, you ought to be, not only was I talking to a top-notch DCI, but I was also having a nice chat with Robert Vere. You know, the solicitor chap, as well as chatting to his glamorous girlfriend, the very lovely Yvonne Clarkson. Her being there as well was a real bonus.' Noakes laughed, thoroughly enjoying himself as Overstone struggled to get a word in edgeways. 'Just think of that,' he went on, 'my dad, so frightened by a beautiful girl that he wanted to kill her!' In the pause that followed Overstone could hear the background noise made by busy traffic as it rumbled by the phone box.

'Oh yes,' Noakes smiled again, chatting conversationally and happy to rattle the unseen Overstone. 'Those two, and the police. Well, so I'm told, they know about you as well, thanks to your friend Drysdale. Yes, just before they hanged him in Pentonville, he was busy writing away. Okay, he was only the getaway driver but, nevertheless, they hanged him for your murders.' A long silence followed, before he began talking again. 'You know what? Vere's got the notes left by Drysdale. They've spent the last fifty odd years in Canada, unopened, but now they're back here, very much open and the police have a copy.' Noakes laughed, 'so, I guess you're looking over your shoulder quite a bit now,' he continued, thoroughly enjoying himself. 'Right then, let's cut out the crap because I know you're Buchanan and I know how to contact you.'

Reeling under the onslaught Overstone fought desperately to collect his senses. He knew that he must try and win time - time in which to work out a plan. Time was his major asset, but he must use it wisely as the truth dawned on him that he now faced four enemies: Vere, Clarkson, Terry Noakes and the police. Firstly, he knew that the threat from Noakes was paramount and that he had to die. But, before that, he must believe that I'm willing to meet his crazy demands while, at the same time, the police must remain at arm's length. This, he knew, would give him the time needed to eliminate the young couple before making his escape. All of this being necessary before any one of them, or all of them, could stand between him and next Monday.

'Okay then, Terry,' he said calmly. 'You win. You want twenty-five thousand for your silence. Is that correct?'

'Bloody wrong,' he snapped back, 'I want twenty-five grand for losing my dad, compensation like. We can talk about the price of my silence later, as we develop a cosy relationship.' He laughed again. 'You'll like that won't you?' Noakes said bullishly as Overstone muttered to himself. He's too clever by half and, just like his old man, he's signed his own death warrant ..

'Right then, Terry, that's not a problem,' he replied in a chirpy voice. 'Be on this number at ten o'clock tomorrow morning. Then we can finalise things.'

'Wrong again,' Noakes snorted, 'you still don't get it do you? We're finalising nothing. In fact, we're only just getting going. First off, I want twenty-five grand for my dad, then we'll sort out a monthly payment to make sure I stay quiet. That's the only way you can keep yourself out of jail,' he chuckled, 'I'm your stay out of jail card! That should be worth a bob or two, but I can't answer for Vere and Clarkson, what they might know, or could even be telling the coppers as we speak.' He added the last bit, unable to resist the temptation.

'Okay, Terry, we'll do it your way. As I said, be on this number at ten tomorrow morning so I can tell you how we'll play it. I want you to have your first instalment, the twenty-five thousand for the loss of your father within days. I'll get onto my bank, right now and tell them to get the money together for you.' Before he could add anything further the line went dead.

Ah well, Noakes thought, let him play the big man but I've got him by the balls, and he knows it. Meanwhile time for a drink to celebrate because, by this time next week, I'll be rolling in it. Cheers Mr Buchanan.

CHAPTER 47

THOUGHTFULLY OVERSTONE REPLACED the telephone, managing to smile briefly. Greed, he thought, it always works. He's like a mouse, back for another nibble at the cheese. And, like the mouse, you'll come back for just one more delicious nibble then BANG! The trap springs shut. Greed versus caution, no contest he laughed. As for thinking that I'll pay him twenty-five grand for his old man, plus a monthly fee for his silence. What planet's he on? Cheeky little bugger, he'll be asking for a monthly banker's order for his silence, he scowled. Oh, you'll be quiet all right. That's one thing that I can guarantee he promised, taking a large-scale London Underground map from a desk drawer.

Minutes later, as he fleshed out his plan to eradicate a second Noakes, his mind wandered back to Vere and Clarkson. Was I wrong to dismiss them as mere lightweights and being of no consequence? Yes, they're involved somehow but what information do they have? What had that silly little twerp Drysdale written all those years ago? And why has his wretched last testimony been over in Canada for so long? Have I underestimated the lot of them?

Unable to settle, he kept thinking back to exactly what Noakes had said, especially about Vere and the girl. *Did they know enough to impact on my plans?* Just as sulphuric acid will eat its way through copper to detonate a bomb, this uncertainty gnawed away inside him. Dealing with Noakes would be straightforward. He's blinded by greed and anger, a heady cocktail that would override logic, dispel caution and leave him vulnerable.

But no, Vere and Clarkson are the ones that worry me. Might they know something that could bring about my downfall? A question that occupied his mind until he accepted how they had become a threat to his freedom.

Like George Noakes, Overstone found himself weighing up the odds, deciding how the strength of an unknown threat, from Vere and Clarkson, might disrupt his carefully planned escape strategy. *Hope for the best and plan for the worst* he wondered. But no, he concluded, a pre-emptive strike against them now would leave Monday's escape plans intact. Disposing of young Noakes would not be a problem, nailing Clarkson and Vere would take far more guile, something he'd never be able to delegate to Dukes at such short notice.

With Monday's deadline coming ever closer, killing Vere and Clarkson had now become urgent. With the place and equipment for their deaths ready and waiting, he knew that he had to derive the strategy needed to get them there, ideally one at a time. Settling back in his chair he began visualising exactly how his theory would become a reality. *It's worked before,* he told himself, *and it'll work again.* Originally a minor irritant, by now he'd convinced himself that the couple had now become a major threat to his survival and had to be eliminated.

Next, he began rechecking next Monday's departure. A carefully planned exercise geared to knowing that the best place to hide a tree was in a forest. So, he'd elected to disappear into a crowd, being just *one* person in an exceptionally large and transportable crowd. And the best people for transporting large crowds were the cruise lines, operators specialising in being able to off-load and embark thousand passengers very quickly.

What was just one traveller, equipped with a false identity in amongst such a crowd? Trees and forests! One amongst thousands, unseen, unrecognised and undetected. Perfect, a large liner was due to sail on the very day his bank-fraud money reached his company's account. With the transaction confirmed for next Monday he'd made a last-minute booking, selecting an inside cabin on a liner leaving Southampton for the Baltic and Saint Petersburg. Next morning the ship was to dock in Amsterdam, just a short taxi ride to the airport at Schiphol and his pre-booked flight to Panama. Then, by the time the ship's logging system declares me missing, I will be halfway across the Atlantic, he laughed.

***

Next morning it was an eager Terry Noakes who snatched up the telephone, virtually on the first stroke of ten o'clock. 'I'm impressed,' he said, 'bang on time.'

'Hello, Terry, good to hear you,' Overstone started conversationally, 'punctuality is important in business. And, of course, Terry, we are now in business, aren't we?' He smiled as he spoke, knowing that a smile affects the voice tone, softening it and making it sound friendly.

'Yeah, that's right,' Noakes responded, his voice surly, although pleased by Buchanan's compliance.

'Good, now the first step is to get you your twenty-five thousand pounds, isn't it?' Overstone spoke softly, imagining Noakes growing in confidence as he believed that he was really controlling events.

'Yeah, that's what I said,' Noakes replied.

'Of course, Terry, I fully understand. Since we last spoke, I've been onto my bankers in the city who're making up a package of notes for you, tens, twenties and fifties. All in used notes and ready for you to collect first thing tomorrow morning. You okay with that used notes business?'

'Best way,' he confirmed, hardly able to believe his luck.

'In fact, the only way,' Overstone laughed lightly. 'Can you get up to London early?' Overstone waited, knowing that if he'd suggested meeting on the far side of the moon, Noakes would have been up for it. Oh, the power of greed!

'Sure, not a problem. Where do we meet?' Overstone smiled, knowing that Noakes would be coming from Reading.

'Right, but you must come alone, Terry. No friends, no coppers. Muck me about and all bets are off, oh and don't think I can't find you.' Overstone added his own little sting, just letting Noakes know that he wasn't handing over control entirely.

'Course I'll be alone, I want my bleeding money, don't I?'

'Play by my rules and you'll get it. And, as we said earlier, there will be plenty more where that came from for you.' Oh, there I go again, playing the greed card, he thought, barely suppressing a smile.

'Right, let's get down to business. Be in Piccadilly Circus tomorrow morning, eight forty-five exactly. Do you know the place?

'Well, yeah I can find it, I guess. I'd look a bit silly if I couldn't. What with all that money at stake,' he laughed.

'Wouldn't you just,' Overstone shared the laughter, knowing the more confident he allowed Noakes to become, the easier his task would be.

'Okay, that's it then, the corner of Glasshouse Street and Shaftesbury Avenue, eight forty-five. Be on time, be alone then we can get your money. By half nine you'll be twenty-five thousand pounds better off, and on your way home. Now that can't be bad, can it? Oh, and while we're in the bank, I'll make the arrangements to pay you a monthly sum of money, for your continued silence. Agreed?'

'How can I agree?' Noakes responded angrily, 'when don't I know how much you're going to bloody well pay me each month?'

'Ah, yes, sorry about that, Terry. I'm proposing to pay you three thousand a month, for the rest of my life, providing you keep quiet and I stay out of jail. Does that sound reasonable?' As Overstone expected, the silence was lengthy as Noakes's faltering brain took in the figures. Twenty-five grand now and thirty-six grand a year for as long as Buchanan lived or stayed out of jail. Now that's what I call *hitting the jackpot*, he thought excitedly.

'Okay, Buchanan,' Terry finally managed, almost mesmerised by the figures. 'I'll be there, but no tricks, like.'

'Terry,' Overstone said patronisingly, 'you're the one in charge. I just want to make very sure that you're on my side. I need to stay out of prison. Satisfied? Now, if you're happy with that, just one more thing before we hang up. How will I recognise you?' Overstone posed the obvious question. But, for reasons unknown, Noakes had to pause briefly before answering.

'Well, I'm forty years old. I'll be wearing jeans, combat jacket and army boots. I've got close cropped hair, greying a bit. Now you know what you're looking for, I'll be there, eight forty-five tomorrow morning.' This time, it was Overstone left hanging onto a disconnected line, Noakes foolishly believing that by hanging up first he was asserting his authority. A gesture completely wasted on Overstone since this pathetic little mouse was coming back for just one more nibble at the cheese. As fatal for the mouse as for Noakes.

CHAPTER 48

'SO,' BAXTER ADDRESSED Crowland, placing his plastic coffee cup down onto the DCI's desk, 'we've still got nothing worth getting excited about, have we, sir?'

'No, we damn well haven't,' Crowland sighed with frustration, 'DI Robson's handling the Acton shooting which, I'm guessing will turn out to be a dead end - excuse the pun,' he raised his eyebrows. 'Anonymous, in black motorcycle leathers, black helmet and black visor. It could be anyone.'

'Fair enough, but what about the Wayne, Archer and Noakes set up?' Baxter questioned.

'Nothing there either. Archer was purely a leg man for Noakes, getting Wayne to pass on the information about Clarkson's car. But, while we're on that subject, did the Acton lads manage to pick up anything on the motor bike, you know from the CCTV and number plate recognition cameras?'

'No, sir,' Baxter replied gloomily. 'Okay, they got a selection of good shots from the cameras and were able to check out the bike's number. Led to a massive overkill I'm afraid. An armed SWOT team, suited and booted, descended on a seventy-something born-again biker in Hemel Hempstead. Poor old so and so. He'd just walked back from his allotment and was having tea with his misses. Usual heavy-handed bully-boy approach, shouting and screaming, forced the terrified old couple onto the floor. Searched the house, found nothing except a gleaming black Honda VFR in the garage with the same registration number. But that's where it ends, the bike's not been used for months. Even had cobwebs on the tyres, so I'm told.' Baxter shrugged his shoulders and Crowland knew that he had just hit another dead end. 'Okay, but what about Vere and the girl?' Baxter asked brightly.

'Nothing there either. Yvonne, as you can imagine, was really upset by Terry's performance the other day. Bit of a cock-up on my part I suppose' he reflected thoughtfully. 'Anyway, I understand she and Vere were together in Shiplake over the weekend, and where everything remained quiet,' he smiled. 'Bit of a first for them of late, but' he added, leaning back in his chair, 'let's be grateful as there's no way that we can keep them under surveillance. Buchanan's still at large, out there and unknown to us. As for Terry Noakes, what he's up to is anybody's guess. He's not got the brains to be trouble yet, on the other hand he's thick enough to get himself into trouble. We know the little sod's been lying to us, delusional enough to think he can outflank us. If so he's way off course with that one. What do you think?' The unanswered question hung in the air as Baxter commented.

'Too flaming clever by half would be my best guess, sir'

***

He was just another tourist, idly spending time minutes by the base of Eros in the centre of London's Piccadilly Circus. Anonymous, in a lightweight raincoat and busily making use of a small digital camera fitted with a powerful telephoto lens. Anonymity. That was exactly the impression Miles Overstone wanted to create in the guise of Alistair Buchanan, comfortable and unobtrusive. The subterfuge was complete, greying black hair beneath a flat cap, moustache, heavy black rimmed glasses and with the foam rubber pads enhancing his cheeks. With the collar of his raincoat turned up he felt secure, unseen and unremembered. One amongst thousands.

After jostling with a group of Japanese visitors he edged his way around to the north side of the plinth. Making use of the telescopic lens he was able to look above the streams of converging traffic, studying the pedestrians on the far pavement. Repeatedly returning to look intently at the people swirling around the junction of Glasshouse Street and Shaftesbury Avenue he was, at face value, a snap happy tourist. Yet, for Overstone, the powerful lens permitted him to make regular and discreet sweeps in his search for Terry Noakes. Not one of the healthiest places to be he murmured, taking in yet another lungful of diesel fumes and his eardrums hammered by the pounding traffic.

Just after eight-forty he spotted Noakes leave the shadowy confines of Glasshouse Street and move cautiously onto the wider pavement. As described: army boots, jeans, tough-guy haircut and a combat jacket. Just another piece of dross trying to give the impression of being something he had never been, a battle-hardened soldier. At least he's on time Overstone thought, pleased that after a further two minutes of careful observation he became confident that Noakes was alone. Satisfied with progress so far he prepared to implement the next part of his plan. Turning suddenly, he grabbed the arm of a nearby rat-faced youth wearing jeans, trainers, and a soiled T shirt, the outfit completed by a worn leather jacket with studs and tassels. The youth had greasy shoulder length hair and, where exposed, his neck displayed garish tattoos. Not the type of person you'd want your daughter to bring home for tea, Overstone reflected as he tightened his grip on the puny arm.

'Here, watch it, mate,' the youth snarled, flinching under the intensity of the grip. With his other gloved hand, Overstone pulled an envelope from his pocket with a ten-pound note clipped to it.

'The notes yours. Give the envelope to the bloke over there in the combat jacket. Okay?' His eyes bored deeply into those of the unpleasant looking youth, his scrawny features tense as he struggled to come to a decision.

'Alright then,' Denny Briggs growled, accepting that ten pounds was a fair rate of return for walking across the road, 'but let go of my bleeding arm first.'

After watching Briggs set off on his errand, Overstone got busy with the camera, reassured that making a direct approach to Noakes would not have been wise. Might the police have offered Noakes a reward for leading them to me? Was he working both sides of the street? Not worth taking any risks as Terry seems to be playing this straight, so far. But I need more time to be sure he told himself, watching the nail-bitten fingers of Denny Briggs carry the next part of his plan.

Inside the envelope was a typed message, instructing Noakes to go down into the gleaming circular concourse of the underground station. Once there he was to wait by the large World Time map where, at nine o'clock sharp, he would be contacted.

Overstone watched the handover, seeing Briggs dash off as an open-mouthed Noakes stared at the envelope in surprise. Seconds later he tore it open, sliding out the typed card which he read before looking around, as if anticipating a further contact. Unsure, he remained stationary, painfully aware of the role reversal taking place. Now *he* was following instructions, rather than giving them. Greed versus caution, opposing emotions that kept him rooted to the spot as Overstone watched, sighing deeply as Noakes eventually pushed the envelope into a side pocket but still didn't move.

A further sixty seconds elapsed before Noakes took his first hesitant steps towards the nearest entrance to the underground station, his head turning from side to side. Is he looking for a friendly companion or is he just aware that I'm watching him? Overstone asked himself before widening his field of vision. This time double-checking to see if any pedestrians had suddenly become immobile, staking out the uncertain Noakes or looking for another contact. No sudden movements, no searching glances. He breathed out slowly as everything seemed to be normal, no obvious followers. Satisfied that Noakes was performing to plan he slipped from the crowd in pursuit of his target.

Minutes later an angry and confused Terry Noakes had located the World Time map, telling himself that it wasn't supposed to happen like this. Buchanan's the one in the crap. *He should be doing what I say, not ordering me about.* By now I'd hoped we'd be in a taxi heading for his bank, with me calling the shots. His brow furrowed with concern as he scanned the stream of humanity moving slowly through the concourse. Anxiously, he looked from face to face, almost desperate to see one making for him, complete with smile and a ready handshake. Hold on, he told himself, this is the bloke who got my dad shot. No, bugger the smiles and handshakes, this sod's going to bloody well pay for what he's done, he told himself in a bullish effort to boost his flagging confidence.

All around him the flow of bodies continued unabated, passengers arriving and departing, most bound for their places of work, offices, banks or shops. Which one was Buchanan? Desperation! Hell, he could be anyone. Heads down and with their feet shuffling the moving procession of humanity passed him by. While most made their way to the platforms, others were simply using the concourse to avoid the busy roads above. Despite his best efforts to spot a potential contact nobody was obvious, making him wonder if he was on a wild goose chase. Then, on the verge of giving up he visibly jumped when addressed by a voice beside him.

'Glad you made it okay, Terry.'

'Where did you come from?' Noakes spluttered, amazed that someone had managed to get that close to him unobserved. 'And what's with this messaging lark, then?' Noakes stared hard at the man beside him. He was thin, tall, and with dark hair showing traces of grey protruding from underneath a cloth cap.

'Precautions, Terry. I simply cannot take risks. I need my freedom.'

'And I need my money, so let's stop mucking about,' he blurted out nervously.

'Okay, Terry. You're right, no more messing about. But, before we go any further, start earning it!'

'What do you mean?' the anxious Noakes spat back.

'Only this, what do you know about Robert Vere and Yvonne Clarkson? You've met them both. What do they know about me?' He glared intently at Noakes, asserting silent authority.

'What you want to know that for?' Noakes demanded. 'Stuff them. I want my money.'

'Straightforward enough, are they a threat to me and my freedom? I need to know. So, tell me what you know then we'll go and collect your money,' he persisted, again using the lure of money.

'Well, yeah, but it's not much really, I suppose,' Terry shrugged. 'The bird works for a women's magazine, got an office near Vauxhall Bridge, I think. Lives in Westridge Green, that's a tiny village, someplace near Reading.' Then, moving into a more comfortable area, he continued with a grin. 'Mind you, that Vere bloke's knocking her off you know.'

'Well, I'd worked that out already,' Overstone said sarcastically. 'But what do you know about Vere?'

'Not much either. He's got a place at Shiplake, that's near Henley. He's a solicitor, says he's got offices in Cavendish Square. That's up West here somewhere, isn't it?'

'Yes. But when you saw them in Reading, did they say anything about me?'

'Hang on, mate,' Terry snapped back. 'I was in custody, interviewed by the police and helping them with their bleeding enquiries, so they said. It wasn't a social gathering, no cucumber sandwiches and China cups. All I know is this. The guy they hanged for driving for you and my old man, left a bunch of notes that have now come to the surface.'

'And' Overstone probed impatiently.

'Not sure, but whatever was in them notes allowed that smart-arse Clarkson to find my father, and now he's dead. So, if she's smart enough to do that, could she be sniffing around after you,' he laughed, enjoying the obvious discomfort his remark caused. 'Anyway, I guess they're all scratching around for a lead of some sort to find you.' Noakes added the final words with a touch of spite. Then remembering something from the Reading interview, he continued. 'Hey, tell you what. They've got a set of your fingerprints.' Overstone feigned surprise, turning towards Noakes as he took time to assess his position.

'What do you mean? A set of my fingerprints.'

'Yeah, when you gave my dad his cut from the robbery all those years ago, the night before Drysdale's execution, dad kept the envelope because it's got your dabs all over it. Now, that wasn't very bright of you, was it?' he sneered.

Overstone pondered the information, already aware of the envelope thanks to George Noakes. What he'd laughingly referred to as his insurance policy. Overstone smiled briefly. So, the police have the wretched envelope. Not a problem there, logical reasoning taking over from mild concern.

'Alright, they've got my prints?' he smiled, relaxing as he continued, 'No worries there then. Had they'd matched anything on their database the police would be all over me by now. They'd be like flies round a pile of dog dirt on a summer's day! No, Terry, they're not going anywhere with that one.'

'Says you,' Noakes smirked.

'Alright, enough of that. You need your money and I need to stay clear of the police. Okay, although they don't know me now, I need it to stay that way. Therefore, I'm relying upon your continual silence for which I'm willing to pay you handsomely. Your money's safe and the monthly payments will continue for the rest of my life, or just so long as I stay out of prison. You do understand that as you'll have to stay quiet forever?' The last words had no significance for the greedy Noakes who grinned and waited anxiously for Overstone to make the next move.

'Yeah, course I understand.' Noakes confirmed.

'Okay, time to take the tube, travel up a couple of stops, cross onto the Central Line then into the city. That's where my bank is and, more to the point,' he laughed, 'where your money is waiting. You happy with that then?'

'You bet,' Noakes agreed, thrilled to be that much closer to his money. Twenty-five grand, he thought. So easy, I should have asked for more, but I'll see about putting the screws on him for that later, he consoled himself. 'So, you're Buchanan then?' he asked a little belatedly, as they stepped away from the map to join the passing procession of humanity. 'Not a jumped-up lackey working on his behalf; trying to act big and throw me?'

'No, Terry, I'm the real deal; Alistair Buchanan in the flesh.' Overstone grinned, pulling the two tickets he'd purchased earlier from his inside pocket knowing how only one of them would be used. But, for a result, cheap at twice the price!

CHAPTER 49

TERRY NOAKES WENT unsuspectingly to his death, alone yet surrounded by hundreds of commuters. Motivated by greed, and the lure of easy money, his simple brain could see no treachery. No danger here, just a fantastic opportunity to pick up some much-needed money. My silence in exchange for keeping this old git out of jail. Safe as houses he thought, moving onto the escalator behind the ageing Buchanan. No, I've cracked it. He's just an old bloke determined to stay free and unfettered. Suits me, quick trip to his bank, get the old fart to set up the promised monthly payments for three grand a month. In less than an hour I'll have twenty-five thousand in my pocket and be on my way home. Might even upgrade my ticket at Paddington, travel fist-class. He smiled at his thoughts. Could get myself a nice little car, move to a better place in a village outside Reading. Now, that'd be nice, somewhere like where all those posh people live. However, as he revelled in the prospect of his imaginary new lifestyle anxiety struck.

This bloke, he thought looking down on the upright figure before him on the escalator, had my dad killed yet here I am taking him on trust. Was that really the smartest of moves? he asked himself, quickly countering the doubt by wondering just what sort of damage this old bloke could do to a big strong chap, down here in a public place or even in his bank? Okay, I'm a bit exposed. Once back home I'll write it all down, make notes on how to contact this Buchanan chap and leave them with a mate. Should anything happen to me, folks will know where to start their hunt. That'll be my first job once I'm back in the flat he told himself. Readjusting his grip on the moving handrail he glanced across, watching commuters on the ascending escalator opposite, most clutching briefcases or handbags. The handbags, he noticed, ranged in size from the small to the absurdly fashion-conscious supermarket checkout sized bag. God knows what women find to put in them he thought, feeling the temperature around him begin to rise he watched Buchanan prepare to step off the escalator in front of him.

'This way,' he ordered, guiding him into a tightly bunched crowd of people making their way through to the platform. Once there the passengers dispersed, many of whom were talking with companions while others looked across at the far wall lined with advertisements. Films, banks, insurance companies, wine merchants and department stores were all represented. Each one hoping that their strategically sited posters would have travellers reaching for their wallets or mobiles. Noakes, unused to the pressures of peak-time tube travel, looked around uncertainly while trying to take it all in. Buchanan, maintaining the initiative, managed to guide him through the thinning crowd towards the far end of the platform, ending up amongst a gaggle of assorted passengers eager for the next train.

'Won't be long now, one'll be along in a minute,' he shouted, holding his mouth close to Noakes's ear as they heard the distant rumble of an approaching train. Like a giant piston in a cylinder, Buchanan thought, as the train pushed before it a great plug of dry and dusty air. Peering into the tunnel he started to calculate the angles needed while factoring in the disposition of the passengers close by them.

'Move up a bit,' he shouted to Noakes, 'try to get closer to the edge of the platform. Once the train stops it'll be a scrum-down, people trying to get on fighting those trying to get off. We don't want to miss it, do we?'

'No way,' Noakes called back over his shoulder, greed dispersing any thoughts of danger. Buchanan, by peering between the heads of neighbouring commuters managed to see a little way into the tunnel. Briefly he caught sight of the approaching train's lights and a fleeting glimpse of the bored looking driver through the cab's window.

Around them the crowd surged as Buchanan, taking advantage of the movement, allowed himself to be pushed back to end up directly behind Noakes. Amid a squeal of brakes, the train emerged from the tunnel as Buchanan made his final adjustments. Leaning forward he pushed his right arm between the two nearest forward-facing passengers he gave Noakes a monumental shove in the back, propelling him forward violently. Taken completely by surprise he burst from the crowd yelling in disbelief. With arms flailing wildly he plunged into the train's path to vanish from view beneath its murderously slicing wheels and the high voltage rail.

Buchanan didn't wait. Ducking low and pushing hard into the wall of passengers surging forward to board the train he fought his way off the platform. Behind him those nearest the edge were still screaming, having witnessed the helpless Noakes plunge to his death Sickened, they frantically pushed against the passengers behind them who, determined to board the train, remained completely unaware as to what had just happened.

The driver, reacting quickly, slammed on the brakes and brought his train to a shuddering halt. Within seconds passengers further down the platform realised that something had to be wrong as only the train's first three carriages had emerged from the tunnel. Concerned, yet unaware of events, they knowingly attributed the delay to a technical problem rather than a sudden death.

Amid the noisy clamour Buchanan stayed low, battling against the pushing wall of commuters. Eventually breaking clear he stood upright, finally able to walk towards the ascending escalator, unnoticed and unconcerned. Back in the concourse he walked into the 'gent's' toilet, found an empty cubical and snapped the catch closed behind him. Off came the cap, the greying toupee, the phoney moustache, the heavy glasses and the two pads of foam rubber from inside his mouth. Lastly the lightweight raincoat, fully reversible, went from fawn to dark blue in an instant. From an inside pocket, he withdrew a folding walking stick, opening to its full length as his "Buchanan accessories" were slipped into the vacated pocket. Moments later a semi bald man in his seventies stepped unsteadily onto the concourse, walking with the aid of a stick and muttering quietly. Impudent young pup, fancy being naive enough to think he could blackmail me.

Below, on the platform, a depressingly and well-practised routine had swung into operation. With all passengers having to leave the platform the train, still with passengers on board, reversed a short distance back into the tunnel. Then, once informed that the power had been switched-off, two paramedics stepped down onto the track and immediately pronounced Noakes dead. Death by electrocution or horrific injuries? the final verdict resting with the pathologist. Meanwhile the police took custody of any personal items they had found on the body while a police photographer recorded the scene Once completed the police gave permission for the removal of Noakes's body after which a station operative used sand to cover the blood stains.

Power was reconnected, so allowing the train to finally occupy the full length of the platform, allowing those on board to follow instructions and leave the carriages. Such incidents have an immediate knock-on effect, forcing tailbacks down the tunnels as dozens other trains came to an enforced standstill across the network. At Piccadilly announcements said that the station would remain closed until the police and Health and Safety staff had completed their investigations.

'Most likely to be a suicide,' an official said to one of the disgruntled passengers forced to reschedule his journey. 'It's unfortunate, but we get a number of jumpers each year.'

CHAPTER 50

BY NOON MILES Overstone was back in his office, enjoying a cup of coffee whilst scanning down a column of figures on his computer screen that gave him a feeling of overall satisfaction. A mood which improved considerably when the BBC News website carried a report on a suspected suicide at Piccadilly tube station that morning. The victim, so far unidentified, had died at the scene with the police saying they considered this to be nothing more than a tragic suicide. No witnesses, and with the deeply shocked driver unable to add to the information already to hand, suicide it would remain. 'The bloke just shot out of the crowd, like a cork out of a blasted bottle, then fell under my train,' he told the interviewer.

Overstone smiled as he closed the browser on his computer, comfortable that the police considered the incident as an unexplained suicide with *No Further Action* stamped across the file. Excellent, he smiled, with the Noakes problem resolved he turned his attention to the perceived threat posed by Vere and Clarkson. With only four days to go any interference would be disastrous. Just as my failure to act now could prove to be equally disastrous.

***

Robert Vere picked up his buzzing mobile phone, annoyed at the interruption and answered it curtly.

'Mr Vere,' DCI Crowland announced, 'sorry to trouble you in the office, but I think you should know about something that happened earlier today. You okay to talk for a minute?'

'Oh yes, sorry if I was a trifle sharp just then, but I'm under pressure to get an important contract finalised. Anyway,' he sighed, 'enough of my troubles. What gives?'

'Have you heard the news today?'

'No, not really, read my paper on the way up to Town this morning. Nothing in there with my name on it,' he laughed.

'Okay, this'll not make the headlines. Earlier this morning, not that far from your office, an unidentified man fell to his death in front of an underground train.'

'Oh, that's rotten, but sadly it happens,' Vere replied, a little surprised at what sounded like unimportant news.

'Well,' Crowland paused, 'the victim's been identified as Terry Noakes.'

'Bloody hell,' his reaction was spontaneous as the news grabbed his attention. 'That's terrible. What do you make of it?' he questioned, falling silent as Crowland recounted how the police had later recovered a wallet and driving licence, so able to confirm the victim's identity.

'First reports reckon it was suicide. Witnesses say he took a ruddy great jump off the platform. But, with nothing more than an open mind, I'm wondering if there may have more to it than that,' the DCI said thoughtfully.

'What makes you say that?' Vere questioned, before continuing with another question. 'Hold it, this happened in London, so how'd you get to hear about it so quickly over there in Reading?'

'There, for a change, we had a modicum of luck. Standard practice, the West End police filed the incident on the national computer system. Minutes later a sharp-eyed copper in Acton saw it. Recognising the name Noakes he made the connection, notifying DI Robson who, in turn, had the decency to give me a call.'

'Ah,' said Vere.

'Oh, it gets better,' Crowland added, explaining how the police had found an open envelope in the dead man's pocket. Inside the envelope they found a typed card directing Noakes to the World timeclock on the station concourse.

'Definite arrangements for a meeting, explains why Terry was in London so early. A great big longshot, but I'm wondering if this meeting could have been with Buchanan. Guess that's too much to hope for, although Robson said forensics picked up Terry's prints on the card. No surprises there but, right in one corner of the envelope, there was another set of prints.'

'Buchanan's?' he asked hopefully, knowing that the police had recently secured a set of his from behind the print in Noakes's gym.

'Hey, steady on, our luck's not that flaming good,' Crowland laughed. 'Sorry, no, he's far too clever for that. These belong to a piece of low life called Denny Briggs, one of Robson's regulars, as she calls them. She's out there now, trying to find him.'

'But where does he come in?' Vere asked, struggling with the information.

'My guess, based on nothing more than instinct,' Crowland said thoughtfully, 'is that Buchanan slipped Briggs a few pounds to pass it on to Noakes. Okay, on its own, not much to get excited about, but there could be a bonus.'

'Which is?' Vere asked in anticipation.

'Hmm, you see, if Robson and I are correct in our thinking, this Briggs character is the only person we know of who's seen the person we believe to be Buchanan. So, once Robson runs the little toe rag to earth, we can get a description. From that, we should be able to get an artist's impression. Next thing we can get it in the papers, and on television which should pull in something?'

'Sounds promising,' Vere offered politely, though far from convinced.

'It's a start, but don't get your hopes up. I've been in this game too long to expect life to be that easy. Not to worry though, I'll keep you posted.' He said helpfully, before speaking again. 'In the meantime, look after yourself and take care of Miss Clarkson.' The DCI paused, before continuing, choosing his words carefully, 'Look, I hope I'm not sticking my oar in here,' he spoke hesitantly. 'You see I still have concerns for the safety of you and Yvonne, what with this unknown Buchanan being around. So, to be on the safe side, is there any chance you could get her to move into the cottage with you for a while? Say a week at most while we sort this mess. If she'll come that is?' I'd certainly be happier with you keeping an eye on her.' He stopped talking, still unsure if he'd overstepped the mark.

'That'll not be a problem, but does that mean you think we're in any sort of danger?'

'Sorry to sound like a surgeon, but I can't make promises. I simply don't know,' he paused, 'but, as a precautionary measure, I'd be happier if you were both together, safety in numbers and all that sort of thing. I'm guessing you could commute together as well.' Crowland waited, hoping his suggestion would be acceptable. "Yes, I'm sure we can manage that, Mr Crowland,' Vere agreed.

'Oh, for heaven's sake,' the DCI gave a soft laugh, 'let's make things easier for ourselves and drop the formalities. On a one-to-one basis, please call me Ted. I've no problem with that.'

'Not got one here either, Ted. I'm, Robert as I'm sure you know.'

'Great, that makes for an easier rapport when we're working informally together. Look, I know you and Yvonne are a couple, but I still have a hidden worry that I'd like to share with you.'

'Which is?' Vere asked, his voice laced with caution.

'Okay, here goes. Let's hope it's not the end of a budding friendship.' Pausing, he took a deep breath before continuing. 'You see, and without putting the finer point on it, our current problems are down to Yvonne's curiosity. Chasing up George Noakes set the ball rolling, fact is her innocent involvement led indirectly to a couple of deaths.'

'Sadly, you're not wrong there, Ted,' Vere conceded, digesting the information. 'I know Yvonne feels just as rotten about it as we all do. The words you used......well they describe things perfectly, innocent involvement and curiosity. As much as I love her, she is a trained journalist.

Okay, not a news hound, but never happier than when chasing a story. Fashion's her thing but, having seen Noakes's hand on the television after we'd read Drysdale's notes, she thought she'd got a story. I didn't see any real connection, whereas Yvonne couldn't see any harm in pursuing what she reckoned could be something. She simply used the time-honoured techniques of her trade, metaphorically speaking that's to build up a bit of pressure in the boiler then look out for the leaks. The same in your line of work I guess and look, if Yvonne could turn the clock back, I know she would.'

'I'm sure, but once she opened up this particular "can of worms" there was no way on knowing where it would take her. In this case, into the unknown and we still don't know who Buchanan is. Although,' he paused, 'by tonight we might at least have an idea what he looks like. That's always assuming Robson can get hold of Briggs.' He stopped talking for a moment, trying to rearrange his thoughts, before continuing. 'But there again, I'm starting to think that Buchanan might now be realising that you two know nothing.' Vere, happy to accept the DCI's thinking, waited as the DCI continued speaking.

'Listen,' he began sounding more confident, 'the more I think about it I reckon he'd have made a move by now if he thought you could damage him in any way. Yes, I think you'll both be okay but do take care and no unnecessary risks. I'll get back to you when we're able to firm up on anything more.' With that they disconnected, Crowland dependent upon Robson for results and Vere left to ponder just exactly who the DCI was trying to reassure.

CHAPTER 51

YVONNE, WHERE HAVE you been?' Vere asked abruptly.' I've been trying to reach you all day. You've been permanently on answer phone.'

'Oh, Robert,' she answered frostily, annoyed at his tone, 'surely you're not checking up on me, are you?

'Of course not,' he replied, trying to stay calm despite the frustration caused by his inability to make the earlier contact he so needed..

'Okay,' she accepted, 'but why so formal. Is there a problem? I've been out of the office since late morning, had lunch with an editor then looked in on an afternoon fashion show Knightsbridge. That's kept me busy, oh and the show's organisers were a fussy old lot. Mobiles banned and all that, even said that on the invitation. So, to avoid problems, I left mine in the office. Fact is the taxi only dropped me off back here ten minutes ago.'

'Sorry, darling, of course I'm not having a go at you, it's just that I'm a bit up tight, could have done with speaking to you earlier on that's all. You see, it's that Ted Crowland called me around lunchtime with the unpleasant news that Terry Noakes met with a terrible accident.' He heard

Yvonne gasp as he explained how Noakes had fallen in front of an underground train. 'Yes,' he confirmed, 'it happened earlier this morning at Piccadilly. Crowland's not sure if it's suicide, an accident or whether foul play might have been involved.'

'That's awful,' she said slowly, absorbing the news, 'not that he was a nice person, but I'd not wish that on anyone. You say there may have been foul play?'

'Not me,' he smiled, 'all we know so far is that it happened just after nine this morning. From what Crowland told me, it looks as though Noakes had arranged to meet with someone, not sure whom, but his money's on it being Buchanan.'

'On no,' she replied, 'this just gets more complicated by the minute. That wretched man's popping up all over the place. But' she paused as a thought struck her, 'what about us? Are we in any danger?'

'Not a problem there, my love,' Vere said with a cheerfulness he knew to be false. 'Crowland doesn't think we are, just advises us to take care. Stick together and avoid isolated places, that sort of thing. Mind you, he did suggest that you move in with me for a while. I didn't tell him that you've already been living in Shiplake since Monday. I think he's got something more permanent in mind, just to be on the safe side.'

'Gosh,' Yvonne giggled, 'that must be a first. What with me being a respectable young lady and ordered by the police to move in with a randy old solicitor of doubtful moral character?' Despite his tension he couldn't avoid laughing at Yvonne's mimicking Eliza Doolittle as visions of My Fair Lady flashing across his mind.

'Hey, less of the old,' he chuckled. 'Seriously though, he suggested that I've got to keep you in order, even suggested taking a firm hand.'

'Promises,' she called down the line, laughing, 'a firm hand indeed. Oh no, does that mean another playful spanking if I misbehave?' More laughter, 'and in answer to your first question, I'm about to leave the office. Too late to do any work now, so I'm on my way.'

'Okay, you little vixen,' he said firmly, his voice without any trace of humour. 'Yvonne, will you please be serious. Do take care. Stay among the crowds. I'm due to leave the office soon and we can decide what to do when you get to Shiplake.'

'Right then, Mr Big Boss man,' she laughed again, 'I like it when you get all masterful. Not to worry, I'll see you around seven.' After disconnecting, Yvonne began to feel uneasy, aware that despite her teasing comments Vere had sounded serious. Just being protective, she wondered, or is he reading more into the death of Terry Noakes than he's letting on? Then again, had Crowland said even more to Robert?'

***

About the time Yvonne was reaching for her coat Denny Briggs walked beside the shell of a burnt-out car, just a mere hundred yards away from where he lived. Home, for Denny Briggs, was a third floor flat he shared with his mother, and younger brother on a sprawling West London estate. Looking up Denny could see lines of washing draped from the railings while around him loud music blared defiantly across the whole area. Denny surveyed the familiar run-down collection of unsightly three and four storey blocks of red brick flats conditioned, by years of experience, to accept its depressing normality. Inside the blocks the graffiti-streaked lifts seldom worked and, when they did, their secondary function as urinals left an appalling smell. Running along the outside of the blocks the external walkways provided ready-made depositories for rubbish, broken bikes, used condoms, empty pill bottles and discarded syringes. At street level countless tired looking and damaged cars, all without hubcaps, simply added to the air of desolation. Across the road a group of youngsters bounced around on BMX bikes whilst others sat on benches smoking and drinking from cans. Typical late afternoon, Denny thought, his confidence high, after a successful day "up West," dipping into tourist's pockets and bags, plus a bit of shop lifting on Regent's Street. Got a bit of decent gear, plus half a dozen good bits of plastic. Pity I didn't get any PIN numbers, but the cards will still fetch a pound or two. Got to move them quickly, no good when the owners have cancelled them. That ten quid, first thing in Piccadilly, got things off to a good start. Overall, a good day and I should make decent money from that lot. Well, he sighed, at least enough to buy some gear from that miserable Greek bastard that I can sell on. Not that I do drugs, but money makes money. So, who am I to complain if smack heads want to blow white powder up every orifice that God gave them? Why shouldn't I make money out of their brainless addiction? No reason at all he assured himself, deciding to sell his spoils in the pub later that evening tonight. Annoyed to find that the lifts were yet again out of order he reluctantly took to the cold, dirty and graffiti strewn communal stairwells to reach his mother's flat. Reaching the third floor landing he moved onto the outside walkway leading towards home. Then, after taking the final corner, he stopped dead in his tracks. Thirty feet away two police constables, with their backs to him, were busily quizzing his

mother in the doorway to their flat. 'Fucking hell,' he exclaimed softly, ducking back towards the stairwell. That was quick. How did they get onto me? Stepping back out of sight he wiped beads of sweat from his face, confused and more thana little frightened. Seconds later a hand grabbed his collar, pulling him backwards through the now open doorway of another flat. Tottering badly, he heard the door slam behind him. Turning, he saw the stubble covered chin and bleary-eyed face of Jimmy Green peering back at him.

'What you been up to, dickhead? Arty rang, said he'd seen the pigs enter the block, pass our place then go straight for yours. Now, they're giving your old lady a tough time. It's a safe bet they want to see you. So, what you been up to?' Denny Briggs turned and then flopped down onto a cluttered settee.

'Just the usual. Been up West, dipped a few pockets, pinched some plastic cards, usual sort of day,' he said nonchalantly.

'So? Why have the ruddy coppers come straight to your place? There must have been something else? he questioned, 'unless you were "clocked" on CCTV somewhere?'

'Ha, reckon I'm too smart for that. Come to think of it, there was this old bloke who slipped me ten quid. Just wanted me to pass a message on to a geezer across the street...............'

CHAPTER 52

ACTON POLICE STATION. Eight o'clock in the morning found DI Robson strutting around the Incident Room, her anger building as she addressed the assembled gathering. Speaking loudly, she explained how her underlying objective was to explore possible connections between the deaths of George and Terry Noakes.

'Noakes senior was shot,' she said, 'right here in Acton, killed by a person unknown. And, while we've several good witnesses to that killing, his son died horribly beneath an underground train yesterday morning. Now, given the circumstances, it's quite likely this was no accident. Mind you it's amazing. There he was, surrounded by dozens of people on a crowded platform and not one of them saw a thing. And, as of now, all we have is a reference to someone called Buchanan.'

'Now, without going into *chapter and verse*, George Noakes and Buchanan did a bank job over fifty years ago. They killed two people then scarpered with the money. Later their getaway driver, person by the name of Drysdale, was taken into custody, tried for murder and subsequently hanged.' Again, she paused, before going on to press home the urgency of finding Denny Briggs.

'We know from the fingerprints that Briggs was handed a message by someone to pass on to Terry Noakes. We found that message in Noakes's pocket. We believe the person who gave Briggs that message could well have been this Buchanan character. And, to the best of our knowledge Briggs is the only person who has had a visual of Buchanan. So, find Briggs and we might be able to find Buchanan. Well at least we might get a half decent description,' she fell silent for a moment, giving the officers a chance to take notes before continuing.

'Be in no doubt, this Briggs is a piece of low life and has been pulled in from here many a time. Christ, if this place were a football ground, he'd have a season ticket!' she ranted but no one laughed, just as she knew they wouldn't. 'And now, the toerag has vanished off the face of the earth,' she stormed. 'I want the despicable little bastard now! Put the word out. He's not in any trouble, but we urgently need to speak to him. Someone must be hiding him.' She paused for breath, glaring from face to face. 'We got a warrant to search his place and I took a team round there last night. Turned it over good and proper. No sign of him though, all we got was a bit of cannabis, pornographic videos and a selection of tasty items even his charming mother couldn't account for.' She looked around the room, searching for signs her requirements had been understood. 'I want that estate raked clean! Warn everybody you speak to that a charge of perverting the course of justice will follow if they're found to be hiding Briggs or holding anything back from us.'

Impatiently she paced in front of the large white boards, liberally daubed with green ink, maps and pictures. The buttons on her jacket under even more strain as she breathed heavily, desperately hoping that someone in the room would produce something positive. Around her all faces remained blank because, and based upon past experiences of her scathing comments and ruthless put-downs, all mouths were staying firmly closed. No one was going to speak. Senior staff realised it was futile while their junior counterparts feared humiliation under the lash of her tongue.

'Well, get to it!' she called out as the officers began to leave the room 'and find Briggs for me.' Her last words yelled above the sound made by scraping chairs, shuffling feet and closing notebooks. Amongst the noisy departures a young constable whispered to his colleague.

'I wouldn't cross the road to piss on her if she was on fire.'

'What was that?' Robson screamed, having seen but not heard the brief exchange.

'Nothing, D I Robson,' the constable said, mightily relieved to scurry away unscathed to his place of work.

***

As Robson ranted in Acton, Vere and Yvonne were on the train travelling to work, having spent a pleasant night together at the cottage. Strictly on police instructions you understand, Vere had assured the giggling Yvonne between the bedsheets. For the first part of the journey to the main line station at Twyford they remained upright, squashed tight in an over-crowded railcar unit. Ten minutes after reaching the junction they boarded a fast train to Paddington, fortunate enough to find seats.

Despite spending part of the previous evening raking over Crowland's comments, they'd come to no useful conclusion regarding personal risk factors. Finally, Yvonne had ended the debate with a measure of logical conviction.

'Oh, come on, that does it! If Sherlock Crowland cannot give us an answer, what chance have we got?' Devoid of any rational response Vere accepted her assessment before manging to persuade her to vary her routines. Still bothered by Crowland's attitude he addressed Yvonne as their train ran through Slough Station.

'Look, while we're commuting together, I'm sure we'll be okay. I just don't want you going off on your own. I know it's a big ask, but it'll only be for a short while. Are you okay with that?' his question brought a smile as she knew his suggestions were based on loving concern. Once at Paddington they stepped down onto the platform and stood still, Vere holding Yvonne tightly to his chest. Two stationary lovers. An island in a moving tide of commuters. Leaning down, he brushed his lips against her freshly washed hair to whisper in her ear.

'Leave the office a bit earlier. I'll meet you here at five. Over there, by the coffee bar,' he waved his arm across the concourse.' In return, Yvonne put her arms around his neck and pressed her lips firmly against his cheek.

'Oh, don't worry, I'll be here,' she laughed as Vere gave her a peck on the cheek. Then she turned and joined the crowd making for the Underground.

***

That evening, as Vere and Yvonne relaxed at the cottage, Miles Overstone was giving the couple thoughtful consideration. It's now Thursday evening he reminded himself, only leaves Friday, Saturday and Sunday, three more days before the money's transferred to m account on Monday. Refusing to let his mind become obsessed with thoughts of big money, and evening drinks under the glorious setting sun in Panama, he focused on the young couple in Shiplake. Surely, if they've given any worthwhile information to the police I'd have known by now. Arrested and taken off to face a barrage of awkward questions. These he knew would be a mixture of what the police knew already, what Vere and Clarkson might have told them and sheer police guesswork.

Deep in thought the brash voice of Terry Noakes cut through his mind like a laser, was it only yesterday he'd told me how friendly they'd been with DCI Crowland? Damnation, he fumed, had Noakes been taunting me, or had he stumbled across something far more threatening? As for the notes left by Drysdale, what had they contained? After all these years, had the police somehow got hold of my DNA? No, not back then, there was no DNA. Did I leave anything in the car when we abandoned Drysdale? Did they still have any of our clothing? No, but we did leave the balaclavas in the car. Oh God, he sighed, knowing that any hairs left in them would contain traces of DNA. Overstone stopped his pacing, trying to control his racing mind. No, they've got nothing, he reassured himself. Even if they've managed to lift DNA samples, they count for nothing. They've got sod all to match it with as mine isn't on file. But could those two still be a threat? Questions without answers. Raging inwardly, he was desperate for a solution. Then, as Thursday moved towards Friday, he had the answer to his quandary. He had been right all along, based upon the balance of probabilities. While the pair did not pose a known threat, they may certainly pose an unknown one. No, he told himself, its high time to start taking risks to safeguard my plans.

CHAPTER 53

YVONNE SIGHED, STRETCHING out in the big double bed, relished the prospect of a relaxing weekend free without having to worry about Buchanan, DCI Crowland or the death of Noakes and his son. Pushing herself up into a sitting position she eased back onto the pillows, pleasantly aware that noises from downstairs told her that she was in for a treat. Ah, breakfast in bed she thought, what better way for a girl to get Saturday off to the perfect start.

Later, and propped up on even more pillows, they slowly worked their way through cereal and four rounds of toast and marmalade. Giggling and joking they made a considerable effort to keep crumbs away from the bed sheets, only to soon realising the enormity of their task. Coffee followed, one black, one white with no sugar. Then, with appetites satisfied, they gave attention to the daily paper that Vere had tossed across the bedclothes, sharing pages and passing comments.

Later, and seeing no urgency to get moving, they turned to each other and where no words were necessary as they eagerly pushed aside the discarded papers and straightened the sheets. Soon settling into tender and intimate foreplay during which their fingers and tongues advanced and retreated as they revisited familiar territory. Every excursion being enjoyed as if it were for the very first time. Their lovemaking, at first gentle, soothed away the stresses of the last few days before easing one another into powerful and shared exhaustion. Shortly after that they took a shared shower, an exercise where there could only be one inevitable outcome.

Later, happy, satisfied and deeply in love, they spent enjoyable hours in the Jaguar driving around the outlying villages in a search for antique shops. Not that they were serious buyers, Yvonne content to imagine how pieces of old furniture might blend in at the cottage. Whereas, for Vere, it was the attraction of copper and brass that held his attention. Eventually, they settled for an old Victorian copper bed-warming-pan on a solid wooden handle.

'Look well in the hall,' he commented as they drove away in search of a pub able to serve them a late lunch. This they found in an olde-world timbered building that had once been a coaching inn. There, and over pie and chips, their conversation turned to the following day where Vere expressed an interest a London exhibition of ancient Egyptian artifacts. But, for Yvonne, dreamy eyed and in love the thought of another day together easily overcame her lack of interest in four-thousand-year-old relics.

'Of course, we'll go,' she confirmed, willingly submitting to his wishes, although he had raised something of a precondition.

'That's great, but I'm a bit worried, what with having had so much time off work lately. Truth is I'm well behind with my workload and I've got these papers that need checking for a client meeting on Monday. Must be right because we're in court the following week. So, if we're off out tomorrow, I'll have to spend time on them this evening. Are you okay with that?'

'Of course, darling,' she agreed, content as the big Jaguar purred its way back to Shiplake, both unaware of what fate had in store.

***

Miles Overstone looked absently down the long lawn leading to the river, his focused entirely on cold-blooded murder. Clarkson first then Vere, he said to himself as he considered the prospects for success. That woman he fumed! What does she know, turning up at such a critical moment? I need to separate her from Vere, but how? For a while he pondered the problem, before returning to his desk.

Once seated he pushed emotion to one side and considered the facts. Ideally, he needed to tackle Clarkson on her home ground. People are always more relaxed on their own turf but, to do that, I need an advantage, but what do I have?

Thoughtfully he reached for pen and paper before starting to jot down the salient points needed to consolidate his plan. Address in Westridge Green, yes I've got that and her mobile phone number as well, al courtesy of Noakes's trawl of information. Known facts, he said to himself. Right now, she's most likely to be at Vere's place, but I need to get her alone and ideally over at Westridge Green. But what might compel an attractive young lady to abandon her "love nest" and return home on a Saturday evening? Deep in thought he absently doodled on the paper as his mind battled with the problem. Well, he smiled, I cannot rely upon her walking out after they've had a blazing row. An impossible prediction but there is one thing that might just work. Would she respond to a domestic emergency? But, even if she did, would she come alone?

Discarding a row as being completely unpredictable he gave attention to a domestic emergency, gas, electrical or plumbing. Which of those would bring about the required and immediate response? Convinced that he was on the right track he eliminated gas, not even sure if she had it in the house. Next electricity. She'd certainly have that but, short of a power cut defrosting her freezer, anything else would keep until Monday. So, that leaves plumbing and the nightmare of unexpected water leaks? Ruined carpets, damaged furniture, sodden floorboards, soaked plaster work and short-circuiting electricity. Now there's an idea, he smiled knowing that thoughts of that scenario would generate an immediate response. Not the sort of risk she'd be wanting to leave until Monday he laughed, aware how the fear of water sloshing around in her house would get the meddlesome lady back home soon enough.

CHAPTER 54

BY EIGHT O'CLOCK that evening Yvonne was settled in the lounge, aware that Vere working in the kitchen was the price of a day out together tomorrow. Relaxed, she fiddled with the television remote-control in the hope of finding something mentally stimulating. Disappointed when none of the channels managed to hold her attention for long she was interrupted by the buzzing of her mobile phone. Responding, she reached down for her handbag and withdrew the phone and looked at the screen, noting how the caller's number had been withheld. Momentarily she regarded it as a nuisance call, anything from PPI, a fictious accident injury claim, bank scammers or the collection of a bogus parcel. Modern technology was never invented for this, she thought, about to press the Do Not Accept button before having a change of heart and pressing the accept button. Make a change from television channel hopping she thought, despite anticipating the usual recorded message. Yet, on this occasion, it was a man's voice that caught her attention.

'Miss Clarkson?' an unfamiliar voice enquired.

'Yes,' she answered uncertainly.

'Oh, hello. Look, I'm sorry to trouble you but I'm glad I've managed to reach you. My name's Jackson and I'm an engineer with your water company. I'm sorry to be troubling you at this late hour, but we've got a problem in your area. As you're not answering the phone at Westridge Green you're not at home I thought I'd try your mobile.!

'Yes, Mr Jackson, you're correct. I'm not at home so what's the problem?'

'Please,' he said softly, 'let me explain. Earlier this afternoon there was what we call a pressure surge in the system, in and around the Westridge Green area. So far it's not proved to be that serious, but it can well blow out weak or suspect fittings in people's homes. You know like stopcocks, old taps, radiators or header tanks. But look,' he said reassuringly, 'I'm guessing you'll be okay, but appreciate that we always err on the side of caution.

Unfortunately, in these cases, rare as they are the risk of flooding can be a strong possibility. Fact is I've spent all day up here to make sure that your neighbours are safe, and I'd really like to check everything at your place as well. It won't take me long – fifteen minutes tops. Any problems, I can get a team of plumbers out to you right away, at no cost to you of course. Anyway, as you're not at home, is there any chance you could get back here to let me in?'

'Well, not really,' she said, hesitantly before having a sudden thought, 'but my next-door neighbour could, she has a key to my place. She'll let you in.'

'Hmm, well that used to be fine,' he said affably, 'but, under new legislation, we're not allowed to enter premises unless the owner is present. I know it's a load of old guff, but there you are. I'll be up here for another hour or more so, if you could make it back here, that would be great.' Yvonne took in what Mr Jackson was saying, fearful that some of the older fittings in her house might not be up to surviving the unexpectedly high pressure he mentioned. Then, like any good salesperson, Jackson went for closure. 'Forgive me, but I'm instructed to point out that if you fail to respond to this call, within a set time, our Insurers may reject any claims made against us in the event of your home being flooded.

'Oh dear, yes I can understand that.' she answered carefully, 'but how do you have my mobile number?'

'Oh, that was the easy bit,' he laughed. 'You gave it to us. Do you recall that we wrote to everybody asking for your help to update our records? And they're all on the laptop computer I've got in my van, along with my sandwiches and flask of coffee,' he joked. 'But' he became more serious, 'do you think you'll be long?'

'No,' Yvonne she replied, having reached a decision, 'about forty-five minutes should do it. That okay?'

'Great, many thanks and I'll see you then.'

After disconnecting Yvonne walked slowly from the lounge and stood in the kitchen doorway, peering down at the seated Vere. In silence she took in the scene, mildly amused as he had managed to cover the entire table with files, dockets, folders and legal pads. Cunningly leaving just enough space for a bottle of wine and a glass.

'Robert, can I interrupt?'

'Of course, sweetheart, what is it? Need another drink?' he smiled, tapping the bottle.

'No, it's a bit strange really. I've just had a man on the mobile, said he's from the water company, name of Jackson.'

'And?' he questioned, 'is there something of a problem?'

She shrugged none-committedly, stepping forward to pull up a chair on the other side of the cluttered table. Once settled, she passed on to Vere what Jackson had said

about the pressure surge in her area, explaining that in some cases it could leave serious leaks inside properties. Lastly, she told him how Jackson needed her there to let him in, explaining how this was now a legal requirement.

'True,' he agreed, 'and yes I can see the legal take,' he nodded.

'So,' she smiled, 'if it's okay with you, can I take the Jaguar and nip home and sort this out? Anyway,' she laughed, 'it could be providential as I'm in need of some more clothes. I've got two big meetings next week, plus a trip up to Nottingham for a major fashion show. And' she laughed again, 'guess what, I've got nothing to wear.'

'That sounds fun,' he laughed, giving her a wicked grin, 'that's not a problem and I'll come with you. After what Ted Crowland said I think I ought to,' he announced as Yvonne glanced down, taking in his tired face and the pile of papers on the table. Then, before he could say more his mobile phone rang. Pushing aside some files, he extracted the instrument and pressed it to his ear. Two minutes later the decision was made.

'That was one of the senior partners,' he pointed to the phone, 'he's been out all day and just got back in to find an urgent Fax. The court case for this lot,' he waved his hand across the table, 'has been brought forward to Wednesday. That means Monday's meeting, with the client, is now the final pre-trial check. Damn the bloody lot of them,' he fumed, pushing his chair back.

'Right, that clinches it,' she said firmly, 'this lots now priority number one for you. So, don't worry, if I slip off now I can be back soon after ten. Half an hour each way, half an hour in the house for Jackson to check the plumbing while I round up some dresses and shoes. Then I'll go around to see Mrs Frobisher. Make sure she is okay, what with all this water board business.'

'Well, if you're sure,' he said a little half-heartedly. 'I'd really appreciate some time on this lot now. In fact, after that phone call from up on high, I ruddy well need it.'

'Hey, don't look so sad. I'll be fine and back in time for a night cap. Are the car keys still in your jacket, out in hall?'

'Yeah, help yourself and take care. Love you.'

'Love you too,' she called back from the hallway, before closing the door behind her. Vere looked up, left with the tantalising aroma of Chanel No. 5 inside while outside he heard his car crunching slowly over the gravel.

CHAPTER 55

THIRTY MINUTES LATER Yvonne eased the Jaguar onto the grass verge outside her house, surprised to see an unoccupied white Range Rover already parked there. Intrigued, but not bothered, she went inside switching on lights and pleased to find no evidence of water leaks. Then she went upstairs, collecting the extra clothes she'd be needing and placing them into a small suitcase which she carried down to the hallway. Next she went into the kitchen where she turned her attention to the fridge. Her inspection led to a quantity of doubtful looking milk being poured away before she then took stock of the vegetable situation. Any vegetables, unlikely to survive her extended absence, went into a plastic bag which she then took next door to Mrs Frobisher and to let her know she'd be away for a little longer.

'Oh, I'm not sure about this,' she said shortly after entering her neighbour's house. 'Earlier this evening, on, over at Roberts, I had a man on the phone from the water people. Something about a pressure surge in this area, asked me to come back home so he could look at my plumbing. You know, just to make sure there were no leaks, hence me being here on a Saturday evening.' Pausing, she expressed surprise when Mrs Frobisher expressed surprise at the pressure surge and had certainly not had any callers. 'Not to worry,' Yvonne smiled, 'I reckon he'll be along shortly, knowing that I'm coming back. Meanwhile,' she joked, 'who's your boyfriend?' referring to the parked Range Rover outside her house. 'It's obviously not the water man, told me he was in a firm's van.'

'Not with me I'm afraid,' the elderly widow replied brightly.

'Odd,' Yvonne commented, 'we don't get many strange cars around here. Not to worry, I'll make a note of the number and scribble it down - just in case,' she smiled. 'Anyway, I'll call round to say hello when I get back. Looks like I'll be away for a few more days, home by the end of the week I guess,' she called out cheerily as she left. Walking back through the darkness to her house she noticed the Range Rover was still there. Curious, and knowing that the owner was not with Mrs Frobisher, she made a mental note of the car's number. Once inside, and with the door closed behind her, she wrote it onto a pad which she then pushed firmly behind the telephone on the hall shelf. Making sure that both the kitchen and lounge lights were off she returned to the hallway. Just as she was about to pick up her case the doorbell chimed, momentarily startling her. Jackson, she assumed, stepping forward she opened the door to find an older looking man in dark blue overalls smiling pleasantly at her.

'Miss Clarkson?' he said brightly, 'I'm Jackson, we spoke earlier about this wretched pressure surge.'

'Oh yes, of course, do come in,' she offered, swinging the door open and stepping to one side. 'Haven't found any leaks so far,' she pointed out cheerfully, turning to walk towards the kitchen and saying over her shoulder, 'most of the plumbing bits are down here, and the boiler's.......' Her words cut short as Jackson, now standing right behind her, thrust his left arm over her left shoulder and across her throat before pulling her backwards. Wearing high heels, she was immediately unbalanced, tottering backwards with her arms outstretched in search of a handhold. Jackson, anticipating this, held her tightly against himself with his left arm, using his right hand to pull a thick cotton wool pad from his overall pocket.

Holding this tightly across her nose and mouth caused her to cough violently as fumes from the chloroform-soaked pad entered her airways. Futile resistance continued for a second or two before her legs begun to buckle and she lost consciousness. Discarding the pad Jackson used both arms to catch Yvonne as she fell backwards. Taking the weight, he gently lowered her onto the carpet before kneeling to wrap strips of Velcro around her wrists and ankles. From ringing the doorbell to reducing Yvonne to a comatose captive had taken a matter of seconds. Still on his knees, he placed sticky surgical tape across her mouth in preparation of making his next move.

Minutes later, when his breathing and heart rate had returned to normal, he opened the front door a matter of inches. Cautiously he peered across the garden, then out towards the roadway. Not a sign of danger anywhere. Returning to the hallway he stooped down, manoeuvring Yvonne into a sitting position against the wall, before starting to slide her upright. Leaning forward he pushed his left shoulder into her mid-riff before drawing her across his shoulder and standing up. The classic fireman's lift he thought, feeling his legs wobble under the unaccustomed weight. Upright, he stepped outside and turning awkwardly with Yvonne across his shoulder, managed to close the door and heard the locking mechanism engage.

Releasing the Range Rover's tailgate with his right hand, he then slid the unconscious body onto the floor space behind the rear seat. Work for a younger man he thought, breathing heavily as he leaned against the rear of the vehicle, pausing to look around. Still all quiet, no twitching curtains, no dog walkers and not even a late-night jogger in sight. Leaning across Yvonne's inert body, into the space behind the seats, he retrieved a leather bag from which he took out a small hypodermic syringe filled with a colourless liquid. Moments later, after sending the fine spray of liquid needed to dispel air bubbles from the needle, he squeezed an area of her upper arm into a small mound, into which he inserted the needle muttering, 'sleep well,' over the recumbent body.

Minutes later and happy to discard his Jackson fakery he drove away from the darkened hamlet, satisfied that any further danger from Clarkson was now in the past and was a problem he now intended to solve on a permanent basis. But, in his haste to leave the cottage, he had failed to see the pad wedged behind the telephone.

***

For Vere, the evening passed quickly enough as he diligently read the legal papers, making copious handwritten notes as he did so. Deciphering the sworn testimony had been mentally draining, then trying to find loopholes in it even more so. Taxing in the extreme. Pausing, he looked up at the kitchen clock and was amazed to see just how quickly the time had gone. Ten-fifteen already, he sighed. Pushing his arms outwards, he stretched to ease the dull ache in his shoulders. Looking to his right the low level in his wine bottle caused slight alarm. Have I drunk that much already? Ah well, no point in leaving that last drop is there? Glass full, he settled down to re-read his earlier notes, comparing them against the sworn statement submitted by one of the land grab protagonists.

By eleven o'clock, with Yvonne still having nor returned, he was starting to feel a little anxious. But, deep down, he was unable to see any real cause for alarm, easily visualising Yvonne 'popping' next door, as she called it, to see her elderly neighbour. No doubt off-loading perishables from her fridge and having a good old natter with Mrs Frobisher. He smiled, having already classified the water company man as being of no importance. Relaxed, he knew that Yvonne had a key to the cottage and would return when she was good and ready. His mind, tired through work and wine could see no danger, just so long as the Jaguar's okay, the thought tinged with mild humour.

Wearily, he made his way up the narrow staircase, ducking automatically under the now painfully familiar low ceiling beam that crossed the landing, several feet in front of the main bedroom door. During his early days in the cottage his head and that *beam* had become all too well acquainted.

Eventually, and after such encounters, naming his bedroom the 'Nutcracker Suite' had been an obvious choice. Now, drunk or sober, he instinctively ducked when passing the offending piece of timber. Minutes later he quickly made it into bed, soon falling into a deep alcohol-induced and dream-free sleep.

CHAPTER 56

AWARENESS, LIKE THE dawn, crept slowly over Vere and it was well after eight before he was anything like awake. Then, stirring reluctantly, he was immediately aware of two things. A dry throat and a compelling need to visit the bathroom, blaming both on the previous night's excesses. 'Damned red wine,' he cursed, pushing himself into an upright position.

On unsteady legs he tottered along the corridor, instinctively ducking on his way to the bathroom. Gulping down a welcome beaker of chilly water his sluggish mind registered an urgent message. *You've just left an empty bed!* Struggling to digest the information he knew it was correct, the sight of Yvonne's neatly folded nightdress on her side of the bed being proof enough.

Close to panic he rushed back into the bedroom calling out her name, knowing full-well that she was not going to be there. Stopping abruptly, he looked down at the empty space, the neatly folded garment reigniting his worst fears. *No, she's not here!* the garment seemed to shout back at him. Something must have gone dramatically wrong. Yvonne's missing! She would never stop out all night, not without letting me know he told himself. Frantically he stared down at the bedside 'phone, his bleary eyes desperately seeking a flashing red light. Had Yvonne called and left a message? One not heard in my exhausted state. No flashing red light - no message! Had she had an accident? Had she decided to spend the night at her place? Permutations flashed across his mind, endless and unanswered.

Reaching across the bedside table he grabbed his phone, frantically dialling Yvonne's mobile number. Seconds later he was listening to her familiar voice asking him to leave a short message. Sheer agony. *So near, yet so far.*

Clearing the call, without leaving a message, he desperately redialled, this time using her home telephone number. No answer, just an impersonal electronic buzzing noise, as if the phone were out of order. For one moment he thought of ringing Mrs Frobisher, soon realising that was not an option. Ringing an eighty-something widow, this early on a Sunday morning was neither kind nor practical. Frantically he scrolled through the contacts stored in the phone, selecting DCI Crowland's number. Half a minute later a drowsy voice growled down the line.

'Ted! Robert Vere. Sorry about the hour, but I'm close to a blind panic. Yvonne's gone missing.'

'What?' Crowland rasped, propping himself up on one elbow. All thought of further sleep vanishing. 'Okay, hold on. Tell me what happened?' In the background Vere could hear a grumpy female voice muttering away. Doubtless the antagonised Mrs Crowland registering a strong protest at such an intrusion that early on a Sunday. 'Well, go on then,' Crowland insisted, ignoring his wife's plea to go back to sleep. Vere, in response, outlined the events of the previous evening. As he was finishing off Crowland cut in.

'Right, get over to her place. That water thing sounds highly suspect. What were you thinking of, letting her go over there on her own?' he scolded, anger and frustration in his voice. Then, more calmly, he continued. 'Get yourself over there, that's where we start. I'll ring Baxter and spoil his Sunday morning lie-in. See you there at ten. Meanwhile I'll get the station to check on any overnight traffic accidents, hospital admissions, that sort of thing. Just in case,' he added tactfully before disconnecting.

***

Badly distracted, Vere managed two cups of strong black coffee before leaving for Westridge Green in his MGB. On arrival he pulled up outside Yvonne's small semi-detached house, stopping directly behind Crowland's car with Sergeant Baxter standing beside it. Beyond that he could see his Jaguar.

'Morning, sergeant. I'm sorry to muck up your Sunday. Where's the DCI?' he asked, nodding to Baxter as he climbed out of the sports car.

'No worry, sir, he's just looking around the outside, suggested I wait here for you.' Hearing voices, Crowland appeared around the side of a hedge.

'Mr Vere, good morning. Have you got a key?

'Sorry, no, but Mrs Frobisher, the lady next door has one. Good neighbours. Mrs Frobisher keeps an eye on things when Yvonne's away'

'Got it,' he said turning to his sergeant, 'see if you can get the key. Be polite, remember she's an old lady, but be quick about it.' It took Baxter less than two minutes to return with the key.

'She might be old, but she's up and about. Fully dressed and quite with it. Told me Yvonne had called round to see her last night, about nine. Said she'd mentioned something about a chap from the water people, name of Jackson. Said she'd be away for a little while. Gave her a bunch of salad stuff from her fridge. Didn't want it to go to waste, she'd said.'

'Okay, cut the Master Chef stuff. Mr Vere's told me about this Jackson chap, don't like the sound of him one little bit. Where's the key?'

'Right here, Gov.'

'Good, then let's have a look inside.

***

Once through the door evidence of a scuffle having taken place in the narrow hallway was clear to see. The centrally placed rug, now crumpled, lay to one side while the contents of an open suitcase lay scattered across the foot of the stairs. Further down the hallway Vere spotted Yvonne's handbag, picking it up before Crowland could stop him looking inside.

'Her wallet's still here, as well as her mobile,' he called out.

'What about cash and cards?' Crowland snapped back, a little annoyed at Vere's interference.

'Looks to be okay. Fifty in cash plus her cards, Nat-West, Amex and Barclaycard, along with her company credit card. Oh, and her railway season ticket.'

'Did she have any other cards?' Baxter asked.

'Not that I know of,' he confirmed, his faced lined with concern.

'Looks like we can rule out robbery,' Crowland said softly.

'Of course, we can,' Vere said forcefully, 'she's vanished without a trace. Abducted and we know by whom. Buchanan's now working for the water company!' Before Crowland could comment there was a loud banging on the still partially open front door.

'Sorry to be a pest,' the grey-haired Mrs Frobisher announced, stepping inside uninvited, 'but is something wrong? I mean, with a police officer wanting Yvonne's key.' She looked quizzically at Crowland, before continuing. 'And I suppose you're a police officer as well?' she peered up unflinchingly at Crowland.

'Yes, Mrs Frobisher, that's right. I'm DCI Ted Crowland,' he told her, pushing out his right hand. Then, as Baxter moved from her line of sight, she spoke again.

'Oh, Robert, I didn't see you there.'

'That's okay, Mrs Frobisher,' he managed to smile, stepping forward to greet the old lady, 'but it looks as though Yvonne may be in spot of bother and, right now, we're not sure where she is.'

'Oh, how dreadful, she's such a beautiful girl, perfectly charming and really kind to me.'

'I'm sure,' Crowland said, a little patronisingly. 'But can you tell me what happened last night, you know when she came to see you?'

'Well, yes, but there's not that much to tell really, she wasn't with me for long. She told me about a man from the water people, said he was coming to see her, something to do with a pressure surge whatever that is, and the possibility of leaks. After that she was planning to go back to your place,' she said, looking up at Vere. 'But, thinking about it, she did seem to be a little bothered about a strange car, parked right outside. Thought it might belong to someone visiting me.' She laughed, 'I ask you, eighty plus and getting visitors after nine at night. I should be so lucky.' Both men smiled politely.

'Yvonne said she'd write the number down, when she got back home, just in case it was something out of the ordinary.'

'Baxter,' Crowland said quietly, putting an arm around the frail shoulders of the old lady. 'Please take Mrs Frobisher back home,' he said, steering her towards the still open front door. 'Oh, Mrs Frobisher,' he said as she moved away with the sergeant, 'could you be a dear and make us a pot of tea? I think we might be here for a little while and a cuppa would go down a treat'

'Yes, of course,' she said cheerfully, 'and sergeant I can find my own way back home. I might be old, but I've not lost my marbles, well not yet anyway.' Baxter smiled, returning to the hallway as Crowland stepped by him to go outside, mobile at the ready.

'Sergeant, I'm ringing for back up. You and Mr Vere have a quick look around, ask him if anything looks to be out of place. I'll be back in a minute, but don't touch anything.'

'Right, sir,' he called after his departing superior before turning to Vere. 'Pretty sure the DCI will designate this as a crime scene, probably onto Forensics now,' he added as they moved through into the small lounge. Later they went upstairs, taking quick glances into all the rooms.

'Seen anything out of the ordinary yet, sir?' Baxter asked.

'Not that I can see, but this is driving me crazy. It's clear Yvonne's been abducted, and by this so far unknown Buchanan. We can't do anything here. We must get out there and start looking.'

'Okay, sir,' Baxter said patiently, 'I know what you mean, but let's finish the inspection first. To find Yvonne, I mean Miss Clarkson, we must start from here, it's the last place where we know where she was. There'll be clues, and we need to find them, so look for anything out of the ordinary.'

'Okay, you win, but I'm not what you'd call a regular here. Although we've been together for over a year now our time together, in the main, has been over at my place.'

Five minutes later, they were back down in the hallway, just as Crowland came through the front door.

'Anything?' he asked expectantly.

'Not that I could see, all looked okay to me,' Vere said to Crowland who did little to hide his disappointment.

'Hang on a minute, sir,' Baxter asked, 'wasn't Mrs Frobisher saying something about an unusual car being outside last night?'

'That's right,' Vere said excitedly, 'she mentioned that Yvonne was going to make a note of the number somewhere.

'Let's get looking! Mr Vere, as you've already been in her handbag, have another look? See if you can find anything? Notebook, diary, a scrap of paper, anything she might have written it down on. Oh, while you're in the bag,' Crowland added, 'let me have her mobile, you said it was in there.'

'What for?' he asked the DCI.

'Just thinking about what you said earlier. That call, you know, from the "so called" water board man. Yvonne took it on her mobile you said, so I'll get the technical people to see if they trace the phone's number. They might get something,' he remarked as Vere handed him the phone. 'Meanwhile, I'll have a look in the kitchen, Baxter take the hall, then the lounge.'

'Yes, sir,' the sergeant acknowledged, moving away from the stairs and towards the front door later, and after giving careful attention to the small glass shelf with the telephone, he looked up and shouted for Crowland.

'Sir, come and have a look at this.' Further down the hallway Vere, hearing the urgency in Baxter's voice, looked up as Crowland emerged from the kitchen.

'What is it, sergeant?

'There's a pad here, sir, wedged tightly behind the telephone.' Slipping on a rubber glove, he carefully slid the pad from its place of semi-concealment. 'This is it, sir! There's a number written on it.' Crowland stepped forward, staring down at the pad and studying it carefully.

'Good spot, sergeant. Mr Vere,' he called out, 'can you tell if this is Yvonne's writing? Because, if it is, that could be the car number Mrs Frobisher mentioned.' The DCI pointed, waiting for Vere's verdict.

'Yes, without a doubt,' he confirmed, staring down at the writing.

'Great stuff, that's one smart girl. I'll check it out now,' he said snapping open his mobile phone and punching in a number. After a pause, lasting little more than a couple of minutes, he closed the mobile.

'Car belongs to one Miles Overstone, he's got a big house up near Wallingford, by the river.'

'No way, Gov! That's not right, no way,' he shook his head in disbelief. 'He's a local millionaire, entrepreneur, philanthropic charity donor and, no doubt, a freemason to boot. No, she's made a mistake there,' Baxter stated emphatically.

'Sergeant,' Crowland asked slowly, 'you've met Miss Clarkson now - on what - three occasions, haven't you?'

'Yes, sir, you know that. You were present at all of them. Here, after the fire bombing, again at Mr Vere's place and then days ago at Castle Street.'

'Right then, and based upon those experiences, would you say that Miss Clarkson was a capable person? Someone able to remember a car number and write it down correctly? Also remember this is a lady who sees things and writes about them for a living. So, I ask you again, would you say that Yvonne wrote this number down correctly?' Crowland asked quietly, but with a hint of sarcasm.

'Well yes, sir I would,' Baxter agreed while casting alternate glances at both men.

'Right then, let's see if our Mr Overstone is at home to visitors shall we.'

CHAPTER 57

YVONNE'S HEAD WAS spinning. The crazy dream just went on and on. She was flat out on her back in hospital and a masked man was leaning over her brandishing surgical instruments and mouthing meaningless platitudes. She tried to cry out, unable to understand why her words would not come. Frantic with worry she wanted to run, but her legs wouldn't move. Was this masked man a surgeon? Desperate and unsure she tried to push him away, confused as her arms refused to work.

Bit by bit the hazy dream began to fade as, like a photographic slide coming into focus, her eyes adjusted to reality. This was not a dream. The surgeon slowly faded, replaced by a figure from recent memory, her late-night caller from the water company. She wanted to cry out, but words were impossible, stopped by the large strip of plaster across her lips. She wriggled helplessly, unable to move either arms or feet.

'Ah, we're awake are we, Miss Clarkson? Good morning.' The strange voice lanced through Yvonne's woozy mind. Panicking, and flat on her back, she wondered why she was unable to use her arms to push herself into a sitting position.

Speechless and tightly restrained she felt vulnerable, lying helpless before this scary stranger. Further efforts to move her arms were unsuccessful, only producing the metallic rattling sound of her dreams. Giving up the battle with her arms, she slumped backwards and looked intently at the face peering down at her.

'Well,' the thin balding man spoke slowly. 'Now we're all alone that nasty tape can come off, no one can hear you outside this room.' Without warning he whipped his hand across her face, tearing off the tape in one swift movement that sent a blazing pain through her lips and cheeks

'God!' she spluttered, the pain giving way to shocked recognition. 'The man from the water company.'

'Well, not quite, but it worked didn't it, Miss Clarkson?'

'Worked, what do you mean, worked?' she asked in confusion. 'Why am I here? Where am I?' she challenged despite feeling so helpless.

'Why indeed,' Overstone said mildly, 'but let's start with the easy bit shall we? As to where you are, well that's straight-forward enough. You're in my house just outside Wallingford, a nice little place beside the river.' The thin wrinkles on his face creased slightly, caused by yet another sickly smile. Then, by tilting her head further back, she could see wrists attached to the brass bedhead and were firmly held in place by a pair of handcuffs.

'As to the why, as in why you are here?' The man stood upright, looking dispassionately down at the restrained body in front of him. 'You see, I'm a double act. Today I'm the nice Miles Overstone, property developer, local millionaire, benevolent charity donor and, well, everybody's friend.' He shrugged his shoulders. 'Then, on other days, I'm my true self. Bank robber, drug runner, abductor of females and a murderer.' The words hit Yvonne like a bucket of freezing water. Desperately, she pulled at the handcuffs. Next, she tried to move her legs, again no reaction. Looking down she saw why. A large black Velcro strap had been bound firmly around her ankles. She went limp, terrifyingly aware that she now lay at the mercy of a killer. Tears began to roll down her cheeks, fuelled by rage and impotence.

'You see,' Overstone continued, 'over recent years I've established a financially rewarding lifestyle, one that is due to improve even more dramatically tomorrow. But, in the meantime, as you and your boyfriend have the capacity to cause me trouble I must have you both removed. That, my dear lady, is a euphemism for being killed. You understand?' he said this quietly, pulling up a chair and setting it down beside the bed. 'I need to be rid of trouble-makers, well, in this case you and Robert Vere.' Horrified by what she was hearing Yvonne sobbed, helpless and terrified.

'Very cleverly you found Noakes, frightening him so badly that he hatched his hair-brained scheme to fire-bomb your car. Such a shame that a nice old man from the garage died in the fire. But now, as you know, that should have been you,' he chattered away without a trace of malice. 'Then,' he smiled, 'just when things looked like getting back to normal, along comes Noakes junior. You'll be pleased to know that he told me how you and your boyfriend are snuggling up to the police, telling them all sorts of things about me. He even told me that the police have a set of my fingerprints. Then, and you can hardly believe this, he told me all about the notes Stephen Drysdale left behind.' Pausing for effect he watched as this information soaked slowly into Yvonne's brain, like water into a sponge, as she finally recognised the awful truth.

'You,' she gasped, 'you,……you're Buchanan,' she writhed on the bed, giving her arms another desperate pull.

'How astute,' he said bitingly. 'Just as the Noakes duo sealed their fates by interfering, your meddlesome antics have done the same for you,' he grinned, savouring the moment. 'Well, not for a while, so relax. I want your boyfriend here to partake in the final ritual as you're both going to die in a place where no one will ever find your bodies!' His voice rose as he finished the sentence.

'No!' she shouted, horrified by what she had just heard. 'Robert will come for me,' she cried out, more in hope than anger.

'Oh, he'll come all right,' he told her reassuringly, 'I'm relying upon him to do just that. It's so sweet, and all because he loves you. Why, I'm sure he'd walk over red-hot coals to reach you. But' he paused, stroking his chin, 'don't worry about that. There won't be any red-hot coals where you're going.' He laughed at his joke. 'I'll even leave the front door open because I know he'll come dashing to your rescue – the misguided fool.'

'We don't know who you are, or anything about you.'

'Oh, come now, don't be so modest. You did well to find George Noakes, but now your meddling has got in my way. Please understand, tomorrow evening I'll be sailing into the sunset, with millions of pounds of someone else's money in my pocket. After months of preparation,' he sighed, 'I'm ready to start a new life, poised on the cusp of success you might say.' He smiled before pulling a face. 'Then you two arrive on the scene. Interfering and dragging in the police,' he whispered softly, leaning forward on the edge of his chair, 'even at my ripe old age a new life awaits. But not for you, I'm afraid.' Yvonne groaned in desperation, the full meaning of his words striking home as more tears rolled down her cheeks.

'Don't worry,' Overstone addressed her cheerfully, rising from the chair, 'you've still got a little while to compose yourself. Meanwhile, you'll remain tied to the bed. Then, later, I'll bring you something to eat, of course freeing your hands to eat and then letting you visit the bathroom which is just over there,' he pointed to a doorway. 'Don't get any ideas about escape. As I said a minute ago, you are an unwilling guest in my house, not that I expect you to enjoy it,' he laughed. 'This room,' he waved a hand, looking around, 'is hermetically sealed and sound proofed.' He smiled, 'the builders assure me that an orchestra could play the 1812 Overture in here, cannons and all, and no one outside would hear a thing. Oh, and the windows are bullet proof,' he added nonchalantly.

'But' Yvonne spluttered, desperately trying to find a way out, 'we don't know anything about you, nor do the police.'

'Miss Clarkson,' he smiled, 'you don't expect me to believe that do you?' his eyebrows raised. 'Don't insult my intelligence! For a fact, I know you've seen DCI Crowland repeatedly, at your place and at Vere's. Not only that you had lunch with him the other day, doubtless helping them with their tactics.' He paused, expecting an interruption, but as none came, he continued. 'Oh yes, I know all about your afternoon meeting with Terry Noakes, all of you tucked up nicely at the police station. Anyway,' he continued, revelling in his self-importance. 'Did you know that I pushed Terry

Noakes in front of an underground train? No?' he sneered, 'why should you? He was rubbish and was stupid enough to think that he could intimidate me.' Sliding back the chair he stood up, staring down at the limp body, recognising utter defeat when he saw it.

'Oh,' he said turning to the door, 'and let's not forget your little sessions with the charming DI Robson. No,' he said reaching for the handle, 'as you and Vere know too much I dare not go taking any risks right now. No hard feelings, but you must die.' With that he was gone, turning the key in the door and leaving Yvonne sobbing uncontrollably while crying out Robert's name.

CHAPTER 58

'NICE CAR,' BAXTER nodded towards Vere's MG as he and Crowland drove away, leaving the white suited forensic and fingerprint specialists hard at work inside Yvonne's house.

'True,' Crowland offered, 'if you like museum pieces, but okay on a day like this with the hood down. Mind you, he's got that Jaguar for his proper driving,' Crowland nodded, pointing a thumb over his shoulder at Vere's other car. 'Anyway, let's see what Miles Overstone has to tell us.'

Five minutes later they were driving slowly down the long hill that took them into the village of Streatley, Baxter at the wheel.

'Just over there,' Crowland pointed to the steep hill on his left as their car stopped at the traffic lights, 'is part of the Ridgeway.'

'What's that when it's at home?' Baxter asked.

'It's an old route, used by cattle herders up to five thousand years ago, and later by Roman soldiers. It's a pathway running from Avebury in Wiltshire through to Buckinghamshire, handy knowledge for use in pub quizzes. At Avebury, you'll find the largest ancient stone circle in Europe.'

'Thought that was Stonehenge,' Baxter commented, as he turned left, having negotiated the traffic light-controlled strip of road beside the Bull public house.

'Well, for your sake, let's hope they haven't added history to the exam for inspectors.'

'So,' Baxter asked, keen to get away from the lecture, 'this Overstone guy, how do we play it?'

'Just follow my lead, sergeant,' he replied, carefully taking a compact silver case from his top pocket. Baxter, while keeping his eyes on the road, managed to see him open the case and carefully withdraw a small number of his police business cards. Intrigued, he was able to see the DCI select one card from the middle of the bunch, handling it only on the edges. Curious, he managed to catch a glimpse of the card being turned over before the DCI wrote a telephone number on the back. Satisfied with his work he replaced the card, face up on top of the other cards which he then returned to the silver case.

'What's all that in aid of then, Gov?'

'Watch and learn, sergeant, watch and learn.' Twenty minutes after leaving Westridge Green, Baxter pulled up outside the closed and imposing gates leading down to Overstone's palatial looking house.

'What a place,' he exclaimed, 'bit beyond a sergeant's pay,' he said, stepping from the car.

'And mine,' he heard Crowland say through the open car door as he moved to use the gate-mounted intercom system. Moments later he heard a low-pitched humming noise as the heavy wrought iron gates began to swing open. Seconds later he was back behind the wheel, moving the car slowly down the long driveway towards the white-painted house.

'Do come in,' Overstone said warmly, welcoming the two police officers under the imposing entrance porch. 'But I must confess to being somewhat curious,' he remarked, before guiding his unscheduled visitors through the elaborate entrance passageway, complete with the two sets of glass doors. Reaching the main hall itself, he turned and looked closely at the officers before examining their identity cards. 'And now, to what do I owe this visit?'

'Well, sir,' Crowland smiled, addressing the sharp-eyed Overstone, 'it's probably nothing but, as the jargon goes, we need to eliminate you from our enquiries.'

'Enquiries, you say. Goodness me, of course I'll do anything to help. It all sounds like they say on those television programmes,' the immaculately dressed Overstone joked. 'Do tell me more?'

'Not much to tell, right now, sir,' Crowland replied. 'it's just that there was an incident last night, over at Westridge Green. Do you know the place, sir?', Crowland asked with the hint of a challenge in his voice, hoping to unsettle Overstone's relaxed composure.

'Hmm,' he thought before answering, 'let's say I've heard of the place, but I don't know it. But' he paused to question Crowland, 'what do you mean by an incident?'

'I can't say too much at present, it's just that a young lady seems to have been abducted over that way last night.'

Abducted!' Overstone responded quickly, a little too quickly Crowland thought, detecting tension in his voice.

'That's right, sir, abducted. So, just to tidy things up, I need to ask you where you were last night, say round about 9 o'clock time.' Both men remained silent, watching Overstone intently.

'But why are you questioning me about this?' he asked indignantly, his back stiffening noticeably. 'Of course, I'll do everything I can to help you. I don't want to appear uncooperative and upset your superintendent, or heaven forbid, the chief constable himself. Do I?' His polite laughter doing nothing to hide his veiled threat.

'Quite so, and I do understand,' Crowland parried, bristling with anger at Overstone's loaded words. 'It's nothing really, standard procedure at times like this because, as I said, sir, I'd like to eliminate you from our list of suspects. Fact is,' he continued before Overstone could add more bluster, 'a sharp-eyed neighbour noticed an unfamiliar vehicle parked for a while, right outside the house we're interested in. Being a public-spirited citizen, he wrote the registration number down, handing it to one of my lads when they were checking the area earlier this morning. A call to the vehicle licensing people showed it up as belonging to you, a white Range Rover,' Crowland read out the number Yvonne had written down.

Yes, that's my number,' he said dismissively, 'obviously a mistake as I was at home all evening. Well,' he paused, 'not strictly correct I suppose,' he added, 'I had dinner up at the golf club, somewhere around seven. I went up there alone, ended up dining with the club secretary, after that I came home. Got back here about nine, I think.'

'Anyone verify that, sir?' Baxter asked, notebook at the ready.

'Well, the Golf Club secretary of course.'

'That's fine, but what about back here, at home, sir?' Baxter persisted.

'No can do. I'm a confirmed old bachelor, live all on my own so no alibi there I'm afraid.'

'No worries,' Crowland shook his head, 'as you say, sir, the nosy neighbour got it wrong. However, if you do think of anything else, can you give me a ring please, sir? I'll leave you a card. You'll find my office and mobile numbers printed on it.' Baxter watched as his superior withdrew the small silver case and, by using his forefinger and thumb, carefully passed the top visiting card to Overstone.

'As I mentioned sir, if you think of anything at all, give me a ring.'

'Of course,' Overstone nodded as the police officers took their leave and headed for the doorway, Crowland paused, mid-stride, before turning to walk back towards Overstone.

'Oh, hang on a minute, sir. I've just had a horrible thought. That card I've just given you, can you flick it over to see if I've scribbled anything on the back? Terrible habit of mine, jotting phone numbers on the back of my cards. Can you check it for me please?' A startled Overstone turned the card over in his hand.

'Oh, yes. You're right, there's what looks like a number on the back,' he confirmed, handing back the card.

'Oh, thanks, bad habit of mine,' Crowland smiled, taking the card back and looking at the number he'd written on it. 'Oh good, that's for a chap called Buchanan. Didn't want to mislay that one, although it's got nothing to do with our abduction enquiries.' he smiled, disappointed at seeing no change in Overstone's expression. 'You know how it is,' he continued, 'suddenly you need to write something down and there's never a piece of paper handy. Anyway, if you let me have that back, here's another card.' Overstone took the replacement card, before casually turning it over.

'You're safe this time, Chief Inspector. No state secrets on the back of this one.' Bemused by the exchange, and the mention of Buchanan, Baxter watched as his DCI accepted the card back, holding it only by the edges before sliding it into his jacket pocket. Back in the car Crowland spoke first.

'What did you make of our friend there, sergeant?'

'Well, he's rich, powerful and has friends in high places. As for believing him, I just don't know. But what was all that about a neighbour clocking his car number, then giving it to one of our chaps? As for a list of suspects, you've got me confused. And that's without pitching Buchanan's name into the conversation. Damn nearly made me jump.'

'Glad to hear it, hopefully it threw Overstone as well. Let him think that at least one person saw him at Westridge Green last night. I wanted to try and rattle the bloke, see how he reacted to the word abducted. Trotting out Buchanan like that was a last-minute idea.'

'Yeah, he twitched a bit at abduction, icy calm when you mentioned Buchanan though,' Baxter remarked, moving the car slowly up the driveway. 'Mind you, one thing's for sure.'

'And what is that sergeant?'

'If we're to go head-to-head with that guy, we'll need a heck of lot more than a car number plate.'

'True,' the DCI muttered as Baxter swung clear of the heavy gates, before heading through the rolling countryside towards Reading.

'While I think of it, sir, what was all that business with the cards?'

'As I said watch and learn because, thanks to that, we now have a perfect set of Overstone's fingerprints. Therefore, should our people find any of those in Yvonne's house he'll need to do some explaining. Like you, I didn't believe him for a moment. He's too smooth by half, gave the impression he could have been expecting us. Hoping to head us off at the pass as they say in all the best cowboy films. Anyway, I need more information before I dare go for the throat. For the time being I want to unsettle him, keep him guessing. Behind all that gloss, I'm betting he's a shifty bastard with a fair amount to hide. Now let's get the ball rolling and see what the honourable secretary has to say for himself, over at the golf club. Chances are he should be there on a Sunday morning, checking all is well in his little empire.'

From the lounge window it was a badly troubled Overstone who watched as the police officers left his property, aware that the DCI's almost casual mention of Buchanan was no slip of the tongue. It had been deliberate, convincing him that his decision to eliminate Vere and Clarkson had now become a priority.

CHAPTER 59

VERE FELT USELESS, watching as the two police officers drove away while behind him white-suited forensic specialists scoured Yvonne's house for evidence. But, for him, there was nothing; no information, nothing he could be doing and, worst of all, *still no Yvonne*. Did their failure to find a body, or even bloodstains, in the house confirm that she'd been abducted? If so, might the next move be some sort of ransom or blackmail demand? Yet, for that to happen communication from the abductor was essential. But so far silence. Had this unknown Buchanan really been here and seized Yvonne? And what about this Overstone fellow? Had Yvonne made a mistake recording the Range Rover's number? But what if she'd been right and it was Overstone's car? What was he doing up here in Westridge Green? It's either bloody suspicious, or is there a perfectly logical explanation?

'Robert,' the frail voice cut into his wildly racing mind, 'why don't you come round for a cup of tea? You can't help dear Yvonne by standing there,' Mrs Frobisher said kindly. Tea, Vere thought, turning to face the elderly lady, the English panacea for every known problem.

'That's kind of you, Mrs Frobisher, a good cuppa is probably just what I need right now.' Vere recognised the widow's genuine concern, knowing full-well that it was based upon her deep affection for Yvonne.

Three hours later and he was back home, feeling a little more motivated as he left a voice mail for Mary, his secretary at Regency Law, explaining that he would be away from the office for a few days. Unable to say more he disconnected. Afterwards he made a second call, leaving a similar message on the answer-phone system in Yvonne's office. For a man of the law being untruthful went against the grain. Even so, putting her absence down to illness was better than saying she'd been abducted so, to appease his conscience, he said he'd call back in the morning, after she'd seen a doctor. No sooner had he finished making those calls than his mobile demanded attention.

'Oh, hello, sir. It's Gary Baxter here, DCI Crowland has asked me to give you a call.'

'Yes,' Vere answered, a wave of hope surging through his body.

'Sorry, but there's not a lot to report. We visited this Overstone fellow, at his place near Wallingford. Didn't deny that the car number is his but was unable to explain how it was outside Miss Clarkson's house. Said it must have been a mistake, saying he'd had dinner yesterday evening with Major Forbes, the golf club secretary. The major confirmed this, although times vary a bit. Overstone said seven, but the secretary reckoned it was nearer half-six. Either way, Overstone was gone from the Club before eight. Said he went straight home but, as he lives alone, no confirming witnesses.'

'Okay then, he could just as easily have been at Yvonne's before nine,' he remarked hopefully.

'Possible, I guess, but we need more to go on. Anyway, stay close to the phone. I'll get right back to you if we get anything further to go on.'

'But what about that water company fellow – Jackson or whatever his name was? Did you get anything off Yvonne's phone?

'Not really, okay it recorded the call being made, but it showed up as number withheld. Our technical boys had a good look, traced the call back to one of those pay-as-you-go phones. Useless to us, I'm afraid.'

'Yes, but what can I do?' Vere pleaded, 'there must be something.'

'Not right now, sir. Just leave it to us. We're getting things moving over here.' Baxter presented this crumb of comfort, in the hope of placating Vere yet knowing it to be worthless. 'Stay near the phone. I understand how you feel,' Baxter offered diplomatically

'Don't patronise me, sergeant! Vere shouted belligerently as the line went dead, further fuelling his mood of depression.

Disconnecting the line Baxter looked across the office at his DCI, perched on the edge of his chair, elbows on the desk and head in his hands.

'Poor sod, he's gutted. His girlfriend's been lifted, and he can't do a thing.'

'Well, we're not much better either, are we? It's Sunday, we've a missing girl and not a clue between us.' Crowland replied, raising his head as he thought back to his attempt to get his superintendent to grant him a warrant to search

Overstone's place. 'Good God, man!' he'd raged at the DCI. 'Have you taken leave of your senses? Miles Overstone is a millionaire, pillar of the community, charity supporter and a mason. For God's sake,' he'd fumed, 'I play golf with him and he's a friend of the Chief Constable. Now you want to go barging in there, turning his place over on the flimsy basis of a car registration number. I'll wager the silly girl made a mistake in the first place. No, you'd better come back with something a lot stronger than that if you want my backing for a warrant.'

Crowland, forced to accept the inevitable, had felt crestfallen and frustrated. A feeling triggered by the thought that his superior might be trying *to circle the wagons.* Was his reluctance to back me genuine or a move designed to preserve harmony at the golf club or amongst the masons? And that's without upsetting the local *establishment*, the ranks of which his upwardly mobile superintendent was desperate to join.

'If only we could find some trace of the girl, even a strand of her hair in the back of his Range Rover,' Baxter persisted.

'Gary,' the DCI said slowly, 'with me, you're pushing against an open door. But, with that lot upstairs, it's welded shut! Imagine trying to get a magistrate to sign off the warrant? They'll all be in the same blasted clique, garden parties at Buckingham Palace and everyone a mason!' he said sarcastically. 'And you never heard me say that.'

'Say what, sir?' Baxter said slowly 'but shouldn't we be asking the obvious question here?'

'Which is?'

'Why would an ageing millionaire be abducting a beautiful girl like Clarkson? Fair enough, I thought he looked crafty but we can't pull him in for that, can we, sir?'

'No way,' Crowland laughed, 'the cells would be full to the brim. But look,' he said seriously, 'aren't you missing the obvious here as well?'

'How do you mean, sir?'

'It wasn't, as you said, a girl like Clarkson that got abducted, it *was Clarkson*. So, why would a supposedly respectable millionaire need to abduct Clarkson? That's the nub of the problem. Find me a link between

Overstone and Clarkson, then you'll have your answer? That's assuming it was Overstone who abducted Clarkson, in the first place. And, if he did, why?'

'There you have me, sir,' Baxter replied thoughtfully, 'in fact it's all rather tricky. We need to dig out the evidence, as much to clear Overstone as to pull him in. But, for whatever reason, the boss man won't allow us to go near it. So, until we can eliminate him we have no other leads worth a light.'

'In a nutshell,' Crowland sighed, flopping back in his chair as Baxter began talking again.

'What if we did turn Overstone's place over, you know and found nothing? Profuse apologies all round. Good enough for everyone else in the Thames Valley, but not acceptable to friends of the top brass. Let's hope this doesn't go belly-up. We'll end up with an enquiry, into an enquiry, and the super will struggle to save his arse.'

'Right now, sergeant,' Crowland laughed, 'the only arse I'm interested in is Miss Clarkson's, and don't you dare take that the wrong way or traffic becomes a certainty.'

'No, sir,' Baxter gave a wicked smirk, unseen by the DCI.

'Right,' Crowland sat bolt upright, 'staying with the vernacular, get your arse in gear and see if forensic have produced anything useful out at Clarkson's place. That's apart from being able to tell me that her milkman smokes a bloody pipe! Go!'

***

Later that Sunday afternoon DI Robson and her subservient sergeant drove deep into the estate where the search for Briggs was in full swing.

'It's no good,' she shouted, 'I want results. It's time to get out there and crack heads,' she ranted as the sergeant parked their car under the watchful gaze of a young constable. 'Keep your eye on this car,' Robson barked as she left the vehicle, 'look the other way for ten seconds and the bloody wheels will be gone.' Turning on her heel she headed further into the bowels of the estate, followed by the luckless sergeant. Already under acute pressure because of the overtime costs, she needed to fire up the teams of officers conducting the house-to-house search for Denny Briggs.

'For God's sake, somebody must have found something by now,' she raged at her sergeant as the teams returned unable to pinpoint Denny Briggs. Later, and still in a positively volatile mood, she was confronted by a uniformed sergeant noted for his outspoken attitude.

'Look, Gov, my boys and girls are doing their best, so don't keep harassing them. If there's anything there to be found, they'll find it.'

'Sergeant,' she stormed, 'when you're a DI you can tell me how to run this search, until then shut up!' Completely unabashed, he stared coldly back at the DI before replying.

'Of course, Gov, you know best. But knowing best and getting the best are two different things altogether,' he said peering down at the angry face glaring at him. 'So, if you want the best out of these guys, you'd better change your bloody attitude, and change it now.' Robson's jaw dropped, momentarily stunned at receiving such a painful dose of her own medicine.

'And, before you utter another word,' the sergeant added, pressing home his advantage, 'I'll deny ever having said this. But it`s time somebody told you to go and take a running fucking jump because your attitude stinks! You're a disgrace to your uniform, *and to the Force*. In fact, I'm ashamed to be associated with you.' Without further ado he turned on his heel, walking away to join a young WPC, leaving Robson fuming with indignation and lost for words.

***

In a shabby apartment, not that far from where Robson glowed incandescent with rage, the root cause of her fury faced a worried Jimmy Green.

'Look, mum says you can stop here for a while longer. She's already told your old lady that you're okay, but this can't go on, you know.'

'What you mean?' Denny asked, confusion showing on his face.

'See outside - the whole place is crawling with coppers. We've never had this many before, not even when young

Julius knifed that old geezer, in the pub a year back. Fuck me, we're in lockdown.' He dropped onto the sofa, his feet swinging up onto the coffee table. 'Look, Denny, no one can deal. Blokes are desperate to score. Nobody can make

any money, they're scared witless! There are coppers all over the bleeding place. Hell, even the hookers are out of work and getting ready to claim Job Seeker's Allowance.' Green laughed at his own joke, as Denny remained silent. 'Come on,' Green continued. 'Old Sid, down the way, reckons the landlord of the local boozer says opening up's a waste of time. Says none of the regulars will go near the place. Everyone's scared, like, knowing it could be invaded by the plod at any minute. No, Denny, it's time for you to the police. You've done brilliantly, staying clear for days now. So, go and turn yourself in. The coppers want your help. They're not going to nick you.'

'And you believe those lying sods?' Denny snarled back, 'look how they stitched up your Billy, two years back. Promised to go easy on him if he coughed. Then they threw the book at him. Ten years minimum, I ask you. All for nicking a motor and running some silly old bugger down, just as they were driving off. Fuck me, it was an accident, anyone could see that! And you expect me to trust them?'

'Yeah, what you're saying is true, but we can't go on like this. The whole estate's sewn up tighter than a fish's backside. The lads are getting jumpy. Someone will shop you sooner or later, just to get those sods off the estate. Then mum and I will get done for harbouring you, probably get sent down.'

'You reckon?' Denny asked, gently massaging the swastika tattoo on the side of his neck, while giving thought to his friend's words. 'Yeah, you're right I suppose. I could do with moving a load of gear on myself, including a few good cards. Leave it much longer and they'll be stopped - ruddy worthless. Okay' he said, 'put the word out that I'll go to the coppers in the morning.'

'Good man, then we can all get back to something like normal.'

'Okay,' Denny responded, 'that'll stop them moaning,' he smiled and rubbed his hands together. 'Right then, got any more of those beers, and fancy sharing a joint?'

CHAPTER 60

AFTER SWITCHING OFF the MG's ignition system Vere remained seated, having stopped beneath the covered entrance to Overstone's palatial Wallingford home. In the ensuing silence he was surprised to hear a cultured voice deliver a message of welcome although unable to see the speaker.

'Mr Vere, welcome and please do come. Miss Clarkson and I have been expecting you.' Well-chosen words, delivered with precision and raising his spirits, proof positive that Overstone had somehow been involved in Yvonne's abduction, if not solely responsible.

Climbing slowly out of the MG Vere looked across at the ornate pillars, then up at the imposing arched roof they supported. Wearing an old tracksuit and worn trainers he felt a little out of place, hardly the right attire for such opulent surroundings. Bugger what I'm wearing, Yvonne's here and that's all that matters right now. Time to sort out Overstone and get her back to Shiplake. Little could he have foreseen the devastating consequences of his ill-advised and unsupported action.

By three o'clock he had been going frantic, not having heard a word from the Police while any attempts to reach Crowland had gone straight though to his messaging service. Alternatively, when dialling directly through to the police station, his treatment had been courteous but depressingly similar. 'I'll get him to call you back, but you do realise that it's Sunday, sir?' had been the response, time after time. Yet, convinced that a financial demand would soon be forthcoming he'd waited for the call that never came. His optimism shrinking as the hours had ticked by.

Determined to do something, but unsure as to what, he'd looked to his computer for help. If Overstone was the only lead the police had, no matter how tenuous, it had to be worth looking at. An on-line search had highlighted Miles Overstone as a respectable property dealer, operating from offices in Docklands and with a home near Wallingford. Google Earth had shown this to be a mansion, set in its own private grounds with high walling and gated security. The images also showed that the property had a good hundred yards of prime riverside frontage. A bastion of respectability, four-square to road and river, designed to keep people out or, he thought, just maybe to keep people in!

Vere, unaware that the police had earlier discounted the prospect of an ageing millionaire abducting a young woman, had still found the idea valid. Is it a sexual thing? he'd wondered or is he into white slave trafficking? God forbid, he thought, working hard to dismiss visions of people bidding for a scantily clad Yvonne in a middle eastern slave market auction. Farcical ideas he'd dismissed just as quickly. Nothing made sense because, if the police are unable to pin anything on Overstone, it's likely he's got nothing to do with it anyway? Had she simply made a mistake in recording the car's number? But, then again, if not Overstone then who else and why?

These, and countless other thoughts, had tormented him into the late afternoon before he'd decided to confront Overstone head-on. Maybe not the best policy, but with nothing to lose so what? If he's clean, I'll be on my way. Half an hour later he'd backed the MG out of the garage and had driven to Wallingford with just one thought in his mind.

***

Finding the electric security gates open had been a surprise to Vere as, beyond them, the sloping driveway to the house tempted him towards to his next surprise. Everything was unreal as he saw how the heavy wood panelled front door had been swung wide-open as the unseen speaker continued to talk.

'Mr Vere,' the voice boomed again, 'allow me to repeat my invitation. Please do come in, Miss Clarkson and I have been expecting you.' Expecting me? Vere questioned, the relief at hearing Yvonne's name adding certainty to his mission. Cautiously he went through the open door into the passageway where, a little further along, what looked to be a heavy glass door was conveniently held open. Six feet beyond that was an identical glass door, this one closed. Beyond this was the brightly lit semi-circular entrance hall, at the back of which opposing staircases curled gracefully upwards, one either side of the hallway. Positioned centrally on the far wall, between the curving staircases, he saw the sliding doors of a lift . Then, to his surprise, an older looking man in a wheelchair came into view, rolling up to the glass door and holding what looked like a television remote controller.

'Quite a place,' Vere said, seeing no danger from an old chap in a wheelchair. Reaching the second door he gave it a solid push in the hope of coming face-to-face with Yvonne's captor. Surprised the door failed to yield to his effort, he looked down and was about to question the man when an unexpected hissing sound from behind made him turn. The door behind him had now closed.

'Now, Mr Vere,' the man in the wheelchair said, 'I have you where I want you. In fact, and to be frank, you're trapped between two sets of doors made from toughened security glass. Stop a bullet so I'm told, not that I've tried that test just yet,' he smiled. 'Where you are now is an airlock, it's completely soundproofed with just the speaker and microphone high above your head.'

'Very impressive, I'm sure. Quite a welcome, but what do you mean by saying you have me where you want me?' Looking intently at the man in the wheelchair he began to feel the first signs of anxiety. 'I guess you're Miles Overstone, but how do you know my name? I've come here in the hope that you can help me find my girlfriend.'

'Oh, yes, I know who you are, Mr Vere, and let me assure you that Miss Clarkson is here already. And yes, you've come to the right place.' Overstone squeezed a lever on the wheelchair, moving closer to the glass. 'I was certain you'd come, barging in here before too long, ready to grasp the only straw the pathetic police have. Not to worry,' he smiled 'you're both here and you won't be leaving. Not ever!' Vere shivered, struggling to stay calm despite his rising fears.

'What do you mean, we'll never leave? Are you some sort of confused fruitcake?'

'Fruit cake? No, on the contrary,' he laughed. 'I'm a hugely successful entrepreneur on the verge of pulling off an outstanding financial coup or fraud, depending upon your point of view,' he added. 'But sadly, in my hour of triumph, you and Miss Clarkson have got a little too close for comfort, *my comfort* that is.'

'Yvonne?' Vere questioned, calling through the glass.

'Yes, she's here and you'll soon be together for all eternity,' he said softly as Vere watched in astonishment as the man vacated the wheelchair and walked briskly up to the glass panel. 'Look at you,' he sneered, 'you're pathetic. You come charging in here and see an old man in a wheelchair. What harm could he be? You undoubtedly said to yourself, not knowing that others have made the same fatal miscalculations.' Pausing, he turned and paced across the wooden floor before returning to the glass. 'You've heard of George Noakes? He was one such person who made the fatal mistake of underestimating me. But' he smiled, 'right from the word go I knew he never had the balls for that armed robbery, all those years ago. At first, he was useful but, like so many others, he ended up being a dangerous liability and had to disposed of. And now, just like Noakes and his son, for you and Miss Clarkson it's your turn to die.'

'Die!' Vere gasped, stepping forward to place a hand on the glass as he suddenly realised what was happening. 'My God, you're Buchanan!' he called out, shaking his head in disbelief. 'And, by the sound of things, you're still deluded enough to think that murder is the only solution to a problem. How do you think that an old man like you is going to get the better of me? I'm fourteen stone and six foot two.'

'Come now, Mr Vere,' he laughed, 'stop the bragging. I've no intention of tackling you head on as that would indeed be a one-sided contest. One that I could never win. However,' he expanded, 'I always win because I leave nothing to chance. Observe your stupidity. Right now, you're a prisoner in a sealed an airlock into which I shortly vent nitrous oxide. Did you know that was once known as laughing gas? Either way,' he chortled, 'you'll not be finding much to laugh about,' he smiled contemptuously.

'And then what?' Vere asked, desperately trying to hide the fact that the latest bit of information had terrified him. 'It won't take long for the police to come looking for me!'

'Ha, the police you say,' Buchanan grinned through the glass, 'why, they've been here already,' he laughed, shaking his head, 'you really are way behind the times. My friendly superintendent, the one I play golf with, kindly rang me. Told me his DCI, a chap called Rowland, or something like that had taken the liberty of asking for a warrant to search my house. The nerve of the chap! Can you believe it, a snotty little DCI wanting to search my house? Anyway,' he mocked Vere, 'my tame superintendent told me that he'd sent his over ambitious subordinate packing. Search warrant indeed! The cheek of the man. Doesn't he know that I'm untouchable? Sorry, no "boys in blue," you're on your own.' Overstone laughed, happy to boast about his privileged and unchallengeable position. 'Now you're on your own, well not exactly on your own if you take my drift. You and Miss

Clarkson will be together, for a while anyway, before you die. Sadly, I cannot make it a quick ending because I need you both to remain well hidden after I leave.'

'Leave?' Vere asked frantically.

'Oh, yes, I'll be departing tomorrow as well,' he shrugged his shoulders, 'off for a better life in the sun. Whereas, by this time tomorrow, you pair really will know if there's life after death. An interesting point for you to ponder as you spend your last hours together.'

'But' Vere shouted out, 'that's murder!'

'Oh, spare me, Mr Vere. I've murdered people before, and I'll do it again. Now, as I'm going to turn on the gas, I suggest you sit down so as not to incur any injury when you fall. When you recover, well you'll be in an underground room and shackled to the wall where, I'm pleased to say, the delightful Miss Clarkson already awaits your company.

'You can't.......' Vere spoke, his words cut short.

'That's enough, I don't want to hear any more. I'm switching off the microphone. Sleep well,' his final words spoken as he opened a small wall-mounted cupboard beside the glass door, operating the valve that sent gas swirling around Vere in the confined space. Seconds later, as he dropped to his knees, he made one last effort to avoid injury as he lost consciousness.

CHAPTER 61

EARLIER THAT MORNING Buchanan had returned, inviting Yvonne to eat from the small tray of sandwiches and fruit juice he'd brought with him. But to no avail, fear having robbed her of an appetite. Dry-mouthed, and watched over by her captor, she'd been grateful for the fruit juice and had managed to drink all of it. Next, the tape had come off her ankles, leaving her free to walk unsteadily to the bathroom. Upon her return the sight of Buchanan holding a pistol had shattered any last reserves of resistance..

'On the bed, flat on your back now,' he had shouted while brandishing the pistol, 'and with your hands above your head.' Yvonne had complied, terrified and uncertain of what was going to happen. Slowly, Buchanan had then walked back across the room, stopping at the bedside. Scared to move, she had submitted meekly as handcuffs and straps were re-fixed to her wrists and ankles.

Later, as the light had begun to fade, she heard the now familiar sound of the key turning in the lock. Seconds later Buchanan had entered the room, this time pushing a wheelchair which he stopped beside the bed. Reaching into a small bag, hanging from the back of the wheelchair, he withdrew a slim hypodermic syringe. Its significance obvious to Yvonne who, struggled to speak while staring in horror as Buchanan had upended the needle. Pressing on the plunger he'd then expelled a small amount of clear liquid to rid the syringe of any air bubbles.

'No,' she'd cried out in terror, writhing in desperation to avoid the inevitable as, foiled by the handcuffs and straps, she'd felt the sharp stab made by the needle. Smiling, Buchanan had stepped back, taking fiendish delight in watching her struggle before the powerful sedative had delivered oblivion.

Once satisfied that she was unconscious Buchanan had first undone the restraints before moving her across the bed and into the wheelchair. Minutes later, after using the lift, they were in the main entrance hall from where Buchanan had pushed her into a broad corridor that ran alongside an outside wall of the house. Halfway down the corridor he stopped, looking down at where the carpet he'd previously folded back exposed an aluminium panel about six feet long and three feet wide set flush with the floorboards. Dull in colour the panel had a recessed lever to one side, not unlike the fitting used to open aircraft doors. Concealed by the heavy carpet it easily remained undetected by anyone walking over it.

After stopping in front of the panel Buchanan had stepped away from the wheelchair, before kneeling to grasp the recessed lever which he had twisted through ninety degrees. Then, standing upright, he'd lifted the panel on its hinges, through the vertical before pushing it back against the outside wall. On the underside of the panel the cross braced strengthening strips of angled metal were clearly visible while around the four edges strips of rubber made the fitting airtight. This was Buchanan's trapdoor, the sealed access to his hidden cellar of death. After returning upright he had slipped Yvonne from chair to floor, positioning he drugged body by the edge of the opening. Then, by kneeling, he had pushed her into the darkness where she had fallen about four feet onto a pile of foam mattresses.

Knowing how he'd soon be needing the wheelchair again he'd pushed it to one side, stooping to pick up an aluminium ladder he had placed beside the trapdoor earlier in the day. Using this he had then climbed down into the cellar to recover the unconscious Yvonne from the mattresses. None to gently he had dragged her across to the far end of the poorly lit cellar, placing her into a sitting position against the wall. Above Yvonne's head, at what would normally be waist height, hung a length of chain securely welded, at one end, to a metal plate bolted into the brickwork. Then, after taking hold of the other end of the chain, he'd attached this to handcuffs around Yvonne's handcuffs with a heavy padlock. Snapping shut the padlock he knew, with absolute certainty, that he had restrained Yvonne for her last journey.

***

Vere regained consciousness, confused and desperately uncomfortable as he battled to make sense of his surroundings. Its dark, cold and I'm ruddy uncomfortable he told himself after conducting a preliminary audit. Finding it difficult to see in the dimly lit space he returned to his main concern, namely his extreme discomfort. Trying to focus on this priority his befuddled brain supplied the answer. You're sitting on cold, damp concrete. Must get up, he told himself, struggling to rise and confused as to why he couldn't move his hands. One look was enough. Even in the poor light the handcuffs, and the chain fixing them to the wall, were the unmistakable bonds of captivity.

'For God's sake, what's happening?' he called out as realisation gave way to panic, making him pull his wrists against the hard metal. The unexpected pain sliced through his brain, acting as a powerful stimulant forcing him focus on his present predicament. Okay, he thought, that's the easy bit, I'm handcuffed and chained to the wall in a dark, cold and dismal place. But how did I get here? And just where is here?

Slowly, but with agonising clarity, he remembered the events of last Saturday evening, recalling how Yvonne had rushed back home in response to an emergency phone call from a water board official called Jackson. But no, only now do I know that Jackson was a fraud. He'd told me so himself and that there never had been an emergency. Just a plot to get Yvonne alone, his jumbled brain recalling how Yvonne had written down the number of a car parked outside her house. No, there never had been a Jackson. Crowland had said so. The car spotted outside Yvonne's house belonged to a local dignitary by the name of Overstone, someone Crowland had said was beyond reproach. Well, he got that wrong, didn't he, Vere cursed, forced to recognise a mistake when it now affected him and Yvonne so badly.

After that nothing, he sighed. Well not until frustration had sent me charging off to Overstone's mansion where it's all gone so horribly wrong. Seated in a wheelchair, behind a glass door, Overstone had played me for a fool. Initially taunting me by saying that Yvonne was already in the house and waiting for me. And, like a mug, I'd believed that I'd simply waltz out of there with Yvonne on my arm, seeing no danger in an old man in a wheelchair. But then he'd come clean, declaring his dual role as Alistair Buchanan, bank robber and murderer with Yvonne and I next on his list! Then had come total darkness.

'Oh, God,' he sighed, now fully aware as to why he was sitting on a damp concrete floor, with his back against a rough brick wall and driven by the need to do something - anything. With movement hampered by the handcuffs and chain, even managing to finally stand upright was a major achievement. Battling hard to fight off advancing panic he took stock of the situation.

First impressions showed that he was in a smallish room, about fifteen feet square, with whitewashed walls and a bare concrete floor. The basic of basics he concluded, wondering just how any form of escape from this virtual dungeon might be possible. Disheartened, he gave no thought to a couple of square-shaped metal grates about two feet apart in the centre of the floor. Dismissing these as irrelevant he looked up at the ceiling, seven feet above him. It was then that he saw the open trapdoor, away to his left. A sight designed to offer no encouragement to anyone chained up in a cellar where the only way out had to involve that trapdoor.

But I've got to get there first he thought, craning his neck to see more of the open trapdoor. Swung open, and leaning back against the far wall, it admitted a welcome shaft of light into the cellar. Not made of wood he surmised, more likely metal by the look of it. Directly below the opening he could see a pile of mattresses, held in place by cargo netting secured by short metal spikes driven into the concrete floor.

Concluding that this must have been his point of entry, when dropped unconscious onto those mattresses, he wondered if Overstone could be acting alone. Ever grateful for small mercies he welcomed the dim light provided by three light units along the wall to his left. These, evenly spaced and mounted about five feet above floor level cast an eerie glow across the cellar. Next, he noticed the long wooden shelf fitted above the lights, empty apart from what he took to be a small domestic header tank with pipes and wires running into it. Not much to go on, a trapdoor on my right, and three dim lights and a shelf to the left. Slumping back despondently against the wall he accepted their position must be somewhere on the bad side of hopeless.

Straining his eyes to look towards the far end of the cellar he saw a bundled heap of rags or sacking which, to his amazement, seemed to move ever so slightly. At first Vere wondered if his eyes were deceiving him in the poor light. Had there been movement? Curious, he tried to see more, teased again as the bundle gave another sign of minimal movement. Struggling for a clearer view he blinked in astonishment, detecting yet more movement from the far end of the cellar, accompanied by a low groan and the unmistakable sound of chain-links rattling. Frantic with worry he tried to see more, watching in horror as he picked out a familiar and much-loved face in the gloom.

'Yvonne!' he screamed, relief flooding through him as he wrestled with the heavy chain that prevented him from rushing to her side. Again, he shouted out her name. Desperate for a response, the lack of any further movement from the far end of the cellar only serving to increase his anxiety. Stunned by her silence he looked around, seeking salvation in the belief there had to be a way out of their frightening dilemma.

Oh, for fuck's sake,' he cursed loudly, looking at the narrow shelf above the lights in the forlorn hope it might contain the odd tool or two. Such hopes dying at birth as the tight chain reminded him that he couldn't get anywhere near the shelf, not even if it contained B and Qs finest tools! With his eyes becoming accustomed to the poor light, he looked closely at the shelf he'd spotted earlier. Yet, despite further scrutiny, he was none the wiser and unable to see any purpose in having a domestic header tank plumbed in this cellar.

Still feeling groggy himself, he repeatedly called out her name, fear and urgency making him shout even louder. Terrified that she was either dead or unconscious he continued to call out her name, pleading for a response. Pausing, after a couple of minutes, he detected signs of movement at the other end of the cellar, making him redouble his efforts. Moments later his spirits rose at the sound of her familiar voice croaking under strain.

'Robert,' she groaned, 'what's going on? For God's sake, the man from the water board.' She stopped for a moment, gasping for breath as the memories came flooding back. 'He took me by surprise, attacking me and them, well he must have drugged me. Then, when I came round, I found myself handcuffed to a bed. Hours later, more drugs and then ending up here. It's Buchanan! He's behind this. He's completely crackers. Masquerading as Overstone, fooling everybody, but he's really Buchanan. Robert,' she sighed in frustration, where are the police? she asked before falling silent.

'Oh, Yvonne, yes, I'm as okay as I can be,' he answered, before detailing how he'd fallen foul of the deceptively docile Overstone. 'Yes, now I know he's Buchanan and, like an idiot, I came in through the front door. But listen, more importantly, how are you?'

'I'm cold and very scared,' she called back, with a sob she couldn't suppress, 'but better for seeing you, even in this dump.' With an aching heart Vere listened to her words, infuriated at not being able to find any words of comfort for Yvonne.

'Yes, he's pulled the wool over a lot of eyes,' he said vehemently, 'managing to get us chained up in this cellar. Not sure what his game is but I think we're in a bit of a mess,' he replied, convinced that had to be the understatement of the year.

'For God's sake, Robert, he says he's going to kill us. I'm absolutely terrified,' she called back, fear giving an edge to her words that echoed in the bare room. 'Where are the police?' Painfully aware that Yvonne's nerve was close to breaking he searched for encouraging words. But there were none. What could he say? Any offering would come, he knew, from a heavy heart tormented by failure. I mustn't let Yvonne know that my visit here was a solo effort. She must have something to hang onto. How could I have been so stupid? Crowland warned me about doing anything silly. SILLY – what I did was insane. Thoughts he put on hold as he searched for something to say, lies, platitudes – anything.

'Hang on in there, sweetheart. He's all wind and water. He hasn't killed us yet,' he said feigning optimism. 'I'm sure that Crowland's on the case, even as we speak.' He spoke with a bravado he knew to be false, hoping the mention of Crowland's name would provide encouragement. In resolving to hide his own distress, from the woman he loved his hatred for Buchanan simply fuelled his own overwhelming feeling of self-loathing.

CHAPTER 62

WITH VERE AND Yvonne confined in his cellar, Overstone thought about the changes he'd have to make to his escape plans following the visit of the police. Unwelcome as this had been he knew it was time to introduce more diversionary tactics to throw them off scent. Yes, he smiled, I'll give them an entirely new scent to focus on, one that'll have them dashing off on a wild goose chase. A move he knew would buy him the time needed to reach Southampton, board the ship and move the money to Panama. As for those two in my cellar? he thought briefly and without emotion. No sweat, their bodies will remain undiscovered for years. Ha, he chuckled to himself, by the time they're found they'll be unrecognisable.

With the driveway lights extinguished he drove Vere's MG around to the back of the house, leaving the engine running while opening a side door into the garage. Soon he returned pushing an electric bicycle that he managed to juggle into the space behind the MG's front seats since the hood was down. Okay, he thought, not perfect but who'll notice at one in the morning? Having then secured the bike he returned to the garage to collect a retractable tape measure.

After switching off the engine he carefully took a measurement inside the car, before going back into the garage. Minutes later he reappeared, bringing with him a sawn down broom handle, a house brick and a ball of string. Placing these items on the passenger's seat he got back into the car and started the engine. Minutes later, after leaving his property, he urged the eager little sports car through the darkness towards its destiny.

With the headlights cutting a swathe before him he soon reached Streatley where the traffic lights held him up for a couple of minutes. Five minutes later it was another set of lights that brought the MG to a halt, this time the set controlling the flow of traffic on a narrow railway bridge. After the bridge, the road sloped downwards running between the railway embankment and a wildlife centre on his left. Seconds later the river came into view, its surface black under a cloudy and moonless sky.

Slowing down he brought the MG to a stop alongside the river on the approach to the village of Pangbourne. To his left, bordering the road, he knew that the neatly manicured lawns belonged to the houses opposite. With the engine just ticking over he stepped out of the car and lifted the electric bike from behind the front seats. Once released, he placed the bike against a nearby fence ready to make good his return to Wallingford. Returning to the car he then drove forward a little way, pulling onto a ten-foot-wide stretch of grass that sloped down to the river. The single, low mounted, line of plastic chain separating the road from the grass broke easily under the MG's tyres. Leaving the engine running he got out, taking the broom handle, string and house brick with him. Leaning forward, he made use of his torch to position one end of the broom handle on the clutch pedal, pushing down until the mechanism was fully depressed. With the broom handle already cut to size, the other end fitted tightly against the driver's seat squab. With the clutch disengaged he was able to lean into the car and safely select first gear. Happy with this, he positioned the house brick against the accelerator pedal. Then, by making further adjustments with the brick, he was able to keep running fast enough to move the car forward once the clutch was engaged.

Only then did he cut a length of string from the ball, tying an end to the broom handle nearest the seat squab. Standing back, he took one last look around, double-checking that the blackness of the night kept him from public view. With care he then pulled gently on the string, his action easing the broom handle across the front of the seat squab, so letting the clutch up gently enough to prevent the engine stalling. Which, to his relief, it didn't. Slowly at first, the car began to move forward, building momentum as it rolled across the sloping grass before plunging into the river.

Overstone watched, mesmerised as the car, partially floating, drifted away from the bank as the gallant MG battled to stem the forces of nature. Soon, the weight of the engine and in-rushing water dragged the front end below the surface. Immersed, the headlights cast a dull pool of light below the surface while the red taillights blazed defiantly two feet above the water. For a moment in time everything remained perfectly balanced as, while the front half of the car had slipped below the surface, the rear half hung in the air acting as a counterweight. Then it was over. The engine stopped, the electrics shorted out and the car slid from view.

Briefly air bubbles, nature's silent witness, marked the spot for a matter of seconds before they too were gone as the dark and sullen river resumed its journey downstream as if nothing had happened.

With both sets of seat belts left undone Overstone felt sure that first impressions would count in his favour. Tyre marks and the broken chain-link fence would indicate that a car had gone into the river, triggering a recovery operation. Aware that basic checking would show who owned the car he hoped the police would assume that Vere, having found Clarkson, had died alongside her in a tragic accident. Confident with his improvised planning, he knew the absence of bodies would force the police to mount a search downstream and well beyond Pangbourne weir, taking up valuable time and resources.

Mounting his electric bike for the journey back to Wallingford, he was quietly relaxed, wanting the MG's recovery to bring about a futile search for bodies, buying enough time for him to make good his escape. Hell, all I need is another twelve hours.

CHAPTER 63

'**GOOD MORNING, SIR,**' Baxter said perfunctorily, entering the DCI's office with the first coffees of the day. 'Anything in about the Clarkson?' he enquired before setting down the two plastic cups.

'No, nothing at all so far,' Crowland replied. 'I've just run another check to see if anything came in overnight, but nothing – just a blank.'

'But hang on, sir, this just doesn't ring true,' Baxter stated, drawing up a chair opposite Crowland. 'A good-looking girl like that can't just vanish,' he said in frustration. 'We know exactly where she was, and the only lead we've got is that Overstone fellow.'

'Don't even go there, or we'll both get flaming mad. Anyway, I'm having all the usual avenues checked, ports, airports and hospitals, but so far nothing. I've tried ringing Vere but he's not answering his mobile.'

'That's odd,' Baxter remarked, right now 'I'd have had him down for answering on the first ring. Tried the cottage, sir?' Baxter suggested.

'No joy there either. More to the point, I'm surprised he's not been pestering us,' the DCI muttered as he picked up his plastic cup. 'Forensics find anything at Yvonne's place?'

'Sadly no, sir, just bits and pieces, nothing of any real significance for us to go on. No helpful fingerprints. Okay, male footprints in the hallway but without a shoe to match them against they're no good to us. They could belong to anyone. Oh, what I'd give for that search warrant,' Baxter sighed taking a deep pull on his coffee.

'You can forget about that,' Crowland said despondently. 'I'd like to search Overstone's place, just to get him out of the way. I know we've not got anyone else in the frame, but there's something about that bloke that bugs me.'

'I know what you mean, Gov. Too clever by half and friends in all the right places.' The ringing 'phone prevented further comment, Baxter watching it pensively as his DCI answered tersely.

'Oh, good morning,' he said, covering the mouthpiece to whisper 'D I Robson' to Baxter. For a full thirty seconds, the DCI listened in silence before speaking. 'Fine, many thanks for that and keep us posted, please,' he said replacing the phone. 'Ah,' he said, looking at Baxter, 'that might just be a little bit of progress.'

'What do you mean by progress, sir?'

'Robson tells me that Denny Briggs, the chap they think saw Buchanan, turned himself in at eight o'clock this morning. Robson says she's had the estate virtually locked-down for four days now. All to no avail and now he's turned up of his own free will. Anyway, she's convinced that some *helpful person's* been sheltering young Briggs.'

'Nice of them,' Baxter said sarcastically.

'Well yes. Robson's guessing that the large police presence on the estate has put the lid on all illicit operations. Tells me how none of the villains have been able to ply their unlawful trades and, as the dealers can't deal, that's left smack heads to start going cold turkey. She's sure the big lads have put pressure on young Briggs, you know, come clean or we'll do it for you.'

'That's a start then, sir,' Baxter acknowledged, 'perhaps we can get a photo fit of some sort from him.'

'Maybe,' Crowland rubbed his chin. But do you know what. The so-and-so has even had the nerve to tell Robson that he wouldn't say a word well, not until he knew all the officers had left the estate! Anyway, he's talking now, so we'll have to wait and see what he produces. Robson tells me she'll put the frighteners on the little sod, charge him with aiding and abetting a murderer and wasting police time if he doesn't come clean.'

'Should cure his constipation,' Baxter's brief smile faded as he spoke again. 'But changing tack, sir, has DI Robson got anything more on the George Noakes's shooting?'

'Not really. We spoke yesterday,' Crowland replied thoughtfully, 'she said it looked like a professional hit. No prints, no DNA, motorcycle courier all in black, complete with helmet. They recovered the gun, wiped clean and with the number ground off. Mind you, they did match the bullets to a killing in the city a year or so back. Nothing there either, that's now classified as an unsolved case for now.'

'I'll bet Buchanan's in there somewhere,' Baxter offered, and was about to continue when the 'phone rang again.

'Crowland,' the DCI acknowledged curtly.

'Sir, it's the Incident Room. We're just getting reports of a car going in the river, up at Pangbourne, late last night or early this morning.'

'What happened?' Crowland asked out of curiosity.

'Not sure, but a local dog walker saw the tell-tale evidence round about eight this morning, you know, broken chain-links and tyre tracks leading into the water. He phoned us and, so far, we've just had a keen young copper wading out to have a look. The rivers about six feet deep there, I'd guess,' he said helpfully. 'Oh, and they've organised a recovery truck, it's on its way there now, sir.'

'Thanks, sergeant, but why are you telling me all this?'

'Oh, sorry, sir, I nearly forgot. Our man in the river reckons it's a white M, sport car job. Didn't you mention such a car at the briefing?' Crowland sat bolt upright.

'Yes, you're right. Good man, sergeant. You're spot on there, that's high on my list of things I need to find. Have they found any bodies?' Crowland asked impatiently.

'None reported to my knowledge, sir, but they're getting a team out to scout the riverbanks downstream, just in case.'

'Sergeant, we're on our way there now. Thanks for taking the initiative and letting me know.' Crowland replaced the handset and looked across at Baxter.

'Right, sergeant, the waiting's over. They've found a white MG in the river at Pangbourne. No number, but a pound to a penny it's Vere's. Bring the car round and I'll meet you out front.'

CHAPTER 64

FOR VERE AND Yvonne, it had been a long and miserably uncomfortable night. Their only relief coming from the dim lights remaining on since the trapdoor had remained open. Looking towards the opening Vere had recognised the truth. So near yet so far. Close but unobtainable he'd fumed, pulling at the rusting links, inflicting more pain on his wrists.

Earlier, hearing the unmistakeable sound of his MG's straight-through exhaust system, his spirits had risen. The deep throaty rumble had, at first, seemed to come from one direction. Then, moments later, it had faded to a gurgle, left ticking over perhaps. Ten minutes after that it the sound had reverted to a steady growl before fading away into the night.

'He's taken my car and cleared off,' he'd shouted to Yvonne, his outburst unanswered in the semi-darkness. No, he reasoned, Overstone must come back. Hang on Overstone's a fake. He's really Buchanan. Even Yvonne knows him as that. Underneath that veneer lurks a killer. Hardly comforting thoughts for us he cursed, languishing in his cellar, manacled and with no means of escape. Even so, if Buchanan intended us to die down here, he would have shut the trapdoor. No question about it.' Slumping back onto the floor, he called across to Yvonne but again received no reply. He guessed that she'd relapsed into a long and reclusive silence after pleading with him to do something. Do something! Like what? He thought, looking across at his distraught and bedraggled girlfriend. Bereft of ideas, he shuffled closer to the wall and closed his eyes, desperately trying to think.

An eternity later a voice cut into his troubled sleep, dragging him back to the realities of captivity and helplessness. 'Ah,' it boomed. 'Miss Clarkson and Mr Vere!' the voice resonated around the cellar. Lifting his head, Vere looked towards the source of the sound, aware that it had to have come from above. Peering upwards at the trapdoor he could see the head and shoulders of their captor. Kneeling alongside the opening Buchanan was taking his body weight on his outstretched arms as they spanned the opening. Thrusting his head well forward, until he was able to see them both, he addressed his victims. 'No doubt an uncomfortable night,' he called down, 'which really is a shame as it was your last!'

'Stop crowing!' Vere responded, aware of Yvonne stirring against the other wall.

'Indeed, I will, as it's now time for me to be leaving. Something I just couldn't do without saying a fond farewell.' He paused, leaning a little further over the opening. 'Anyway, just in case you haven't worked out what will be happening to you, allow me to explain.' Vere continued to look up, but Yvonne was too exhausted to even bother. Dishevelled, she sat on the floor with her knees slightly raised, her left shoulder against the wall, her handcuffed arms hanging from the short chain.

'I'm sure you'll have noticed the metal grilles in the floor,' Buchanan began, conversationally. 'Well, before long, water will start to flow up through them, rising slowly until you are both drowned. The water flows in here under gravity, comes from my large ornamental fishpond out there on the lawn. When the level rises above your heads, it'll float the small ball cock on the shelf. You can see it up there;' he waved his arm down into the cellar. 'The ball cock, when it floats, will activate an electrical circuit to shut off the flow. Can't have my fishes going completely short of water, can I now?' Receiving no reply, he went on. 'Sadly, neither of you two will be doing any floating.'

'For God's sake, Buchanan, this is sheer cold-blooded murder!' Vere roared, pulling harshly on his chains in desperation.

'Yes. I suppose it is. But there you are, I try to think of everything. You see, in the small hours, I dropped your precious MG in the Thames over at Pangbourne. Yes, once found that'll leave the police to think you found Yvonne and crashed into the river shortly afterwards. Absolutely tragic, then the police will start a massive search downstream for your bodies. Drowned at Pangbourne or drowned here, what's the difference? Either way you're dead. So, goodbye, Mr Vere and Miss Clarkson, I'll be closing the trapdoor in a minute but first the lights will go off. So, you may care to take one last look at each other before I throw the switch, leaving you to drown in total darkness.'

'Look-wait!' Vere cried out in desperation, 'at least let Yvonne out.'

'Oh, come now. Do you think I'm that naive? Your Miss Clarkson can identify me, as indeed can you. No. You've left me with no choice. Goodbye!'

'You're a murdering bastard!' Vere screamed back, 'if I ever get out of here don't be around.'

'Not a threat to worry me, Mr Vere. Not only will you die down here, but you'll also rot here as well. This trapdoor is airtight. You see, as the water rises, it will push the air in here out through a small vent pipe through the house wall.' Buchanan passed on this information, almost displaying a degree of pride in describing his apparatus for murder. His killing machine! Buchanan then pushed himself upright, taking a lingering look downwards before speaking again. 'So, even after I'm away from here, the new owner of this magnificent pile won't be troubled by any bad smells. You see I think of everything.'

Twisting his neck to look upwards through the opening, Vere watched in fascinated horror as Buchanan reached for the light switch, set in the wall alongside the raised trapdoor. 'Yes,' he called down, his finger still on the switch. 'Although I'm assured the light fittings are waterproof, I think I'll turn them off, just in case. You see, I prefer to think of you drowning slowly in total darkness. Far more fun than sudden death by electrocution, don't you think?'

'God,' Vere cried out to the semi-conscious Yvonne, 'the man's a fucking lunatic. He's loving every minute of this.' Turning, he shouted upwards, 'Buchanan, I'll have you for this, you cowardly apology for a man.'

'In your dreams,' Buchanan laughed, 'the Police know me as Overstone but when I leave here, in a matter of minutes, I'll be Buchanan, disguised and in possession of an official passport. Miles Overstone will cease to exist. And, by this evening, Alistair Buchanan will have vanished into obscurity. So, this really is goodbye,' he said, reaching for the switch that would turn off the cellar lights.

Down below the effect of his action was instantaneous, reducing the cellar space to near blackness and leaving them with just a shaft of light coming from the open trapdoor. Moments later that also vanished as the aluminium door dropped solidly into its tailored airtight recess. Any sound made by the locking handle securing the trapdoor went unheard by the pair in the cellar as the all-enveloping blackness held them in it's terrifying embrace.

The effect of losing the lights, followed by the trapdoor closing, stunned the pair into a momentary silence. Broken by Yvonne screaming like an injured animal further tormenting Vere who was already shaking with fear. Yet again he pulled at the chains, distraught at knowing that discovery and escape were now impossibilities. There was no hope, there never had been. For God's sake, nobody knows where we are, this is all my fault, he raged at his own stupidity. If only I had listened to Yvonne, right from the very beginning and told the police what we suspected. Or, why in God's name didn't I go with her yesterday evening? And now, due to my own bloody mindedness, she's here with me and waiting to die. He moaned, dropping down onto the floor and lapsing into silence. Across the cellar Yvonne groaned, before she too fell silent. Minutes later it was a new sound that interrupted his negative and meandering thoughts. The sound of running water! Awkwardly he scrambled upright, shouting to Yvonne.

'Stand up! For God's sake, stand up he's starting to

flood the place.' Although the blackness prevented them from seeing their executioner, they could most certainly hear it. Unseen, it swirled up through the grilles, its murky fingers reaching eagerly across the cellar floor preparing to undertake its allocated task without pity or favour.

***

Above the flooding cellar Overstone replaced the carpet over the closed trapdoor, deciding not to bother concealing the ladder. Everything's going to plan he reassured himself, the water's running, the couple will die slowly while the police conduct a futile hunt for bodies downstream from Pangbourne. Satisfied that his scheme for protracted murder was working well, he went to transition into Alistair Buchanan for the last time.

Returning downstairs, he booted up his laptop, going online to check his firm's bank balance. And there it was, exactly as promised, the perfect swan song, all thirty-two million pounds of it. For a moment he considered transferring the money to Panama right away. No, he thought, that might trigger awkward questions from the company accountant. I'll see to that later he assured himself, a little longer won't hurt so what's the rush?

After snapping down the screen he pushed the computer into its leather carrying case, slipping it over his shoulder. Pausing in the hallway he set the alarm, picked up his suitcase and locked the door behind him. Then, while driving up to the main road, he congratulated himself for upon making the perfect exit. Content, visions of a new life in Panama boosted by thirty-two million pounds, easily countered any sadness at leaving his magnificent home and adopted lifestyle. Relaxing with these happy thoughts he pressed the remote control, shutting the gates for the last time before heading for Southampton. The thought of two innocent people dying slowly in the blackness of his flooding cellar never entering his head.

CHAPTER 65

SERGEANT BAXTER DROVE carefully into Pangbourne, turning right at the roundabout and then under a narrow railway bridge. Shortly after that the road straightened out, running parallel with the river while to their left a line of imposing properties enjoyed prime riverside views. Across the road each of the property owners enjoyed access to their own share of the grass riverbank, each plot identified by short posts connected by rope, chain or plastic links. Crowland paused, taking in the scene and noted how three cruisers, moored to the bank, rocked gently in the wash left by a decorative canal barge as it travelled upstream. Carefully, Baxter slowed down as they approached a set of temporary traffic lights.

'I'm guessing,' Crowland remarked, 'that those lights should give the recovery people a bit more road space to operate in. Shove the car over there,' he called out, pointing urgently to a small patch of well-trimmed riverbank, 'and bugger the no parking sign!' Baxter complied, aware that a small group of onlookers had already gathered further up the road. Stepping out of the car Crowland nodded to the two local constables.

'Good work with the lights. I see that the recovery trucks here already. Can it pull the car out?'

'Reckon so, sir. Dave, that's the first of our chaps to get here, waded out to check there were no bodies in it. He's gone home to change,' the constable explained, 'and Andy there,' he pointed towards the river, 'that's the big chap in the boiler suit, up to his waist in water. He's the recovery man, good bloke, he's managed these sorts of jobs for us over the years. Says the car's not in too deep, sir. Told me he plans to get canvas belts tied round the rear spring hangers.'

'Sounds fine,' Crowland nodded, acknowledging the technical input.

'Yes, sir, he says it ought to pull out okay. He's brought a couple of steel ramps on which to run it up the bank. Two of his men will help him out with that bit. You know, sir, getting the ramps in the right place on the bank, while he pulls.'

'Let's hope he can get it out all right. My sergeant and I have a strong interest in the car's owner,'

'A suspect, sir?' the constable asked with evident enthusiasm.

'No,' Crowland smiled at the youngster's keenness 'not at all, more of an innocent victim.'

'Oh, I see, sir,' the Constable answered. But Crowland knew that he didn't, and he wasn't about to enlighten him. The constable looked up as a wet and bedraggled Andy approached the three men.

'Andy, this is DCI Crowland,' the constable said, introducing the senior officer.

'Hello there,' Andy smiled, 'I'll not shake hands,' he stated, looking down at his muddy palms. 'Be ready to start pulling, you know once I've got the belts in place. They're hooked onto the wire hawsers. That'll allow me to get the car close to the bank. Once there, my lads can see where best to place the ramps, under the wheels like, to help it up onto the bank.'

'You've done an excellent job there,' admiration showing in the DCI's voice, 'clearly, you don't mind a bit of ducking and diving in the river.'

'All in a day's work, besides, I've done it for you lot before. And, like before, you'll get my bill,' he started to laugh, 'this one will be reasonable. Costs double in winter, damn cold out there in January,' he smiled, looking at the two officers in their smart suits. No going in the river for them, he thought.

'I'll bet,' Crowland nodded, noting how the group of curious bystanders had managed to move closer to the scene of the action, many with mobile phones ready to capture the moment. Then, as Andy departed, ready to resume work Crowland turned to the constable nearest to him.

'Now, if I were you, I'd get those people to move back some way.'

'Why, sir?' they want to see what's going on,' he said, unable to see any danger.

'Well,' Crowland explained, 'once Andy starts pulling, those ropes and wires will come under an enormous strain. Should one of them break under the load,' he paused, 'the end will curl round like a whip! Take somebody's leg off soon as look at them. You don't want to be writing that on your report, do you?'

'No, sir.' The constable blanched at this worrying suggestion, something he had never even considered.

Seconds later he took prompt action, urgently directing the onlookers onto safer territory.

Just behind Crowland, Baxter paced the scene, taking notes and not surprised to see how the temporary lights were already starting to cause a fair amount of traffic to back up in both directions. Behind him Andy, having got the cables placed to his satisfaction, climbed back into the recovery truck. Moments later it settled to its task, the diesel engine growling as, yard-by-yard, the big truck moved backwards, the heavy-duty cables quivering under the strain.

'See what I mean about those cables?' Crowland said to the young man beside him. 'Were one to break under that tension and catch somebody it'd probably be fatal.'

'Yes, sir,' the constable acknowledged, mentally checking just how far back he and the persistent onlookers ought to be for their own safety.

Under Andy's careful control the recovery truck's wheels turned slowly, the low reverse gear ratio giving him complete control of the manoeuvre. Behind him the temporary lights, freeing off the nearside carriageway, provided the space needed for him to reverse into as he eased the MG ever closer to the bank. On the bank itself all eyes watched as the MG's chrome rear bumper broke the surface. Someone gave a faltering cheer as, moments later, more of the car became visible, its white paint already coated with a thin layer of slime.

At that point Andy, having stopped the truck, returned to the riverbank thoughtfully looking at the stricken car, gauging its new position relative to the incline. After further consideration he gave orders to his assistants, instructing them precisely where to position the steel ramps on the sloping riverbank, before then making his way back to the truck.

Baxter, having seen his share of vehicle recoveries, returned to the kerb edge and looked at the traffic. While the lights on his right regulated the traffic going into Pangbourne, the other set controlled the flow of vehicles heading for Oxford and beyond. It was *then* that it happened.

***

No longer able to hear the dirty water gurgling up through the cellar floor, Vere knew it was still rising. Relentlessly it had already crept above his ankles, now creeping inch by inch to towards his knees. 'Is your chain long enough for you to stand up?' he shouted into the darkness, knowing how they'd spend their last minutes. On tiptoe, gasping for air and choking on smelly pond water. 'The water doesn't seem to be rising too fast,' he called encouragingly through the blackness, receiving a strangled sort of grunt in reply. 'Are you standing up?' he shouted, waiting for a response before continuing. 'The last time I looked, before the lights went off, you were sitting down.' Faintly, Vere heard a small croak from the other side of the cellar. 'I'm up,' she screamed, 'and we're going to die! I'm terrified.'

'No, we're not,' he called back, trying to muster a degree of confidence that he simply didn't feel. 'Somebody will find us, there's still plenty of time and the water's hardly up to my knees,' he called out before hearing the rattle of chains in the blackness.

'Okay then, who'll find us?' she challenged in a panicky and trembling voice that sliced into the last meagre reserves of Vere's faltering confidence. 'For God's sake get real,' she shouted in exasperation. 'Nobody knows we're even here so there's not a cat in hells chance anyone will ever find us! So, how long have we got?'

'Absolutely ages,' he called back, doing his best to sound optimistic, inwardly raging at his folly. How could I have been so naive? Thinking I could just swan into Overstone's fortress, then waltz out again with Yvonne on my arm. What made it even worse was the fact that he was bloody well expecting me, getting me to turn up like the proverbial lamb to the slaughter. Bugger me, I was so full of my own fucking self-importance that I didn't even bother to tell Crowland what I was doing. Not that he'd have answered his phone anyway. Now we're left with this. Yvonne's over there, so near but so far, and we're both about to drown. All because I thought I was clever, so clever. God if only I could see! He raged, giving the chains another tug that only made the handcuffs bite further into his chaffed wrists.

Pausing in his self-recriminations he heard a soft thudding sound from across the cellar unable, at first, to fathom out what it was. Moments later he shook in horror, recognising that as the sound made by a human head banging against the brickwork.

'Stop it, Yvonne!' he screamed, desperately worried and almost certain that she was cracking up under the sheer terror of their position. 'Yvonne, talk to me,' he pleaded, only to receive anguished mumblings in reply. Anger and frustration made him pull on the chains again, the effort rewarded by more sharp pains in his wrists.

'Damn you to hell, Buchanan!' he yelled defiantly into the darkness, as around his legs, the water continued its slow and relentless upward progress.

'Yvonne ……. darling,' he pleaded, 'hold on in there. All will be well.' No reply came from across the cellar. Silence, as the icy fingers of real fear closed around his heart. Surely she's not dead already?' he questioned. Then, after a short pause, he heard another voice. Not Yvonne's, but that of a small child.

'Hello, mummy, I can see you now.' Her words making Vere recoil in shock as the unfamiliar voice went on. 'It was such a lovely birthday party. My dress was so pretty, mummy, but I'm going to sit down now.'

'No!' Vere screamed into the black void. 'Don't sit down! You mustn't!'

'But I want to because I'm so very tired. I'm sorry if my dress gets wet, but we can dry it tomorrow. I'm just so very tired.' The child-like voice continued for a little while longer before falling silent. Vere, yelled into the darkness. frantic for more information as Yvonne remained silent, making him realise that she had retreated into something like a secure mental zone where childhood memories blotted out the present.

'Christ, I don't want you to die! Yvonne, stand up. It's your only chance!' Vere yelled tugging at the chains, as the cold and unseen water reached his waist

CHAPTER 66

BAXTER, SUBCONSCIOUSLY REGISTERING that the lights were changing, jumped in alarm as the vehicle that should have stopped at the red light surged forward. With protesting tyres, it lurched forward tearing off in pursuit of the blue car in front that had already "jumped" the amber light. Startled by the outrageous driving Baxter just had time to see the rear number plate, gasping as the white Range Rover accelerated away. For a split second he remained motionless. Stunned before instinct, memory and training took over. Wheeling round he started to run, making for where Crowland was talking to a young lady with a baby buggy.

'Sir,' he shouted to the DCI, 'Overstone's Range Rover - it's jumped the lights and making for Pangbourne.'

'What the hell,' Crowland called back in confusion, startling the lady he had been talking with. 'Was it him driving?'

'Don't think so, looked like a bloke with dark grey hair and glasses.'

'So, who was that? Sorry about that madam, excuse me,' Crowland apologised to the surprised mother before walking over to Baxter.

'Now then, sergeant, are you sure about that?'

'Sure, about what, sir? The driver, or the number? The driver no, but the number yes. Oh, damn!' he exclaimed, as the soft jingle of his mobile made an untimely intrusion. 'Sorry, sir, I need to take this,' Baxter said, leaving Crowland to wait anxiously and watch as his sergeant's face cracked into a broad grin before pocketing the 'phone.

'Sir, you won't believe this,' Baxter said smiling broadly.

'Cut the guessing games, sergeant,' Crowland admonished.

'That was the fingerprint people,' he said excitedly. 'Sir, the prints on that that card you gave to Overstone, and then took back, match the prints sent over from Acton. Overstone is Buchanan!'

'Bloody hell,' the DCI spluttered, 'call in for help. Give them the number, get them to pick up that Range Rover. It can't have gone far!' Pulling out his phone Baxter called Traffic Division, asking them to stop the Ranger Rover while Crowland yelled something at one of the constables before jumping into the car alongside Baxter shouting instructions.

'Overstone's place. NOW! I've got the coppers to hold up the traffic. Go straight through the lights now!'

'What? You want to go to Overstone's, not follow the Range Rover?'

'Baxter, just drive! Friend of the Chief Constable or not, that finger-print evidence gives me enough clout to take his place apart. Traffic can pick up Overstone, alias Buchanan.' The engine roared and the wheels spun, tearing up the soft grass before lurching onto the tarmac.

'Buggered up some rich bloke's lawn,' Baxter laughed before asking, 'but surely we'll need a warrant for that?'

'Stuff the lawn, I've got a bad feeling about this because, right now, we've lost Vere and Clarkson and just seen our prime-suspect disappearing over the horizon.'

'Our only suspect, sir,' Baxter reminded his frustrated superior.

'Don't,' Crowland snapped. 'Just drive and be quick about it. I'll call for backup to join us at the house. We'll get a call out to ports and airports in case he's planning to leave the country. If Traffic can't find him the others might have better luck.'

'Yes, sir, but until we get a proper description they can't just pull in every Buchanan wanting to leave the country. Must hundreds of Buchanan's going abroad every day. As bad as looking for a Smith, I'd say.'

'Yes, thank you, Sergeant. Your negative thinking is, as always, an invaluable help at times of stress.' The DCI's voice, heavy with sarcasm fell silent as he dialled up another number on his mobile. Minutes later, as their stopped at the traffic lights in Streatley, a subdued Sergeant Baxter spoke.

'Sir,' he said thoughtfully, 'now we're certain Buchanan is Overstone, or vice-versa, what do we know about Overstone himself? Okay, at face value he's a pillar of society, a party animal with our chief, but what beyond that?'

'Sorry, Gary, where are you coming from?' Crowland asked, as the
lights changed.

'Not too sure, but given that Buchanan was an out and out crook, are we to believe that Overstone is squeaky clean? I mean is he still *a great big crook* but just not on our radar?'

'Go on, but don't slow down. I'm intrigued.'

'Oh, I don't know, sir. Say dashing off today was part of

his long-term plan, not something spontaneous but part of a grand slam exit? Say he's up to something big, how would we know?'

'And if we didn't, should we have been on the lookout for it? Is that your take on things?'

'Well, as far as it goes, yes sir, but I'm not sure. What if he'd got this planned all along? Then Vere and the girl got in his way. Be honest, if those two can prove he's Buchanan he's got to get away like now. So, is he using them to blind side us from his real purpose?'

'And what might that be?' Crowland asked patiently.

'Oh, I don't know, sir. I'm falling short with this but, were I in his shoes and ready to vanish abroad, I'd make sure that I took more than enough money with me. Alternatively, I'd want to be very sure that I'd got a good stash of money out there, ready for when I landed. Well, wouldn't you, sir? With murder and robbery charges hanging over his head, he'll never come back here. Well, not under his own steam anyway,' Baxter concluded thoughtfully.

'An interesting line,' Crowland admitted. 'Okay, our limited intelligence tells us that Overstone has money, a baronial hall in Wallingford and a property empire based in the City. So, let's assume that he's still a crook, more refined, yet still as hungry for more money. As you suggest, has he been lining up his *great escape* now for quite a while? Then, just at the critical moment, Clarkson and Vere turn up chasing old George Noakes. Are you saying they got in the way, forcing him into striking first?'

'Yes, I guess so, sir, bit like removing a probable threat as opposed to leaving it place where it could become a certainty? Let's face it, we've lost Clarkson, Vere's fallen off the planet and now we've seen Overstone's Range Rover being driven by someone who might just be Buchanan.'

'That's interesting, an alternative view if you like. But to be on the safe side I'll give our serious crimes people in the city a call. Tell them we've good reason to suspect Overstone's on the run and that he's likely to clear off abroad and taking stolen or scammed money with him. I'll tell them it's urgent, get them to examine things and pay a visit to his offices before he's the chance to slope off. You never know, a cosy chat with the accountant *might* just throw up something,' he suggested, punching more buttons on his mobile.

CHAPTER 67

ALTHOUGH NOT NOTED for her patience DI Robson was pleased, hearing that Denny Briggs had come into the station just after eight o'clock that morning. Of course, having to be nice to such lowlife did not come easily to her. But, after years of experience, she was wise enough to know that if needs must you swallowed hard and got on with it. In attempting to overcome Briggs's habitual dislike of the police she'd reassured him that he wasn't in any trouble.

'Yes,' she'd told him after gentle probing, 'all the officers have left the estate and they won't be back.' She'd paused for a moment, recognising that this was a false statement. 'Well, they won't be back until you, or any of your neighbours come to our attention. But look, Denny,' she'd pleaded, 'It's like I told you, this Buchanan's a multi-murderer and gunned down two innocent people years ago in a bank robbery. Now, I'm also certain he used a hitman to murder an old chap called Noakes, and then pushed his son into the path of an underground train. He's a murderer on the loose, he'll kill again and doesn't give a toss! Anybody in his way is fair game, could even be you if he thinks you're a risk to him. Come on Denny, we need to catch him now and you are our best shot. You're the only person we know that's seen this Buchanan person.' And so, for another twenty minutes she'd worked hard, placating and patronising the mentally inhibited Denny.

'Look,' she persisted, 'I know we're normally on different sides, but I'm sure you've got enough morals to baulk at murder. Am I right?' she asked yet again, thanking him for coming forward and explaining how she needed his help in compiling a picture of Buchanan, but it took a long time to wear him down. Eventually, and only after seeing how pretty Sally Palmer was, did he finally agree to sit down with the trained officer. Perhaps helping her to create a computer-generated picture of Buchanan wouldn't be so bad he decided.

'Yes!' she shouted at the departing pair, 'of course I'll send in more coffee and cakes. Just get me that picture.'

***

While Robson felt satisfied with a good result twenty-five miles away Alistair Buchanan, alias Miles Overstone, knew immediately that he'd made an error of judgement. Planning to drive to Southampton, the temptation to make a minor detour through Pangbourne had proved to be irresistible. Naturally curious, he never thought the MG would be discovered so soon, never mind a recovery operation being under way as well.

Yet there it was, a big recovery truck, men in overalls, one of whom was in the river and with two police constables on the riverbank. Forced to a standstill, by the temporary lights, he anxiously watched the vehicles in front crawl forward seven or eight places then stop. Ever nearer the lights and ever nearer what could be official scrutiny. Unable to turn around he knew his irrational decision to come this way could disrupt his plans or even his entire future. Powerless, he watched as his error of judgement became a calamity in a matter of seconds. Tightening his grip on the steering wheel he cursed, recognising the smartly suited man standing on the kerb as one of the two police officers who had called upon him the previous morning.

With the lights on green he swore loudly, banging a clenched fist on the wheel and urging the cars in front to get a move on. But, as with motorists the world over, the drivers crawled through the controlled area determined to feast upon the misfortunes of others. The lights, as they changed from green to amber, caused confusion as the driver in front of Buchanan hesitated, came to a standstill and then accelerated hard into the open space before him. Then as lights changed to red, Buchanan reacted quickly, flooring the accelerator in hot pursuit of the car in front.

Pulling rapidly away from the lights one glance in his rear-view mirror confirmed his worst fears as he recognised Sergeant Baxter. 'Oh no,' he called out, horrified by his discovery sod him. Okay, he knows the car number but cannot know me as Buchanan. Then, risking one last glance in the mirror, he saw Baxter rush back towards the riverbank while waving an arm in the direction of his departing Range Rover.

Damnation, he swore silently, knowing how the police would have every copper on the planet looking for his car within minutes! Angry at his own stupidity he drew comfort from the fact that he could not have been recognised.

Overstone yesterday, Buchanan today, complete with a full set of documentation but driving a car that's very definitely hot. I've got to ditch it now, he told himself, pulling away from the river. On the move they'll get me within minutes. The car needs to vanish, and fast, hide it amongst a crowd of other cars, a local car park, out on the street or over at the nearby motorway services. No, that'd take far too long. They'd have me before getting near the place.

Then inspiration struck. Entering Pangbourne, under the narrow railway bridge, he noticed a quality motor dealership on his left-hand side and swung off the road onto their forecourt. Stepping away from the Range Rover, he walked purposefully into the Service Reception area.

'Hello,' he addressed the smartly dressed lady receptionist. 'Sorry to bother you, but I've got a train to catch, from the station just over the road.' He pointed through the window, towards a flight of steps leading from street to station. 'My Range Rover, out the front there,' again he pointed, 'is in dire need of a service. I'll be away for a couple of weeks, so I wonder if I can I leave it with you for servicing? I'll pick it up when I return. Is that okay with you?'

'Not a problem, sir,' the receptionist smiled, flicking the mouse to activate her computer.

'I know, I should have booked it in but if you can help, well it would be appreciated,' he smiled expansively.

'All in order, sir,' the receptionist looked up, 'I'll just need to jot down your details, then take an impression of your credit card.' Moments later his details were in the computer as, with a flourish, he signed the service authorisation document before presenting a credit card knowing that any payment could never go through the system.

'I've just got my case to collect from the car,' he smiled, informing the receptionist that he'd not left it very well parked.

'Don't worry about that sir, just leave the keys in the ignition and I'll get it taken round the back right away. Our General Manager,' she raised her eyebrows, 'doesn't like to see cars left there for too long. It'll be gone before you reach the platform.' *Hide a tree in a forest*, Buchanan reminded himself as he crossed the road, thinking with the car tucked away in the back of the dealership it could be days before anybody recognises the number plate.

***

While Buchanan was congratulating himself Vere shouted to Yvonne, his voice boring though the total blackness as the murky water continued to rise relentlessly. With the smelly water up to his arm pits he shouted again, only to hear his unanswered words reverberate in the confined space. Has she drowned already? he asked himself, desperation making him shout even louder, while pulling again on the unyielding chain that held him captive. Frustration fuelling the blind hope that something might loosen and offer up the faintest hope of escape. Even if free to move, the trapdoor would be an insurmountable problem. No, he ground his teeth, Overstone's far too cunning to provide a release mechanism from this side.

Drown where I am or miraculously break free and drown in this foul muck because there's nothing to stop the water coming in. Or is there? his mind flashing back to

Overstone's technical lecture on his water-powered death chamber. With remarkable clarity he remembered listening to how the rising ballcock, in the tank, would stop the flow of water. But only when it had completed its deadly task. That flaming ballcock. It's just feet away on that shelf, but it might as well be in the next ruddy parish he fumed, the spectre of defeat looming ever larger in his mind.

Buchanan's won. Nobody knows we're here and he's buggered off, leaving us to die. And, by the sound of things, Yvonne's slipped away already. He sobbed, slumping back against the wall as his knees began to sag, allowing the water wash over his shoulders. Alarmed, he instinctively straightened up, standing tall to keep his head as high as possible above the water. And for as long as possible, dragging out the last minutes of life in the faint hope that a miracle might occur. Even as the flames of this vague hope flickered in his mind the helplessness of the situation told him to prepare for the inevitable. Vere knew people often wondered how their lives might end but, not in wildest dreams, could he imagine anyone planning to take their last breath like this. Chained up inside a flooding cellar and drowning just yards away from their amazing girlfriend who'd already suffered the same fate. And all in total, pitch black, darkness.

***

As Robert Vere faced the inevitable prospect of choking to death on foul smelling pond water, Alistair Buchanan had managed to board a train for Reading within minutes of stepping onto the platform at Pangbourne. In the belief that his Range Rover could stay undetected he began to relax, a mood boosted by the fact that he was unknown in his disguise as Alistair Buchanan.

On the plus side he knew that Alistair Buchanan had not appeared anywhere on the "police radar." Despite that, he began to ask the inevitable "what if" questions. *What if the name of Buchanan had cropped up in any police enquiries? What if that stupid sod Terry Noakes had dropped out the name of Buchanan? What if Clarkson had mentioned the name to the police? What if the police have been able to work out any connections between Overstone and Buchanan?*

Had they done so he knew that all points of legal exit from this country would be subjected to extra vigilance. Anyone called Buchanan, going near a port or airport, would find themselves under more scrutiny that usual. Getting on board the cruise liner might now prove to be difficult, if not impossible. Trying to be logical he reasoned that the authorities, not knowing what he looked like, could not simply haul in or detain every Buchanan passing through an exit terminal.

Positive thinking helped to further sooth his nerves with the thought of how his cruise ship booking would categorise him as a holiday maker, not a suspect on the run. If the passport is valid, which mine is, and the photograph matches the holder, which it does, what could be the problem? Reassured by this, he then set his mind on how he could reach Southampton, in time for his scheduled boarding slot.

CHAPTER 68

'**NOW, DOES THAT** look like the man?' Sally Palmer patiently asked Denny Briggs.

'Yes, I guess so, but, as I keep saying, I only saw him for a second or two. I was more interested in the ten quid he was pushing into my hand like.'

'So, that's the best we're going to get, is it then?' the plain clothes police officer asked.

'Yeah, best I can do. Can I go now? I'm not comfortable here, you know, surrounded by coppers, like.'

'Okay, Denny, you've done well.' Sally Palmer spoke encouragingly, 'we'll just go and check with DI Robson, show her the picture. If she's okay with that, the front door beckons,' she said with a broad smile.

'Oh, no,' he groaned, 'must we go back and see that old witch?' Denny growled. 'Like as not she'll probably nick me, now I've done what she wanted.' Sally Palmer smiled but kept silent, knowing what a rough old bruiser Robson could be. But she does get results, the thought uppermost her mind as she closed-down her laptop. Minutes later, as Denny Briggs stood nervously in front of Robson, the D I looked up from her desk and gave one of her rare smiles.

'You've done well, Denny. We think this is a man called Buchanan, and we need him, like *now*. Anyway, Buchanan is what we'll call him. Now off you go, and don't let me see you back here again.'

'You mean I can go?' he asked, his eyes wide with incredulity.

'Yes,' Robson replied, still managing to smile. 'You've done your bit, so I'll keep my end of the bargain. And, as a bonus, I'll forget about that cannabis we picked up at your mum's place. Now go, before I change my mind.' With that Denny Briggs fled gratefully for the door as the DI turned to Palmer. 'Get that picture on the network now. Say we think he's called Buchanan and, despite his age, he's dangerous. Send a direct message to Reading marked for the attention of DCI Crowland, saying we think this Buchanan is on their patch. Go.'

Seconds later, Sally Palmer followed Denny through the door, before returning to her desk to follow Robson's instructions. Unbeknown to Denny, and thanks to modern electronics, the picture he had created with Palmer was in Reading before he had reached the street. Minutes later a member of Crowland's team in Reading was busy examining it. And, even before Denny had time to roll a much-needed cigarette, the picture was on its way to DCI Crowland's mobile phone.

***

'Break them down! Drive through!' Crowland shouted to Baxter, as their car skidded to a halt outside the electrically operated gates guarding Overstone's house. 'I've got a nasty feeling about this.'

'Okay, sir, but I'm not wrecking the car. We've a tow rope in the boot, I'll tear them off. Two minutes, tops,' Baxter said as he jumped from the car and headed for the boot. Good to his word he was back in the car in ninety seconds, ten seconds after that the gates came crashing down. Moments later, with the tow rope disconnected, he was back in the car, reversing over the fallen gates. Then, once in the driveway, he executed a perfect handbrake turn before powering his way down to stop outside the front entrance. As he leapt from the car Crowland saw two police Range Rovers coming down the sloping driveway, stopping on the gravel to offload a total of eight uniformed officers. Shouting across, he ordered the men to surround the house.

'I want all entrances covered. You, sergeant,' he said turning to Baxter, 'get an impact battering ram. Let's have that door open.' As Baxter raced across the gravel, Crowland felt his mobile phone vibrate. 'Not bloody now,' he cursed as he pulled it from his jacket. After two rapid button clicks the screen displayed a simple message. *Buchanan photo fit attached.* Intercepting Baxter, who was returning with the battering ram, he flashed his mobile screen before the sergeant.

'Overstone dressed as Buchanan,' he shouted, 'recognise him?'

'Hard to say, gov, I only caught a three-quarter rear view of him, as he shot through those lights.'

'Okay, not to worry. This picture will be at every port and airport in minutes. So, if he tries to make a run for it, and if someone's on the ball, we should nail him. I know that's plenty of "ifs" but it's the best we've got.'

'Sir,' Baxter acknowledged, ready to use the heavy tool he was holding.

'Right, get that flaming door open!' Crowland called over his shoulder, as he ran after the departing uniformed sergeant and addressed him.

'Go around the house, tell your men to look for anything unusual. Report back to me when you've done the circuit. Then let me know what they've found. Is that understood?'

'Sir,' he called out, sprinting off after his team as the front door swung open, shattered by the sheer force of the heavy battering ram. Baxter, stepping over splintered woodwork, accessed the first part of the elaborate entrance.

'Bloody hell,' the sergeant mouthed, a little puffed from his efforts on the front door. 'Never noticed these yesterday,' he shouted over his shoulder, referring to the closed glass doors. 'Should be a hell of a sight easier,' he said, bringing the heavy ram down through a swinging arc. Next second he was flat on the floor and swearing loudly. Shocked, the heavy ram had bounced uncontrollably off the glass, doing no damage apart from throwing him completely off balance. 'Polycarbonate and flaming bullet proof,' he spluttered, climbing back off the floor as a high pitched and piercing electronic sound cut short further conversation.

'We've set the alarm system off!' Crowland yelled, rushing outside to escape the noise, turning after fifteen yards to find that Baxter was not beside him. Missing, but still in the building he guessed. Sticking his hands across his ears he made his way back into the entrance corridor, surprised to find Baxter busily attacking the alarm control unit with a hefty Swiss Army knife. Seconds later the noise stopped as suddenly as it had started, Crowland removing his hands from over his ears as Baxter shook his head.

'Noisy. I told you that security course I went on was worthwhile, sir.'

'I thought it was a course for police officers, not one for burglars,' the DCI shot back, nevertheless amused.

'Yeah, well, what's good for one, sir? Now, do you want me to have another crack at those doors?'

'Leave them,' Crowland shouted over his shoulder, rushing outside, 'try a window, we'll have more chance there.'

Down in the cellar Vere heard the alarm, its piercing shriek signalling that Buchanan's fortress may have suffered an assault if not actually breeched. The sound, bolstering his flagging spirits, made him call out Yvonne. 'It's the police,' he shouted excitedly, 'hang on in there. It won't be long before we're found.' Silence. Then he detected a low mumbling sound from across the cellar that made him call again, seriously concerned about her mental state. At least she's still with us, but God only knows what this will have done to her. Captured, drugged and forcibly confined, along with the trauma of being half-drowned. And that's without adding in the effects of delayed shock, all or any of which could be well be devastating. Dear Lord, he prayed silently, whatever state she's in please let it be temporary, one where my love and care will soon return her to normality. Returning to earthly matters hearing the alarm had been a huge boost but, even so, he was realistic enough to know that all bets would be off if the police did not get a move on!

CHAPTER 69

CROWLAND AND BAXTER, knowing how access through the front was now impossible, stepped away from the wrecked front door. Then, while urgently seeking an alternative means of access, two uniformed officers approached them

'Excuse me sir, I think we might have found something.'

'Yes, go on, sergeant. What have you got?' Crowland queried, his attention divided between the sergeant and selecting a suitable window for breaking.

'It's, Atkins here,' he nodded to the young constable beside him. 'He noticed how the water level in the big ornamental fishpond is dropping away, says it has been doing so for some time now, by the look of the wet sides.'

'For fuck's sake,' Crowland exploded, manners abandoned entirely. 'I've got an abducted girl, a missing solicitor and a proven bloody murderer on the run, and you want to talk about fishponds. Now, sod off and I'll deal with you later.' Undaunted, the sergeant stood his ground, full square in front of the DCI.

'I know, but there's more, sir. Tell him Atkins.' The fresh-faced constable shuffled his feet nervously before finding his voice

'Sir, if the water's going down, well it must be going somewhere.'

'So?' Crowland said in sheer exasperation.

'Over there, sir,' Atkins said. indicating the side of the building. 'I found a narrow plastic pipe sticking through the brickwork with air under pressure coming out of it. I'm guessing water from the pond is draining away into an underground space somewhere. Not sure what that'd be, but my guess is that waters flooding in and pushing the air out, sir.'

'Quick! Show me!' Crowland barked, turning to follow the young constable as he drew their attention to a short piece of plastic pipe protruding from the wall.

'You're right!' he shouted, placing the back of his hand across the pipe. 'There's air coming out - under a fair bit of pressure too. Quick, find something to bung in the pipe. A bit of stick whittled down to fit will do. Should stop the air coming out and slow down the flow of water. Get going, man!'

'I've not got a knife, sir,' the constable said helplessly.

'You have now.' Baxter thrust across his multi-bladed knife, 'and I want it back,' he called as the constable headed off to find a suitable piece of wood.

'Sergeant, until Atkins gets back, press your thumb hard onto the end of that pipe. Because, if the lad's right, holding the air back might just slow down the water.'

'Sir,' the sergeant acknowledged as Crowland turned to Baxter. 'Look, we know Buchanan's cleared off and I'm guessing he's left those two trapped down there,' he pointed towards the base of the building, 'and, if we're right they're slowly drowning. Now,' he shouted to the uniformed officer beside him, 'I don't care how you do it, but I want that window out, and now!'

'On it, sir. Tools in the car and with two big lads for a bit of muscle, it won't take long.'

'Good man,' he called out before turning to Baxter. 'You know, if young Atkins is correct, those two could be drowning down there as we speak.'

***

As the cold and smelly water edged ever closer to his throat any elation, felt by having heard the alarm, soon became a distant memory for Vere as he struggled, yet again, with the chains that held him prisoner. A false dawn, he sighed, caused by who? The police? An opportunist burglar? Who the hell knows? Can't have been the police, he reasoned, they don't even know we're here. Shaking with fear he wondered if it might have been Buchanan, making one last visit and setting off his own alarm? Either way nobody has come near us, and the alarm has stopped quickly enough, doubtless by someone who knew what they were doing. With mounting fear of a slow and choking death, the absence of any coherent sounds from across the cellar only heightened his growing sense of foreboding. Should the water level rise any further he knew he'd be struggling to breathe by which time the slightly shorter Yvonne would have drowned, even if she had of been standing up.

***

It took less than a minute for two of the sergeant's squad to break through the selected window, letting Baxter help his DCI through the opening and into the house.

'Where are we in relation to that pipe?' Crowland shouted.

'Down here would be my guess, sir,' Baxter called back, striding off from the main semi-circular hallway into a corridor with windows overlooking the garden. 'We're bang on target, there's Atkins, sir.'

'But there's nothing here,' Crowland shouted in frustration as he joined Baxter in the corridor.

'Okay, but whatever we're after must be underneath us, sir. It must be,' he concluded, staring down at the floor. 'Hang on, look at that bit of carpet sticking up against the skirting board? No self-respecting fitter would leave a job like that. Step back, sir. I'll get my fingers under that lose bit, see what gives.' Surprisingly Baxter felt the carpet move and, with a little more encouragement, it came away from the edge of the outside wall. Then, by pulling it lengthways, Baxter showed how the carpet had been cut right the way across.

'Roll it back,' Crowland shouted, uncertain as to what lay beneath.

'Doing it now, sir,' the sergeant replied. Bending to his task he rolled the carpet further down the corridor. His actions revealing how a dull looking metal panel, fitting flush with the surrounding floor, had replaced the original floorboards.

'Hell's teeth,' Crowland exclaimed, 'what's that?'

'Sort of trapdoor, sir,' Baxter replied, staring down, 'got a release mechanism of some sorts set into it, bit like on aeroplane cabin doors.'

'Open it, for God's sake,' Crowland shouted, terrified by the thought of what it might reveal as Baxter dropped to his knees and twisted the handle through ninety degrees.

'Got it!' he shouted, before standing up and lifting the panel, swinging it through the vertical and leaning it back against the outside wall. Crowland, stepping forward, gaped into the opening, only able to see a rectangle of light reflected from the surface of the murky water around fifteen inches below the trapdoor. Crying out in alarm Baxter shouted at Crowland. 'Sir,' he gasped, pointing to the edge of the trapdoor. 'Look, a rubber sealed. The whole thing's airtight.'

'So?' the DCI demanded, unable to grasp the technical implication of what Baxter had said.

'It's an airtight fit. Now we've opened it the water will be pouring in faster than ever! Having Atkins bung up that pipe won't make any difference now.'

'Oh God,' Crowland groaned. 'So near yet so far.

CHAPTER 70

ALTHOUGH CONFIDENT OF his disguise, Buchanan was undecided as he walked away from Reading station, unsure as how best to reach Southampton. Rail, coach or taxi. The rail option he discounted straight away in case his Range Rover had failed to avoid discovery. Unlikely, but should that be the case, the police would have his description as Buchanan and know that he took the train from Pangbourne, all courtesy of that helpful receptionist. Stations he knew had CCTV cameras and, since the Buchanan disguise was essential to negotiate the Southampton cruise terminal, trains were off the menu.

Next he turned his attention to coaches but, after looking at his watch, he realised that time was not on his side. With having to embark over two thousand passengers, in a matter of hours, the port operators needed to follow a strict boarding schedule. Therefore, as the ship would sail at six regardless, taking a taxi was the only viable solution. Picking up his suitcase he walked across to the rank, quickly finding a cabbie unable to believe his luck. A single fare to Southampton.

'Got to charge for the return trip as well,' the cabbie pointed out, determined to set the rules while hoping not to deter his best fare for ages. Behind him Overstone settled onto the comfortable seat, his suitcase and laptop computer carrying bag beside him.

'Not a problem. I'll pay you cash with a good tip, but I'm not in a talkative mood. I need the docks, the Mayflower Terminal, as I'm boarding a cruise ship for a fortnight's break. I'll give you the drop-off instructions when we get closer to the port. Now let's get going.'

As the taxi cleared the southern side of Reading, and crossed the M4 motorway, he began to relax. Ah, he thought, the driver's making for Basingstoke, before dropping onto the M3 motorway. It won't be long before we're passing the old Duke of Wellington's stately home. The Iron Duke, he thought, victorious in battle but not so successful in politics. During his time as Prime Minister, he'd been financially embarrassed when the nation was on the gold standard. *To beat the duke, go for gold*, the popular rallying cry, urging unhappy people to change their bank notes for gold, a move indicating mistrust in his government. No, he thought, thankful that his own "bank rush" was a far more effective way of generating money. Of course, the property market is fun, but making easy money from the weak, feeble and drug-addled sections of society is far more enjoyable, and far more rewarding.

Not long after that they were on the M3 motorway, making for Southampton and bypassing Winchester. Didn't they used to hang people in Winchester prison he asked himself? The thought making him recall how it had all begun. The cash-strapped Drysdale, two deadly shootings, the hapless Noakes, Drysdale's execution and the bungled bank robbery. No, that's wrong, he thought with a flash of annoyance, the robbery was successful. We got away with the money. Only Drysdale bungled.

***

On hands and knees Baxter angled his body well forward, pushing his head into the limited space of clear air above the rising water level.

'Here!' Crowland called out, passing a small torch forward, happy to leave the first inspection to his younger and fitter sergeant.

'They're both here, sir,' Baxter called over his shoulder after having flashed the light around the cellar, 'but they're in a bad way. Vere's down this end, standing up,' he pointed to his left. 'His head above water, well just, but the girl looks done for. She's down the other end, upright, but her face has dropped forward in the water. I can only see the top of her head and with hair floating in the water.'

'Can't they move?' the DCI yelled down at Baxter, unaware that he was asking the blatantly obvious.

'I'm sure they would if they could, sir, but I'm guessing they're secured under the water somehow, otherwise they'd be floating or swimming, wouldn't they?' Crowland reeled back, horrified that any one human being could do this to another, tied down and left to drown.

With one hand on the edge of the opening for support, Baxter continued to scan the small torch beam around the cellar. As he did so a barely audible sound came from the left-hand end of the cellar, just one word.

'Help,' the conscious Vere uttered, reacting to the unexpected light.

'One's alive, sir,' Baxter shouted up before looking down and calling out across the rising water, thrilled at hearing the sound. 'Hey, well done just hang on in there. We'll soon have you out.' Baxter shouted, before looking up at Crowland for advice.

'Got to – got to - stop the water,' Vere spluttered as more of it swilled menacingly into his mouth, most of which he managed to spit out. 'Ball cock, up there, got to shut it off to stop water coming in. If not, we'll be dead in minutes,' the words horrifying Baxter.

'Fucking hell!' he shouted in alarm. 'Atkins was right, sir, they're being drowned,' he informed Crowland, passing on Vere's faltering message about the ballcock.' Craning his neck to look further into the cellar he scanned the narrow beam of light through the ever-shrinking gap between water and ceiling. 'Got it, sir, it's over there, a ballcock hanging down from a shelf of some kind. We've got to shut that off. I'm going in there now,' Baxter added, adjusting himself into a sitting position by the opening.

'Sergeant, I can't order you to do that.'

'You don't have to, sir. I'll be okay,' he shouted as he pulled off his jacket and shoes. 'If we wait for a useless *jobs-worth* from Health and Safety to come and do a risk assessment they'll both be fucked!' Before Crowland could say another word, Baxter had his legs dangling above the water before lowering himself into the blackness. With the water up to Vere's neck, Baxter was surprised to find himself standing on a surface of spongy material, while the water only reached his lower ribs.

'Reckon I'm standing on something like an old mattress,' he called up to Crowland. Seconds later, as he moved away from the opening above him, he dropped about three feet, staggering as the water momentarily went over his head. 'Oh fuck!' he spluttered on resurfacing, 'at least the torch still works.' Pausing, to rebalance himself, he then waded towards the ball cock that was already beginning to float. With Baxter out of sight Crowland could only imagine what was happening in the cellar, praying that both were still alive. Within minutes Baxter reappeared below, wobbling slightly on the unstable mattresses and spitting out more foul-tasting pond water.

'Fixed the ball cock,' he gasped, 'it's on a shelf, bit above head height. I've held it back with my tie, Christmas present from the wife's mother. Never did like it. I'm going back to look at the pair of them - the girl first.' With that, he vanished from sight.

Stepping back Crowland looked further down the corridor, spotting the short aluminium that Buchanan had discarded earlier. That'll do nicely he thought, moving carefully around the opening to reach it. Returning, he angled one end of the ladder into the water, leaning the other end against the side of the opening. With the ladder safely positioned he knelt to see what was happening, his attention diverted by the uniformed sergeant who spoke to him.

'We're all okay out there, sir. But what's next?'

'Get Atkins back here - right away. And, while you are out there, have you got a set of bolt-cutters in your car?'

'Bolt-cutters?' the sergeant questioned.

'Yes, that's what I said! We've got two people down there, chained to a wall and close to drowning.'

'Bloody hell,' his reaction was spontaneous, 'yes sir

we've got bolt cutters. I'm on my way and I'll get Atkins for you.'

'Also,' Crowland bellowed to the departing sergeant, 'get two ambulances down here and a doctor as soon as you can.'

'Will do, sir!' the sergeant shouted, vanishing down the corridor to leave Crowland peering downwards and praying for a miracle.

***

Alistair Buchanan flopped down onto the king-sized bed, letting out a sigh of satisfaction as he looked around the luxurious cabin. No, a stateroom none the less, exactly as described in the brochure. I've made it! But what a day, stressful, tiring and exhausting. Not to worry, we sail in half an hour. Twelve hours after that it'll be Amsterdam.

Loosening his tie, he knew that taking the taxi from Reading had been the right decision. Blasted CCTV cameras, you can't blow your nose without someone filming you these days. Train or bus, either way he knew that the cameras would have picked him up whereas the back of the taxi offered perfect isolation.

Upon reaching Southampton the view of the ship, seen from Canute Road, had been reassuring as it towered above the terminal building. Although he knew that checking in might be fraught, the sight of so many people on the upper floor of the building was a relief. Normally not one for crowded places this, for Overtone, was different. Surrounded by seated and queuing passengers he was happy to hide in a crowd. Waiting patiently to take his turn at one of the "check-in" desks, soon coming face to face with a smiling young lady seated behind a small computer screen.

Despite his lingering concerns, exposing the whole Buchanan identity to officialdom had passed off perfectly. First his ticket and passport had faced examination, then the clerk had scanned his credit card before taking a small "passport size" photograph. Finally issuing him with a credit card sized card that would, the lady had explained, open the door to his stateroom and function as a charge-card for on-board spending. Every action accompanied by welcoming smiles which he'd returned, even if I am on the run. But no, he'd reminded himself, I'm not on the run. That's for common criminals. There's nothing common about me. I'm a dignified businessperson, implementing my own personalised exit, something I've planned to perfection.'

After that, the journey to his stateroom had been smooth and incident free, interrupted only by the customary hand luggage and metal detector scans in security. From there he'd followed the directional arrows, walking up the sloping ramps to make his way on board. As he joined the ship, and unseen by him, two uniformed officials had walked determinedly from an office behind the check-in desks to speak with the receptionist who had just completed his boarding procedure.

Once onboard, directions from a crewmember had led him to his allocated deck level, reaching it via one of the internal lifts. From there it had been a short walk to his stateroom where his suitcase waited by the door. Around him, in the brightly lit passageway, excited travellers were busily fumbling with their plastic cards, unlocking doors and eager to inspect their accommodation. Moving serenely amongst them a couple of white-jacketed stewards had been courteously offering advice and directions

And now, he thought, swinging his laptop carrying case onto the bed, time to move that money. Within seconds of switching on he was looking at his screensaver, one side of which displayed two dozen icons, one entitled Overstone Properties. Clicking on that took him to the next screen from where he could only access the 'beating heart' of his financial empire by using an encrypted password. Diligently he tapped in his twelve-digit alpha numeric code before pressing the enter key. Then, as the screen flickered, it simply displayed a terse message: ACCESS DENIED. Buchanan gasped in shocked amazement, totally disbelieving the message.

CHAPTER 71

'YOU WANTED ME, sir,' Atkins called down to Crowland who was kneeling alongside the open trapdoor.

'Yes,' the DCI said, moving into a more upright position. 'We're right, two people have very nearly drowned down there. Sergeant Baxter's managed to stop the water coming in, now I want you to find out how we get rid of it. My guess would be a stopcock outside, you know a valve that'll let the water out into the river. Find it, then open it as fast as you can. Report back once you've found it?'

'On my way, sir,' Atkins said brightly as he sped away.

'Sir,' Crowland heard Baxter shout from the far end of the cellar. 'The girls in a bad way. I've got my hand under her chin, just managing to keep her mouth out of the water. She's unconscious. God knows how much of this muck she's taken in already. I can't leave her, or she'll be gone.' Crowland heard a splashing sound, followed by Baxter calling back up. 'Sir, I've just slid my hand down into the water. She's in handcuffs, chained to the wall and can't move. Sir, I need assistance down here and very soon. Doubtless Vere's chained up in the same way.'

'Got that,' Crowland replied. 'Atkins is looking for the outlet that'll lower the water level. That should help a bit and bolt cutters are on the way. Oh, and I found an aluminium ladder and shoved it down into the water. Should help when you get over here.'

'That'll be handy, but I don't know about Vere. He's gone quiet, and I simply can't take my hand off Yvonne's chin.' Waiting for a response from Crowland, Baxter heard a faint voice from behind him.

'I'm okay but, for God's sake, what about Yvonne?'

'Oh good, glad you're still with us, Baxter said cheerfully. 'Yvonne's hanging on in there, barely conscious and completely knackered. On the plus side, I've got a pulse.'……. Well just about, he thought, but he kept that to himself.

***

'I've found the outlet valve, sir;' a breathless Atkins called down to the kneeling DCI, 'and managed to open it.'

'Great, where was it?'

'On the riverbank, like you said, sir. Below the level of the cellar and running out into the river. Flow's not brilliant, but it's running.'

'Gary,' Crowland shouted down, 'Atkins's opened the outlet valve and that should lower the level a bit.' Turning, he glanced up as the sergeant returned holding out a set of bolt croppers.

'Well done,' he said, taking the cutters, 'there are two people down there, chained to the wall and drowning. My sergeant's down, just managing to keep the girl's mouth

434

above water. If he leaves her, she'll die, so he needs those cutters now.'

'I'll take them, sir,' Atkins volunteered briskly, 'I'm not a bad swimmer.'

'Thanks, with your height you'll be able to stand, especially if the water level is starting to drop a bit. But take care, it could be dangerous.' Smiling, Atkins slipped off his helmet, uniform jacket and heavy boots. Then, taking hold of the bolt cutters, he placed a foot on the ladder. Pausing, he looked at Crowland saying. 'Don't worry, sir, I'll not sue if I catch cold.' Despite the tension the DCI grinned before shouting down into the cellar.

'Baxter, Atkins is coming down with the bolt-cutters. See if he can duck down and cut those chains, while you keep the girl's head above water.'

'Got that, sir,' he called back. 'Come on in, Atkins, the water's lovely,' the sergeant teased, watching the young constable step off the ladder to begin wading towards him, up to his neck in the filthy water once he's moved clear of the mattresses.

'Ted,' Vere spluttered, his voice barely heard by the DCI, despite him still having his head lowered through the trapdoor opening.

'Yes, Robert, don't worry, we'll soon have you out,' the DCI replied, trying to sound as reassuring as possible. 'Can you see Baxter, and a young constable down there already? They've got bolt cutters and they'll have Yvonne out in a minute, then they'll be back for you.'

'That's good,' Vere spluttered in reply, then in between spitting out more water, managed to speak again. 'On the wall, beside you,' Vere spoke faintly, 'a switch,' he mumbled.

'Says it does the lights down here.' Looking up Crowland saw the switch, instinctively reaching out for it, pulling his hand away at the last second.

'Who says it does the lights?' Crowland asked, becoming suspicious.

'Buchanan,' Vere mumbled, 'reckons they're watertight, sealed units of some sort.'

'Oh,' Crowland acknowledged thoughtfully, knowing that a bit of extra light down there wouldn't go amiss. Reaching for the switch his hand paused in mid-air, sudden doubt clouding his brain. Should I trust Buchanan? Was this another of his devious schemes, a last throw of the dice designed to snatch success away from last-minute rescuers? Water and electricity. Not the best of bedfellows. One bad connection and I'll have four dead bodies.

'No,' he called back into the cellar, 'I'm not trusting that one at all, we'll just have to manage with the torch. If those connections are dodgy you're all dead. We've got this far with the torch. Let's leave it that way.'

Unsighted from Crowland, Atkins paused beside Baxter and the motionless Yvonne. With a quick nod to the sergeant, he took a deep breath and ducked below the surface beside Yvonne. With one hand he groped around, finding the chain running from the handcuffs to the wall. Unable to see in the murky black water, he used his fingers to guide the jaws of the bolt cutters onto the chain. Then, confident that he'd got a firm bite on the chain he stood upright and drew in a lungful of welcome air.

'Cutting now!' he told Baxter, pushing the two handles together as the cutter's lever mechanism maximised his efforts allowing the two cutting edges to sheer through the chain. The action releasing Yvonne who fell forward onto Baxter.

***

'What!' Buchanan cried out in a reflex reaction, before hitting the return key and frantically repeating the process. The same result, his mind reeling in turmoil as he tried to make sense of what was happening. In frustration, and close to panic, he cursed the silent screen, trying yet again to access his on-line banking and accounts facility. In shock he wondered what could have gone wrong. Why, he cursed, only hours ago everything had been fine? Entry to the system had been normal. The money had been there in the account.

Trying hard to be rational he wondered if this might be yet another of those annoying computer problem, or indicative of something far more serious?' Desperate for information he pulled a mobile phone from his pocket and dialled his office. Seconds later he was reeling in shock as his senior accountant told him what had happened. Disaster, with the power of tsunami, had struck. Officers from the City of London Fraud Squad were in the building and had already cleared out half of the staff. Sending them home, pending further investigations. Stunned by the news and trying to make sense of what he had just heard, he bitterly regretted not having transferred the bank's money to Panama that morning. Too busy by half, he told himself. Damn Vere and Clarkson, but they are gone for good, he told himself.

Thirty-two million down, he gulped, trying to imagine what had gone wrong because, quite clearly, *something* had gone radically wrong. Reeling with shock, he collapsed back onto the bed, trying to juggle sums in his head. Without money in Panama I'll be struggling, but there's still more than enough in the Cayman Islands. Well, that's something, and with more to come courtesy of tobacco tins and mules, I can still manage, he told himself. Recovering slightly, he began to realise that luxury still beckoned, despite this discovery being a severe body blow. Tomorrow was a new day! Amsterdam, Schiphol and Panama City.

Loud knocking on his stateroom door brought him back to reality. New towels for the bathroom he thought, rising from the bed. Padding across the deep carpet pile carpet he unlocked the door to admit the half-anticipated steward.

'Mr Buchanan?' a voice from the passageway grabbed his attention, making him turn back to the doorway.

'Yes,' he gulped, shaken by seeing two uniformed police officers, a steward and a ship's officer.

'Right, sir, can you please come with us now?'

'But why? I've paid my fare and the tickets in order. So why do you want me to come with you?' Buchanan replied, while rapidly trying to work out what was happening. 'What's the problem?' he asked, desperately seeking to bluff his way around the posse of authority facing him.

'Look, sir. Be reasonable, you know the answer to that, Mr Buchanan, or would you prefer Overstone?' one of the police officers stated firmly. 'We don't want a fuss, not in front of all these nice people ready to go on holiday, do we, sir? Buchanan looked back blankly, unnerved at realising the extent of the police's knowledge as the officer continued speaking. 'Thames Valley Police have been in touch, sent us down a surprisingly good electronic image of you. They want to interview you in connection with murder, armed robbery and two cases of attempted murder. We also understand that the City of London Fraud Squad would welcome a chat, something to do with thirty-two million quid that was about to go walk-about. Quite a list, so shall we go quietly then?' Utterly dejected, realisation hit him like an avalanche. It was over. Within a matter of minutes his dreams had been blown to smithereens, replaced now by the certainty of lengthy imprisonment.

CHAPTER 72

'YVONNE'S FREE,' BAXTER called up, 'we're bringing her across to the ladder now.' With the water still at neck-height Baxter, helped by Atkins, shuffled across the cellar supporting Yvonne, shouting across the news of her release to Vere.

'Gary,' he sighed, 'for God's sake take care of her, please,' he sobbed

'Will do, trust me, we'll be over for you in a minute,' Baxter called across, feeling his legs contact the submerged mattresses below the trapdoor.

'Well done you two,' the DCI called down, relieved at their success.

'Sounds like ambulances arriving, sir,' the sergeant called out from behind the still kneeling Crowland. 'I ordered a couple, just in case. Managed to round up a doctor from one of the local practises as well. He's behind you now, sir.'

'Right, you two!' Crowland shouted, without bothering to look up, 'now you've got Yvonne over here, keep her upright with her back against the ladder. When you're ready, try and slide her gently up the ladder. We'll take her from there.' Turning, he looked up at the fresh-faced young man standing slightly behind him. No jacket, sleeves rolled up, ready for action. 'That okay with you, doc?'

'Simon Jennings,' he replied by way of an introduction, 'sounds fine, unless there is a possibility of back or spinal damage. Is there?'

'None that we know of,' Baxter called out, having heard the last remark, 'she'd managed to stay upright despite being semi-conscious. Doesn't know what was going on.'

'Fair enough,' Jennings called back, accepting Baxter's nonmedical opinion. 'Right then, start to get her back against the ladder, very gently now. Once she's in place, take hold of her legs just below the knees and start to slide her upwards. Then, as soon as we can, we'll take over up here.' Crowland stepped back, giving the doctor and the sergeant room to move forward, before dropping to their knees. 'Let's get on with it,' Jennings called down to Baxter and Atkins as they began to slide Yvonne slowly up the ladder.

'Okay,' Jennings called back, 'we've got her now, holding her under the

arms. You,' he said, looking up to Crowland, 'sorry, didn't get your name. But can you just take the weight for a second? That'll let the pair of us get upright and keep her as straight as possible, just in case of any spinal damage. You two down there okay with that. But don't push, just hold her steady while we prepare to lift her up.

'With you, doc.' Baxter shouted back, 'her pulse is barely there, so the sooner the better.'

'Thanks for that's, but we've got her. Now she's upright we can swing her across to the stretcher and lay her flat so I can get a good look at her.' While Baxter and Atkins could not see what was going on above them, they could hear the instructions. It was only a matter of seconds begore the doctor returned to the opening, looking down to ask if they were ready to get the other one out.

'Yes, we're on it now. Soon as you're ready, we'll pass him up. It should be a bit easier this time, what with the water level starting to drop and him being conscious – well just about.'

Ten minutes later, and shivering badly, Vere was leaning up against the corridor wall, his longed-for view of Yvonne frustrated by the doctor and paramedic leaning across her body. Struggling to see Yvonne it was the other paramedic, the one charged with checking him over who demanded attention.

'Sir, will you please stand still,' the green suited paramedic pleaded, 'I must make sure you're all right.'

'Me all right, you say,' he gave a mirthless laugh, managing to stay still for all of five seconds. 'Apart from being tied up, hungry, cold, half drowned and flaming angry, yes, I'm okay,' he snapped. 'Never mind me, what about her? He demanded, pushing against the paramedic. 'Why isn't she moving? They cut her free down there,' he pointed to the cellar, 'before lifting her out. Why isn't she moving?' he repeated, looking helplessly at the shiny foil insulation cover keeping her warm while the doctor and paramedic battled to stabilise her on the stretcher. More agonising minutes elapsed as Vere looked on despondently, watching as they placed Yvonne face down, allowing the doctor to apply firm pressure to her back. Seconds later he was relieved to see little pools of dirty water spill from her mouth onto the floor. Only then was she rolled back over so that the paramedic could apply firm pressure to her chest in a repetitive pumping motion.

'Oh, God,' Vere croaked, having enough medical knowledge to know how the doctor was using CPR heart massage to maintain Yvonne's circulation. After a short while the paramedic stopped, dropping his hands to his side and looked up as the doctor spoke to Vere.

'It's a start,' he said, 'we've got a pulse, very weak, but she's still with us which is great news. Now,' he said, standing up to address the paramedic battling to check Vere over. 'Leave this one to me,' he nodded towards the exhausted Vere. 'Now we've got a pulse, get her off to hospital while I finish checking this one over. Soon as I'm happy, I'll get the other ambulance to whip him across to the Royal Berks for a proper assessment.'

'But why isn't she awake?' Vere pressed the doctor as he stared down at the woman he loved, hardly able to comprehend what he was seeing. Muddy slime covered Yvonne, clinging uncaringly to exposed flesh and clothing while mercifully avoiding he head. To Vere she looked deathly pale, unconscious and hardly breathing. As for that lovely hair, he sighed, now matted and hanging down in an unruly mess. Receiving no reply, all Vere could do was to look on helplessly as the doctor helped the two paramedics lift Yvonne carefully onto the waiting trolley. As they moved down the corridor, he called out a final instruction.

'Keep the oxygen going for as long as you can.'

'How is she?' Vere asked, as the paramedics departed with the trolley.

'Hmm,' the doctor cleared his throat before looking thoughtfully at Vere. Undecided, he wondered just how much he could say to this cold, bedraggled and caring man who had just survived such a nightmare ordeal.

'Hard to be specific,' he replied cautiously, 'only when the hospital has completed their tests will they get the full picture. It's then that anyone provide you with answers. And even they may not be definitive.' the doctor added, reluctant to add hope where they may not be any. Then Vere tried another approach, his emotions raw after such an ordeal.

'Okay, doctor,' he said slowly, 'cards on the table. Let me be honest with you in the hope you'll do the same. You see, from my side, I love Yvonne dearly and we want to get married but now, after this,' he pointed to the cellar, 'what are the chances of her even surviving?' Vere looked pleadingly at Simon Jennings, begging for an answer yet fervently hoping it would not be the one he dreaded. For a moment, the doctor looked patiently at Vere, taking in the obvious distress and his burning need for information before reaching a decision.

'Alright,' he smiled, 'at face value it's a mixed bag. What we do know is that her heart stopped for a while, either at the point of being cut free or while in transition to the ladder. We also know that she's swallowed a lot of mucky water, very nearly drowning in it. But, on the plus side, CPR kept her circulation going until we got her pulse back. So, without beating about the bush, for sure she'll have suffered a temporary loss of circulating oxygenated blood, which I'm guessing occurred during recovery from the cellar. Losing blood-flow like that can, as I'm sure you'll know, bring about the loss of brain function in varying degrees,' he advised cautiously, neither wishing to raise hopes or predict problems. 'Hopefully,' he smiled, 'anything like that will be short-term. But, until we get the full picture, further speculation is pointless,' he paused, 'being positive, she's a young and fit-looking, all of which will act in her favour.'

'Why is she still unconscious?' Vere persisted.

'That could be due to oxygen starvation,' the doctor added, taking care to phrase his words accurately. 'Then again, you know that when the body comes under real strain, or indeed trauma, it tends to shut down any number of its ordinary functions. In that way all available energy can then concentrate on taking care of the basics.......' The doctor's words faded away, as he sought not to alarm Vere unnecessarily.

'So, you cannot commit to anything right now?'

'Of course, you're concerned, you're going frantic behind that professional veneer. Nevertheless,' he paused, 'I'm guessing that you'd not thank me for passing on duff information. The truth is, we just don't know,' he concluded, unable to go any further. 'You'll get better information over at the hospital. So, let's get you into that ambulance. The Royal Berks are expecting two very wet and smelly patients, not just the one.' He smiled at Vere, sticking out his hand, 'good luck to the pair of you.'

'Thanks for your help, doctor,' Vere mumbled as the two waiting paramedics. Guided him towards their waiting ambulance.

***

With Vere on his way to the Hospital, Crowland addressed the small gathering around the open trapdoor. Baxter and Atkins looked a sorry sight, wet through, covered in mud, and dripping water all over the bare boards.

'I suggest,' Crowland turned to address the uniformed sergeant, 'that you get Atkins here a warm drink, and a change of clothes, just as soon as you can.'

'Yes sir. I'll get one of the lads outside to drive him back to the Section House right away.'

'Atkins, before you go,' Crowland looked directly into the eye of the keen youngster. 'I'd like to congratulate you for showing such initiative today and I'll be putting that in my report. Well done.'

'Thank you, sir,' his face flushed a little beneath the thin film of slime covering his skin. With that, he turned and began to walk away with his sergeant.

'Not so fast, sunshine,' the shout coming from Baxter, 'what about my knife?'

'Oh, sorry,' he said, sliding his hand into his pocket and then handing over the knife before walking away with the sergeant.

'And, as for you,' the DCI nodded to Baxter, 'take a pull on that, and don't let anyone see you,' he smiled as the small silver flask passed quickly between the two men. 'You did well down there. Another few minutes and we might have lost them both. As it is, the girl looked to be in a bad way.'

'You're right there, sir,' Baxter acknowledged, gratefully savouring the strong brandy. 'I just hope to God we got to her in time. She's a lovely lady and I'd hate to see her come to any more harm. That Buchanan must be a right animal. Oh, if only I could have him alone for ten minutes.'

'Stay focused, sergeant,' Crowland advised, 'then I'll drive you back home for a change of kit. Do you reckon I'll get earache from Mrs Baxter for letting her favourite husband get all wet?' Both men smiled, as Crowland slipped the flask back into his jacket pocket.

'Oh,' he said quietly, 'while you were doing your good things down there,' he nodded towards the trapdoor. 'I got a call from the "super" - told me he's issuing a search warrant for this place. '

'About flaming time,' Baxter grumbled.

'Anyway, the heavy mob will soon be here, geared up to take this place apart. Better late than never,' he shrugged as his mobile vibrated. Walking a little way down the corridor he took the call, leaving Baxter to appreciate the warming effect of his brandy.

'Interesting,' he said cheerfully, returning to Baxter. 'That was the City financial police on the 'phone. I called them earlier, twice in fact. The second time was to confirm that Buchanan was a murderer, masquerading for years as Overstone. Well, they moved quickly once I told them our man was about to do a runner. The DI heading up that outfit has just let me know the score. Based upon our suspicions they got a judge to make a temporary order freezing all the company bank accounts. Nothing suspicious, but with Overstone going AWOL, and now known to be Buchanan, they thought it best to act right away. They told him what we know so far, and said they needed time to sort the wheat from the chaff. It was your good thinking that set things rolling.'

'Thanks, gov,' Baxter laughed, 'guess that merits some more of your brandy.'

'No, it jolly well doesn't. I'll be needing that the moment Mrs Baxter takes one look at you. Come on, let's get you into some dry gear while I take the blame for you losing your mother-in-law's Christmas present.'

CHAPTER 73

LATER THAT MORNING Vere, now clean and wearing a hospital gown, remained desperately anxious for news of Yvonne. Earlier, and upon reaching the Royal Berks Hospital, a team of medical professionals in the A and E Department had subjected him to endless checks, scans, blood-tests and injections. But now he was alone, occupying a single bed in a side-ward and where isolation only added to his concerns. Diplomatically denied any information on Yvonne it was only the unexpected arrival of sweet tea and a sandwich that brightened an otherwise frustratingly and depressing day. A day not improved when a cheerful young Indian doctor entered his room unwilling, or unable, to comment on Yvonne's condition.

'Ah, Mr Vere,' he said, whilst consulting his notes, 'no lasting damage by the look of things,' the doctor pronounced, adding that he'd be kept in overnight for observation.

'That's as maybe,' Vere replied, pleased to hear the doctor's summary of his physical condition. 'But inside I am shot to pieces,' he told the doctor in the hope of learning more about Yvonne. 'Earlier today an ambulance brought my partner in here unconscious, half-dead after being drowned like a rat in a trap!' tension adding a brittle edge to his voice. 'Now, no one will tell me how she is. It's no wonder my blood pressures off the clock,' he sighed, fuming inwardly as the doctor offered further platitudes before departing.

However, by mid-afternoon success that his pleadings to see Yvonne arrived in the form of nursing sister with instructions to take him to see her. Walking slowly, she had guided him along endless corridors before stopping outside a single room in a quiet part of the hospital. Standing silently in the corridor Vere could see Yvonne through the window as, beside him, the sister remained silent, absorbed in her own thoughts.

'She looks so tiny. Helpless in fact.' he said, feeling the need to say something until a strange prickling in the eyes made him fall silent. Seeing Yvonne like that, motionless in the big surgical bed and her body wired up to various machines was truly frightening. Vere, scanning the scene anxiously, noted how she had cannulas in both arms from which plastic tubes curled upwards to suspended bags of clear liquid. In addition to those, he could see how she had a tube had in her mouth, held in place by two strips of white tape. From her mouth the tube reached, snake like, across to a nearby trolley where a machine that wheezed with a steady and rhythmical beat.

'What are all the tubes and pipes for?' he asked the sister while battling hard to keep his emotions in check.

'Don't worry,' she replied softly, 'they look worse than they are. The drips are to restore bodily fluids, you know lost through dehydration and hypothermia. The poor girl's been through so much. That's why we're putting back saline, plus feeding in antibiotics,' she explained helpfully. 'Now, because we're using a ventilator, that's the pipe in her mouth, she'll remain heavily sedated until she can breathe on her own. With all that dreadful water entering her system the lungs will have suffered badly, so the machine will take the load while her body recovers. The other wires, as you can see, are connected to the big screens up there, showing pulse and blood pressure, a bit like an aircraft's instrument panel. It helps the nurses and doctors see exactly what is happening.'

'I see,' he replied, still confused, and unsure as to when someone would give him definitive answers.

'From what I hear,' the sister remarked, 'she's had a terrible experience but she's now in what we call a critical but stable condition,' she smiled, 'and is holding her own which is a good sign.'

'Thank you,' Vere acknowledged flatly, his voice drained of emotion. 'But thank goodness they've cleaned her up,' he commented, looking at the pale skin and straight hair. 'Did you know that she's a fashion journalist?' He gave a brief smile. 'If she wakes up now, and sees herself looking like that, she'll have a fit.'

'I know,' the sister spoke encouragingly, sensing Vere's need to talk, 'I read her articles whenever I get the chance, that is, and I know the girls here read them as well, during our tea-breaks in the rest room.' Vere smiled, the comforting words helping to restore a measure of normality in his troubled mind.

'As for that the hospital gown,' he said quietly, 'she'd not want her readers to see her in that either.'

'Fear not,' the sister smiled sweetly, 'her secret's safe with us. No YouTube or Face Book around here, I promise,' she added, with a chuckle as Vere felt amazed that he could be having this kind of conversation at such a critical time. Assessing the situation his features hardened, Yvonne was still unconscious as the big screen dispassionately monitored her vital functions. Green, red and yellow figures and pulsing lines lit up various screens where readings appeared to change fractionally, second-by second, or where others remained reassuringly steady. Not unlike the screens on City trader's desks, he thought, continually taking the pulse of the financial markets. But no, these screens were far more important, monitoring Yvonne's life electronically and confirming she was alive. Yet, with her eyes closed, she looked to be perfectly at peace.

'What happens now?' he asked the sister, anxiously seeking out any further crumbs of positive news. 'When will she wake up?'

'Yes,' the sister began, 'as you can see we've got Yvonne in a side ward which is part of the Intensive Care unit. In here we have all the latest equipment and where the doctors and nurses will monitor her twenty-four-seven, but she will have to be kept sedated while on the ventilator. Then, and once the doctors decide that she can breathe unaided, they'll being her round gently. Only then will we know the full story. All we can do now is wait, hope and pray,' she offered kindly. 'In the meantime, I'll get the senior neurological consultant, who's looking after Yvonne, to come and have a word with you. I'm sure he'll be able to answer your questions to give you a clearer picture.'

CHAPTER 74

'MILES OVERSTONE,' MR Justice McKinley addressed the defendant in the dock before him at the Old Bailey. 'Although Overstone may, or may not be, your real name, it is the one under which you have been charged and under which will now be sentenced.' In silence the packed courtroom waited as the judge began to play out the final act of a trial that had attracted massive media attention. Having started in early November the proceedings were now reaching their climax shortly before Christmas. Outside the streets of London were aglow with seasonal lights and decorations yet not a single trace of Christmas had penetrated the sombre courtroom. Seated before the judge defence and prosecution barristers, their jobs done, looked upwards in anticipation of his sentence.

Away to their right, and just a matter of yards from the dock, a dejected Robert Vere watched proceedings, pale, drawn and a good stone lighter in weight. Earlier in the trial he had faced isolation in the witness box, enduring hours of passive and hostile interrogation. Although the prosecution barrister had been helpful and sympathetic, his counterpart for the defence had been belligerent and confrontational, actions that made him question the integrity of his own chosen profession. How could this defence barrister be so openly aggressive when defending what was clearly indefensible? Vere, subscribing to *the fair trial for all* principle, struggled to understand why expensive counsels were wrangling over the validity of every point raised by the prosecution. No, Overstone was as guilty as sin! This whole trial has been a waste of time and money, he concluded, fervently hoping that Overstone had not had access to the Legal Aid system.

Before the trial he had felt confused, needing to grieve for the loss of Yvonne, yet she was still alive! In truth, reduced to a severely brain-damaged shadow of her former self, living out her days in a private nursing home. In need of assistance with the simplest of tasks, unable to speak and incapable of recognising visitors she was an empty shell. Alive, but not living. Dear God, in everything but name she's dead. Surely that must be something to grieve for. His mind snapped back to reality as the judge began speaking again.

'Over recent weeks the jury,' he nodded in their direction, 'have listened to powerful arguments, put by both sides of this case. The prosecution,' he intoned, looking down at Overstone, 'has produced compelling evidence, all supported by verifiable facts. And, in pursuit of their brief, your defence team has done its best to create doubt and confusion in the minds of the jury. Indeed,' he looked around the court, 'a ploy that's most certainly failed, given their unanimous verdict.'

Beside him Vere felt Yvonne's mother stir, sitting upright in anticipation of the judge's sentence. Looking down Vere seethed as Overstone remained impassive, the judge's words washing over him like a disaffected tide. He's robbed me of my true love, transforming Yvonne into to a pitiful vegetable. He's taken her life as surely as if he had killed her, robbing a mother of her daughter in the process. How could Mr Justice McKinley pass any sentence that justly reflected such horror?

Over recent months all medical attempts to restore Yvonne to normality had failed, later abandoned entirely. Yes, Vere thought, barely able to dress herself and shuffling aimlessly from room to room they've given up. Her once sparkling eyes now a lifeless glaze, her beautiful face blank and pale while her memory's gone completely. *Like wiping a computer hard drive*, an insensitive doctor had informed Vere after one visit. Those visits, sitting there with Yvonne, holding hands while talking tirelessly in the hope of triggering a reaction in her fog-bound mind.

'Now,' Judge McKinley spoke firmly 'having heard the jury verdict it is my duty to pass the heaviest sentence available to me. However, before doing that, please allow me to share my thinking with you. Although the jury has found you guilty of attempted murder, namely the cruel attempt to drown Mr Vere and Miss Clarkson, I'm going to highlight the other offences that I'm taking into consideration.' Pausing, he looked around the courtroom for any signs of dissent, detecting none, he continued.

'To begin with there's incontrovertible evidence that you masterminded an armed robbery in which you shot two people. The crime leading directly to a young man's execution because he had the misfortune to drive your getaway car.' All eyes in the court focused on the judge as his words resonated around the chamber.

'Next, there was no doubt in the prosecution's mind that you orchestrated the shooting of George Noakes, your original partner in crime. Prior to this it's certain that you pressurised Noakes into firebombing Yvonne Clarkson's car. A crime of hideous proportions, killing an innocent garage employee. Of course,' he said looking around the court, 'we have no hard evidence for this, otherwise you'd have faced a charge of being an accessory to murder as well. Later,' he paused, 'there's compelling evidence to show that you pushed Terry, George Noakes's son, in front of an underground train, where he died. And, before we come to the two proven charges of attempted murder, we have this. Your audacious fraud to procure thirty-two million pounds from a bank based upon a bogus business venture. Indeed,' he paused to look down at his notes, 'your trail of criminal activity is quite breath-taking. And finally,' he looked around the courtroom, 'your attempt to murder Robert Vere and Yvonne Clarkson by drowning. Ah yes,' he sighed, 'just two innocent people who you decided had to die in cruel and horrendous conditions because they got in your way.' The judge paused, pouring water from the glass carafe beside him into a tumbler. Picking up the tumbler, he took a small sip of the water before continuing.

'In fact,' he spoke with conviction, 'in all my years in the judiciary, I have never come across such callous and premeditated action as this. In a civilised world it defies comprehension. Only by good police work was an absolute tragedy avoided. Yet even that's a huge understatement since Miss Clarkson incurred severe brain-damage from which any form of recovery, even partial, is most unlikely. However,' he snapped, 'we can only deal with the facts as they are and the prognosis for the young lady is not at all encouraging. Robert Vere, Miss Clarkson's partner has been left devastated, robbed of the woman he loves. His "impact statement" could have left no one in any doubt as to his devotion and love for Yvonne. He has been robbed - *robbed* of what promised to be a happy future together, one in which the young couple would, we believe, have gone on to marry and.'

'I'm sure the court would wish me to express our sympathy to Mr Vere and to Mrs Clarkson, Yvonne's mother, for their dreadful loss. And to thank Mr Vere for his concise and irrefutable evidence that has gone a long way to convict you,' he glared down at Overstone as, around the courtroom faces turned towards Vere, silently sharing in his grief.

Further back, in the public gallery, other eyes were also on Vere. Cold, calculating and dispassionate eyes, belonging to three middle aged men in dark business suits. They too, in their own way, were experiencing a loss, forced to contemplate life without their leader. Any lingering hopes of Overstone staying free had disappeared when the jury returned with their verdict. Bernard Nolan, seated alongside his two companions, recognised the inevitable and was already calculating how best to maintain strict control of operations during Overstone's absence. The duration of which he was determined would only be of a temporary nature.

'Miles Overstone,' the Judge continued, 'you are a truly despicable individual and, at times like this, I regret that I'm no longer able to pass upon you the only sentence I'd like to. Indeed, the one that you deserve. However, looking back, your young accomplice Stephen Drysdale died in prison as you also will die in prison!' Just as thunder becomes the outrider of an impending storm all in the courtroom knew there was more to come. 'Back then the law set a date for Drysdale's death and now the good Lord will, in his own time, do the same for you. It will happen, and when it does, you'll either die in a prison cell or shackled to a hospital bed. You will never walk free from your confinement.' Looking down into the well of the Court the judge then fell silent, nodding to an official who stood to address Overstone.

'Will the defendant now stand,' he said, turning back to face the judge. For a moment Overstone remained motionless before slowly rising to hear his fate. Now tired and feeble he waited, towered over by the two powerfully built prison officers standing behind him in the dock. The swagger and bravado had long since gone, replaced by the mantle of total and utter defeat. From his elevated position Judge McKinley took one last look around before passing sentence.

'Having been found guilty of the charge brought against you, I sentence you to life imprisonment, with a minimum tariff of thirty-five years. Be in no doubt, should you survive that long only then will the Parole Board even entertain hearing an appeal from you.' Gasps, mixed with stifled cheers, greeted the Judge's words. Pausing, he then drove the final nail into the defendant's coffin. 'Take him down.' The dreadful words bringing silence back into the courtroom. Predictably, whilst Overstone showed no emotion at the sentence handed down, around him a gentle wave of conversation rolled across the chamber. A warm breeze of approval as Vere, taking Mrs Clarkson's hand, gently eased her upright before heading for the doorway.

'Well, it's of no consolation, but at least the blighter is out of the way for good,' Jean Clarkson remarked. True Vere thought, recalling Shakespeare and the words spoken over Caesar's body. *'The evil that men do lives after them, the good is oft interred with their bones'*. Precious little good to inter with Overstone, but I'm betting there's evil left to live on. Is this really the end or of new beginning? Pausing for a moment on the landing outside the courtroom the pair embraced in silence, the woman pressing her face into the taller man's chest. Despite their emotional turmoil, only one of them felt the luxury of being able to shed tears in public.

***

It was dark when they stepped outside onto the pavement as, away to their left, bright lights illuminated an array of photographers and television news reporters. To Vere everybody leaving the Old Bailey seemed to be fair game for the media, all eager to record reactions and broadcast opinions. In the middle of the throng, he could see Ted Crowland fending off questions as he appealed for calm to deliver a prepared statement.

Managing to avoid the "scrum," Vere took hold of Mrs Clarkson's arm, moving her gently away from the crowd. Pleased at avoiding the press the last thing Vere needed was to face an unfeeling reporter asking questions. *'How do you feel? Are you satisfied with the verdict?'* How could any verdict bring Yvonne back from the shadows? Peering into the gloom, in search of a taxi, he was shoulder charged by a fresh-faced youth in a hooded jacket. Pushing his face close to the stumbling Vere he spoke tersely, words delivered with brutal simplicity.

'You're next. Overstone will be out in months, and you'll be dead!' Too stunned to react, Vere stood rooted to the spot, totally perplexed as the messenger vanished, melting into the darkness.

'What was that?' Mrs Clarkson asked only half aware of anything being amiss.

'Oh, nothing,' he replied, gathering his senses before responding positively. 'Come on, let's go to see Yvonne. We can make Reading in an hour or so, be there just after supper then we can tell her what's happened.'

'Yes, let's do that,' Jean Clarkson replied, painfully aware that any words of theirs, no matter how ell intended, would fail to reach her daughter. In silence they departed, walking away from the crowd in search of a taxi. Just two lonely people moving into the shadows. One who had lost a cherished daughter, the other who had lost a dearly loved partner, yet together they both mourned for someone who had lost the rest of her life.

To my dear wife, Audrey, for her patience and the amazing
support she has provided me with while writing this novel.
And to our sons, Richard and Jonathan, for their
most appreciated interest and encouragement.

PETER WARRILOW

The Far Reaches

A ROBERT VERE CRIME THRILLER

SPRING 2023

RIVERRUN

BEYOND THE FIVE SENSES